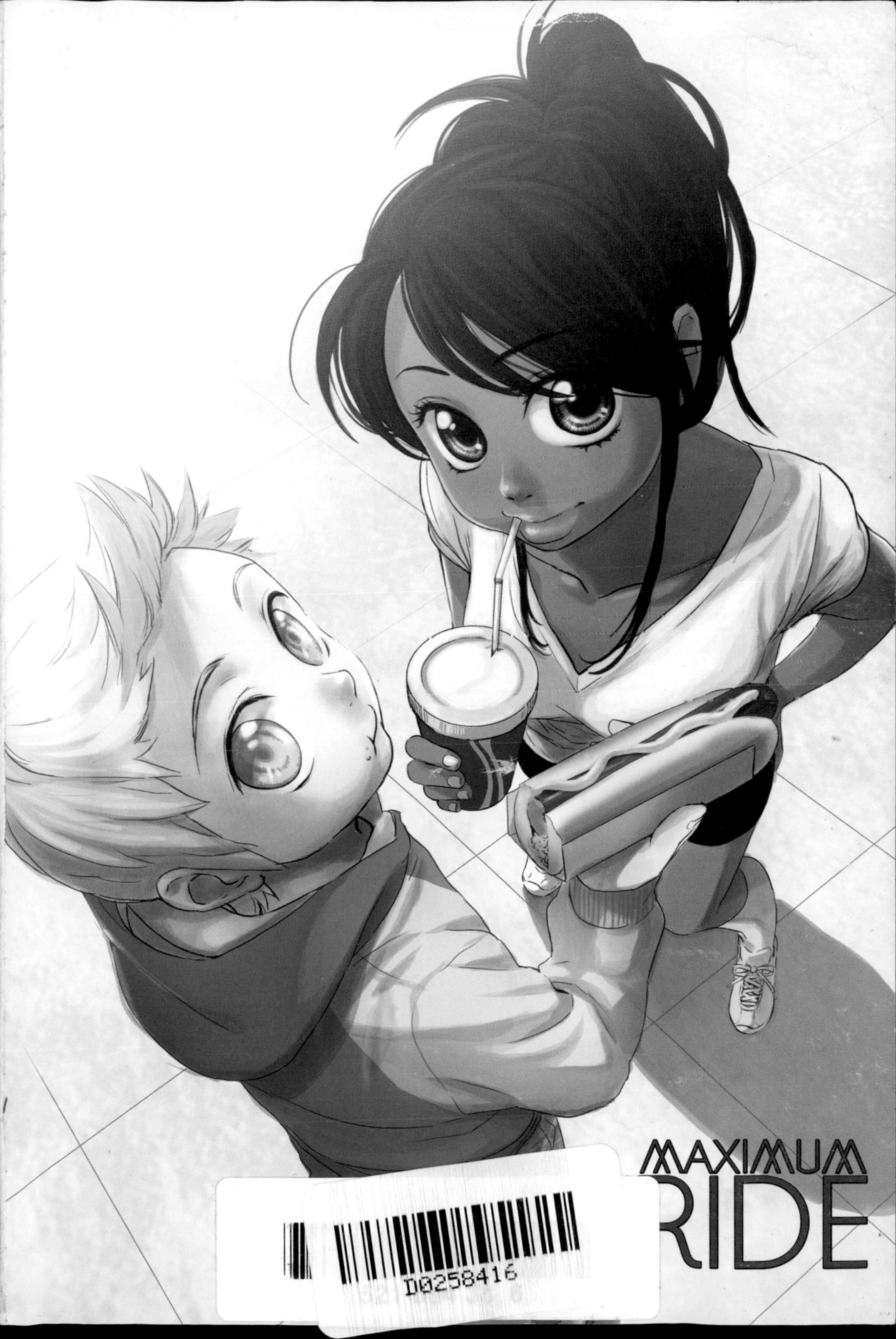
MAXIMUM
RIDE

WHAT CAME BEFORE

Max and her "flock" appear at a glance to be normal kids...that is, if you don't notice the wings!

Instilled with avian DNA in a lab known as the "School," Max and her family escaped confinement with the help of scientist Jeb Batchelder, who they believed perished assisting them. When the youngest of the flock, Angel, is abducted by the lab's foot soldiers – shape-shifting men and women infused with lupine DNA called Erasers – led by Jeb's son, Ari, Max discovers that Jeb is not only alive, but still working with the School! Rescuing Angel, the flock heads to New York City to find the "Institute," which they believe holds the secrets to their past. While raiding the facility, though, they are again confronted by Jeb and his Erasers. The flock manages to get away, but not before Max accidentally kills Ari!

Now the flock is off to Washington, D.C., following up a lead on their parents, but Max can't escape the mysterious voice that's begun whispering inside her head – or Jeb's haunting words that in killing Ari, she may have killed her own brother...

MAXIMUM RIDE

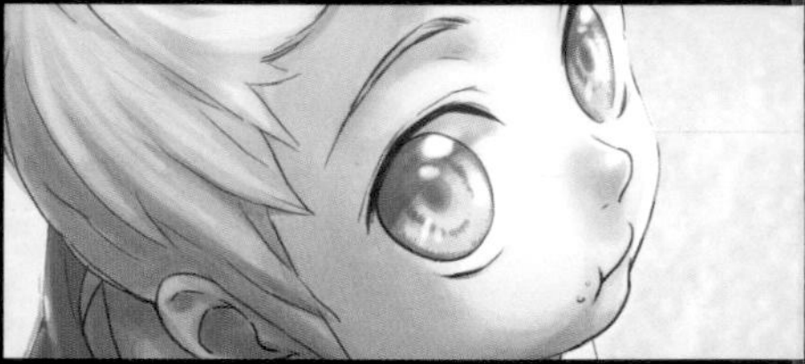

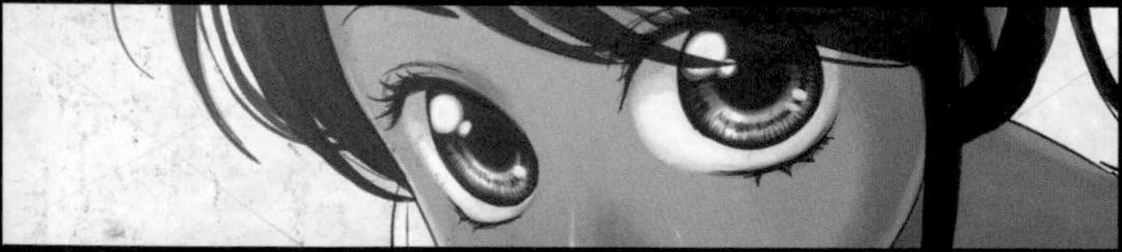

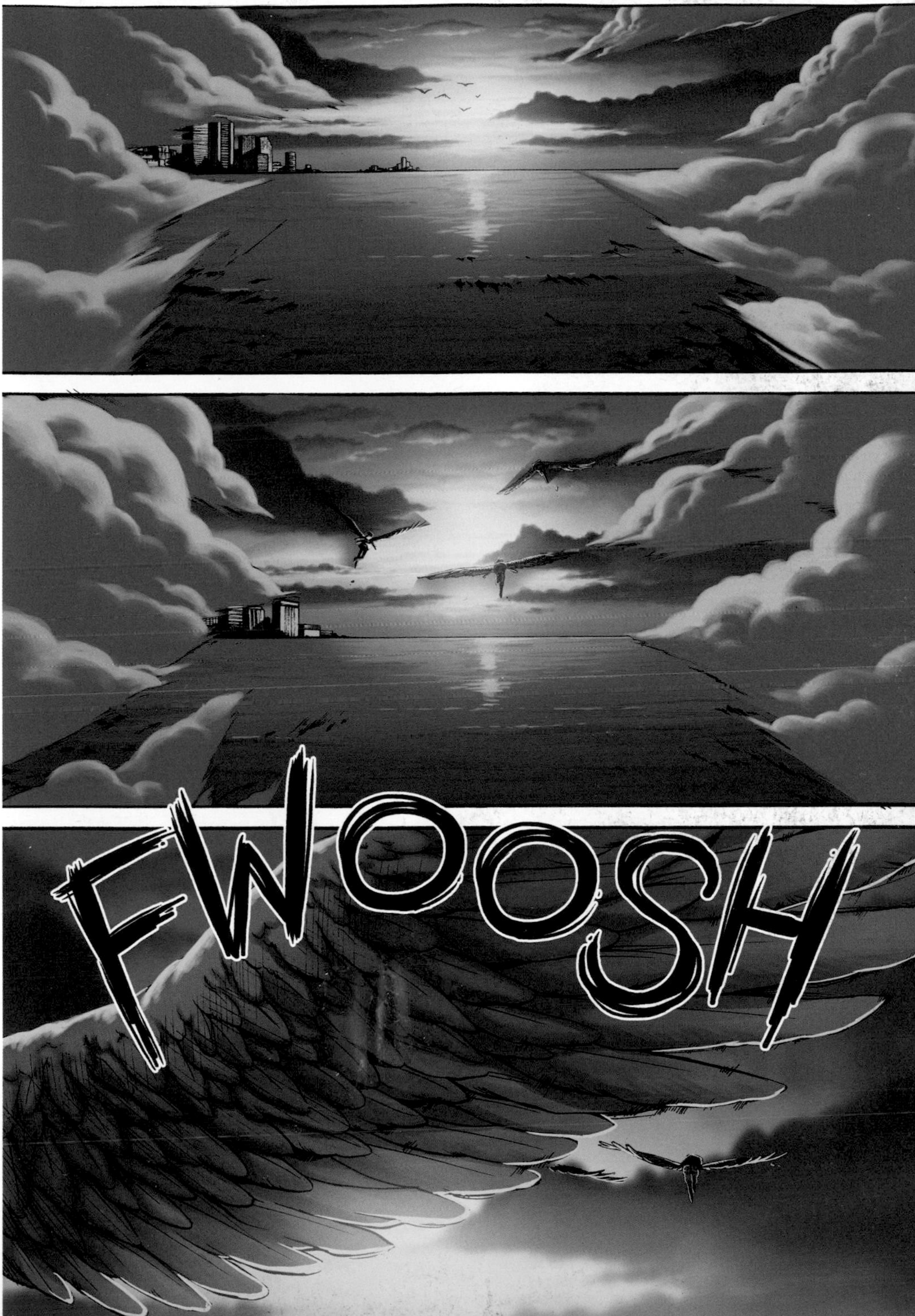
FWOOSH

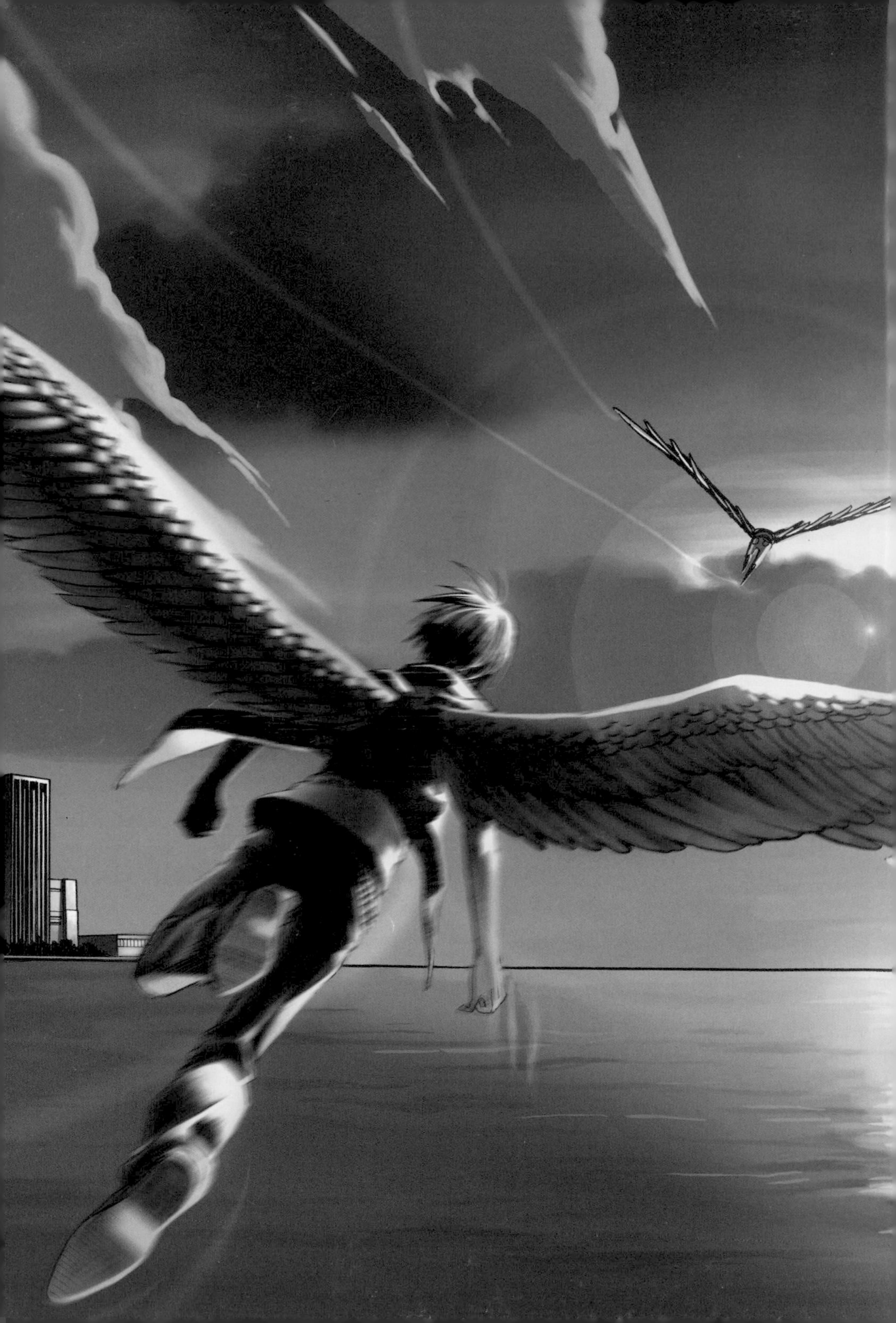

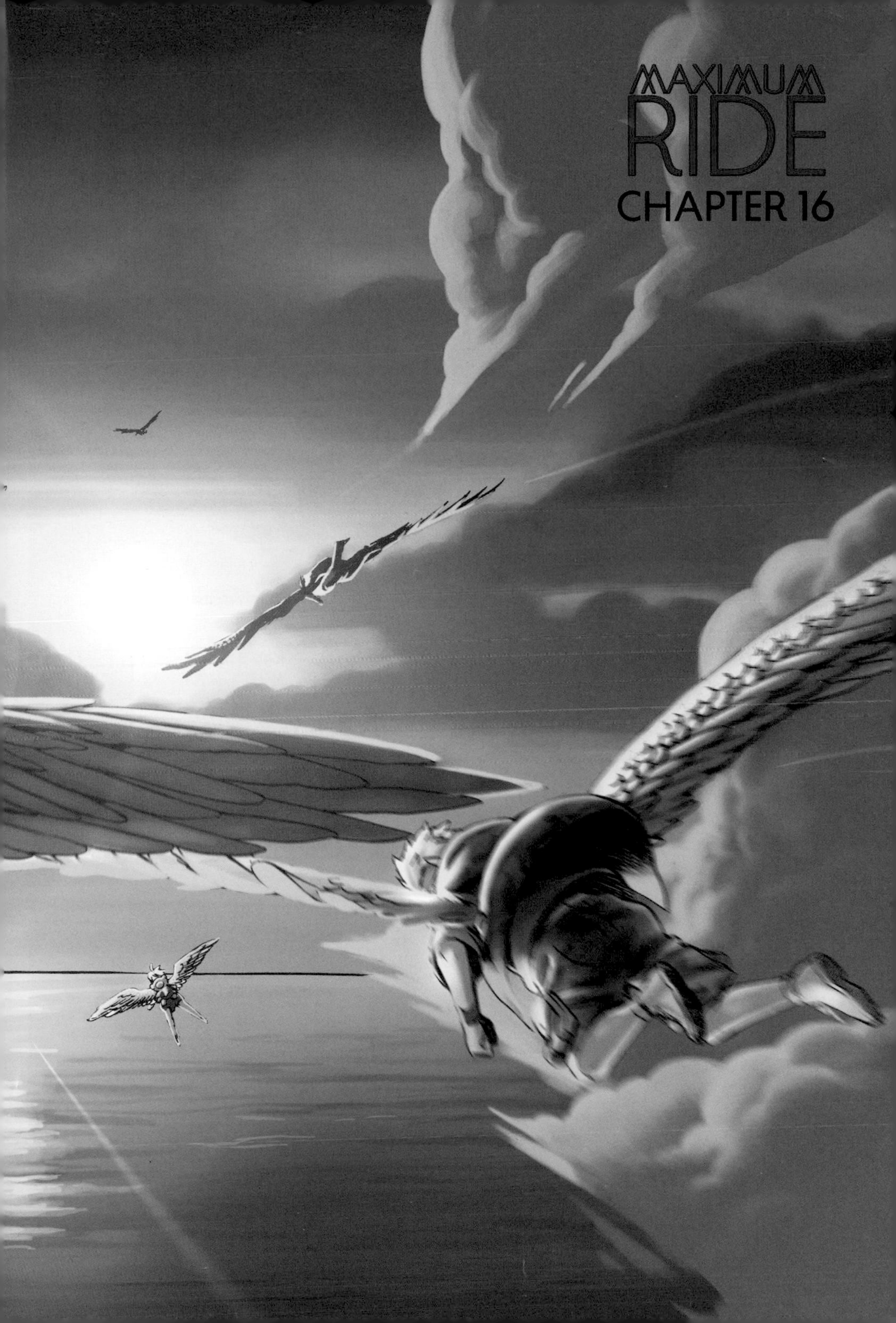
MAXIMUM
RIDE
CHAPTER 16

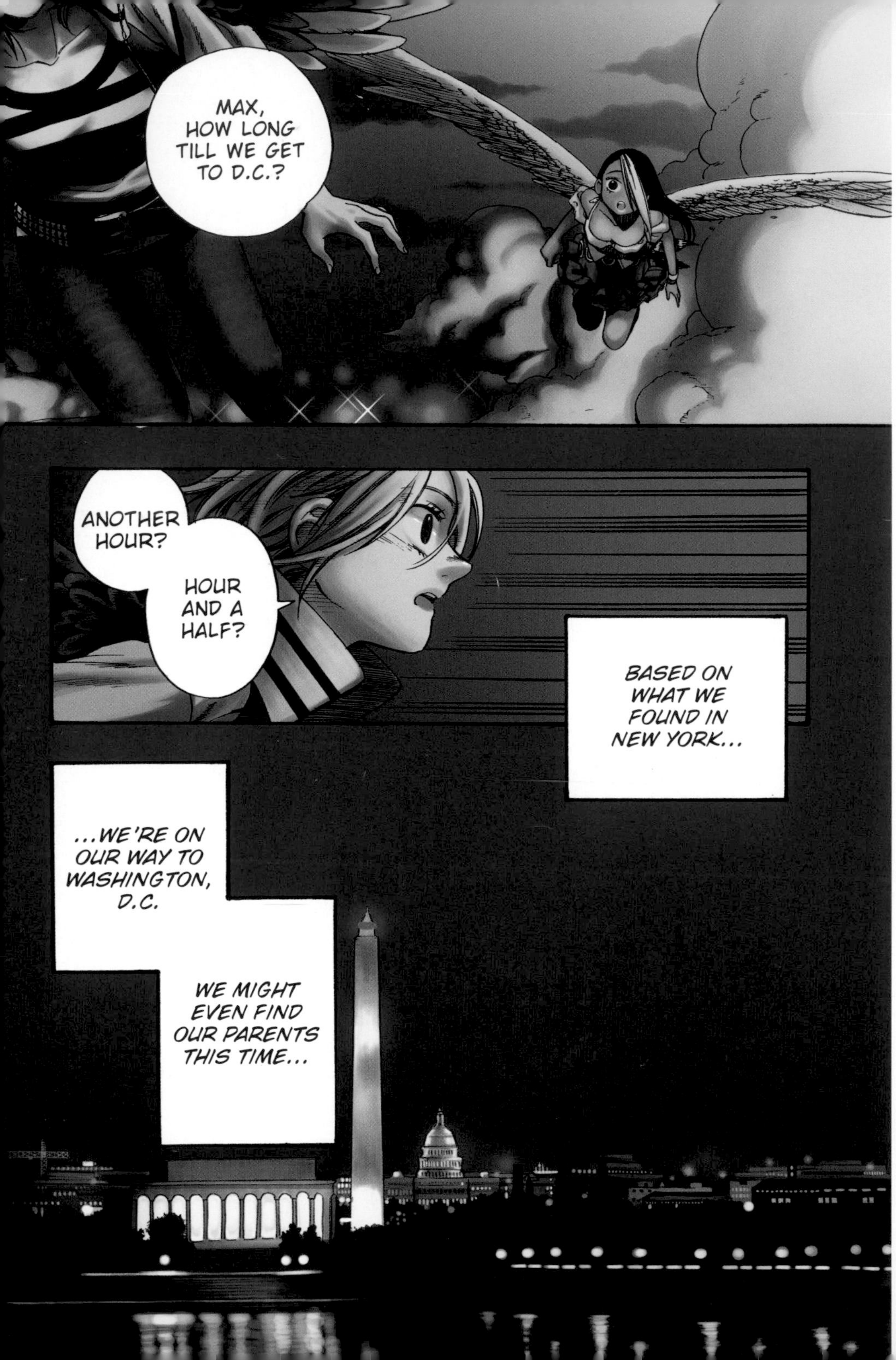
MAX, HOW LONG TILL WE GET TO D.C.?
ANOTHER HOUR?
HOUR AND A HALF?
BASED ON WHAT WE FOUND IN NEW YORK...
...WE'RE ON OUR WAY TO WASHINGTON, D.C.
WE MIGHT EVEN FIND OUR PARENTS THIS TIME...

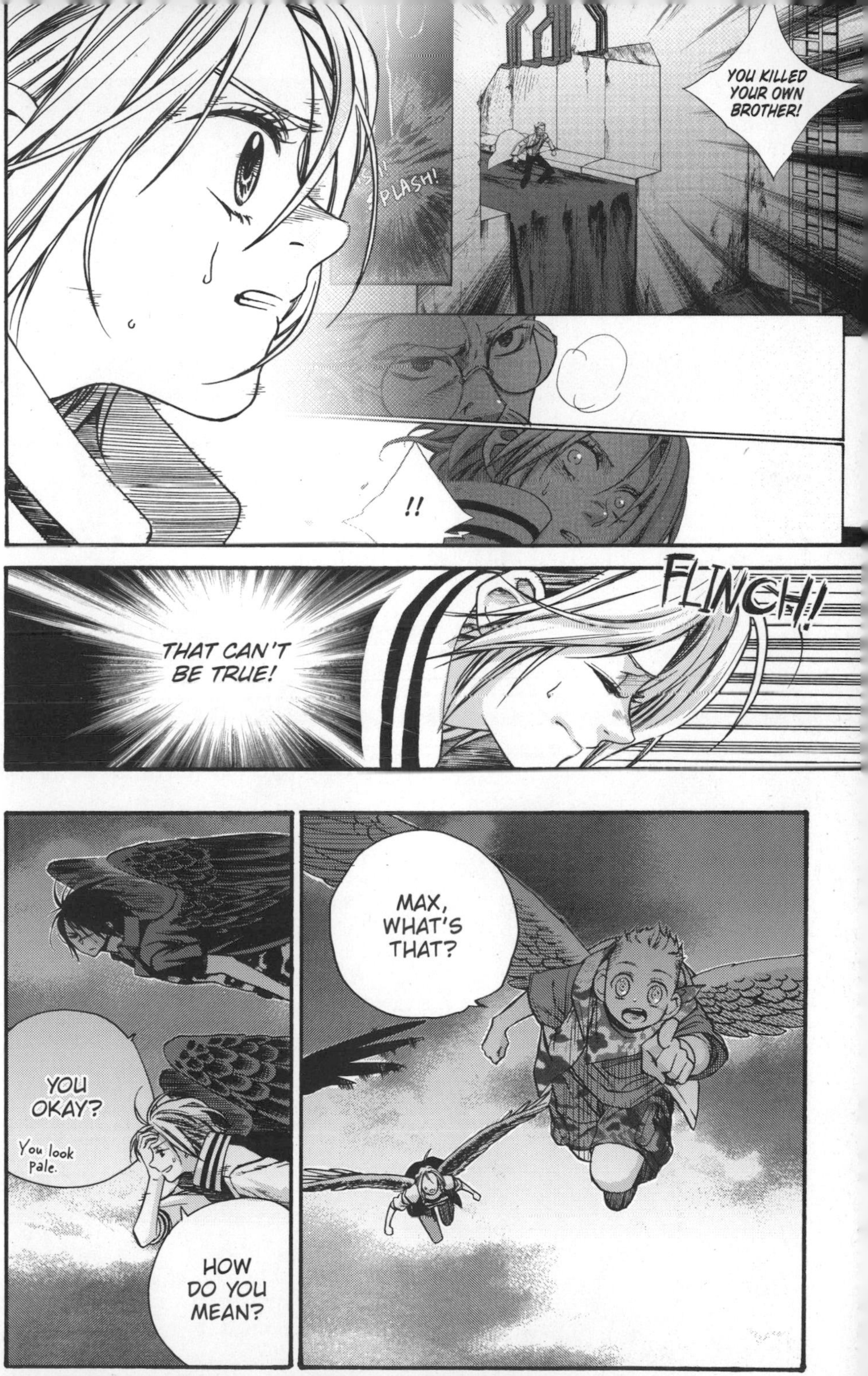
YOU KILLED YOUR OWN BROTHER!
!!
THAT CAN'T BE TRUE!
FLINCH!
YOU OKAY?
You look pale.
HOW DO YOU MEAN?
MAX, WHAT'S THAT?

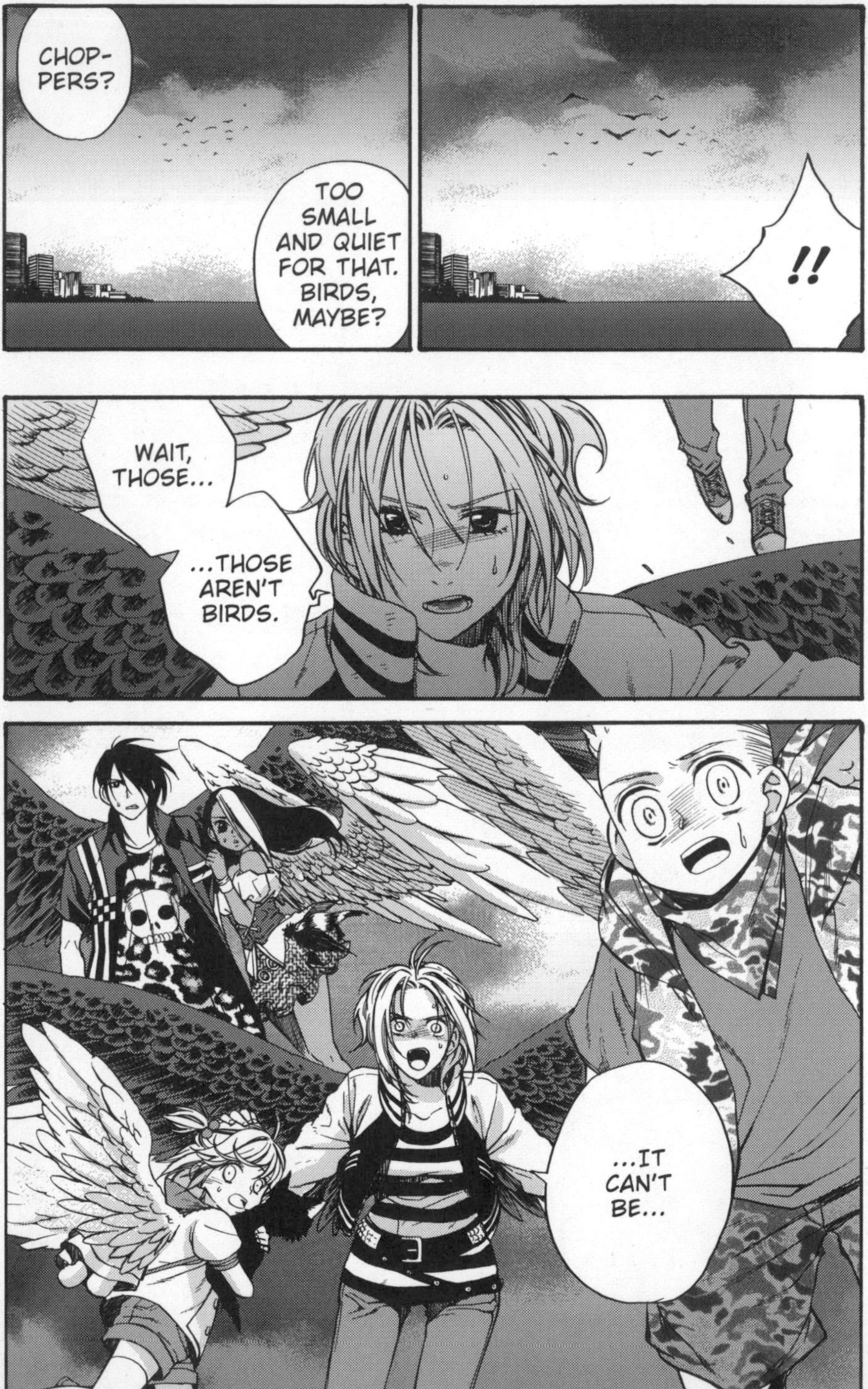
CHOP-PERS?
TOO SMALL AND QUIET FOR THAT. BIRDS, MAYBE?
!!
WAIT, THOSE...
...THOSE AREN'T BIRDS.
...IT CAN'T BE...

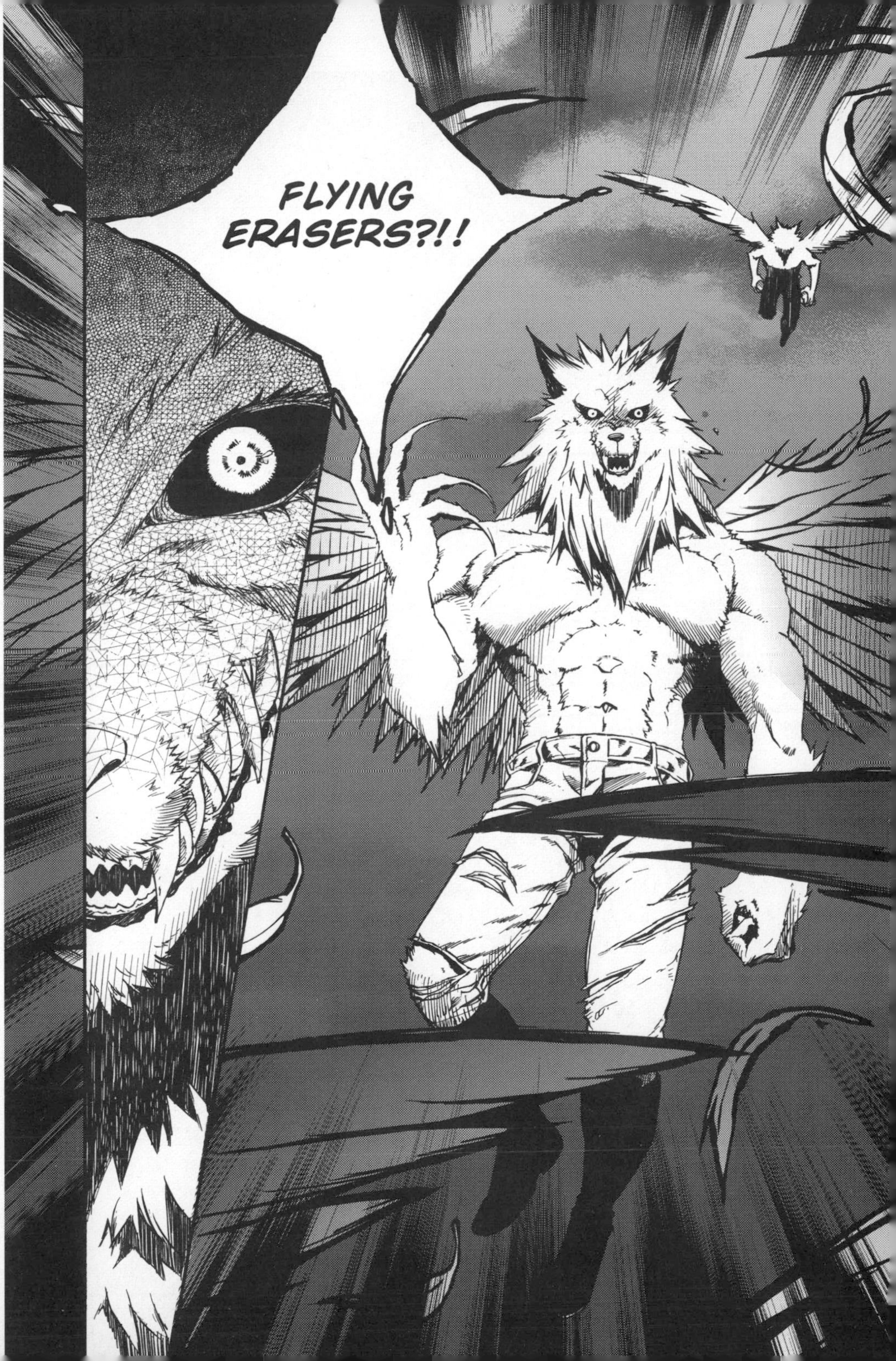
FLYING ERASERS?!!

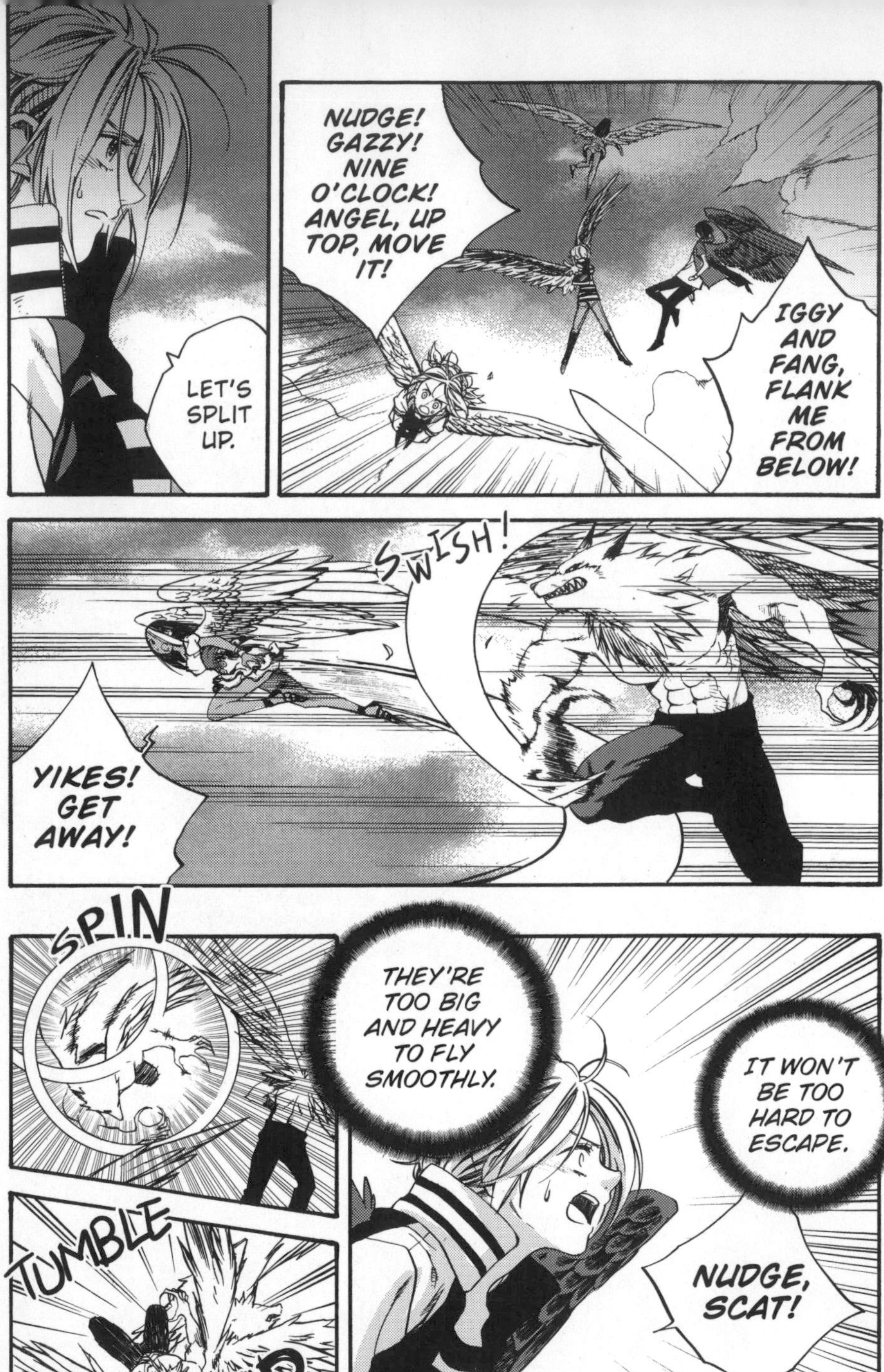
LET'S SPLIT UP.
NUDGE! GAZZY! NINE O'CLOCK! ANGEL, UP TOP, MOVE IT!
IGGY AND FANG, FLANK ME FROM BELOW!
SWISH!
YIKES! GET AWAY!
SPIN
TUMBLE
BUMP
THEY'RE TOO BIG AND HEAVY TO FLY SMOOTHLY.
IT WON'T BE TOO HARD TO ESCAPE.
NUDGE, SCAT!

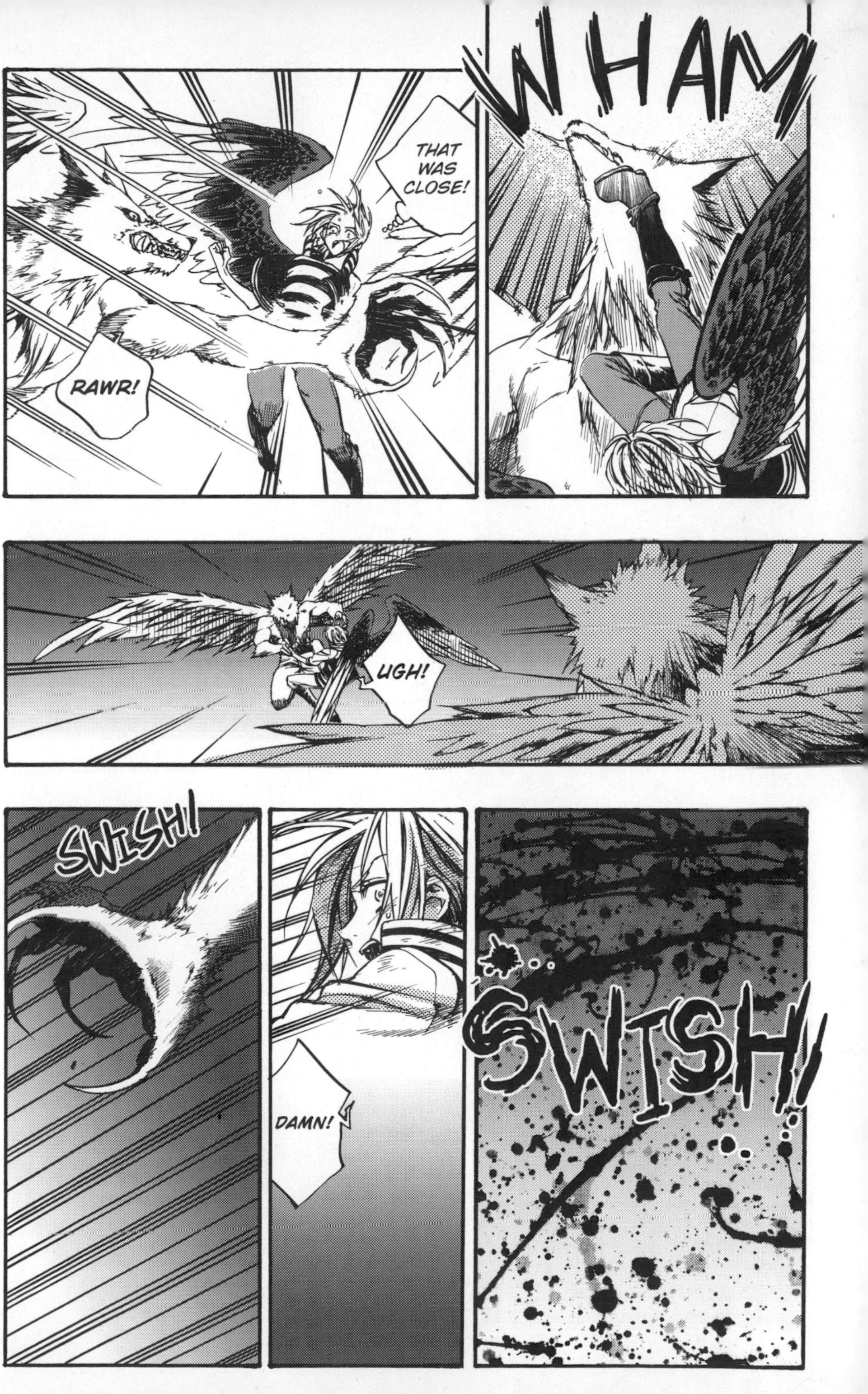
THAT WAS CLOSE!
RAWR!
WHAM
UGH!
SWISH!
DAMN!
SWISH!

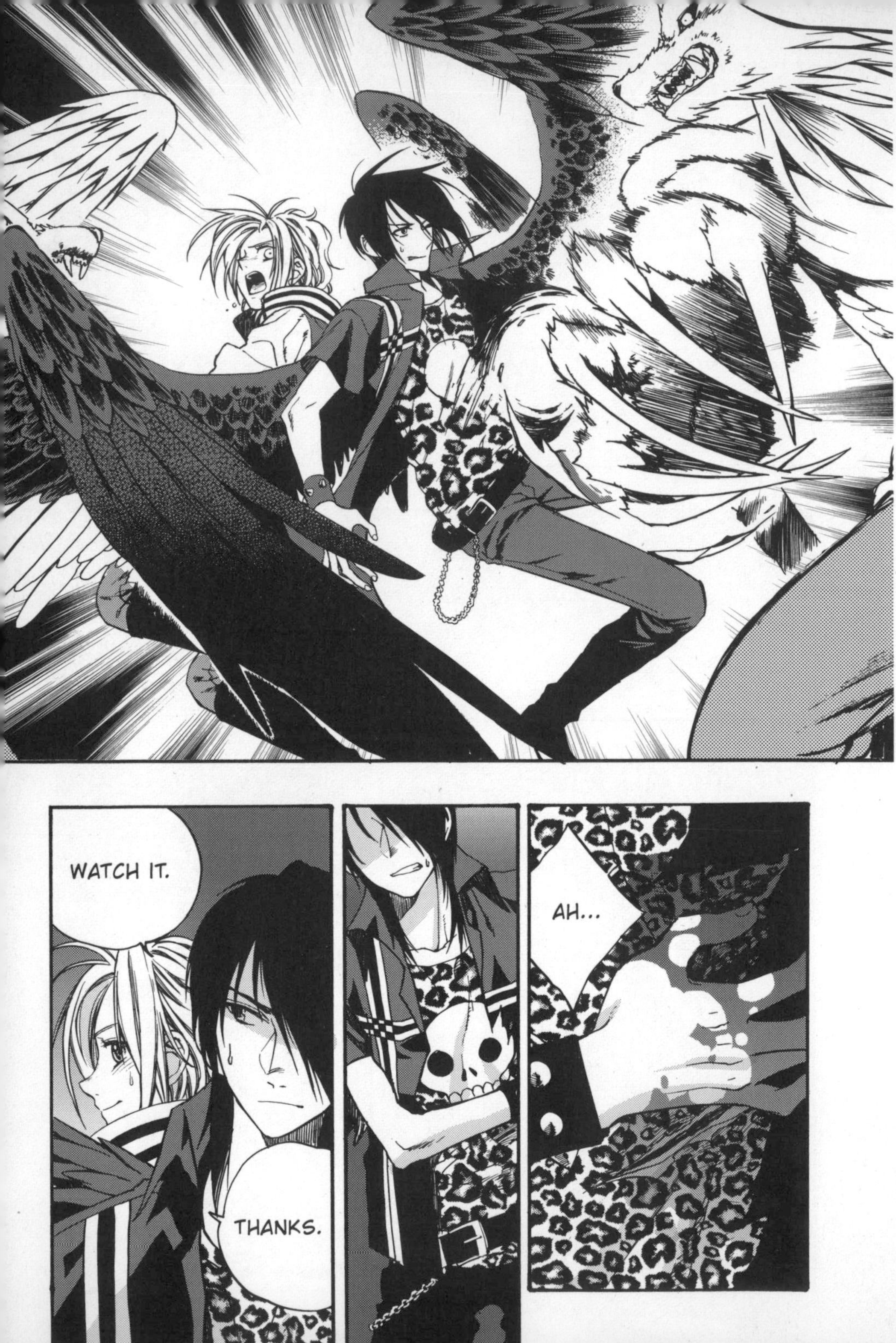
WATCH IT.
THANKS.
AH...

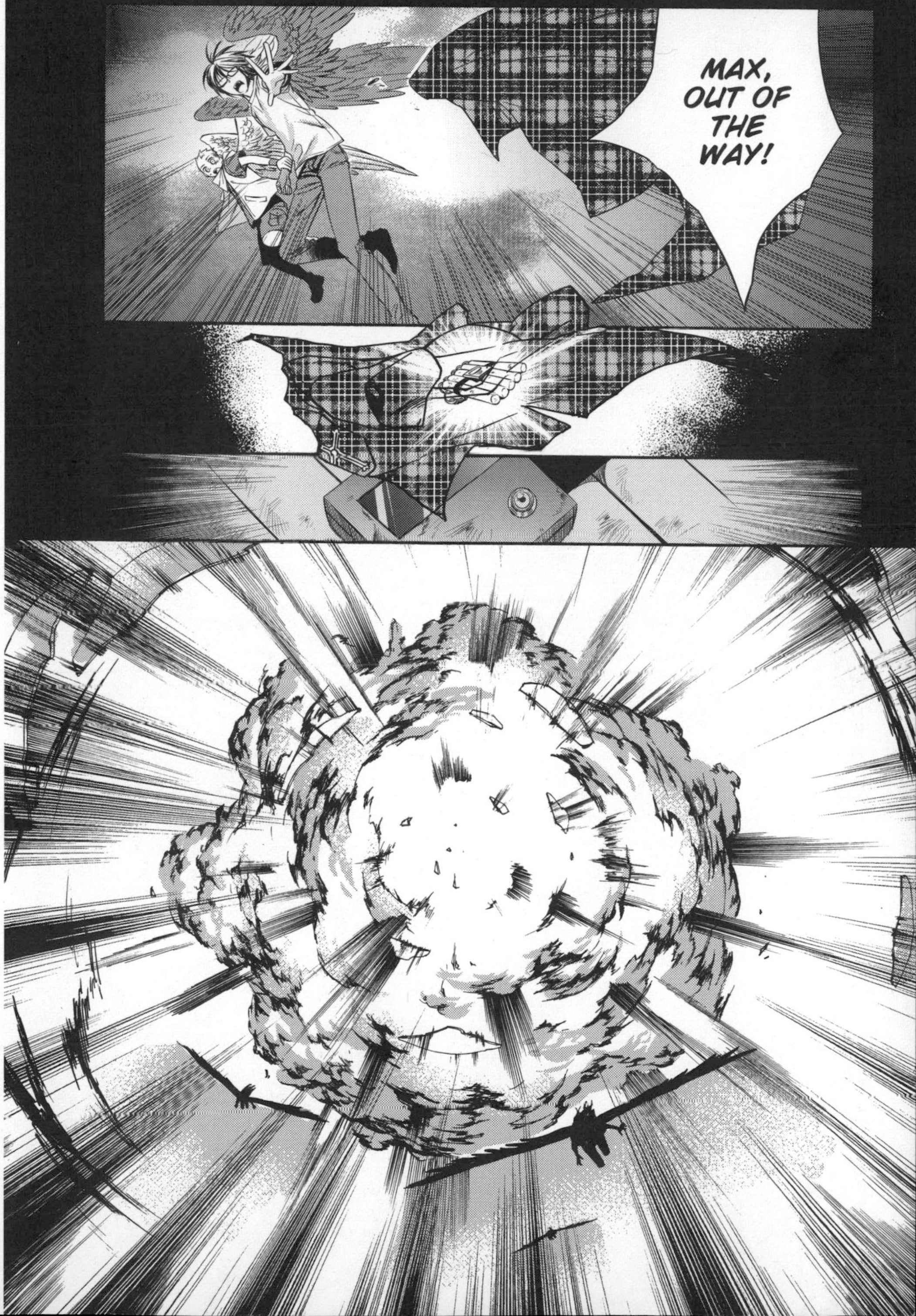
MAX, OUT OF THE WAY!

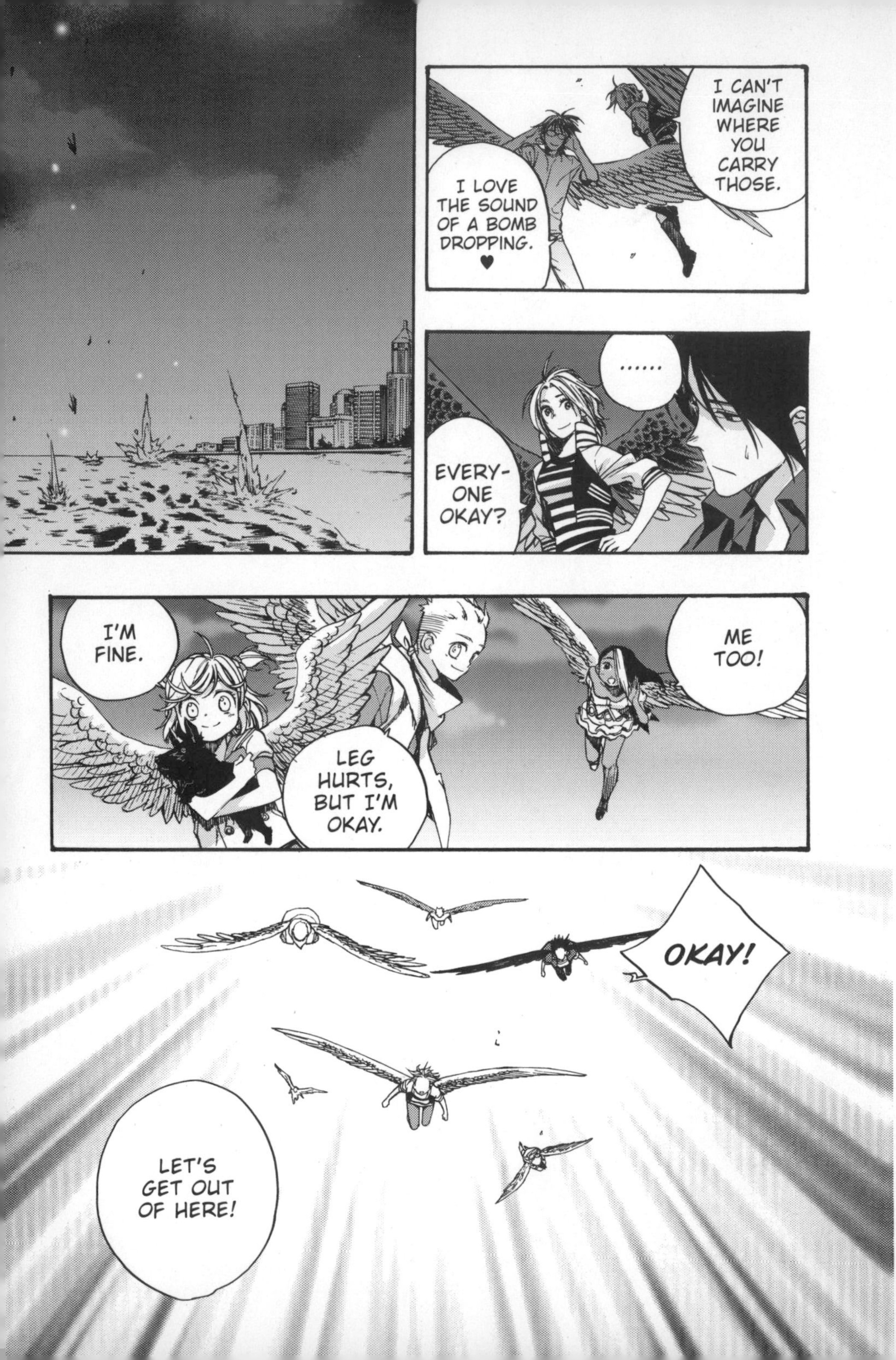
I LOVE THE SOUND OF A BOMB DROPPING. ♥
I CAN'T IMAGINE WHERE YOU CARRY THOSE.
EVERY-ONE OKAY?
......
I'M FINE.
LEG HURTS, BUT I'M OKAY.
ME TOO!
LET'S GET OUT OF HERE!
OKAY!

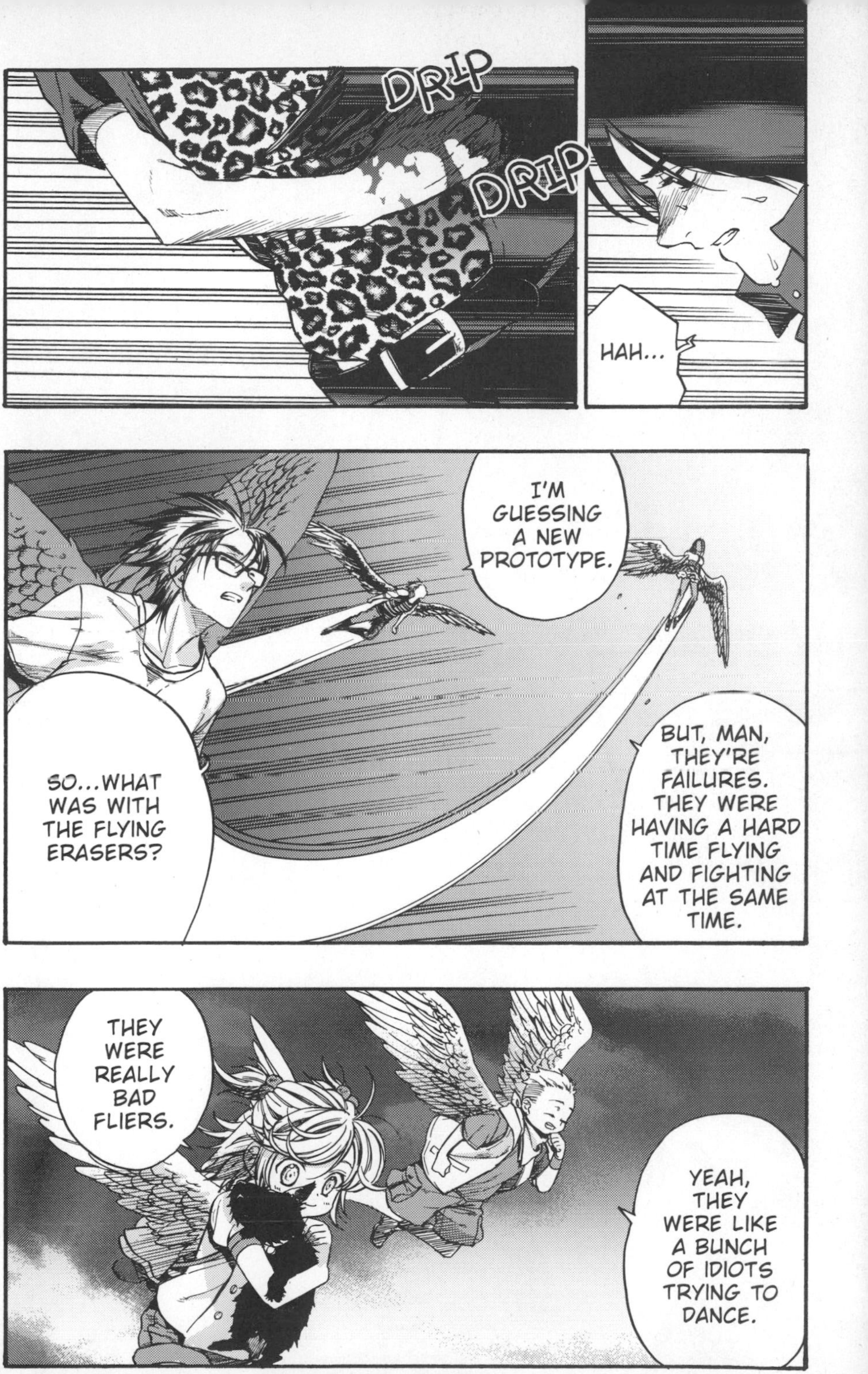
DRIP
DRIP
HAH...
I'M GUESSING A NEW PROTOTYPE.
SO...WHAT WAS WITH THE FLYING ERASERS?
BUT, MAN, THEY'RE FAILURES. THEY WERE HAVING A HARD TIME FLYING AND FIGHTING AT THE SAME TIME.
THEY WERE REALLY BAD FLIERS.
YEAH, THEY WERE LIKE A BUNCH OF IDIOTS TRYING TO DANCE.

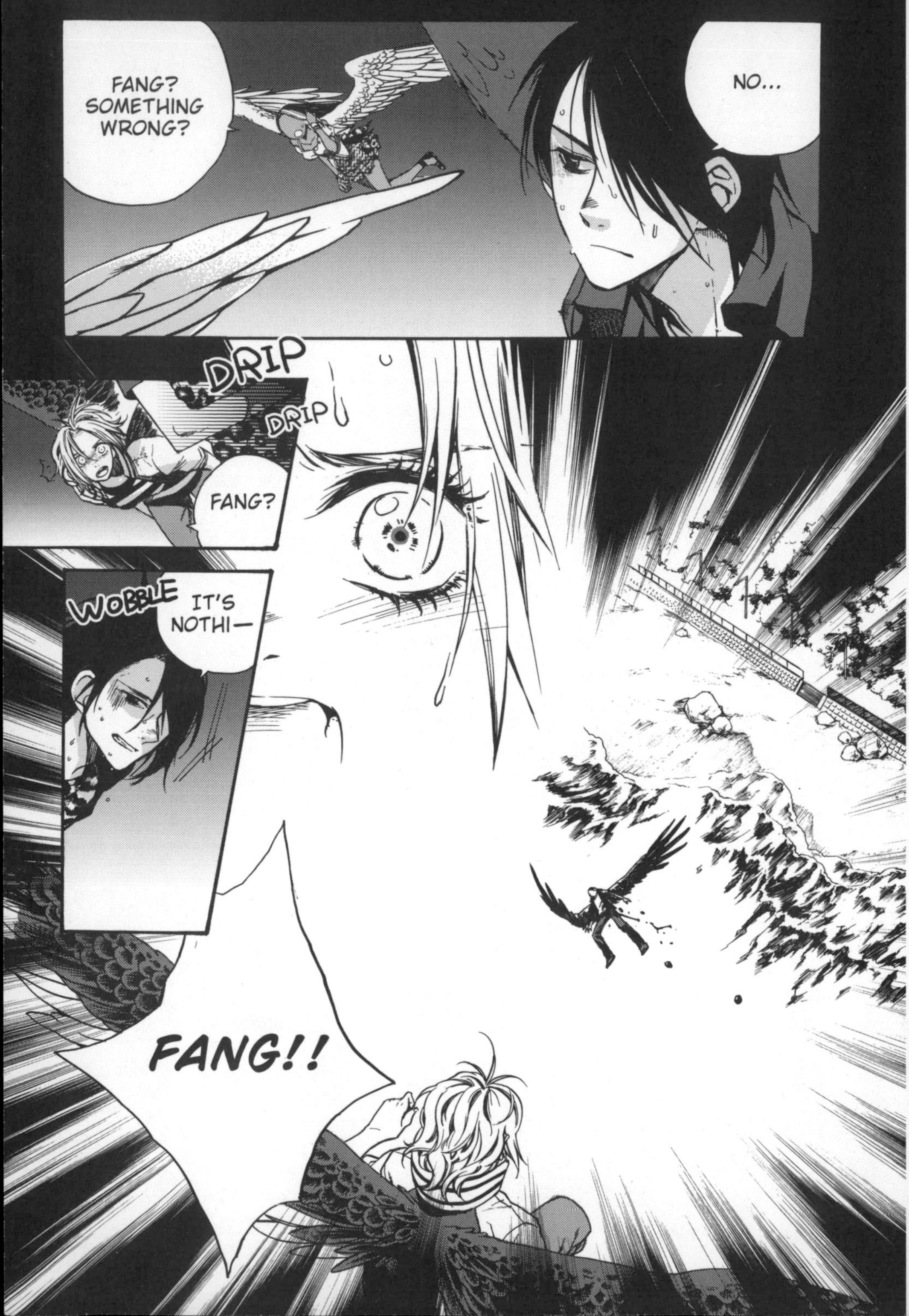
FANG? SOMETHING WRONG?
NO...
DRIP
DRIP
FANG?
WOBBLE
IT'S NOTHI—
FANG!!

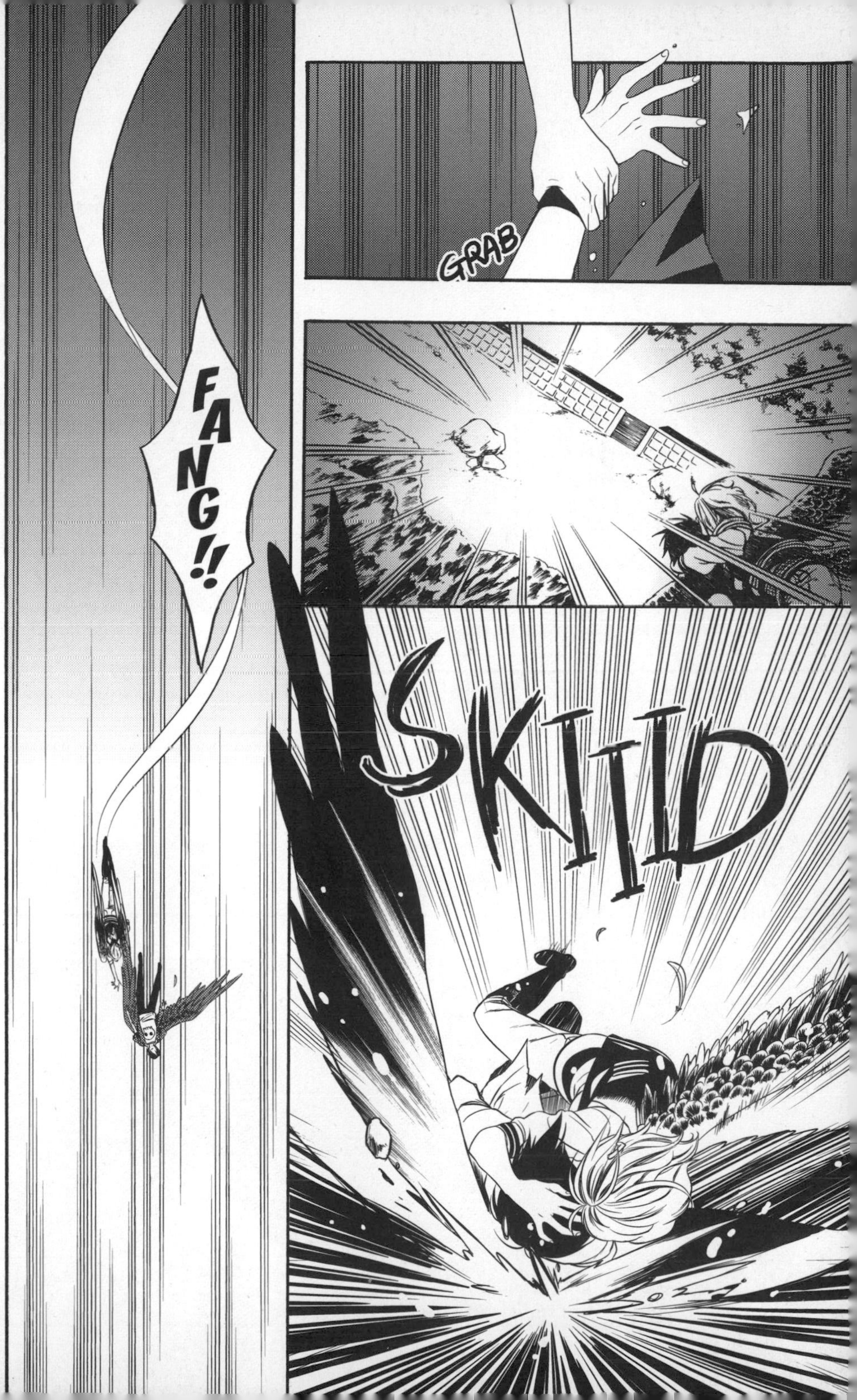
FANG!!
GRAB
SKIID

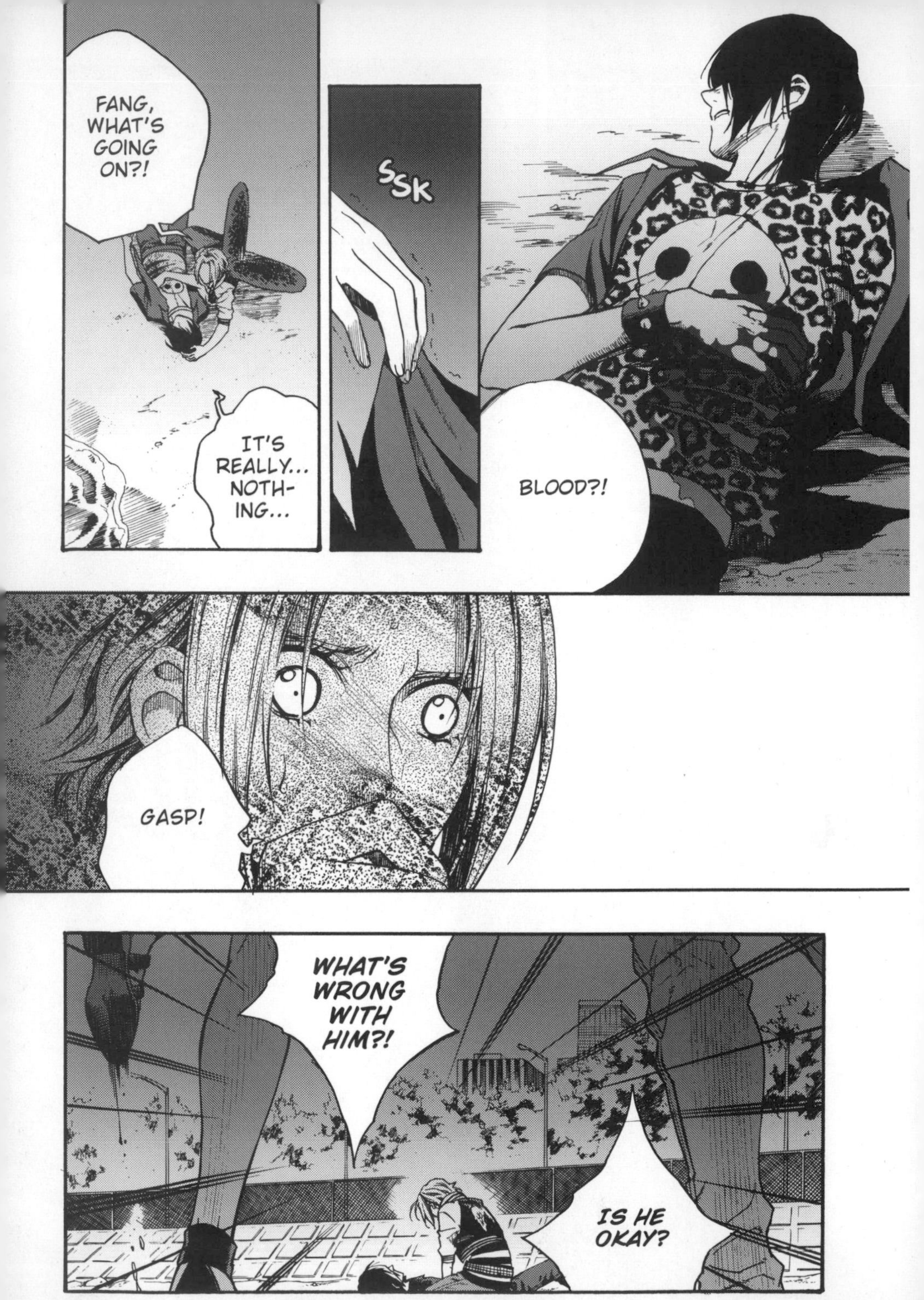
FANG, WHAT'S GOING ON?!
IT'S REALLY... NOTH-ING...
SSK
BLOOD?!
GASP!
WHAT'S WRONG WITH HIM?!
IS HE OKAY?

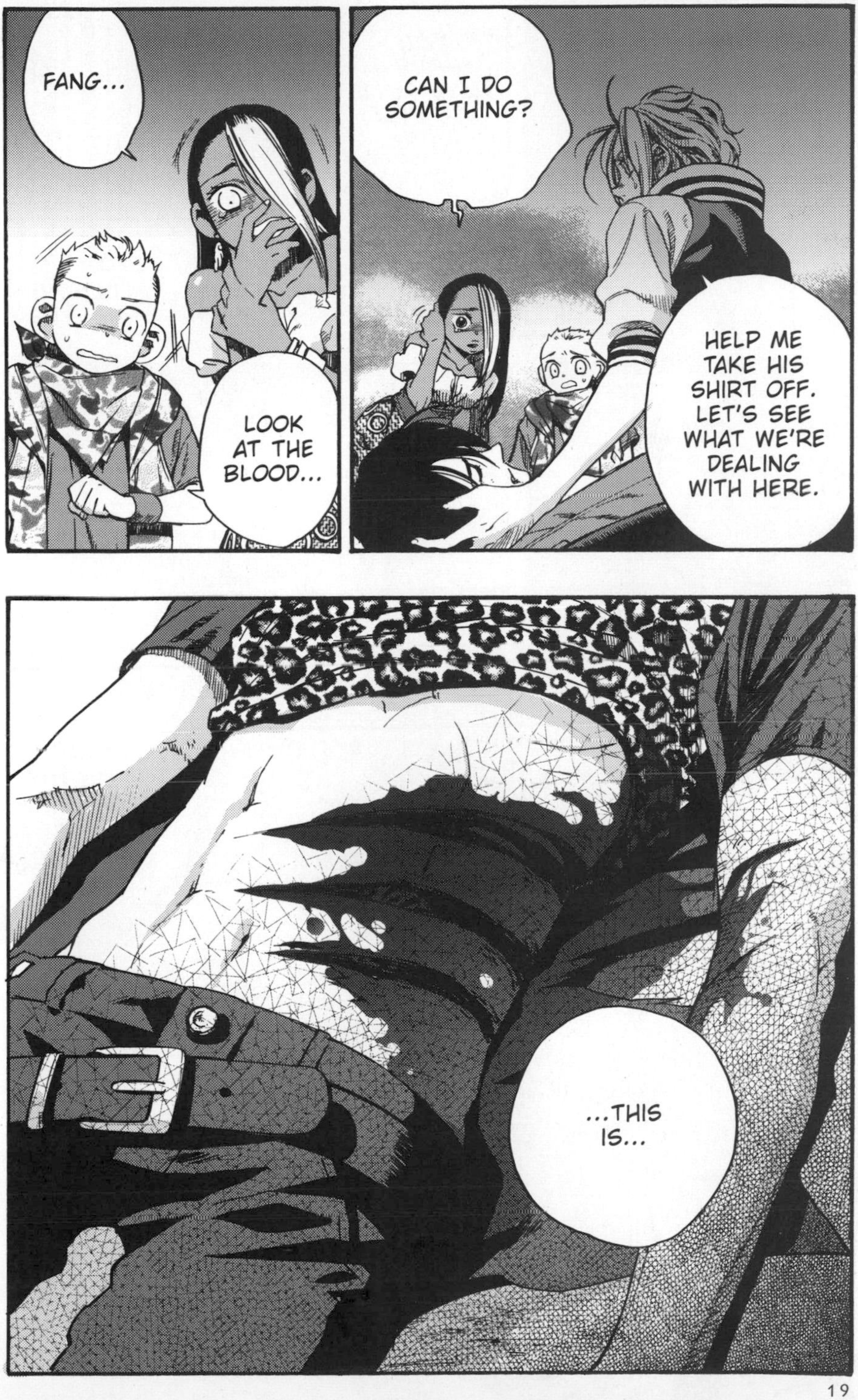
FANG...
LOOK AT THE BLOOD...
CAN I DO SOMETHING?
HELP ME TAKE HIS SHIRT OFF. LET'S SEE WHAT WE'RE DEALING WITH HERE.
...THIS IS...

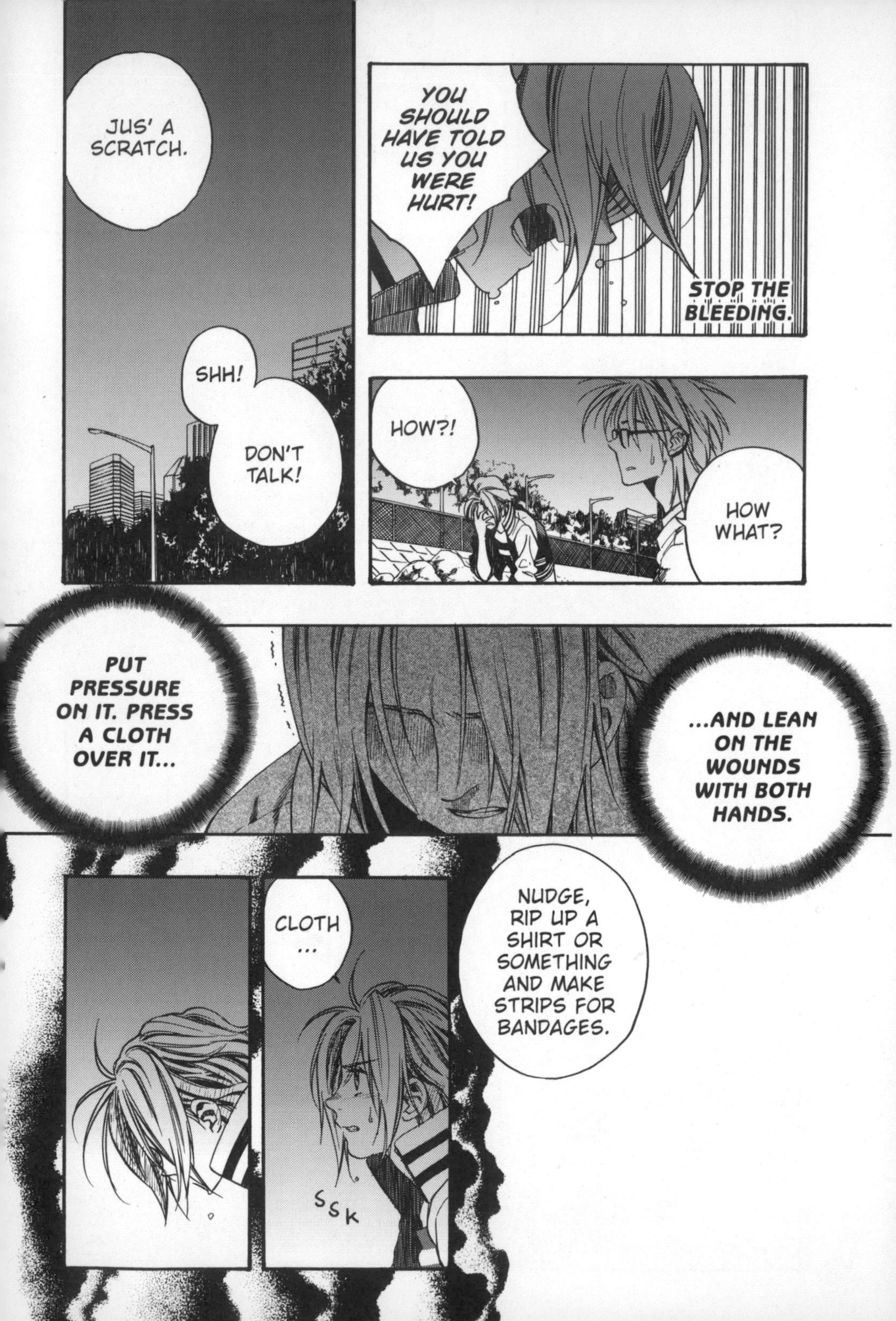
JUS' A SCRATCH.
SHH!
DON'T TALK!
YOU SHOULD HAVE TOLD US YOU WERE HURT!
STOP THE BLEEDING.
HOW?!
HOW WHAT?
PUT PRESSURE ON IT. PRESS A CLOTH OVER IT...
...AND LEAN ON THE WOUNDS WITH BOTH HANDS.
CLOTH ...
NUDGE, RIP UP A SHIRT OR SOMETHING AND MAKE STRIPS FOR BANDAGES.
SSK

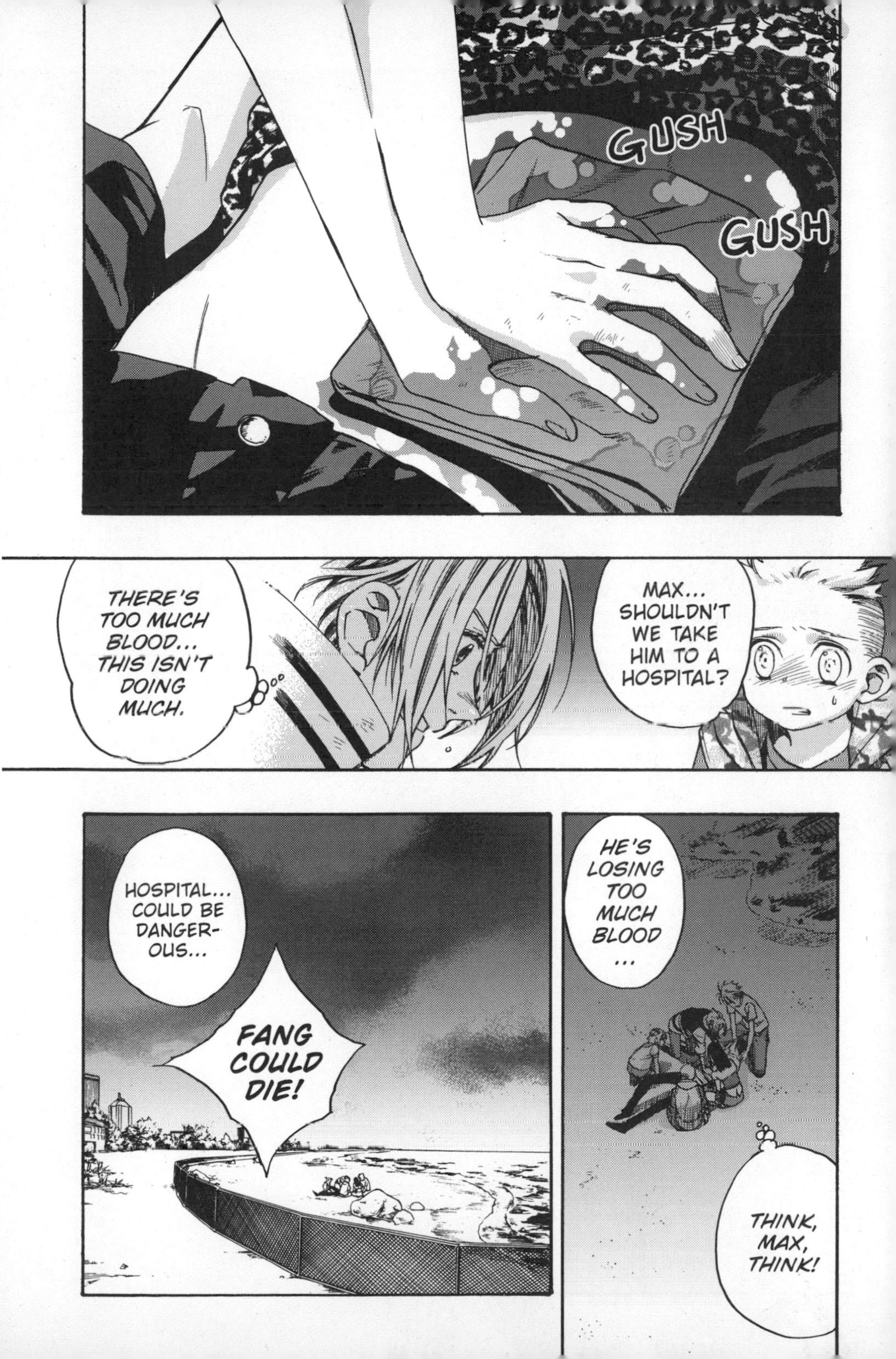
GUSH
GUSH
THERE'S TOO MUCH BLOOD... THIS ISN'T DOING MUCH.
MAX... SHOULDN'T WE TAKE HIM TO A HOSPITAL?
HOSPITAL... COULD BE DANGER-OUS...
FANG COULD DIE!
HE'S LOSING TOO MUCH BLOOD ...
THINK, MAX, THINK!

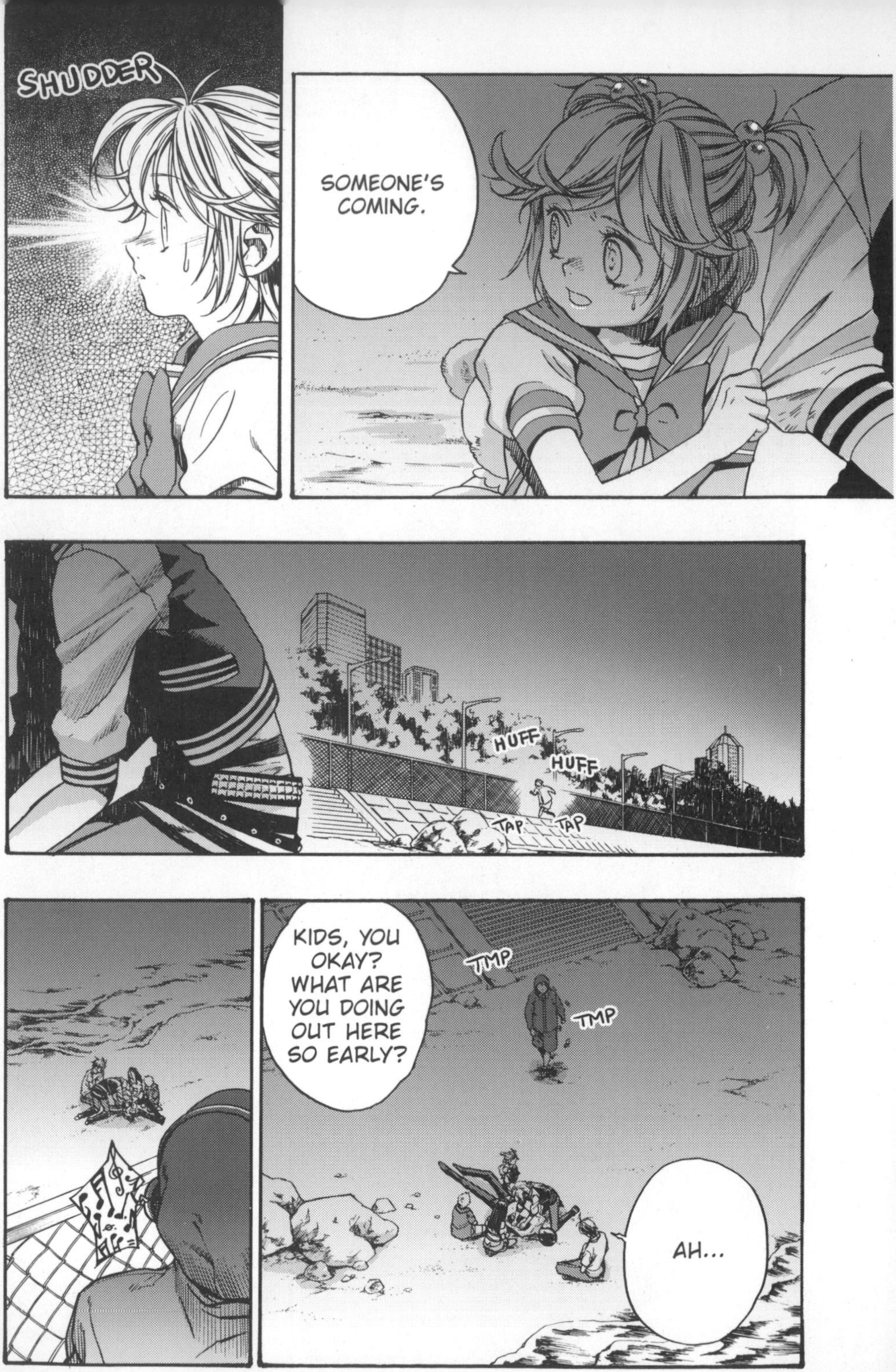
SHUDDER
SOMEONE'S COMING.
HUFF
HUFF
TAP
TAP
KIDS, YOU OKAY? WHAT ARE YOU DOING OUT HERE SO EARLY?
TMP
TMP
AH...

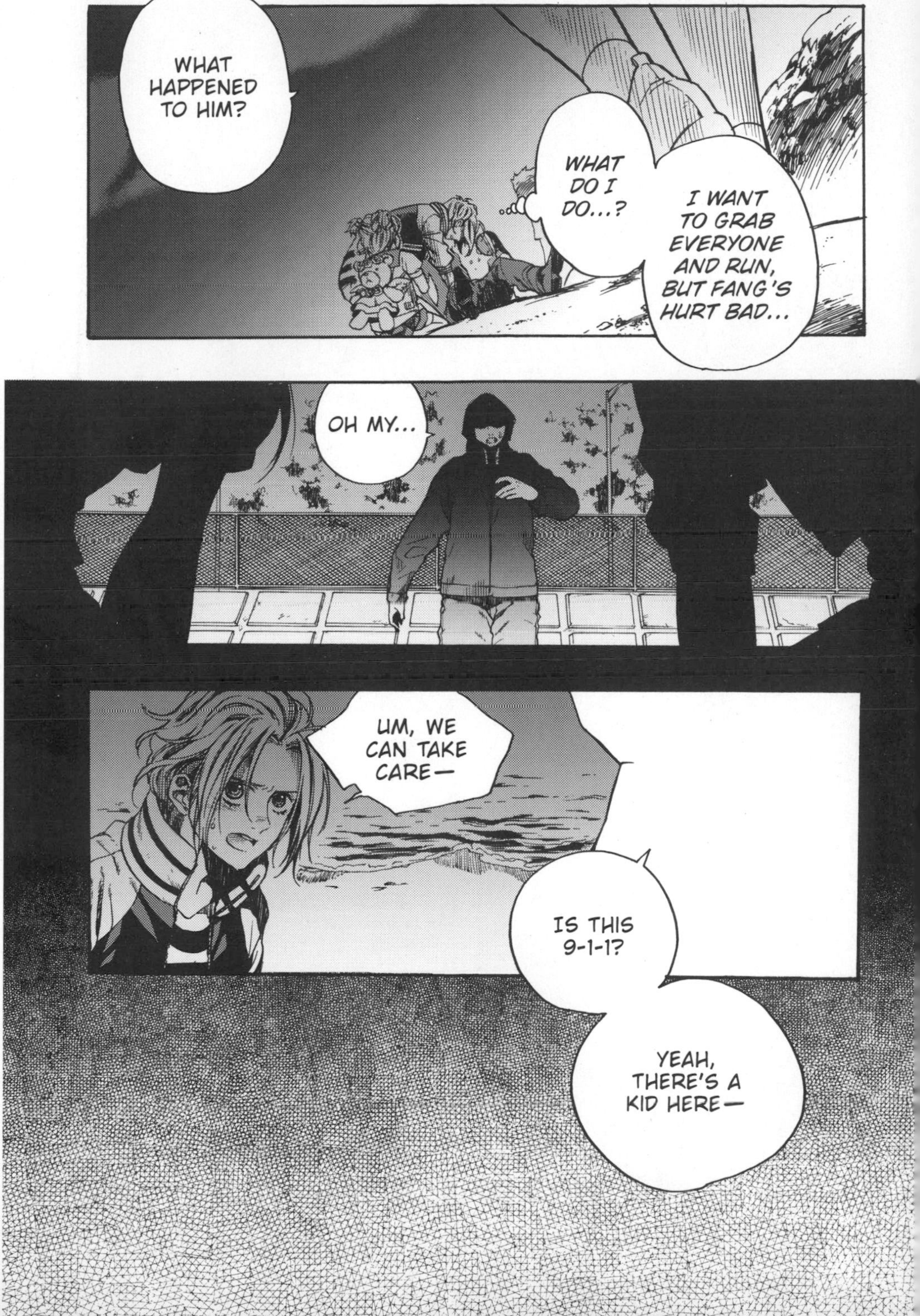
WHAT HAPPENED TO HIM?
WHAT DO I DO...?
I WANT TO GRAB EVERYONE AND RUN, BUT FANG'S HURT BAD...
OH MY...
UM, WE CAN TAKE CARE—
IS THIS 9-1-1?
YEAH, THERE'S A KID HERE—

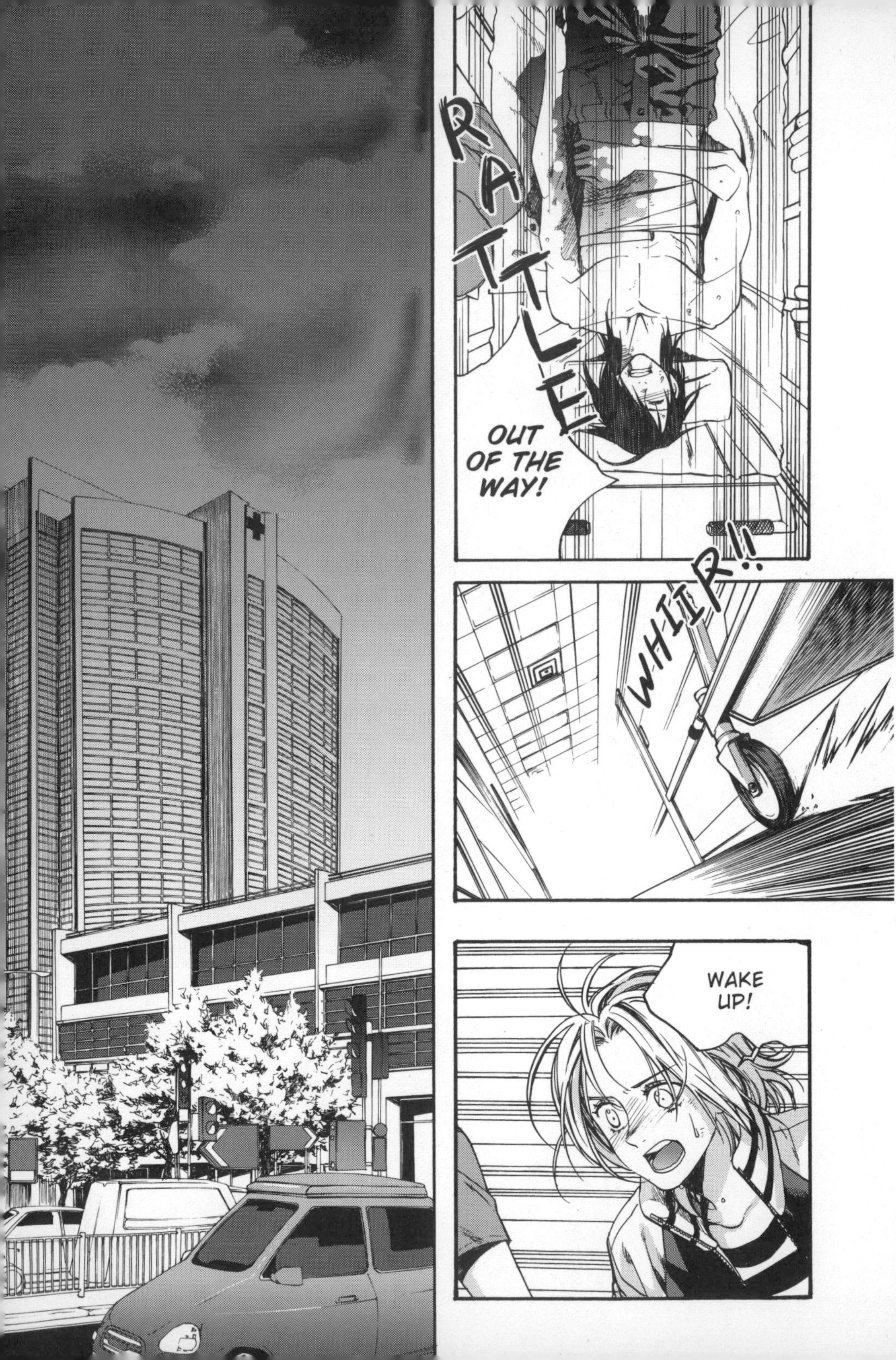
RATTLE
OUT OF THE WAY!
WHIIR!!
WAKE UP!

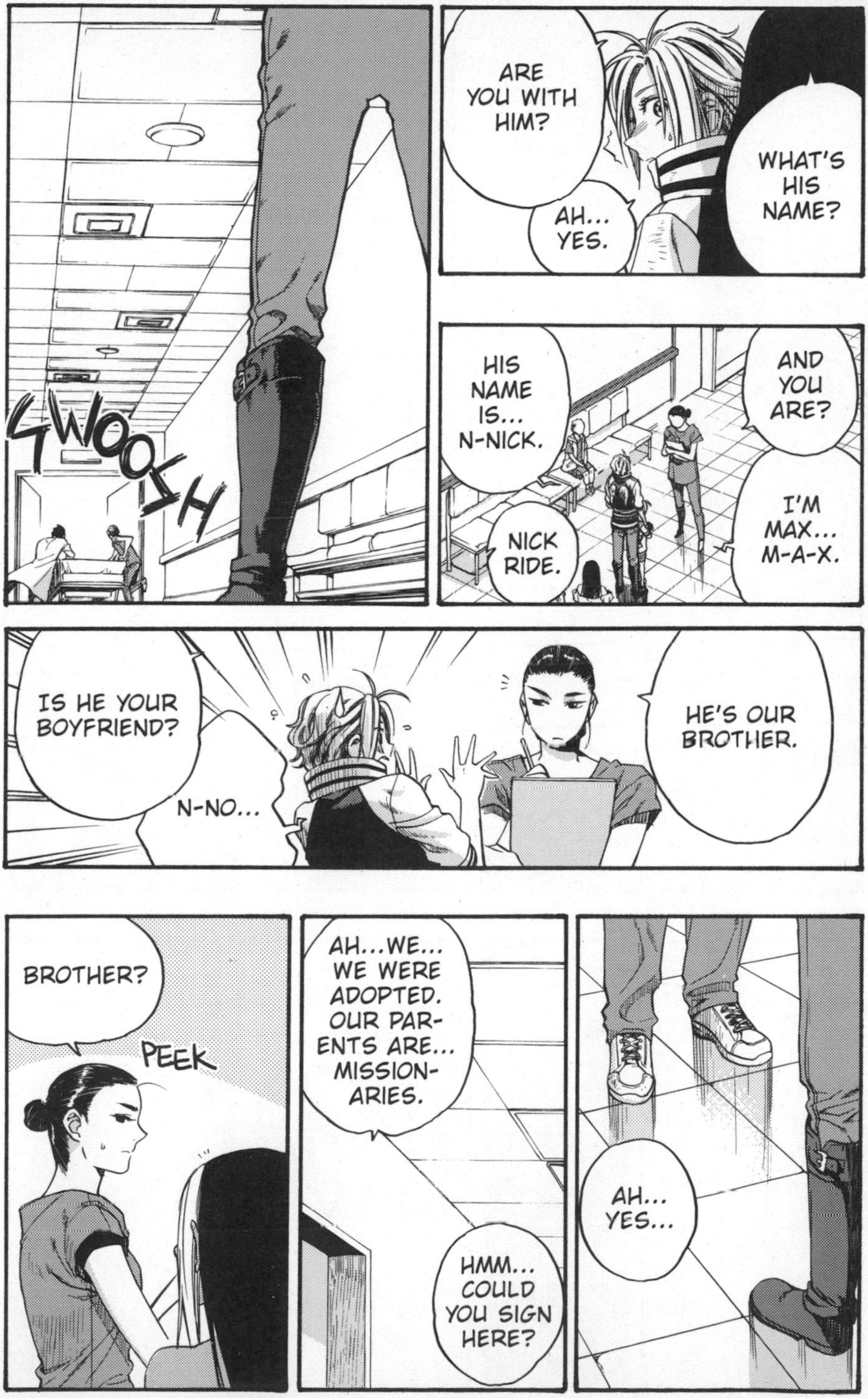
SWOOSH
ARE YOU WITH HIM?
AH... YES.
WHAT'S HIS NAME?
HIS NAME IS... N-NICK.
NICK RIDE.
AND YOU ARE?
I'M MAX... M-A-X.
IS HE YOUR BOYFRIEND?
N-NO...
HE'S OUR BROTHER.
BROTHER?
PEEK
AH...WE... WE WERE ADOPTED. OUR PAR-ENTS ARE... MISSION-ARIES.
HMM... COULD YOU SIGN HERE?
AH... YES...

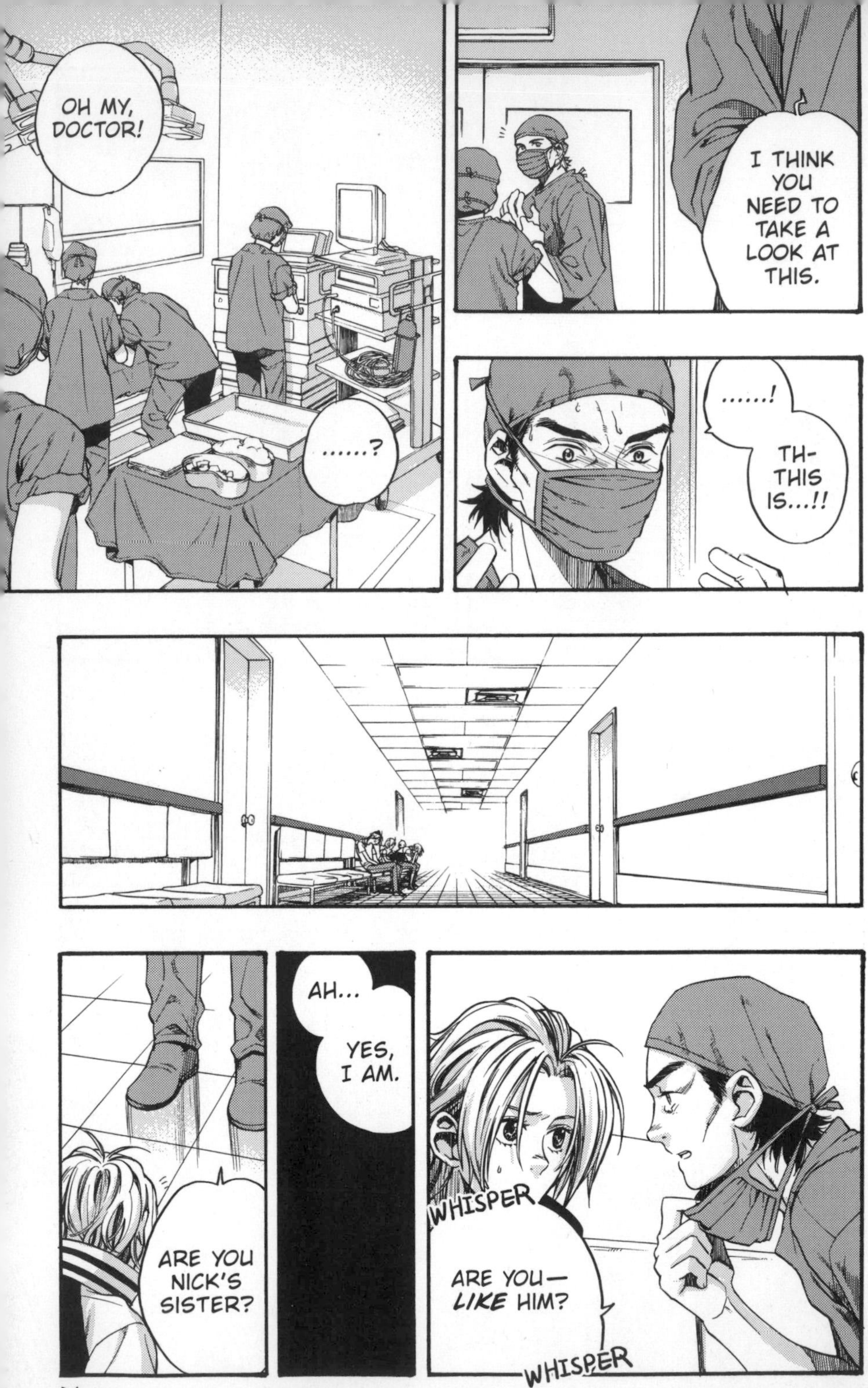
OH MY, DOCTOR!
......?
I THINK YOU NEED TO TAKE A LOOK AT THIS.
......!
TH-THIS IS...!!
ARE YOU NICK'S SISTER?
AH...
YES, I AM.
WHISPER
ARE YOU— *LIKE* HIM?
WHISPER

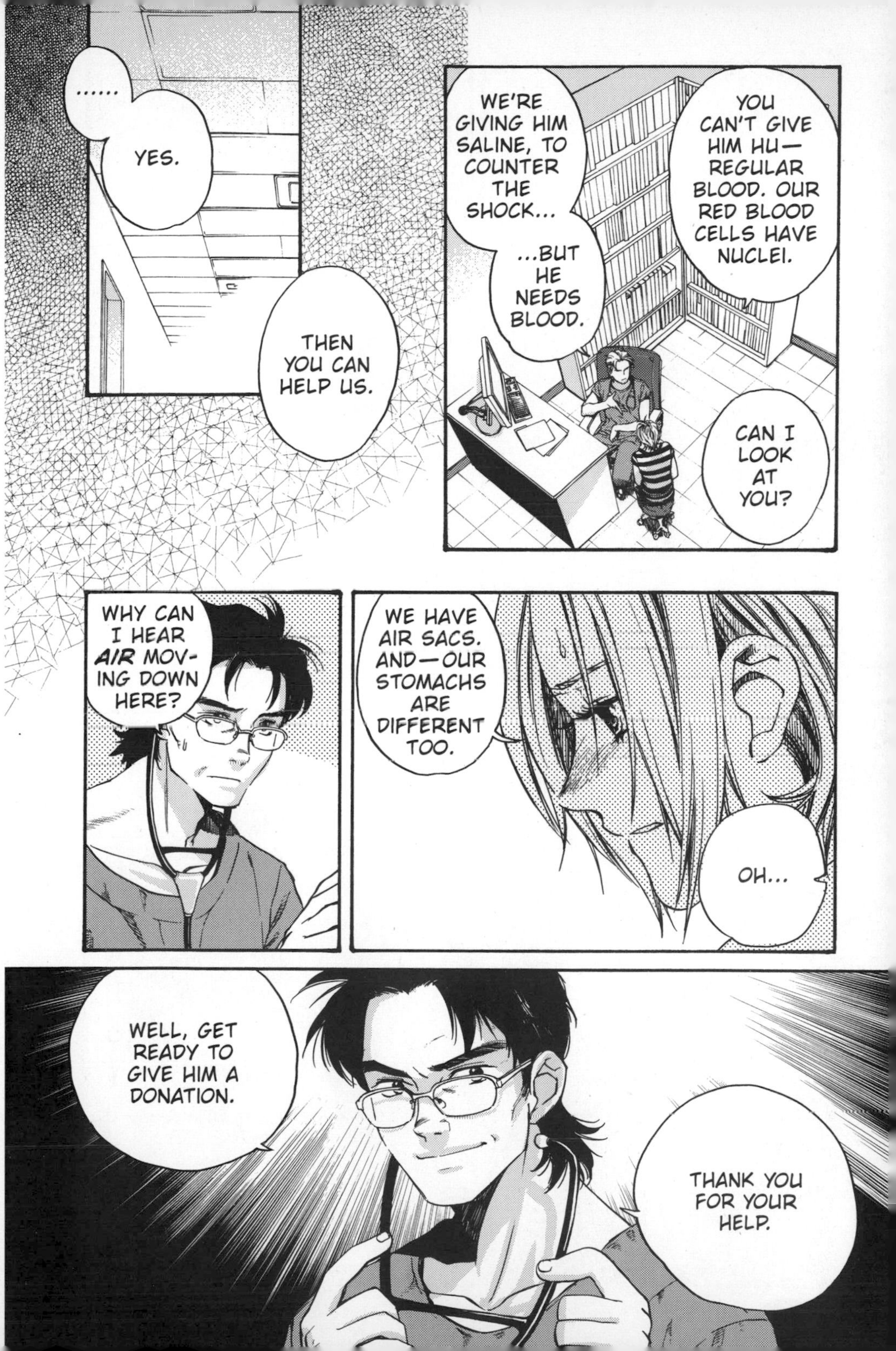
......
YES.
THEN YOU CAN HELP US.
WE'RE GIVING HIM SALINE, TO COUNTER THE SHOCK...
...BUT HE NEEDS BLOOD.
YOU CAN'T GIVE HIM HU—REGULAR BLOOD. OUR RED BLOOD CELLS HAVE NUCLEI.
CAN I LOOK AT YOU?
WHY CAN I HEAR *AIR* MOVING DOWN HERE?
WE HAVE AIR SACS. AND—OUR STOMACHS ARE DIFFERENT TOO.
OH...
WELL, GET READY TO GIVE HIM A DONATION.
THANK YOU FOR YOUR HELP.

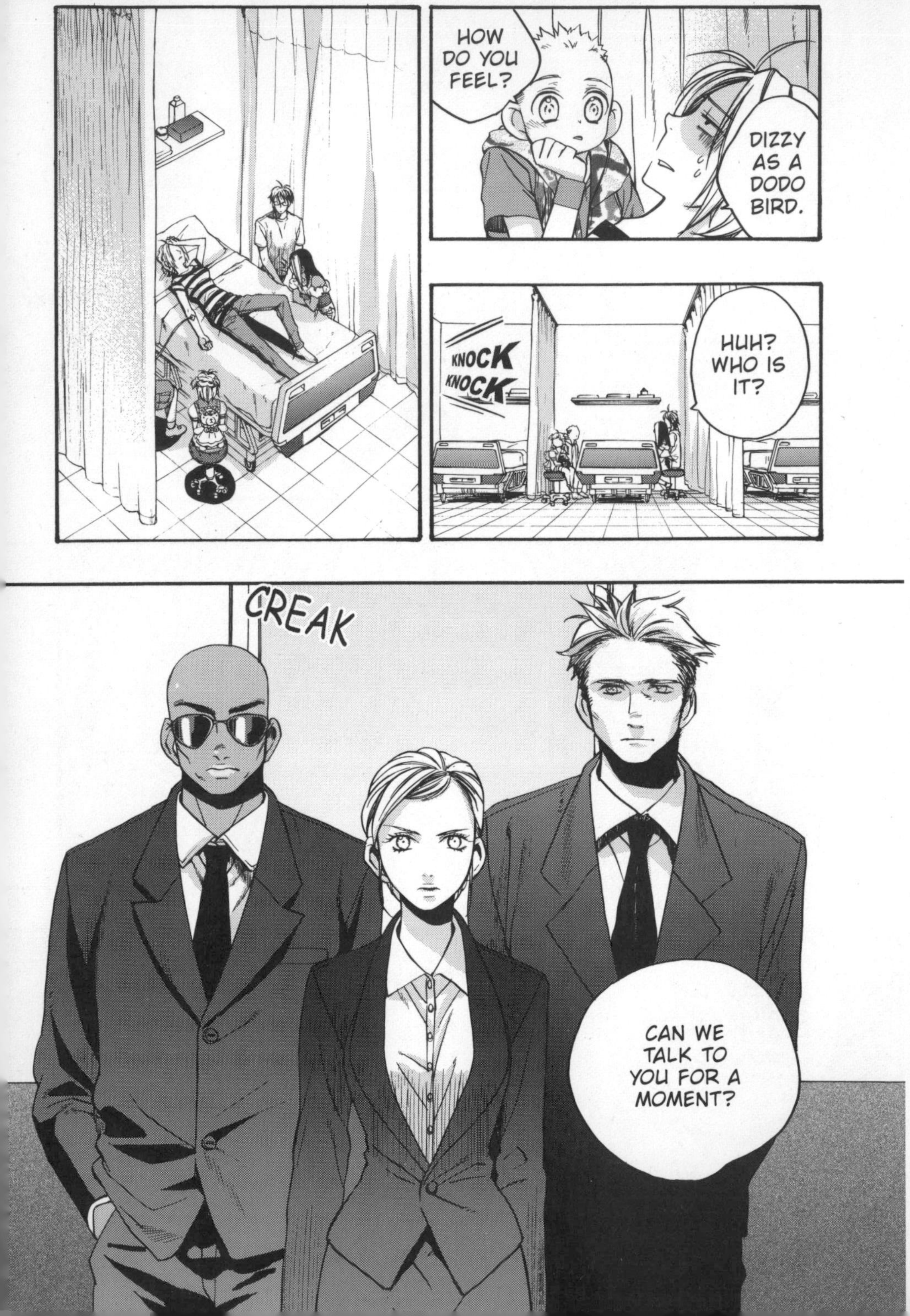
HOW DO YOU FEEL?
DIZZY AS A DODO BIRD.
KNOCK KNOCK
HUH? WHO IS IT?
CREAK
CAN WE TALK TO YOU FOR A MOMENT?

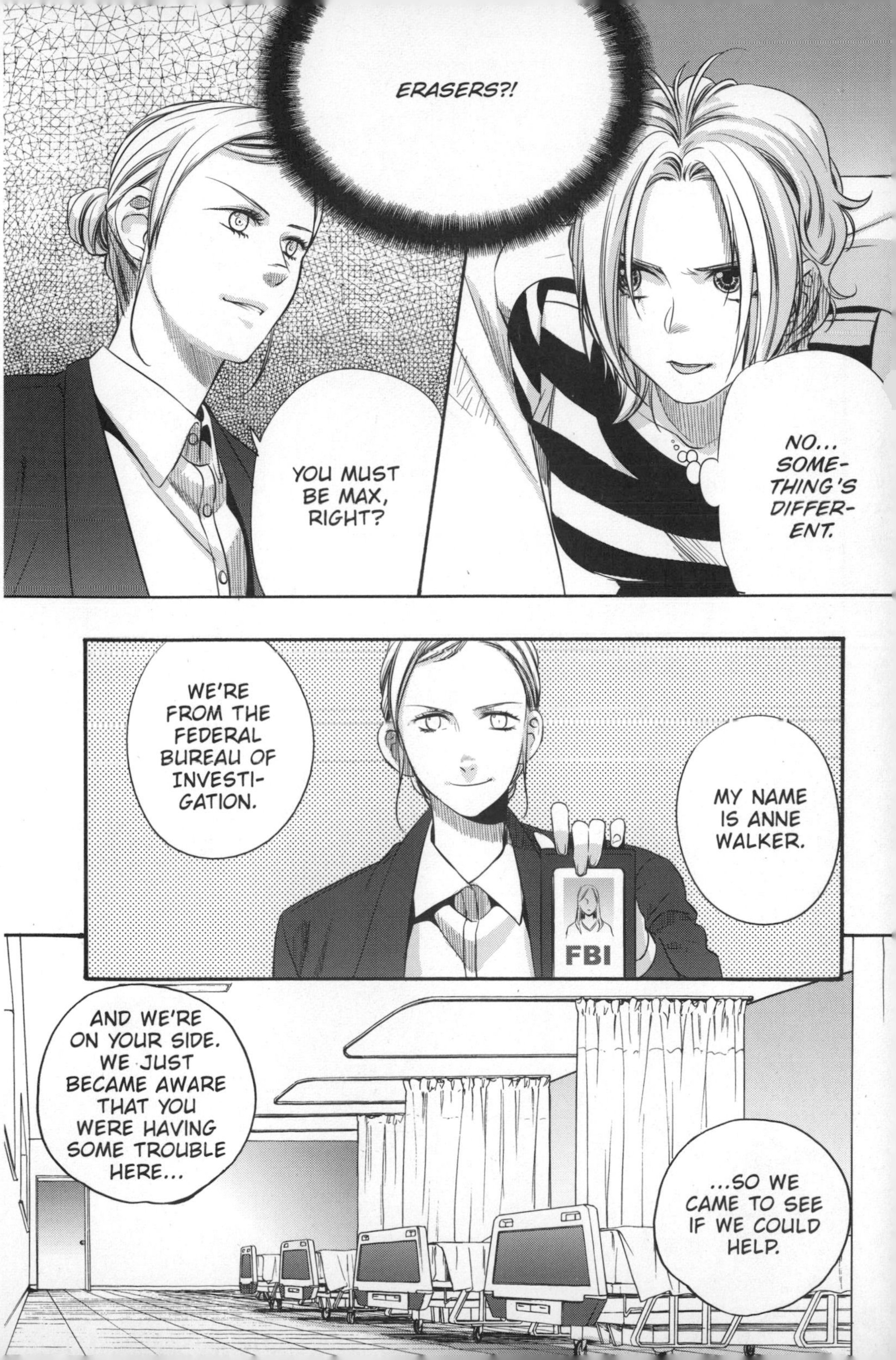
ERASERS?!
YOU MUST BE MAX, RIGHT?
NO... SOMETHING'S DIFFERENT.
WE'RE FROM THE FEDERAL BUREAU OF INVESTIGATION.
MY NAME IS ANNE WALKER.
FBI
AND WE'RE ON YOUR SIDE. WE JUST BECAME AWARE THAT YOU WERE HAVING SOME TROUBLE HERE...
...SO WE CAME TO SEE IF WE COULD HELP.

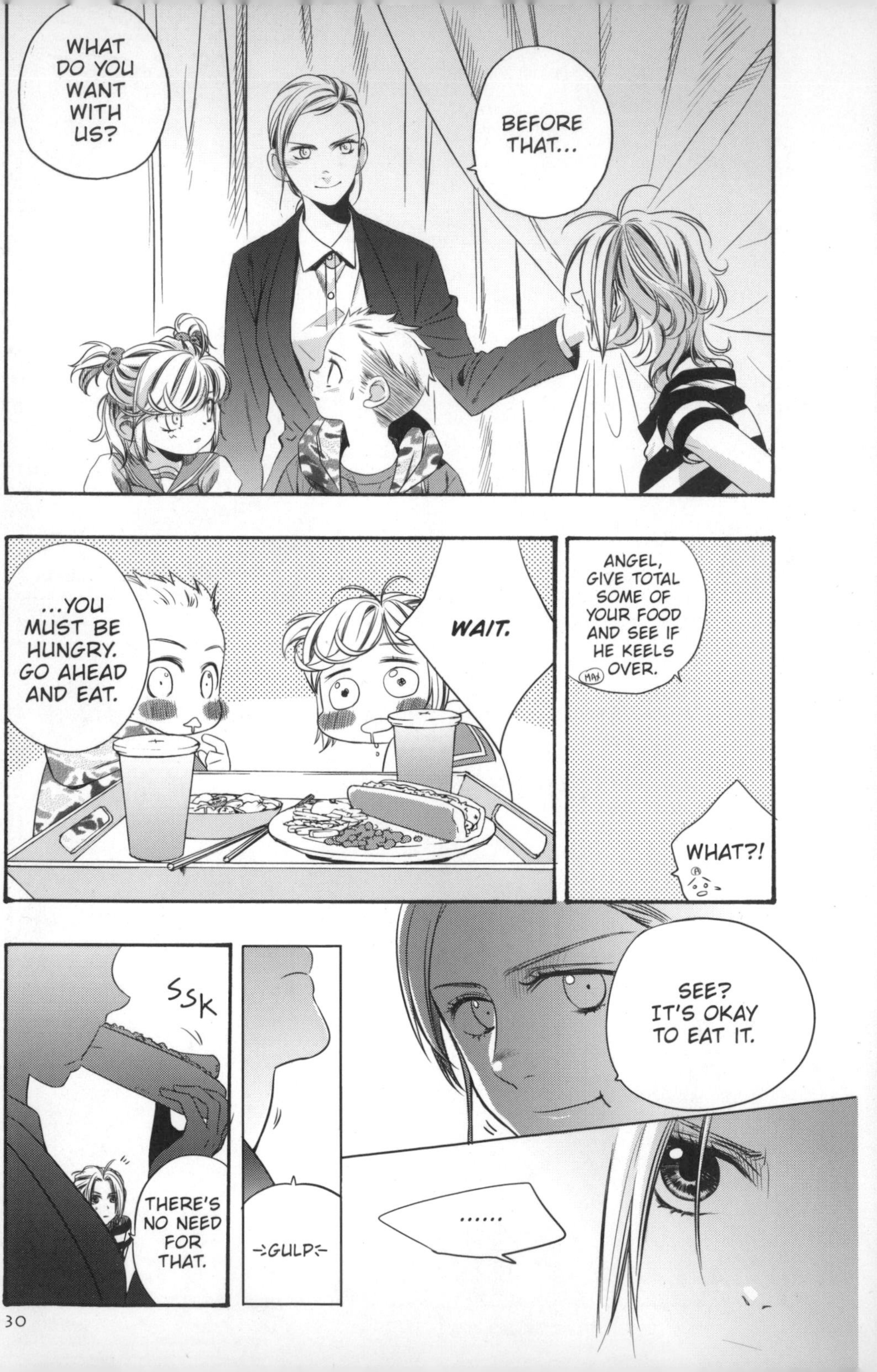
WHAT DO YOU WANT WITH US?
BEFORE THAT...
...YOU MUST BE HUNGRY. GO AHEAD AND EAT.
WAIT.
ANGEL, GIVE TOTAL SOME OF YOUR FOOD AND SEE IF HE KEELS OVER.
MAX
WHAT?!
SSK
THERE'S NO NEED FOR THAT.
GULP
SEE? IT'S OKAY TO EAT IT.
......

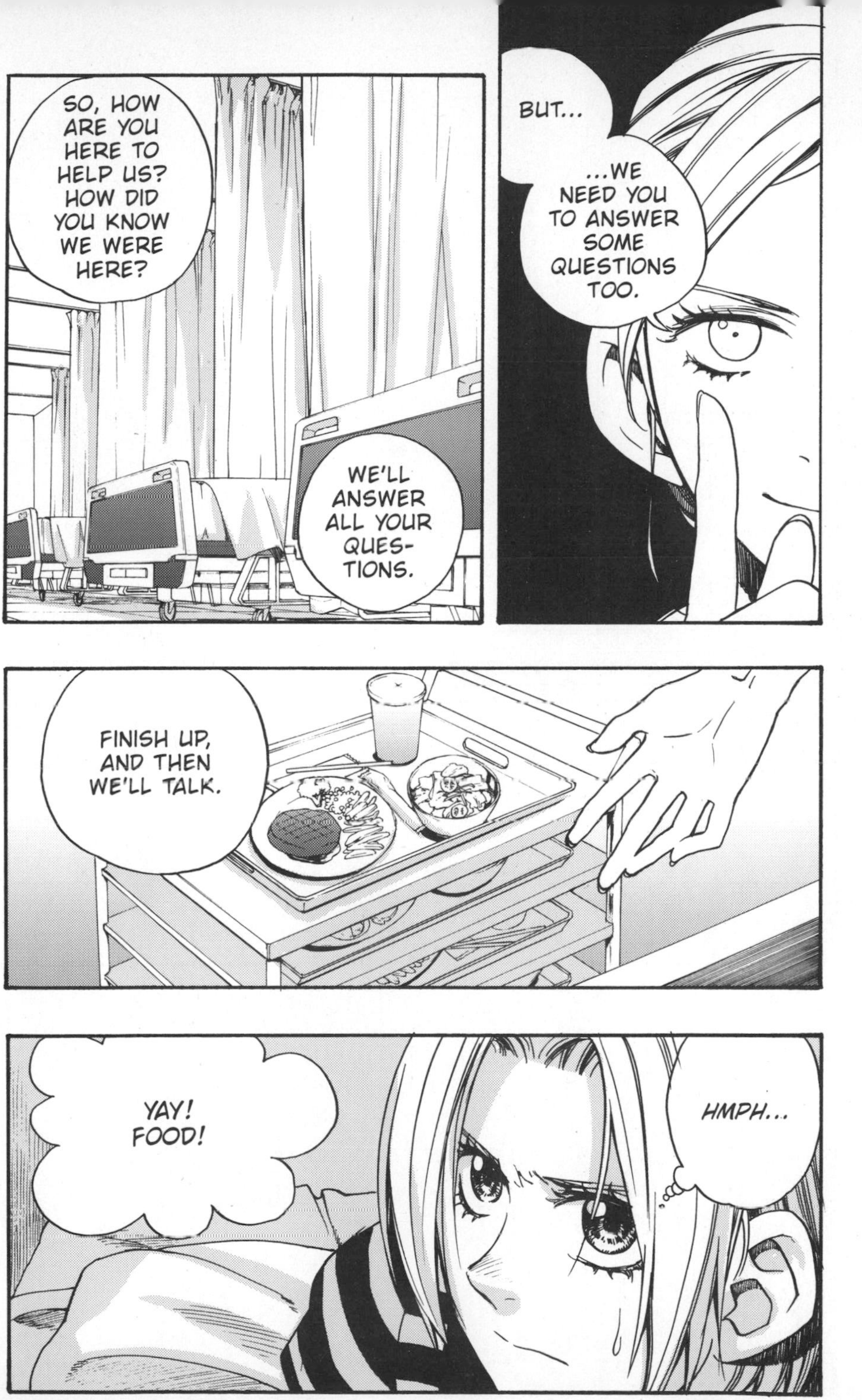

SO, HOW ARE YOU HERE TO HELP US? HOW DID YOU KNOW WE WERE HERE?
WE'LL ANSWER ALL YOUR QUES-TIONS.
BUT...
...WE NEED YOU TO ANSWER SOME QUESTIONS TOO.
FINISH UP, AND THEN WE'LL TALK.
YAY! FOOD!
HMPH...

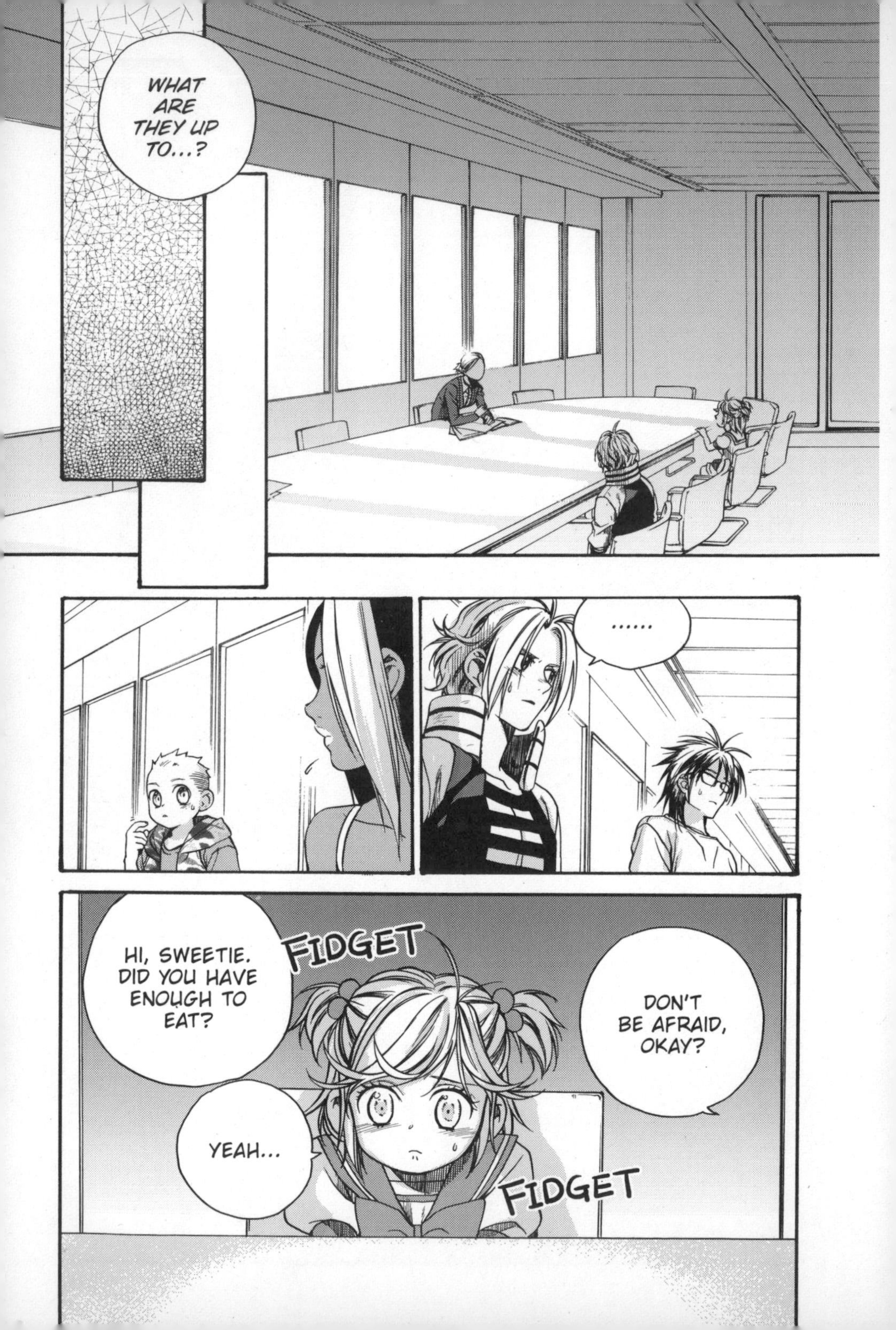
WHAT ARE THEY UP TO...?
......
HI, SWEETIE. DID YOU HAVE ENOUGH TO EAT?
FIDGET
DON'T BE AFRAID, OKAY?
YEAH...
FIDGET

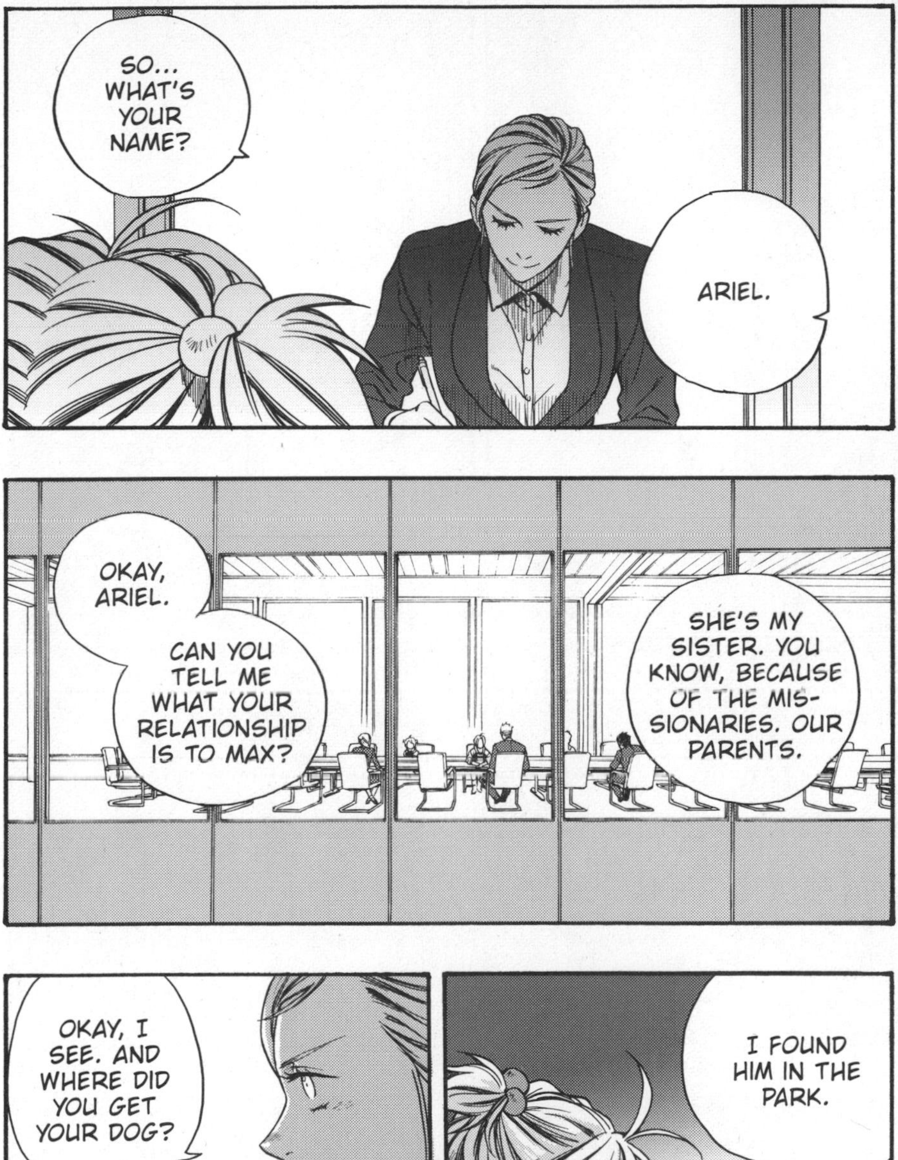
SO... WHAT'S YOUR NAME?
ARIEL.
OKAY, ARIEL.
CAN YOU TELL ME WHAT YOUR RELATIONSHIP IS TO MAX?
SHE'S MY SISTER. YOU KNOW, BECAUSE OF THE MIS-SIONARIES. OUR PARENTS.
OKAY, I SEE. AND WHERE DID YOU GET YOUR DOG?
I FOUND HIM IN THE PARK.
SQUISH

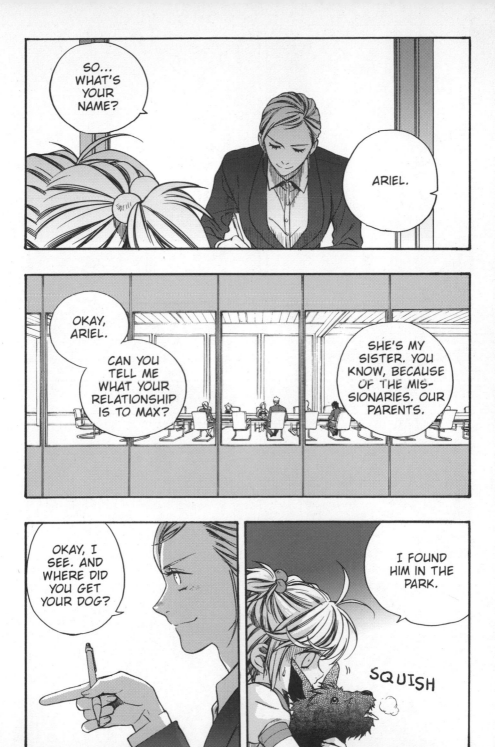

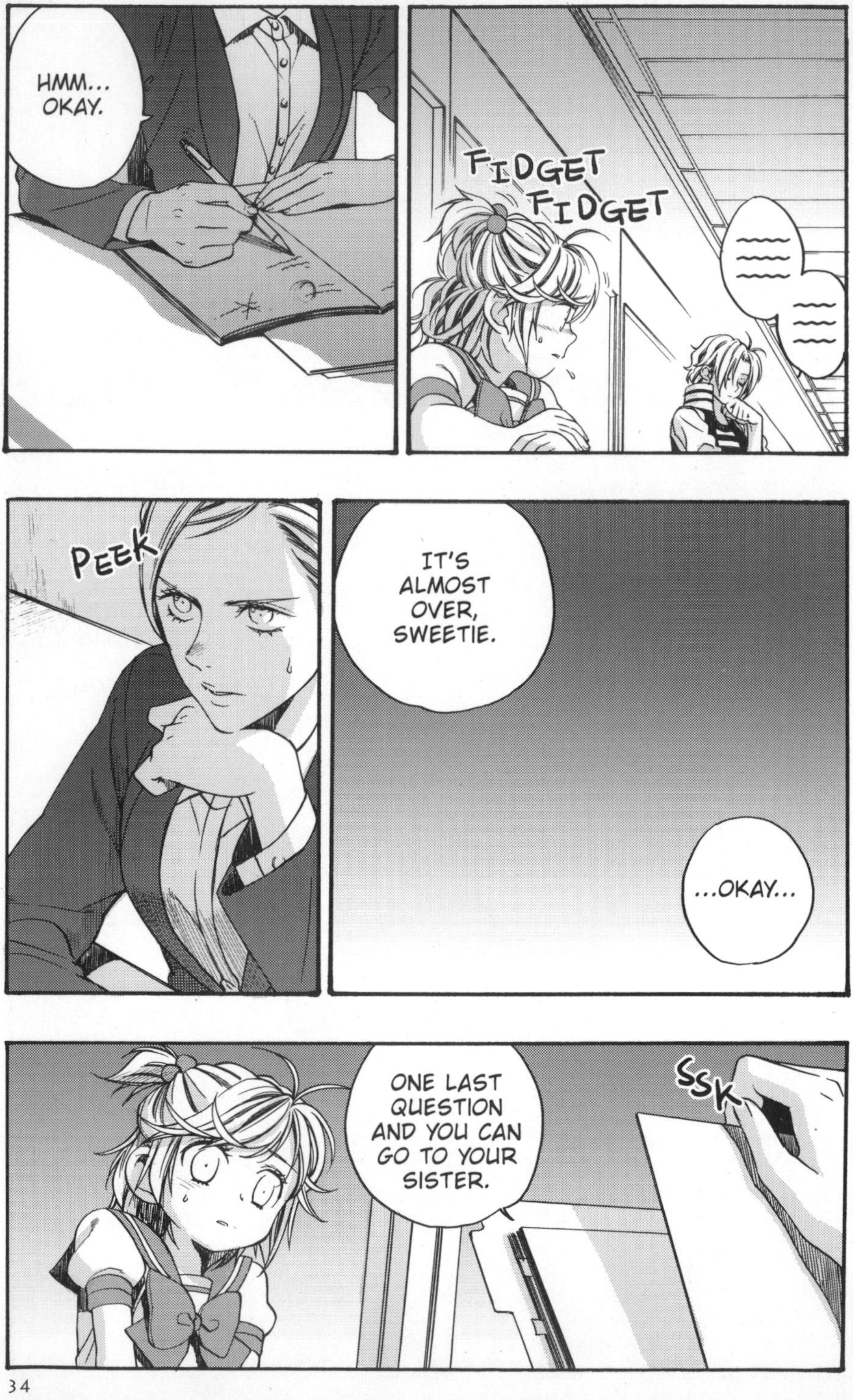
HMM... OKAY.
FIDGET FIDGET
PEEK
IT'S ALMOST OVER, SWEETIE.
...OKAY...
ONE LAST QUESTION AND YOU CAN GO TO YOUR SISTER.
SSK

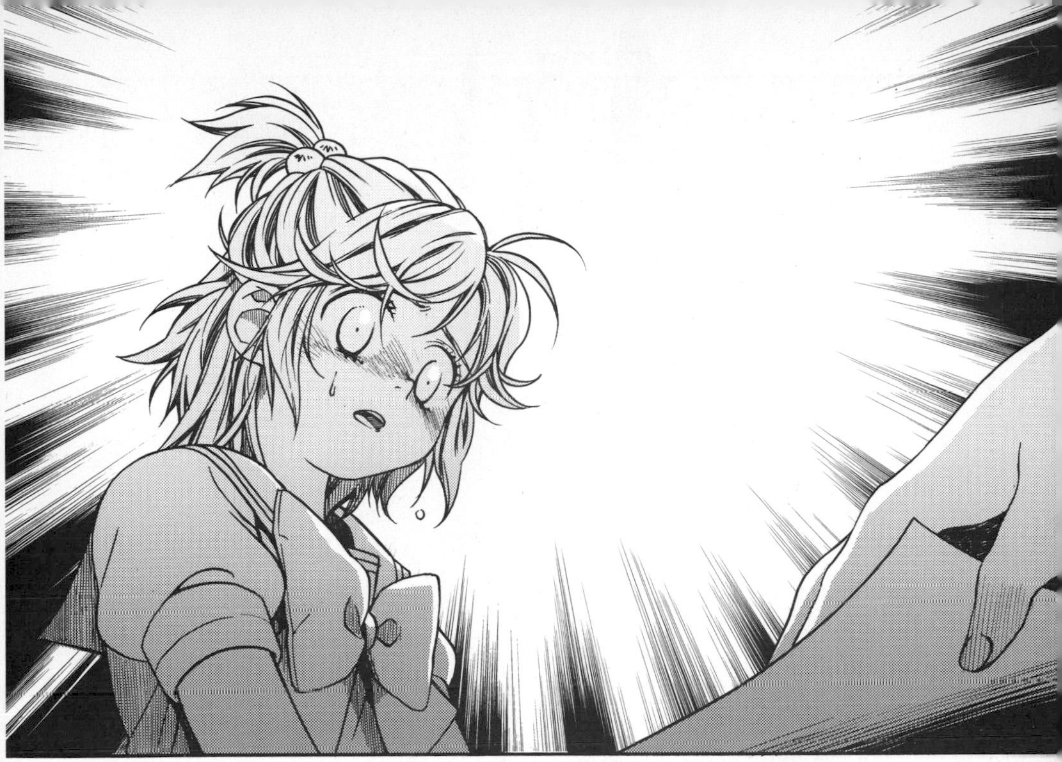

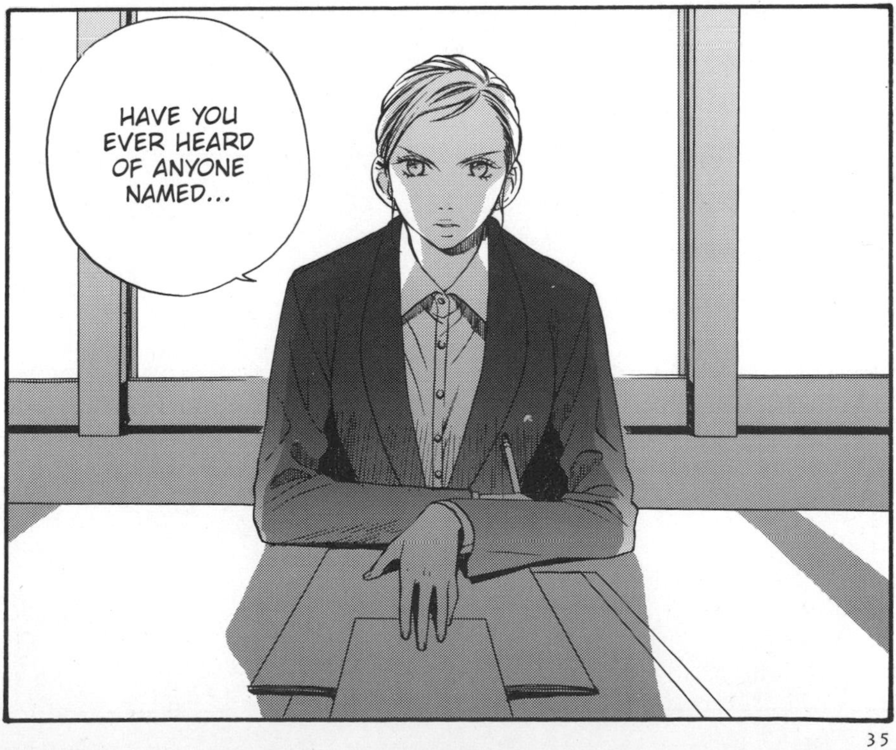
HAVE YOU EVER HEARD OF ANYONE NAMED...

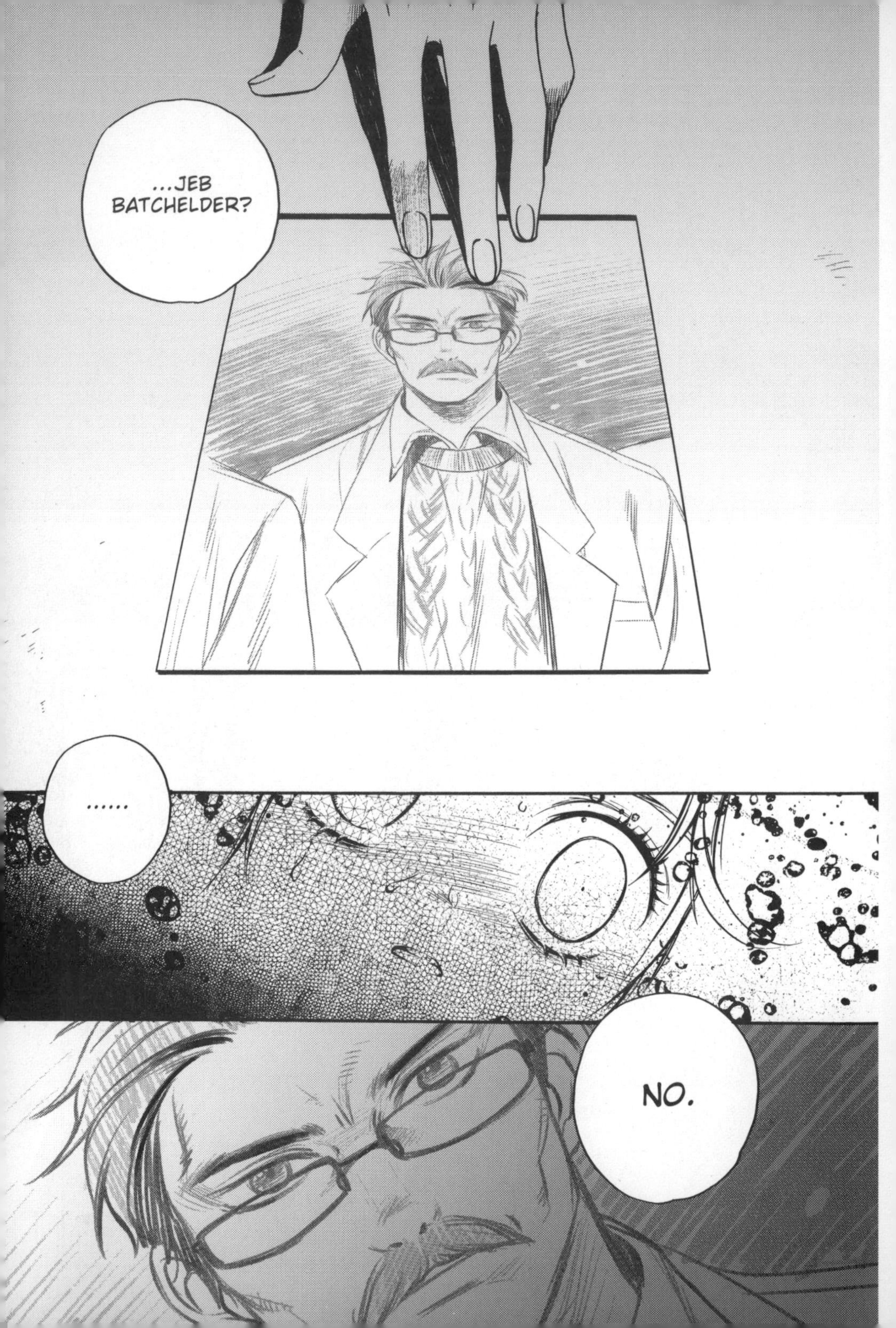
...JEB BATCHELDER?
......
NO.

MAXIMUM RIDE
CHAPTER 17

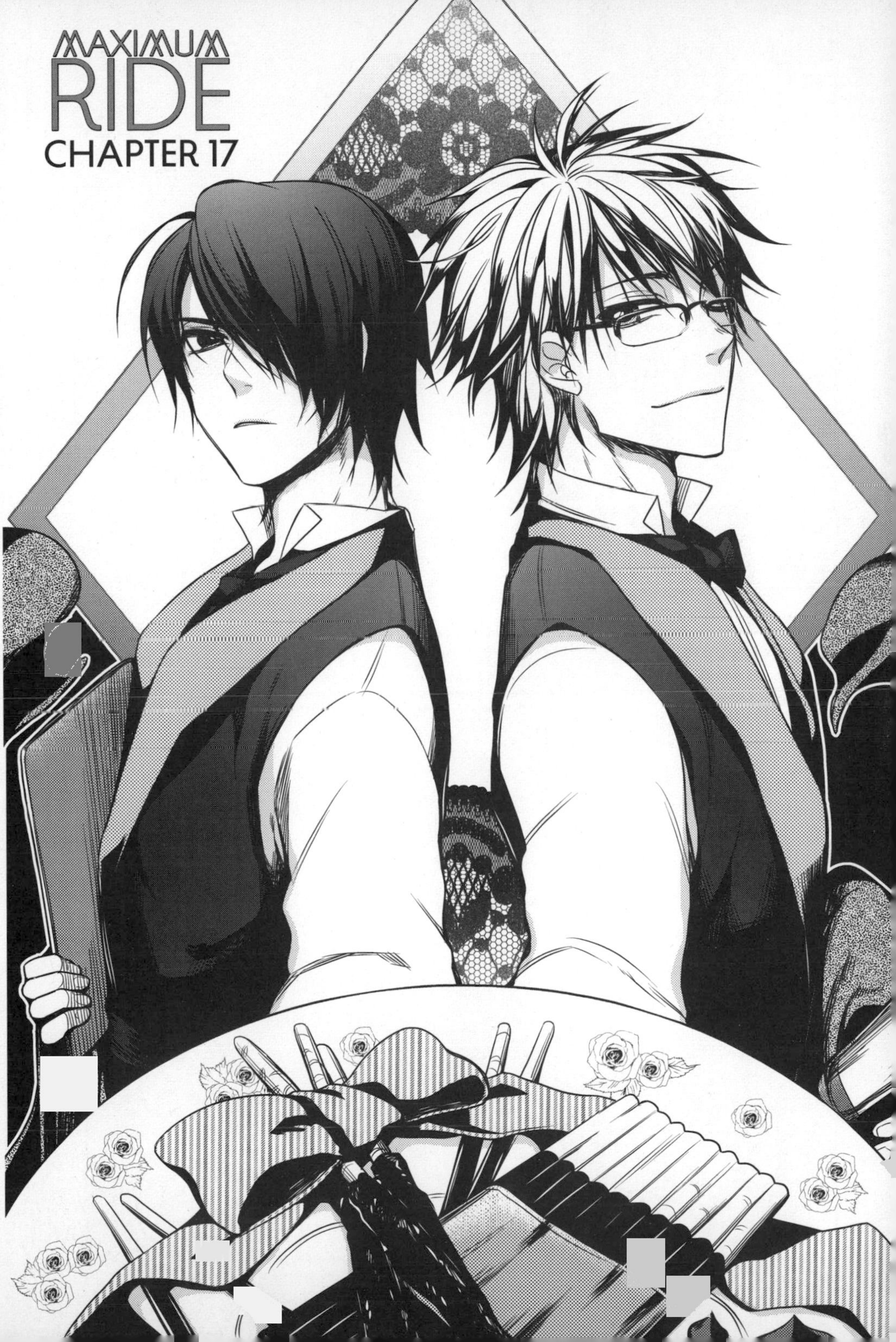

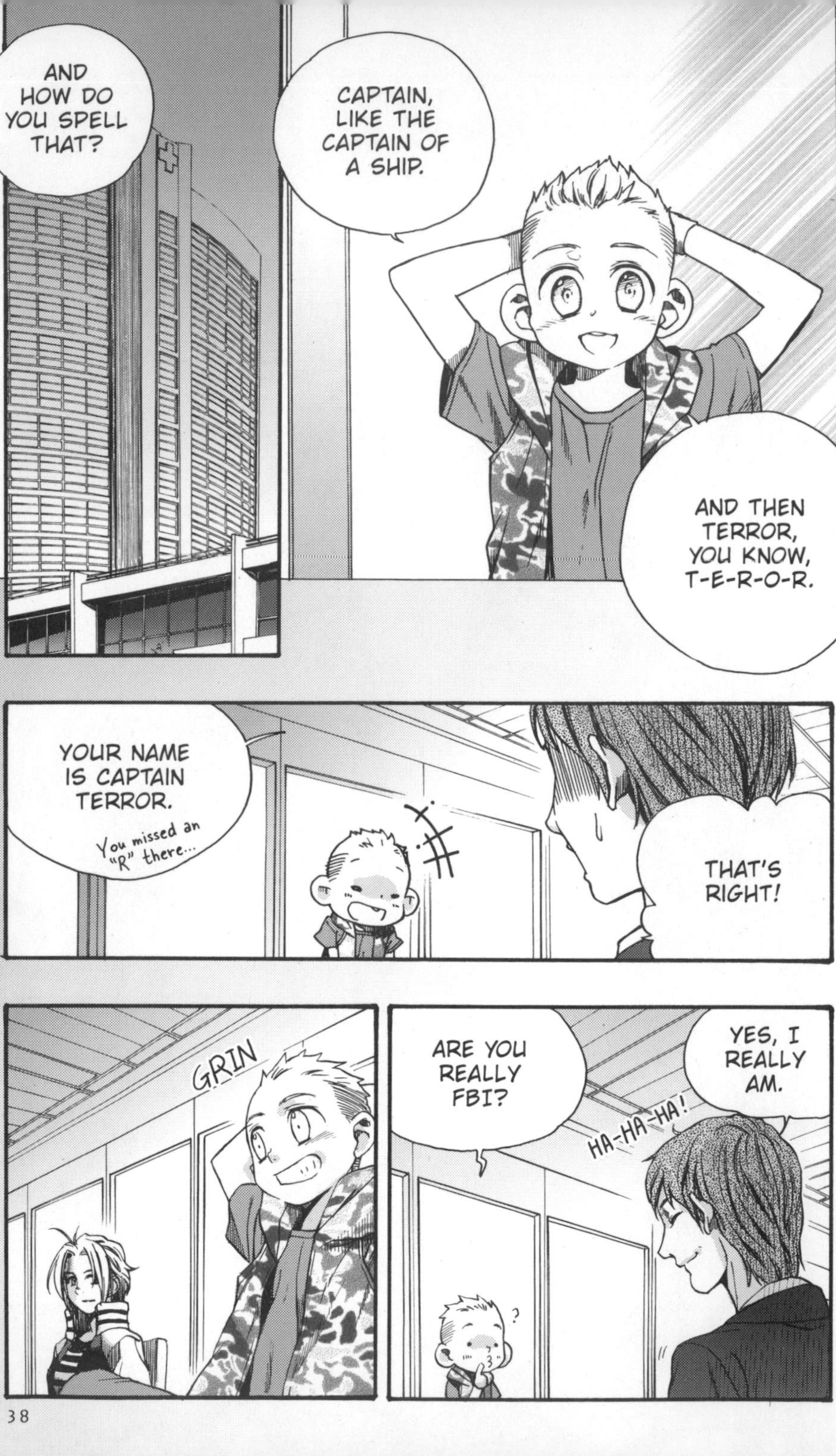
AND HOW DO YOU SPELL THAT?
CAPTAIN, LIKE THE CAPTAIN OF A SHIP.
AND THEN TERROR, YOU KNOW, T-E-R-O-R.
YOUR NAME IS CAPTAIN TERROR.
You missed an "R" there...
THAT'S RIGHT!
GRIN
ARE YOU REALLY FBI?
YES, I REALLY AM.
HA-HA-HA!

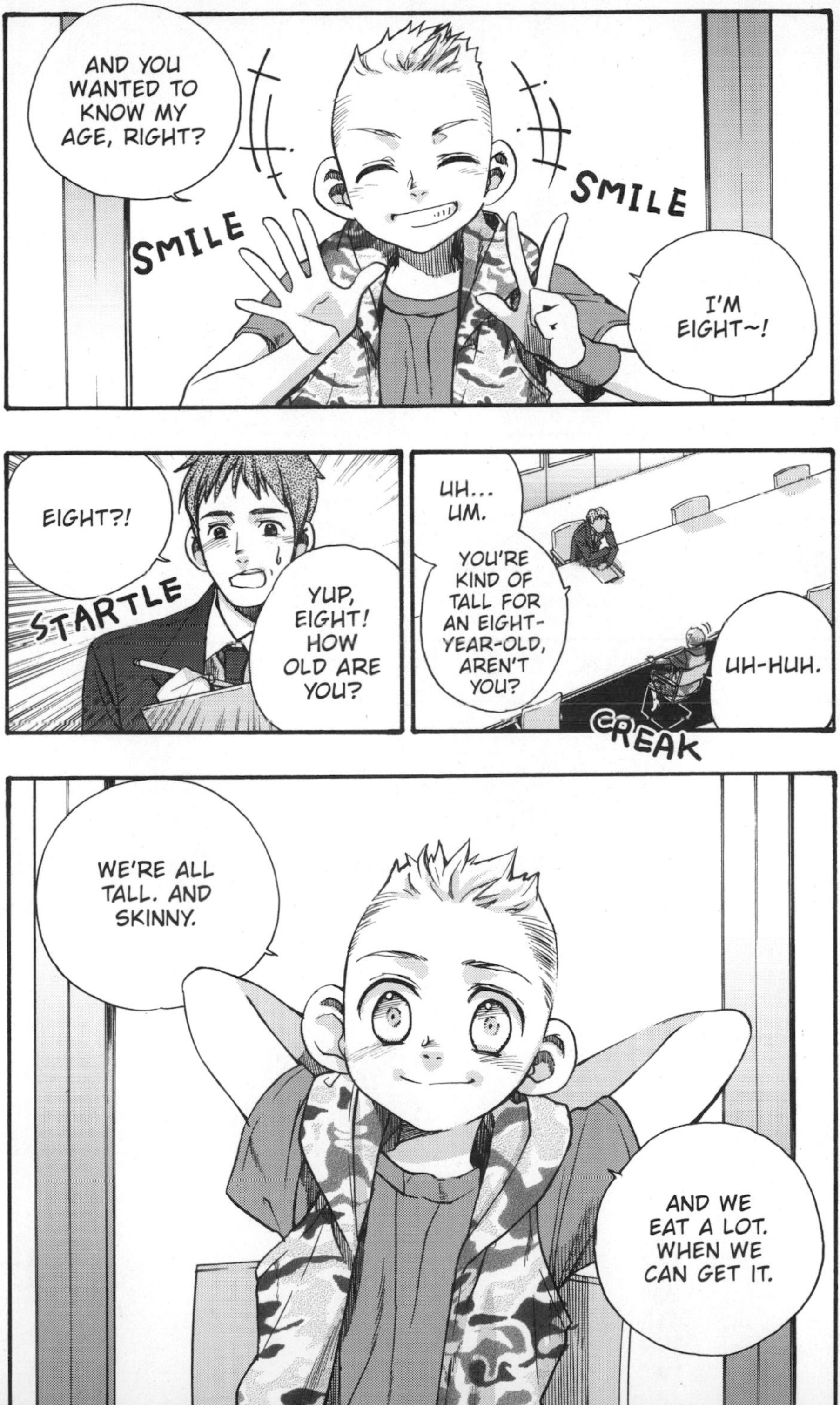
AND YOU WANTED TO KNOW MY AGE, RIGHT?
SMILE
SMILE
I'M EIGHT~!
EIGHT?!
STARTLE
YUP, EIGHT! HOW OLD ARE YOU?
UH... UM.
YOU'RE KIND OF TALL FOR AN EIGHT-YEAR-OLD, AREN'T YOU?
UH-HUH.
CREAK
WE'RE ALL TALL. AND SKINNY.
AND WE EAT A LOT. WHEN WE CAN GET IT.

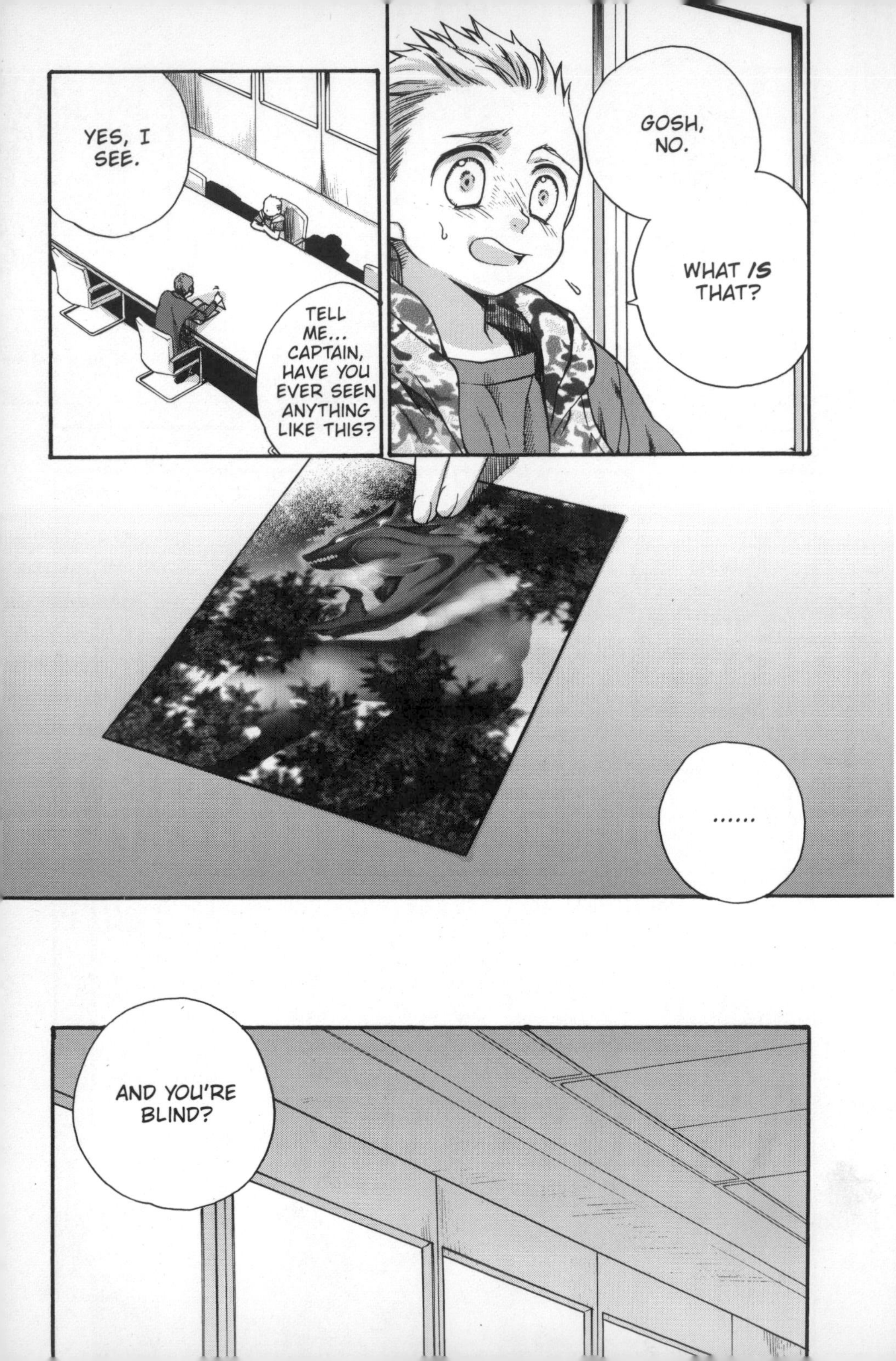
YES, I SEE.
TELL ME... CAPTAIN, HAVE YOU EVER SEEN ANYTHING LIKE THIS?
GOSH, NO.
WHAT *IS* THAT?
......
AND YOU'RE BLIND?

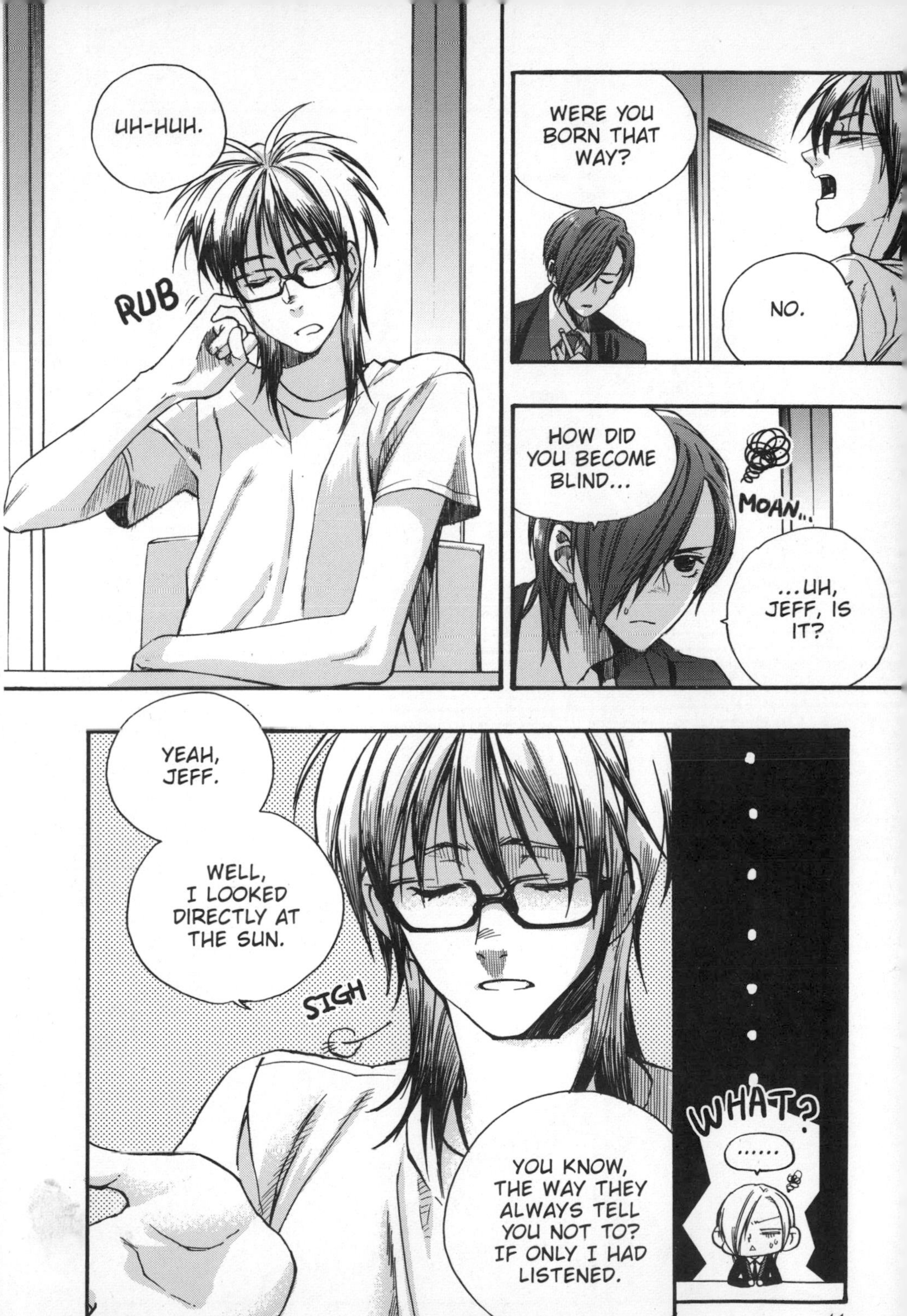
UH-HUH.
RUB
WERE YOU BORN THAT WAY?
NO.
HOW DID YOU BECOME BLIND...
MOAN...
...UH, JEFF, IS IT?
YEAH, JEFF.
WELL, I LOOKED DIRECTLY AT THE SUN.
SIGH
YOU KNOW, THE WAY THEY ALWAYS TELL YOU NOT TO? IF ONLY I HAD LISTENED.
WHAT?
....

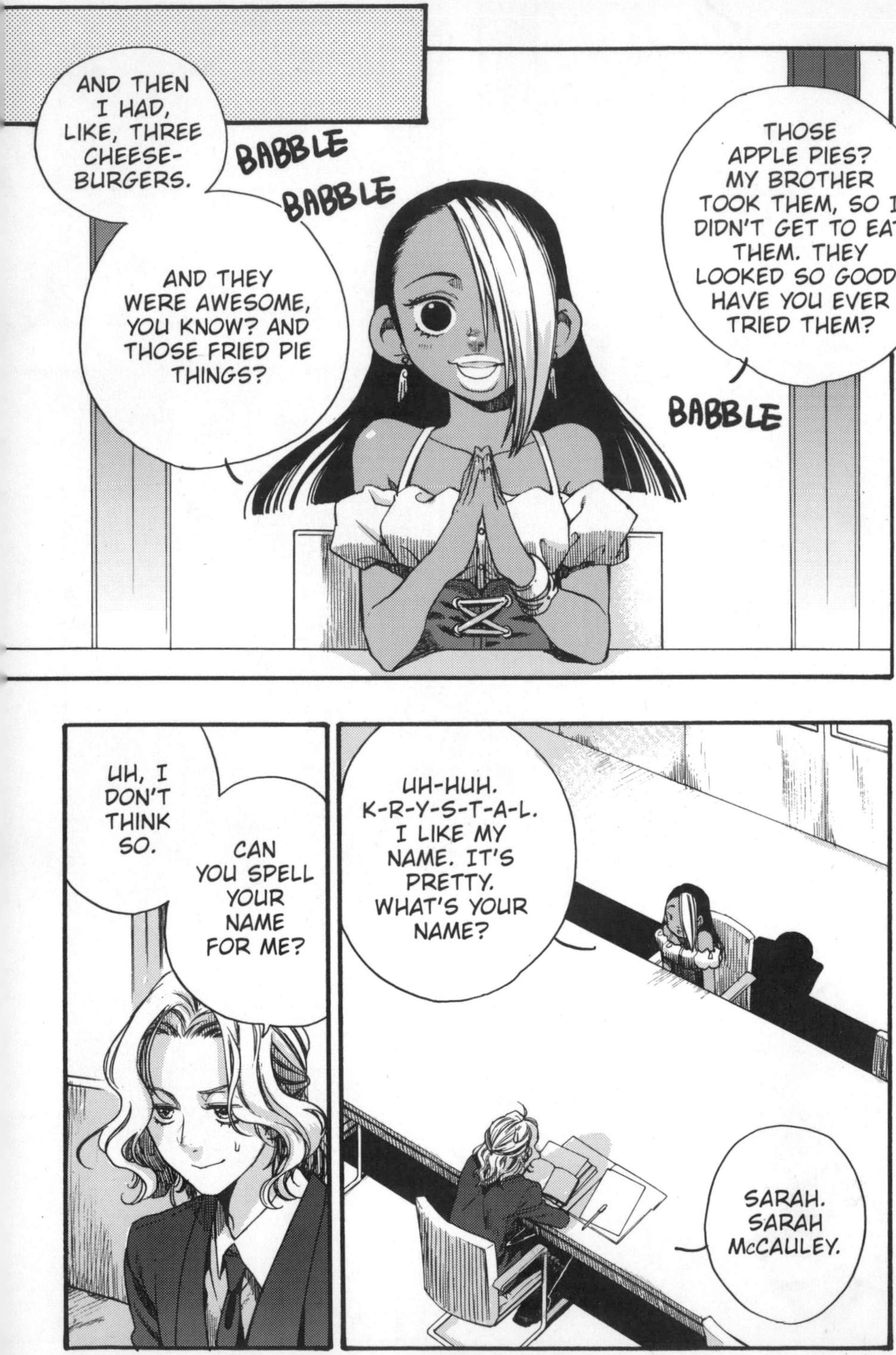
AND THEN I HAD, LIKE, THREE CHEESE-BURGERS.
BABBLE
BABBLE
AND THEY WERE AWESOME, YOU KNOW? AND THOSE FRIED PIE THINGS?
THOSE APPLE PIES? MY BROTHER TOOK THEM, SO I DIDN'T GET TO EAT THEM. THEY LOOKED SO GOOD. HAVE YOU EVER TRIED THEM?
BABBLE
UH, I DON'T THINK SO.
CAN YOU SPELL YOUR NAME FOR ME?
UH-HUH. K-R-Y-S-T-A-L. I LIKE MY NAME. IT'S PRETTY. WHAT'S YOUR NAME?
SARAH. SARAH McCAULEY.

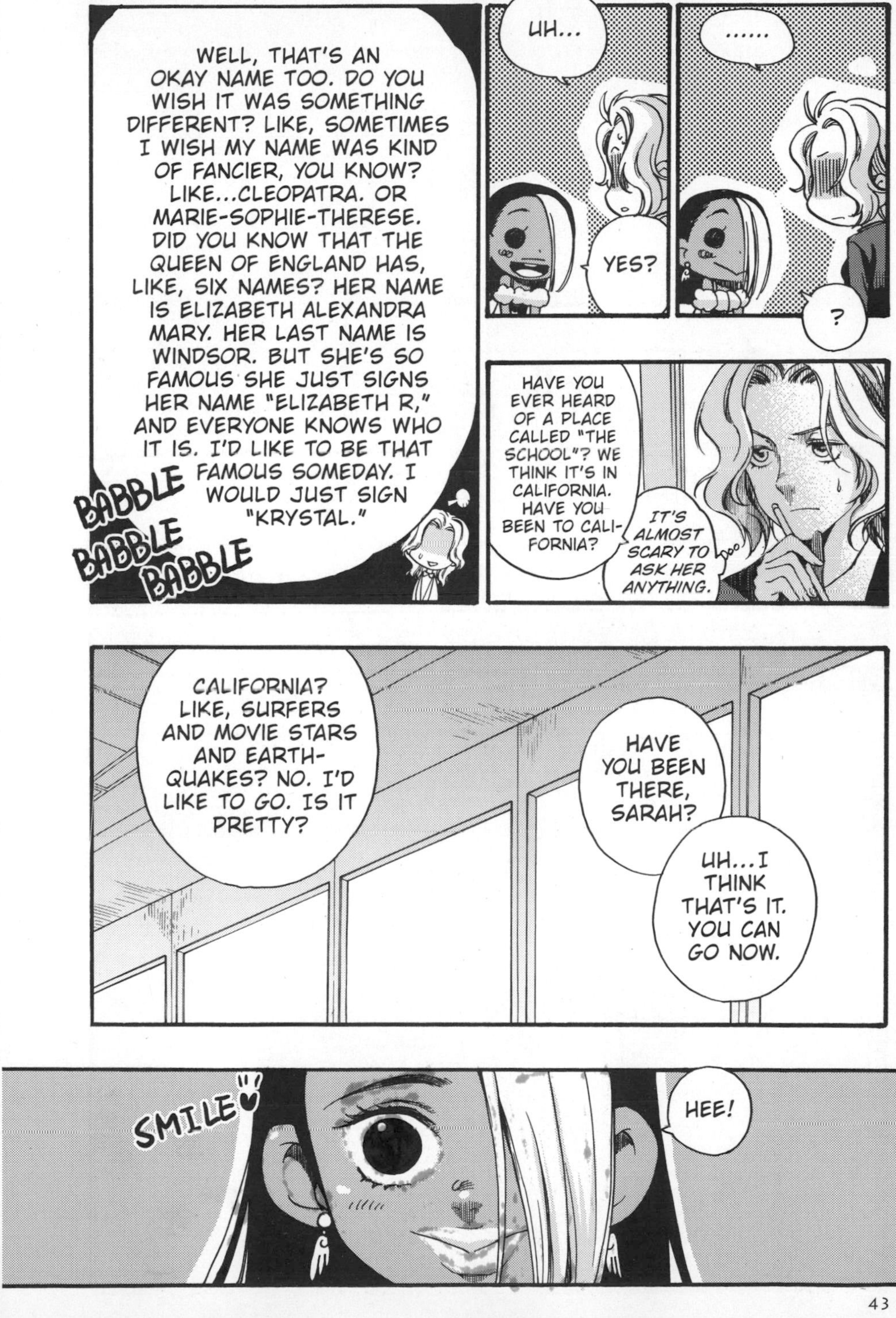
WELL, THAT'S AN OKAY NAME TOO. DO YOU WISH IT WAS SOMETHING DIFFERENT? LIKE, SOMETIMES I WISH MY NAME WAS KIND OF FANCIER, YOU KNOW? LIKE...CLEOPATRA. OR MARIE-SOPHIE-THERESE. DID YOU KNOW THAT THE QUEEN OF ENGLAND HAS, LIKE, SIX NAMES? HER NAME IS ELIZABETH ALEXANDRA MARY. HER LAST NAME IS WINDSOR. BUT SHE'S SO FAMOUS SHE JUST SIGNS HER NAME "ELIZABETH R," AND EVERYONE KNOWS WHO IT IS. I'D LIKE TO BE THAT FAMOUS SOMEDAY. I WOULD JUST SIGN "KRYSTAL."
BABBLE BABBLE BABBLE
UH...
YES?
......
?
HAVE YOU EVER HEARD OF A PLACE CALLED "THE SCHOOL"? WE THINK IT'S IN CALIFORNIA. HAVE YOU BEEN TO CALI-FORNIA?
IT'S ALMOST SCARY TO ASK HER ANYTHING.
CALIFORNIA? LIKE, SURFERS AND MOVIE STARS AND EARTH-QUAKES? NO. I'D LIKE TO GO. IS IT PRETTY?
HAVE YOU BEEN THERE, SARAH?
UH...I THINK THAT'S IT. YOU CAN GO NOW.
SMILE
HEE!

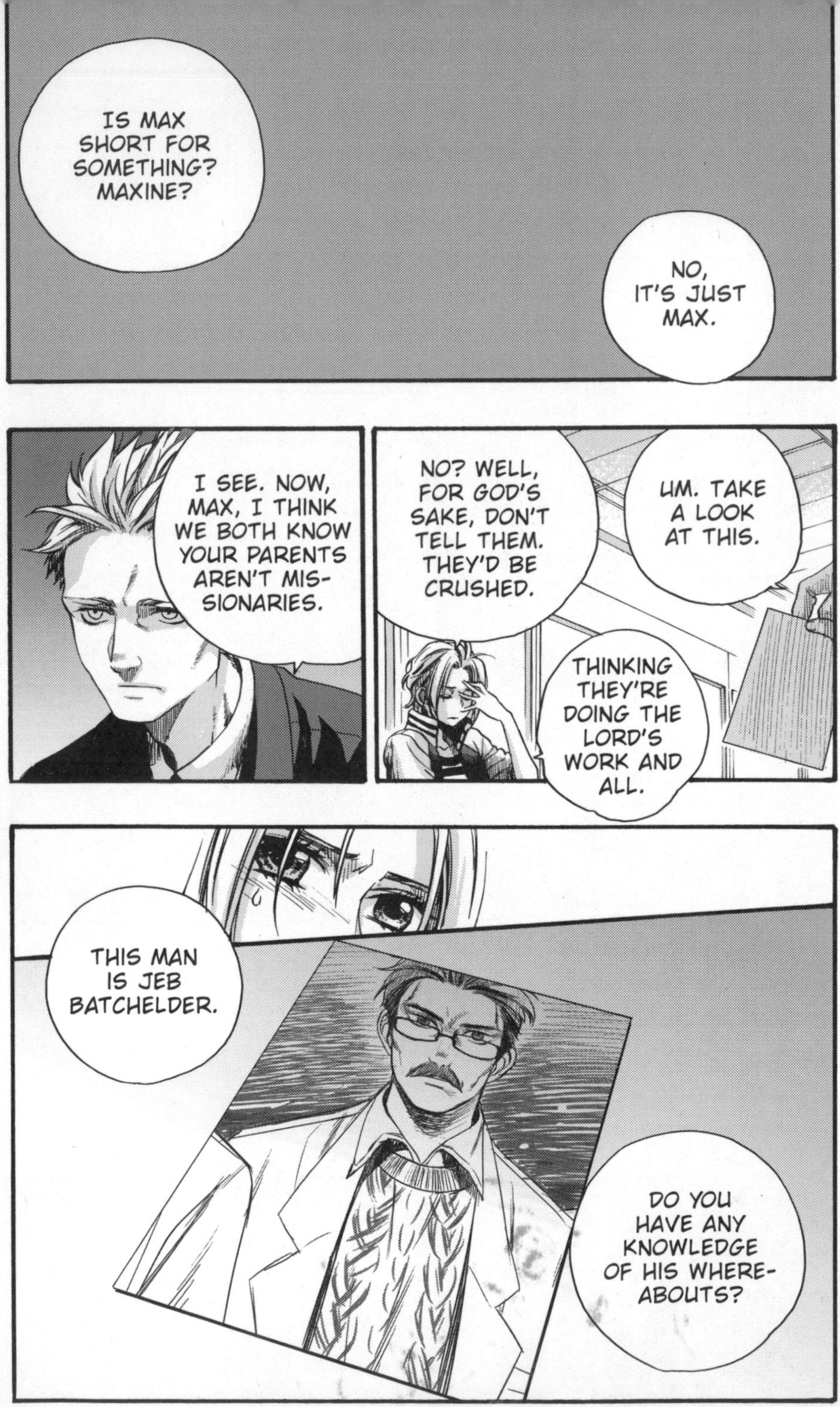
IS MAX SHORT FOR SOMETHING? MAXINE?
NO, IT'S JUST MAX.
I SEE. NOW, MAX, I THINK WE BOTH KNOW YOUR PARENTS AREN'T MIS-SIONARIES.
NO? WELL, FOR GOD'S SAKE, DON'T TELL THEM. THEY'D BE CRUSHED.
THINKING THEY'RE DOING THE LORD'S WORK AND ALL.
UM. TAKE A LOOK AT THIS.
THIS MAN IS JEB BATCHELDER.
DO YOU HAVE ANY KNOWLEDGE OF HIS WHERE-ABOUTS?

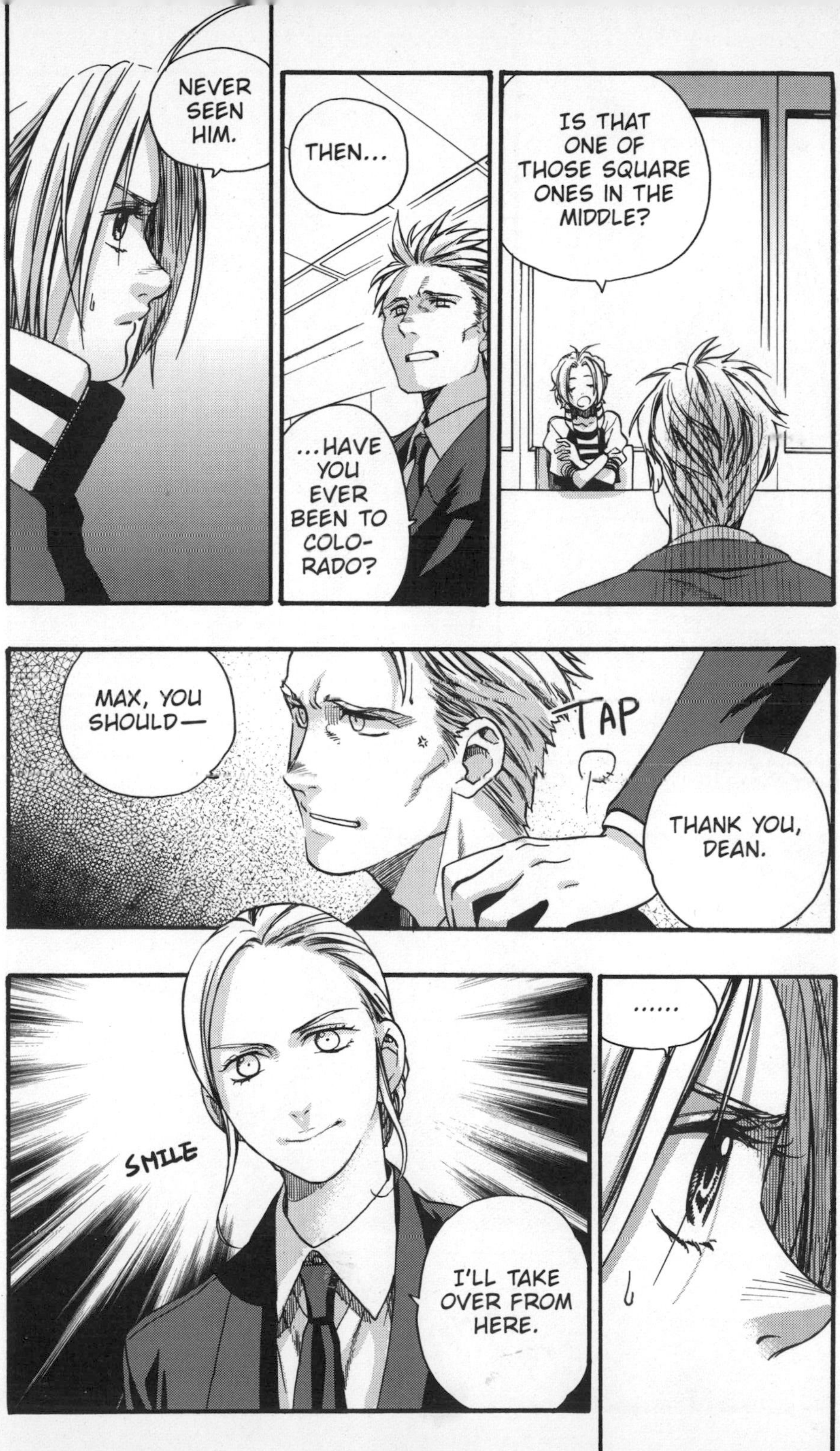
NEVER SEEN HIM.
THEN...
...HAVE YOU EVER BEEN TO COLO-RADO?
IS THAT ONE OF THOSE SQUARE ONES IN THE MIDDLE?
MAX, YOU SHOULD—
TAP
THANK YOU, DEAN.
SMILE
I'LL TAKE OVER FROM HERE.
......

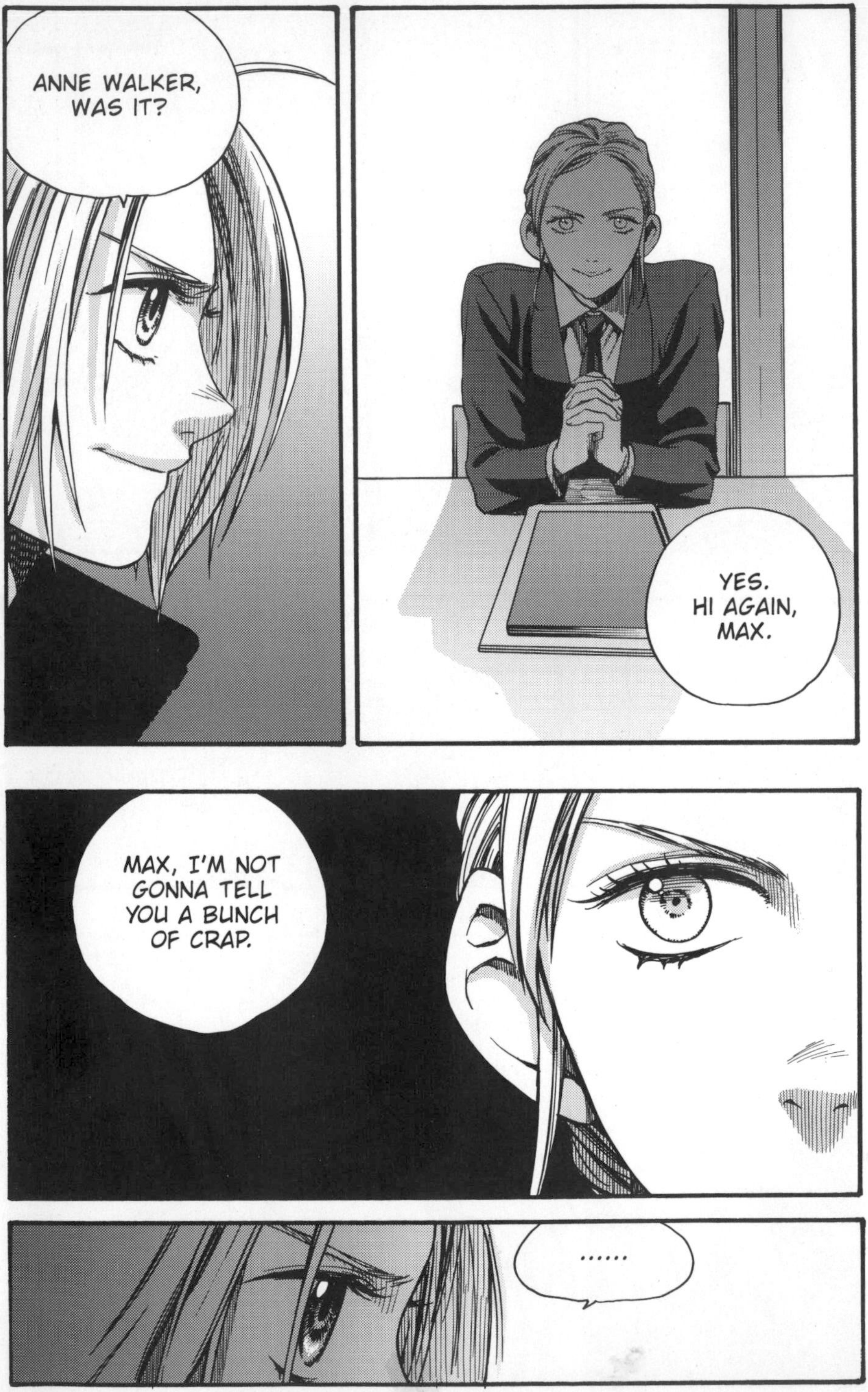
ANNE WALKER, WAS IT?
YES. HI AGAIN, MAX.
MAX, I'M NOT GONNA TELL YOU A BUNCH OF CRAP.
......

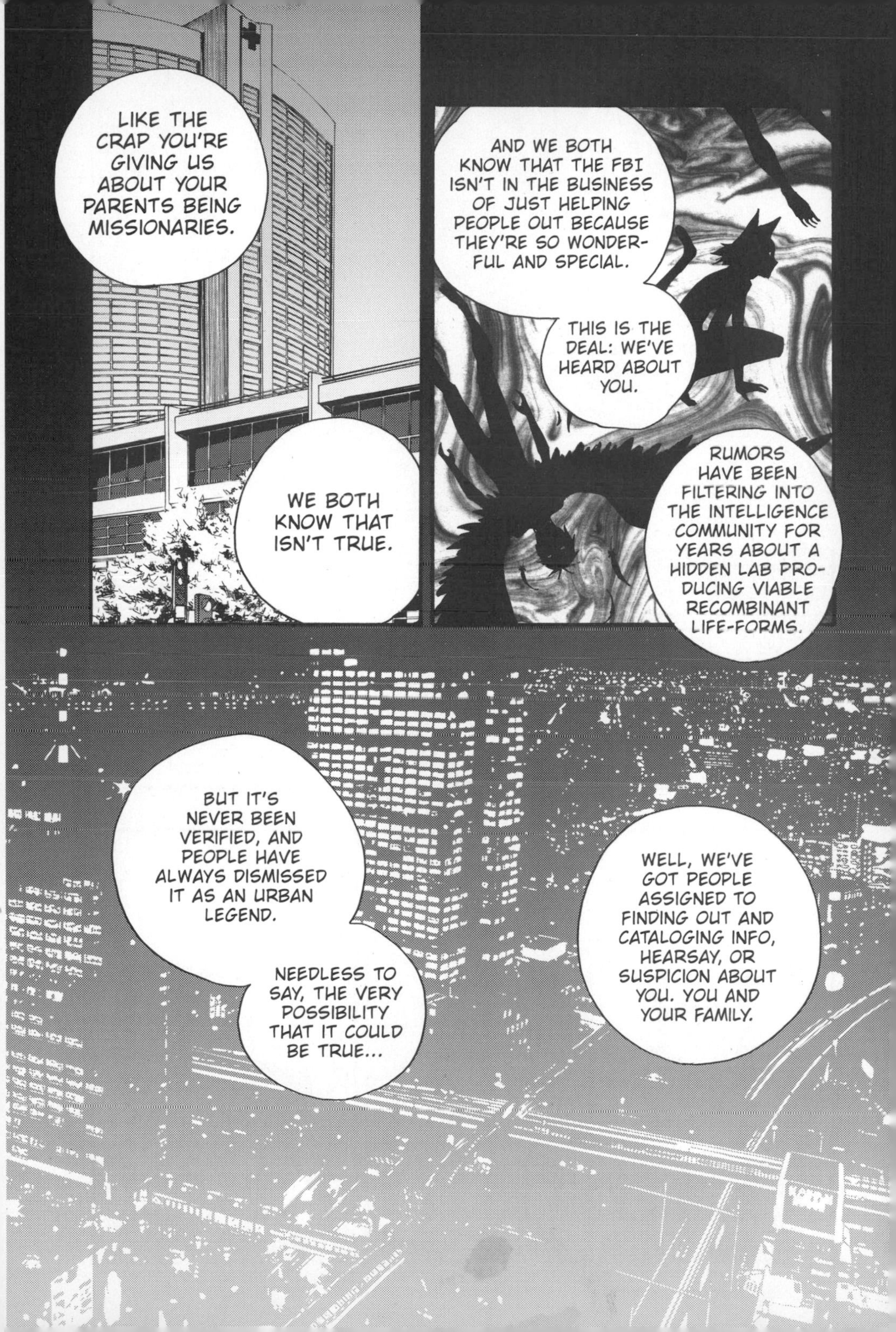
LIKE THE CRAP YOU'RE GIVING US ABOUT YOUR PARENTS BEING MISSIONARIES.
WE BOTH KNOW THAT ISN'T TRUE.
AND WE BOTH KNOW THAT THE FBI ISN'T IN THE BUSINESS OF JUST HELPING PEOPLE OUT BECAUSE THEY'RE SO WONDER-FUL AND SPECIAL.
THIS IS THE DEAL: WE'VE HEARD ABOUT YOU.
RUMORS HAVE BEEN FILTERING INTO THE INTELLIGENCE COMMUNITY FOR YEARS ABOUT A HIDDEN LAB PRO-DUCING VIABLE RECOMBINANT LIFE-FORMS.
BUT IT'S NEVER BEEN VERIFIED, AND PEOPLE HAVE ALWAYS DISMISSED IT AS AN URBAN LEGEND.
NEEDLESS TO SAY, THE VERY POSSIBILITY THAT IT COULD BE TRUE...
WELL, WE'VE GOT PEOPLE ASSIGNED TO FINDING OUT AND CATALOGING INFO, HEARSAY, OR SUSPICION ABOUT YOU. YOU AND YOUR FAMILY.

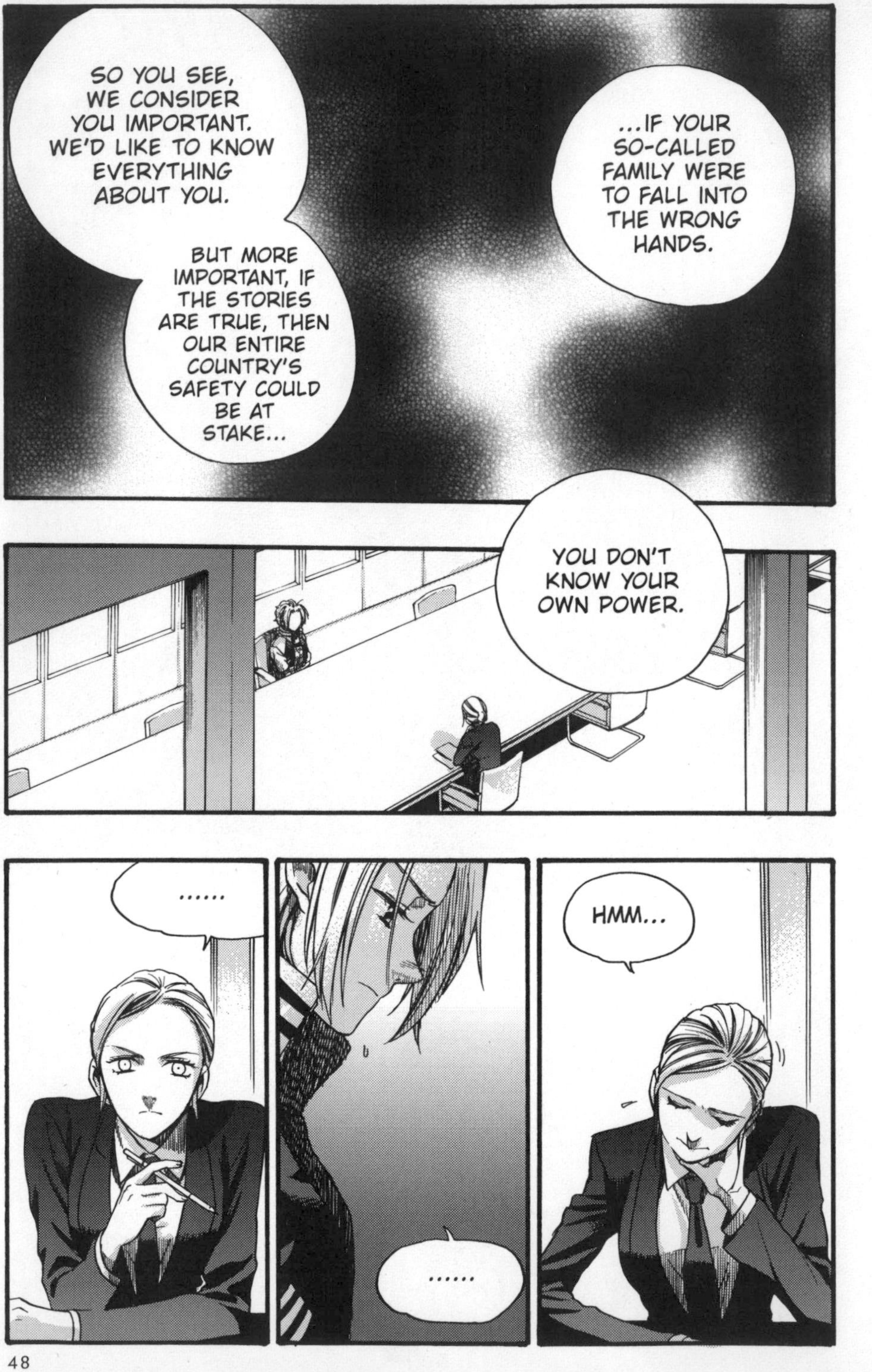
SO YOU SEE, WE CONSIDER YOU IMPORTANT. WE'D LIKE TO KNOW EVERYTHING ABOUT YOU.
BUT MORE IMPORTANT, IF THE STORIES ARE TRUE, THEN OUR ENTIRE COUNTRY'S SAFETY COULD BE AT STAKE...
...IF YOUR SO-CALLED FAMILY WERE TO FALL INTO THE WRONG HANDS.
YOU DON'T KNOW YOUR OWN POWER.
......
......
HMM...

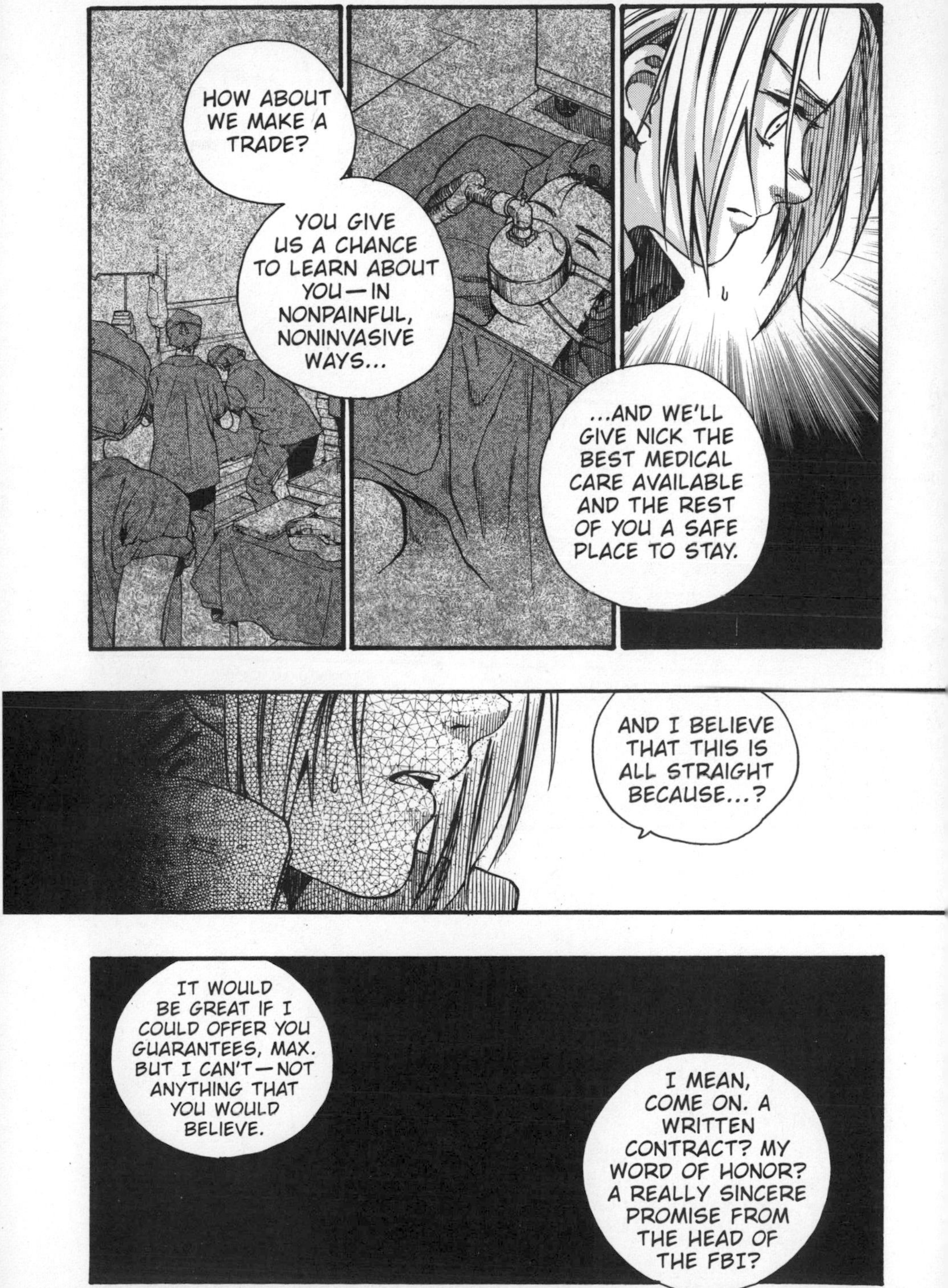
HOW ABOUT WE MAKE A TRADE?
YOU GIVE US A CHANCE TO LEARN ABOUT YOU—IN NONPAINFUL, NONINVASIVE WAYS...
...AND WE'LL GIVE NICK THE BEST MEDICAL CARE AVAILABLE AND THE REST OF YOU A SAFE PLACE TO STAY.
AND I BELIEVE THAT THIS IS ALL STRAIGHT BECAUSE...?
IT WOULD BE GREAT IF I COULD OFFER YOU GUARANTEES, MAX. BUT I CAN'T—NOT ANYTHING THAT YOU WOULD BELIEVE.
I MEAN, COME ON. A WRITTEN CONTRACT? MY WORD OF HONOR? A REALLY SINCERE PROMISE FROM THE HEAD OF THE FBI?

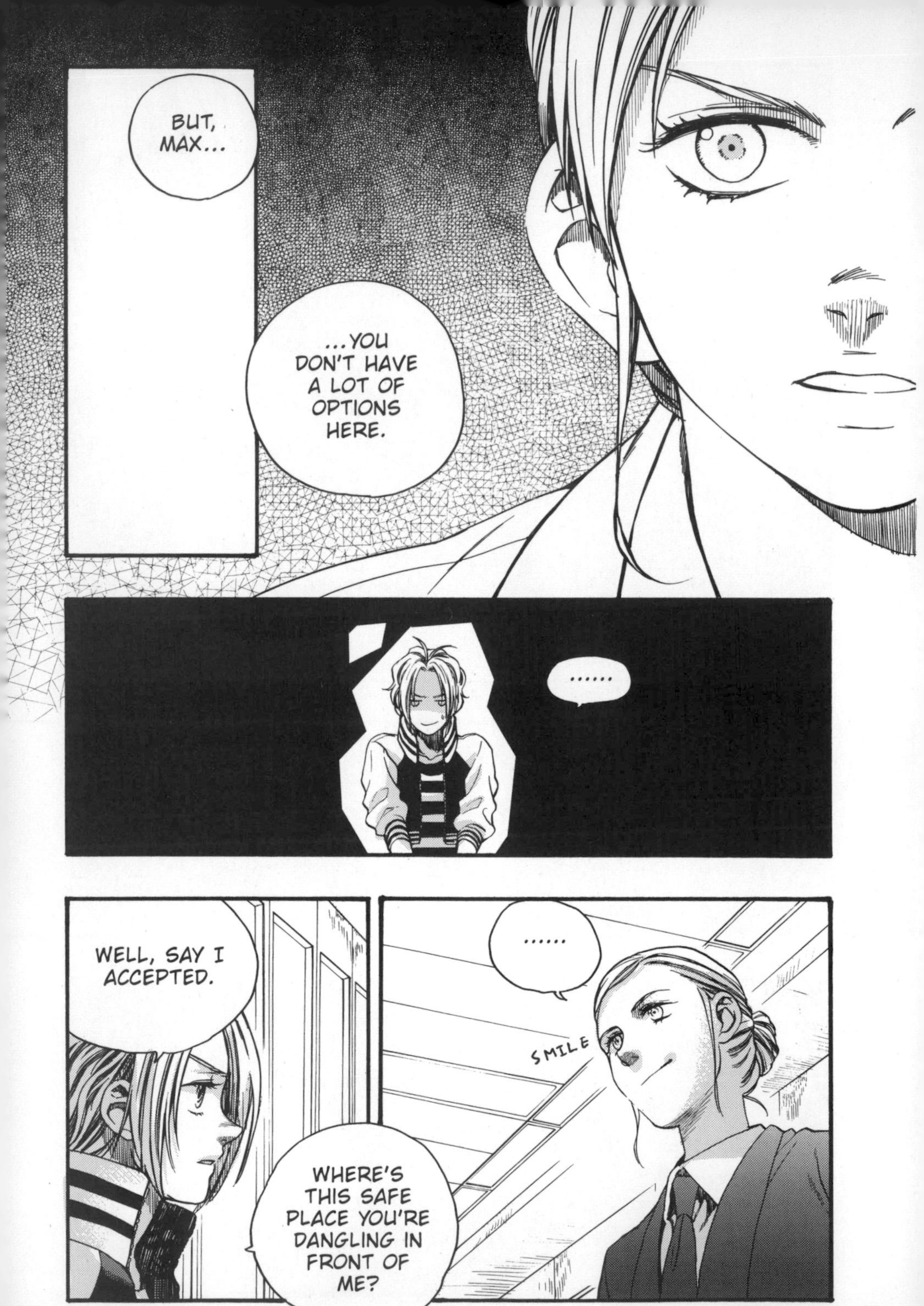
BUT, MAX...
...YOU DON'T HAVE A LOT OF OPTIONS HERE.
......
WELL, SAY I ACCEPTED.
WHERE'S THIS SAFE PLACE YOU'RE DANGLING IN FRONT OF ME?
......
SMILE

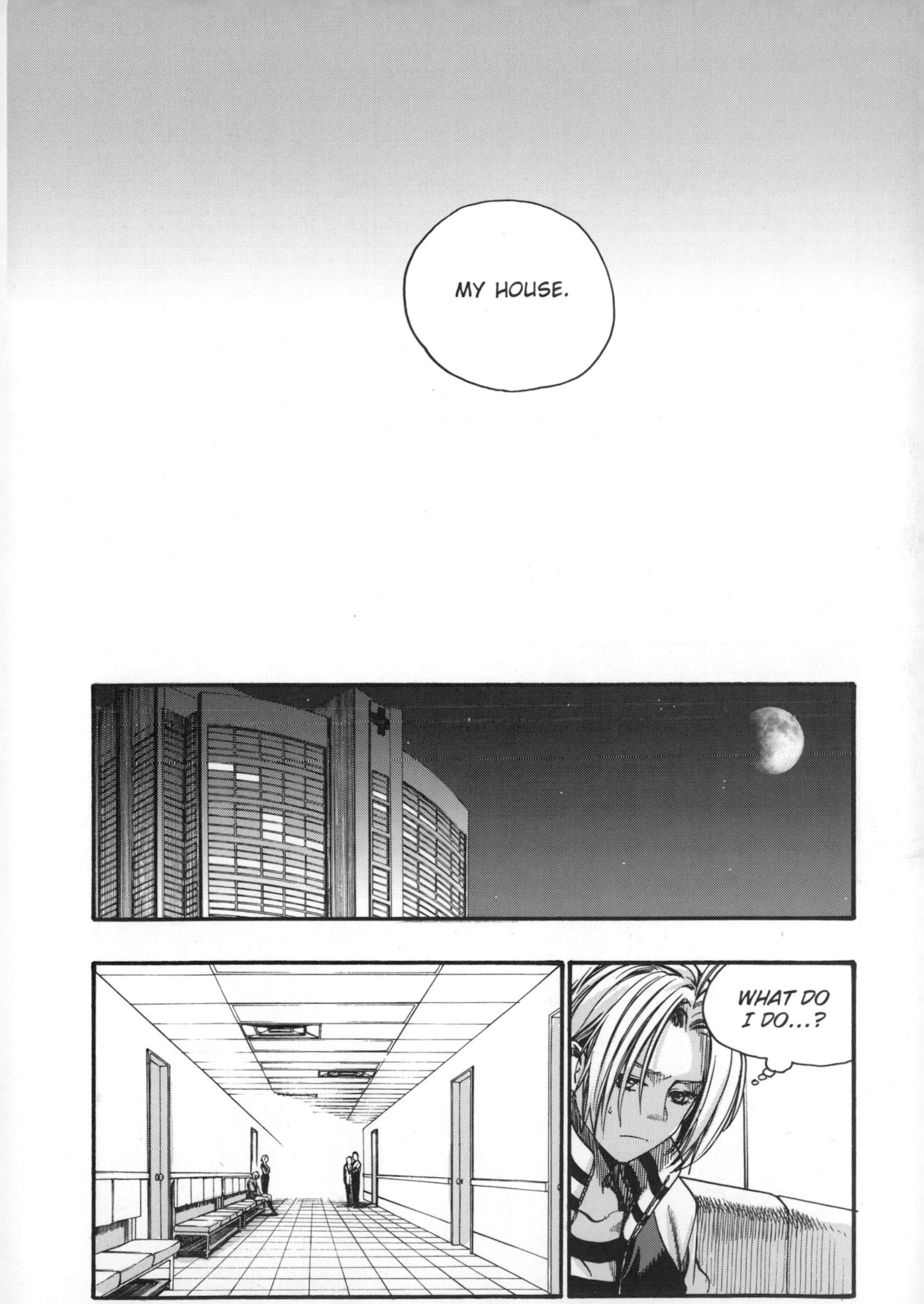
MY HOUSE.
WHAT DO I DO...?

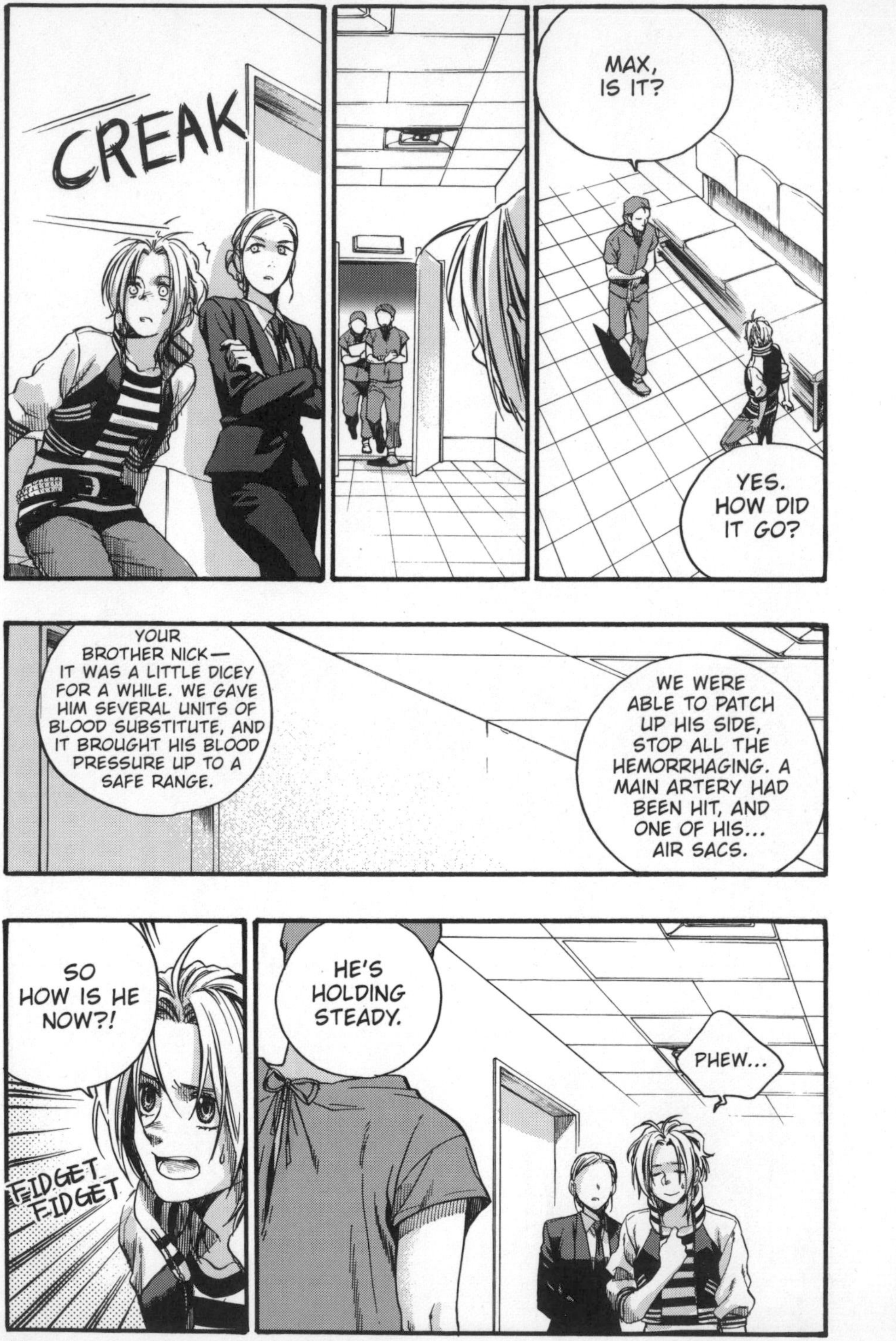
CREAK
MAX, IS IT?
YES. HOW DID IT GO?
YOUR BROTHER NICK— IT WAS A LITTLE DICEY FOR A WHILE. WE GAVE HIM SEVERAL UNITS OF BLOOD SUBSTITUTE, AND IT BROUGHT HIS BLOOD PRESSURE UP TO A SAFE RANGE.
WE WERE ABLE TO PATCH UP HIS SIDE, STOP ALL THE HEMORRHAGING. A MAIN ARTERY HAD BEEN HIT, AND ONE OF HIS... AIR SACS.
SO HOW IS HE NOW?!
FIDGET FIDGET
HE'S HOLDING STEADY.
PHEW...

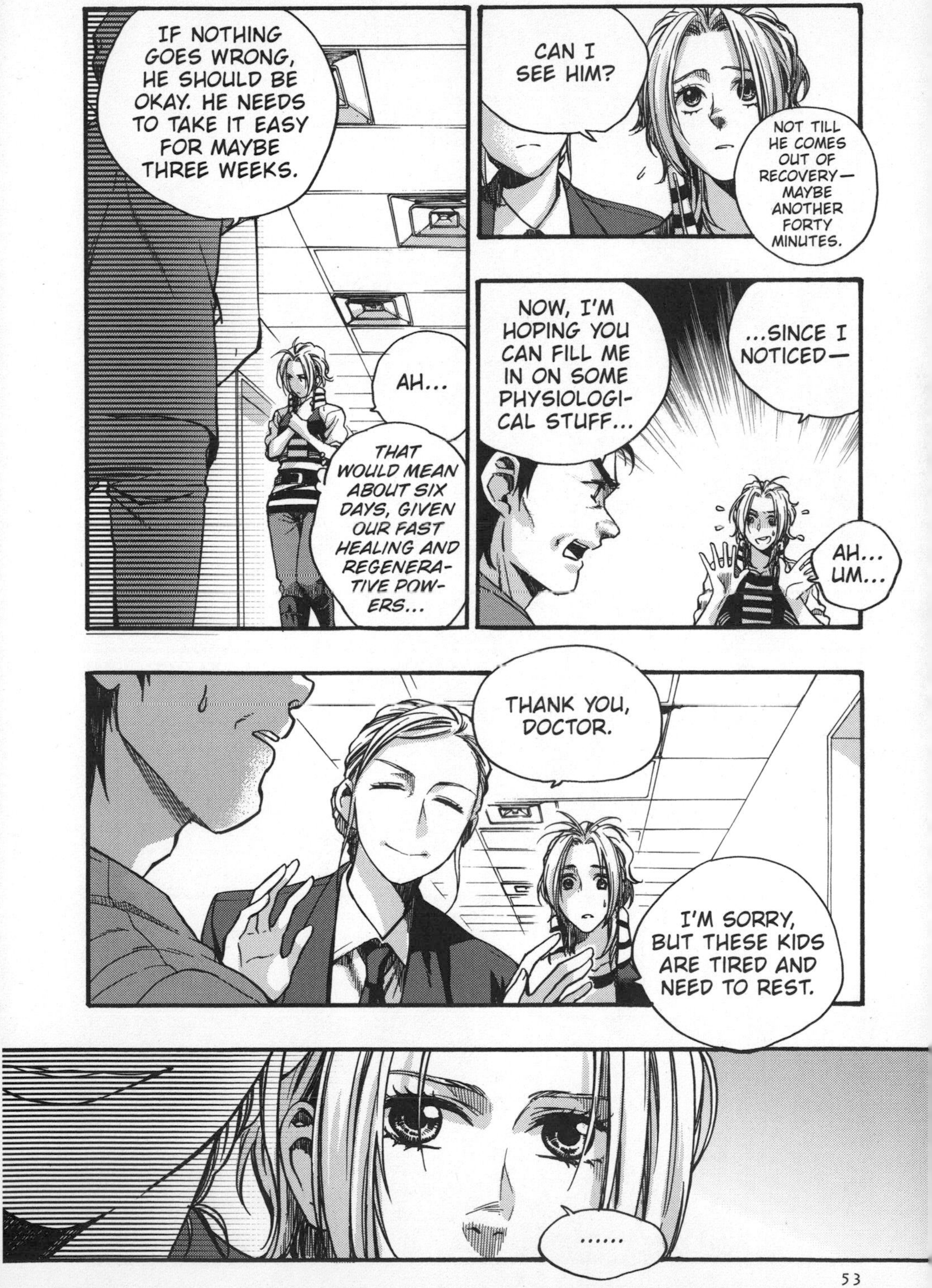
IF NOTHING GOES WRONG, HE SHOULD BE OKAY. HE NEEDS TO TAKE IT EASY FOR MAYBE THREE WEEKS.
AH...
THAT WOULD MEAN ABOUT SIX DAYS, GIVEN OUR FAST HEALING AND REGENERATIVE POWERS...
CAN I SEE HIM?
NOT TILL HE COMES OUT OF RECOVERY—MAYBE ANOTHER FORTY MINUTES.
NOW, I'M HOPING YOU CAN FILL ME IN ON SOME PHYSIOLOGICAL STUFF...
...SINCE I NOTICED—
AH... UM...
THANK YOU, DOCTOR.
I'M SORRY, BUT THESE KIDS ARE TIRED AND NEED TO REST.
......

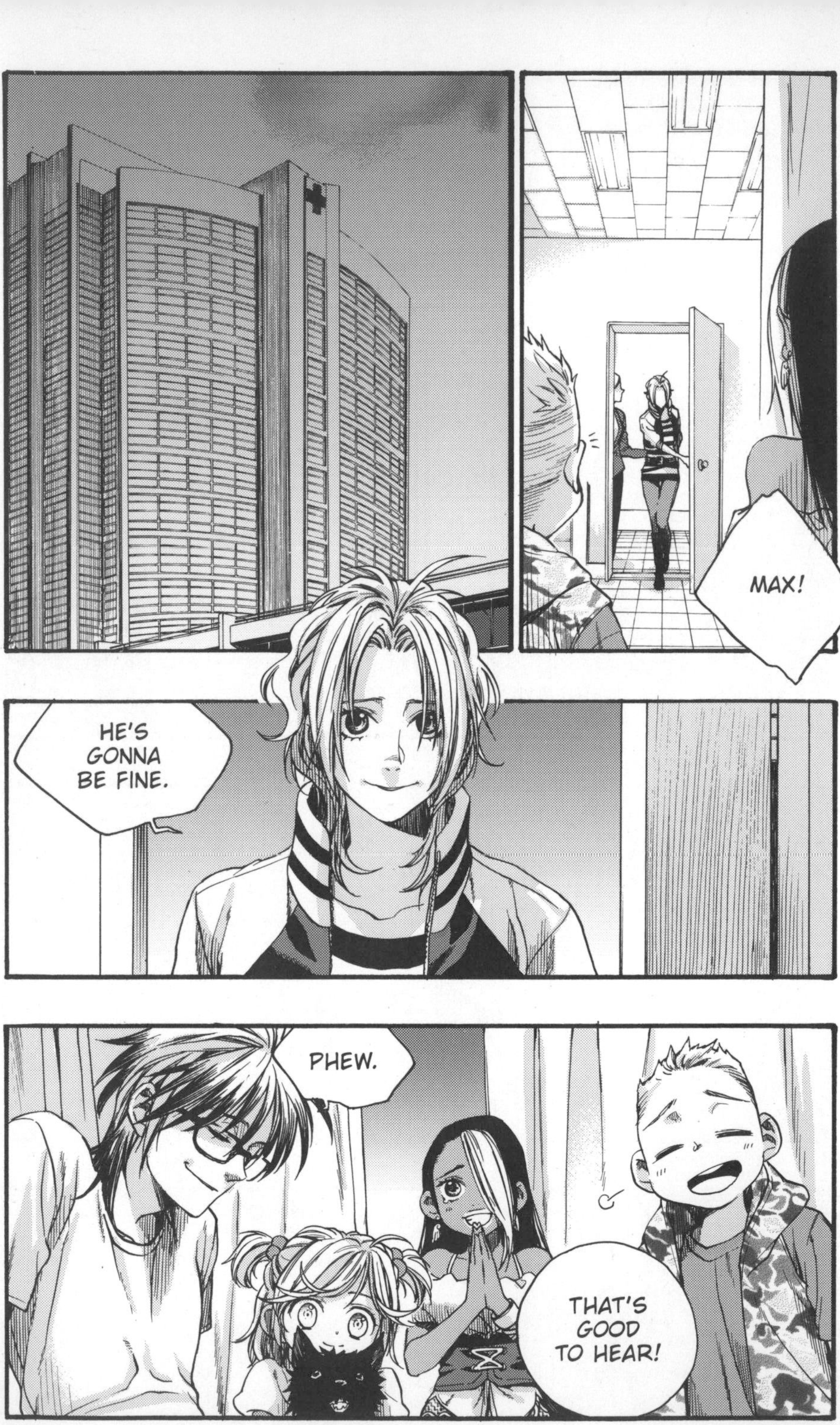
MAX!
HE'S GONNA BE FINE.
PHEW.
THAT'S GOOD TO HEAR!

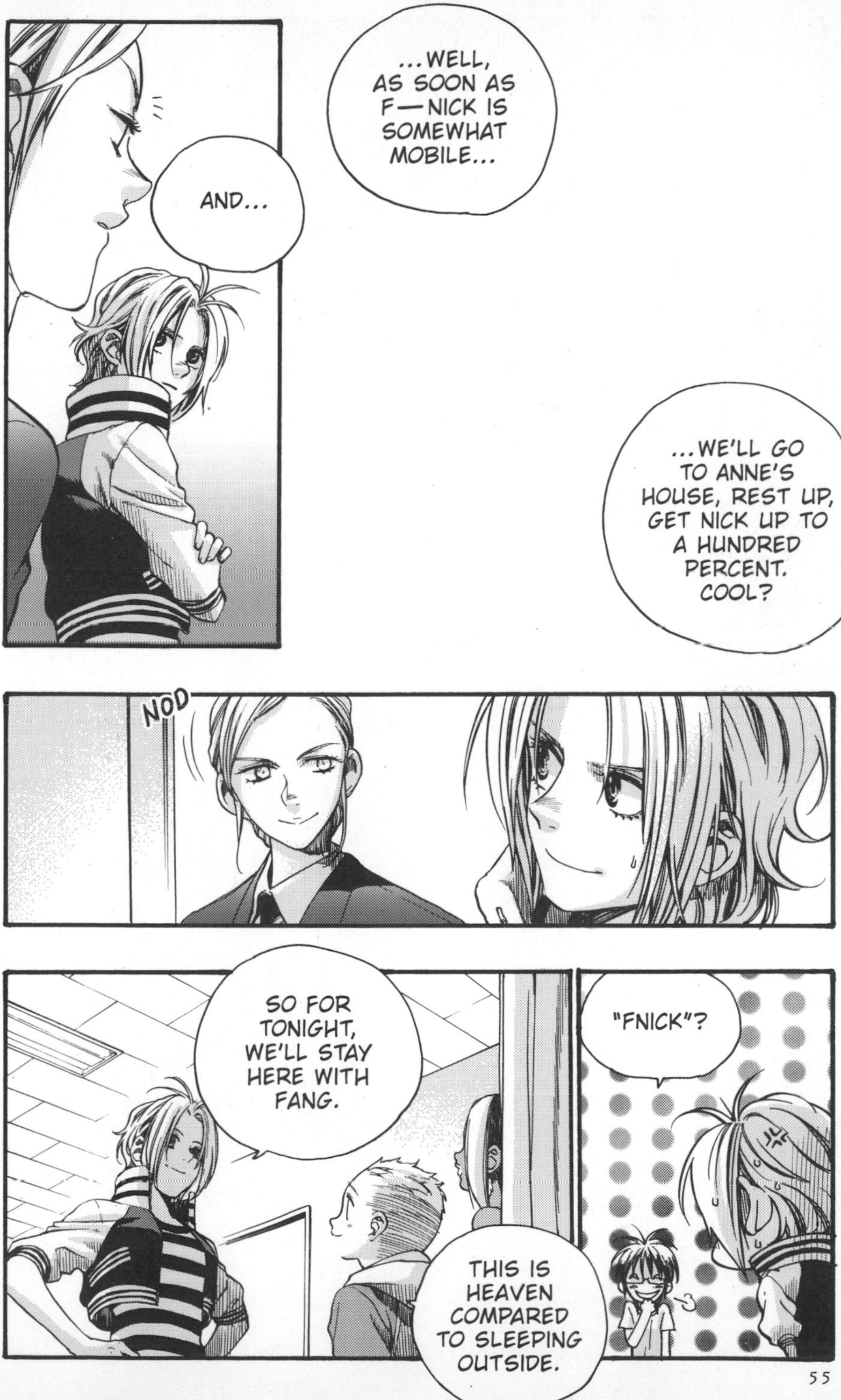
...WELL, AS SOON AS F—NICK IS SOMEWHAT MOBILE...
AND...
...WE'LL GO TO ANNE'S HOUSE, REST UP, GET NICK UP TO A HUNDRED PERCENT. COOL?
NOD
SO FOR TONIGHT, WE'LL STAY HERE WITH FANG.
THIS IS HEAVEN COMPARED TO SLEEPING OUTSIDE.
"FNICK"?

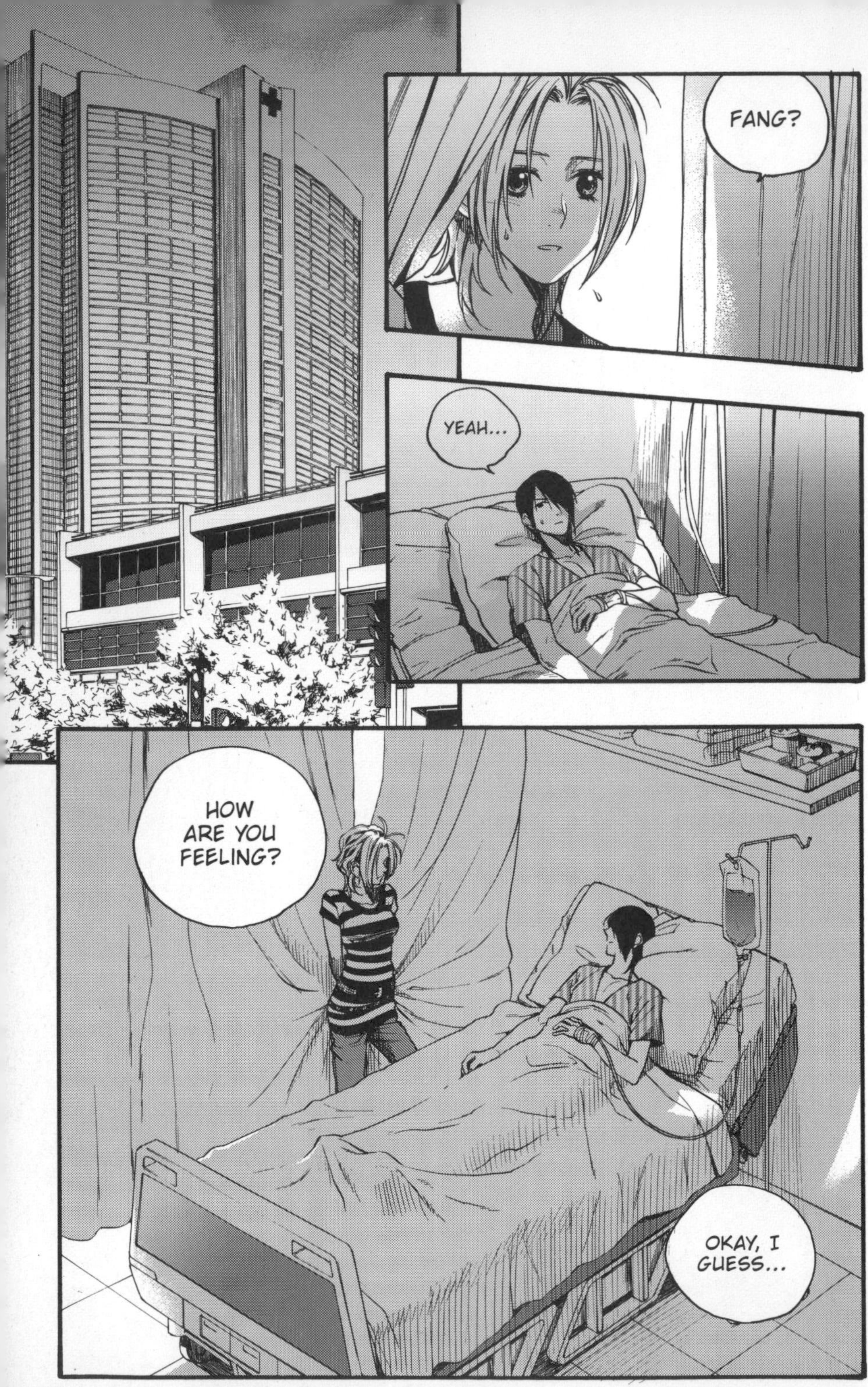
FANG?
YEAH...
HOW ARE YOU FEELING?
OKAY, I GUESS...

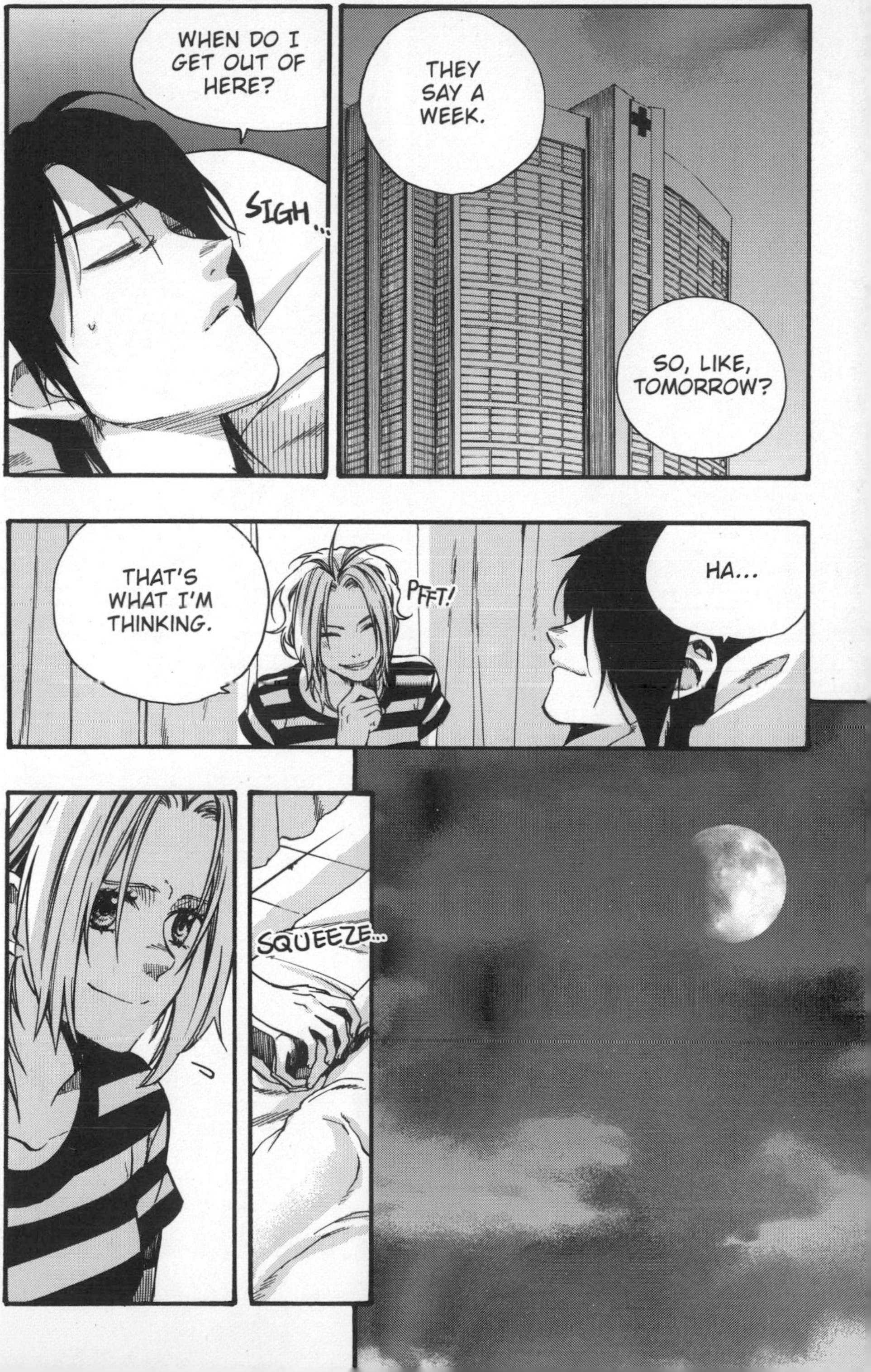
WHEN DO I GET OUT OF HERE?
SIGH...
THEY SAY A WEEK.
SO, LIKE, TOMORROW?
THAT'S WHAT I'M THINKING.
PFFT!
HA...
SQUEEZE...

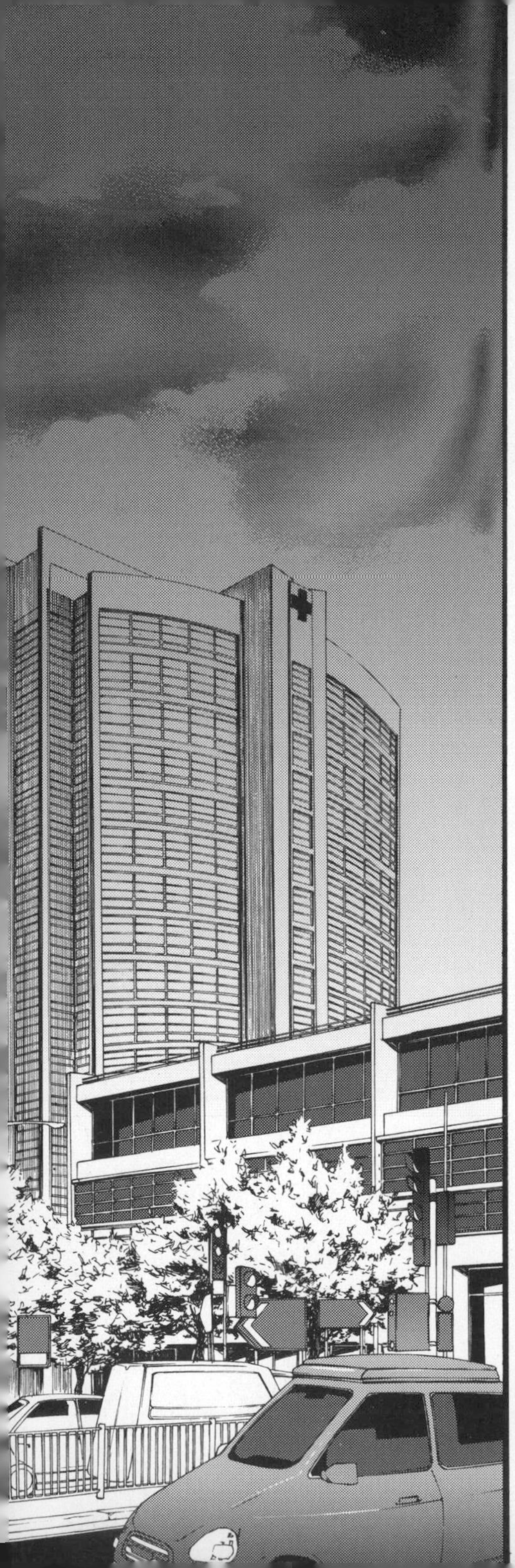

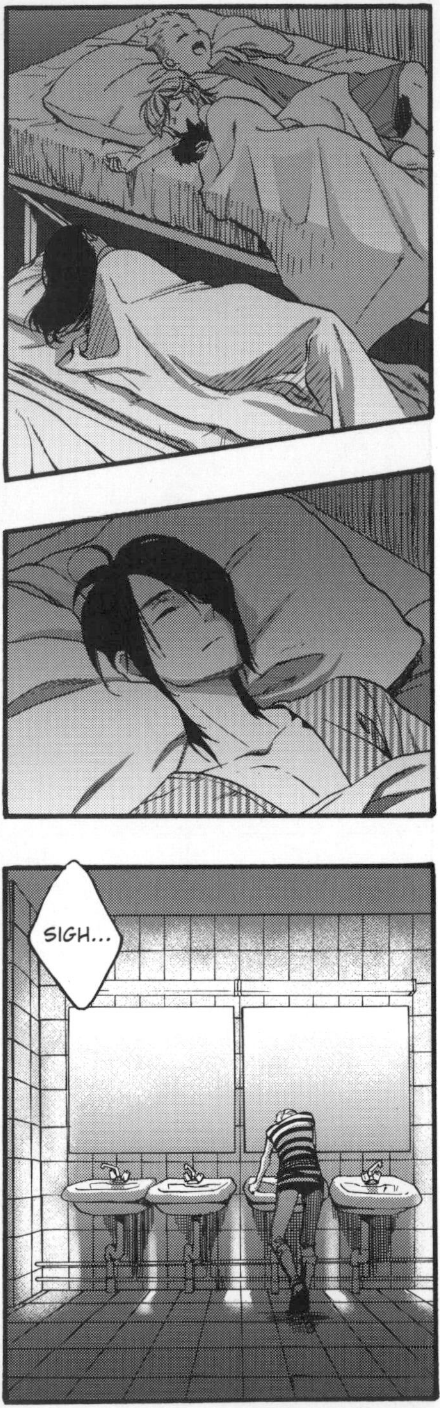

SIGH...

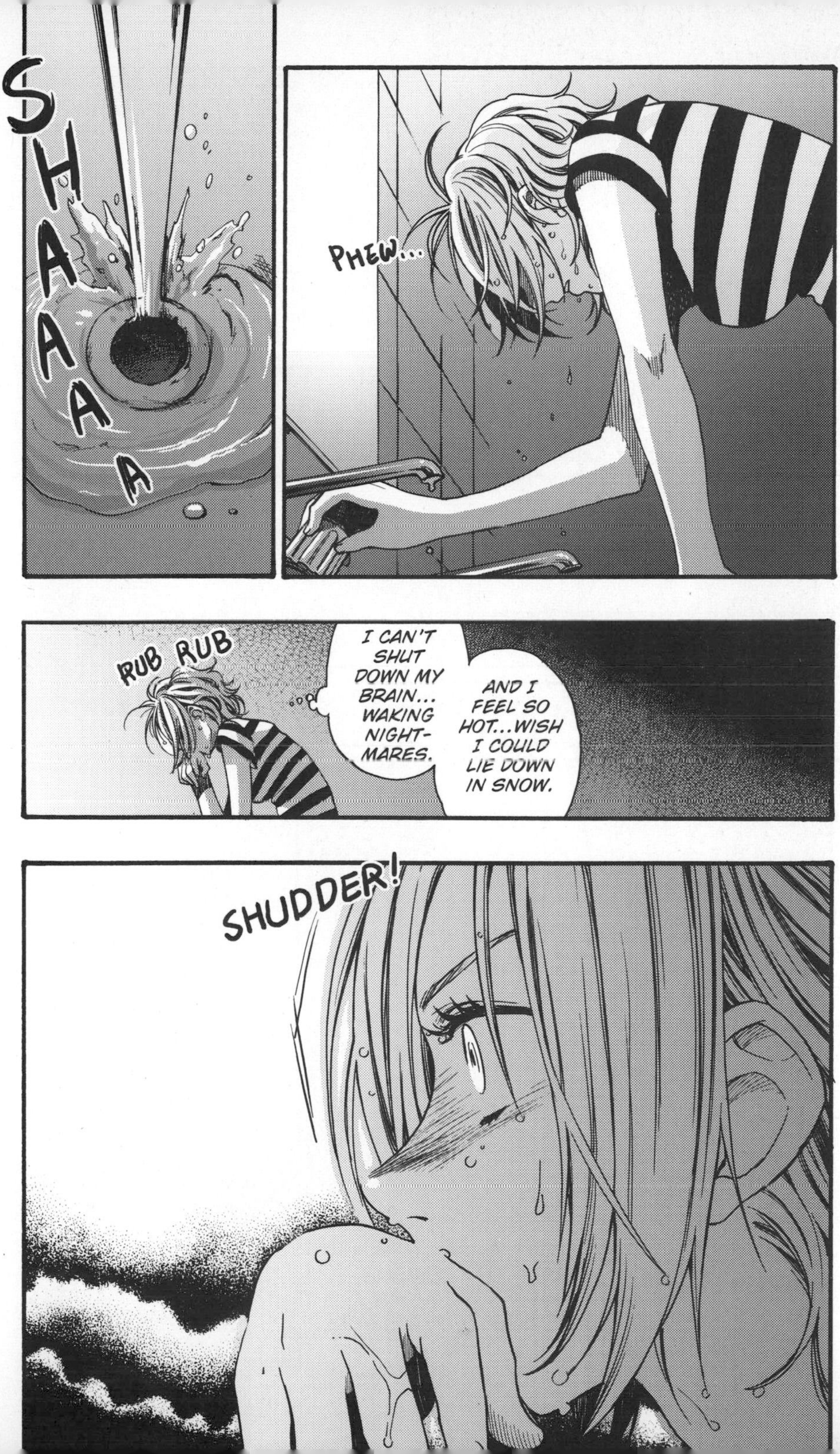
SHAAAAA
PHEW...
RUB RUB
I CAN'T SHUT DOWN MY BRAIN... WAKING NIGHT-MARES.
AND I FEEL SO HOT...WISH I COULD LIE DOWN IN SNOW.
SHUDDER!

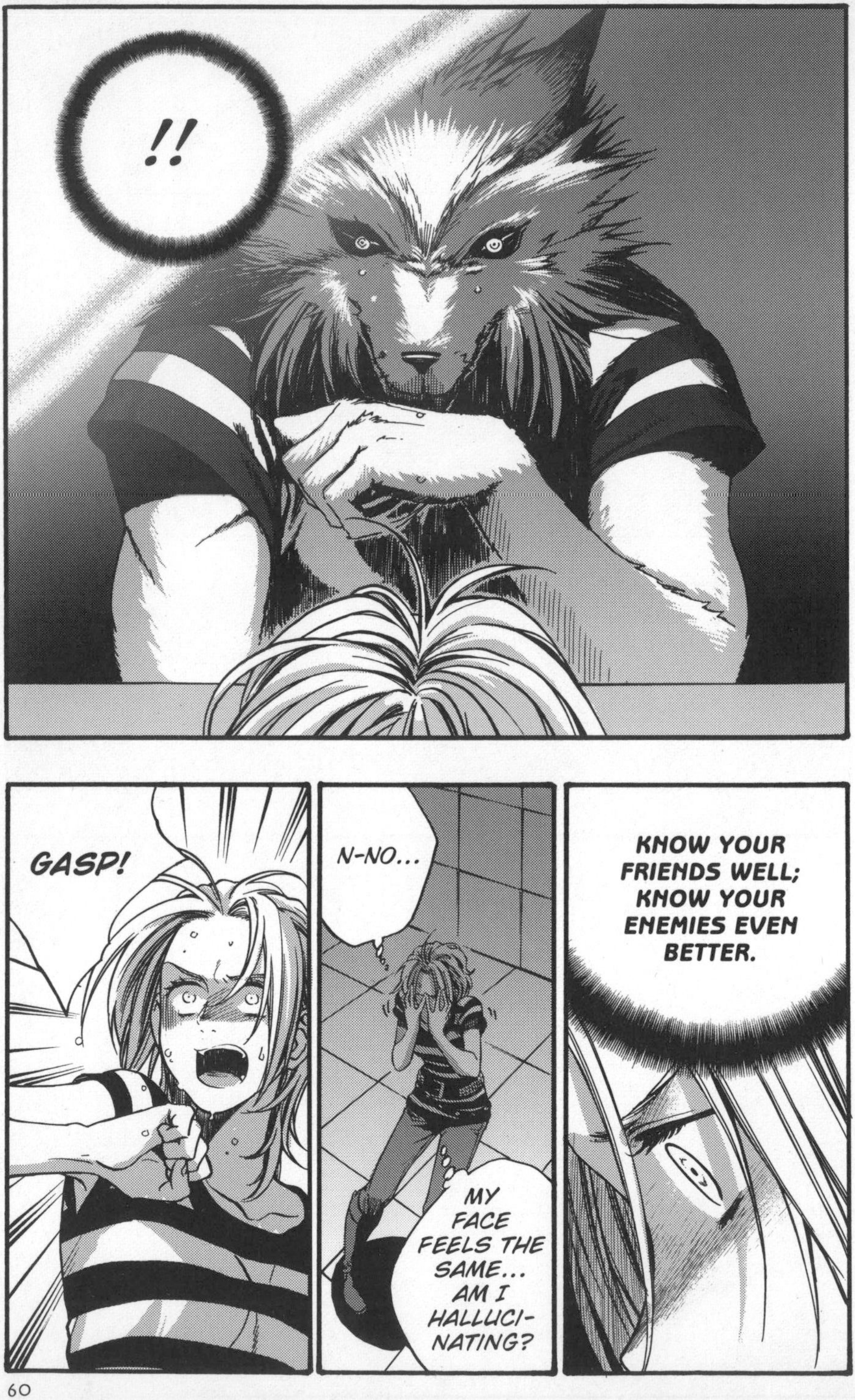
!!
GASP!
N-NO...
MY FACE FEELS THE SAME... AM I HALLUCI-NATING?
KNOW YOUR FRIENDS WELL; KNOW YOUR ENEMIES EVEN BETTER.

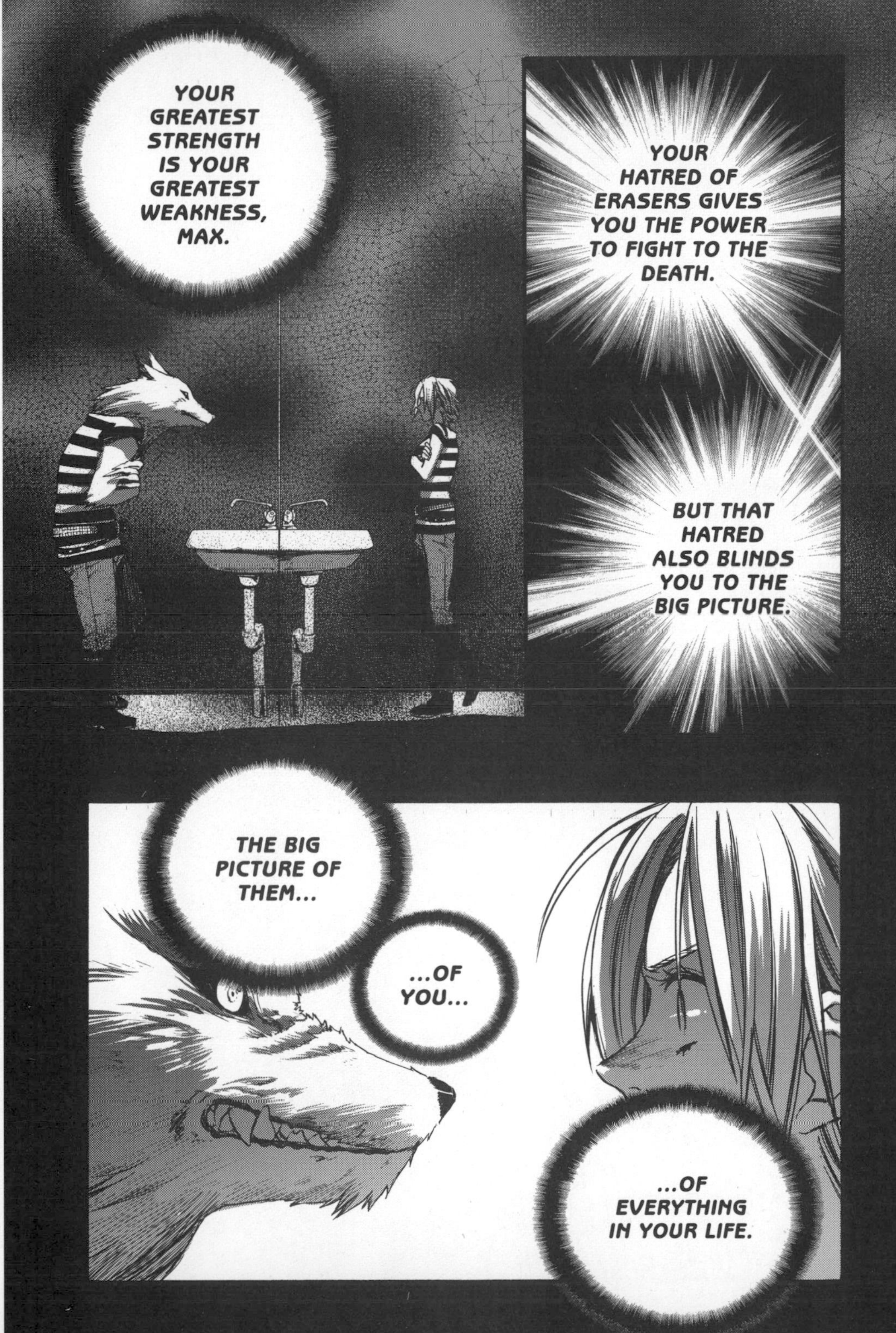
YOUR GREATEST STRENGTH IS YOUR GREATEST WEAKNESS, MAX.
YOUR HATRED OF ERASERS GIVES YOU THE POWER TO FIGHT TO THE DEATH.
BUT THAT HATRED ALSO BLINDS YOU TO THE BIG PICTURE.
THE BIG PICTURE OF THEM...
...OF YOU...
...OF EVERYTHING IN YOUR LIFE.

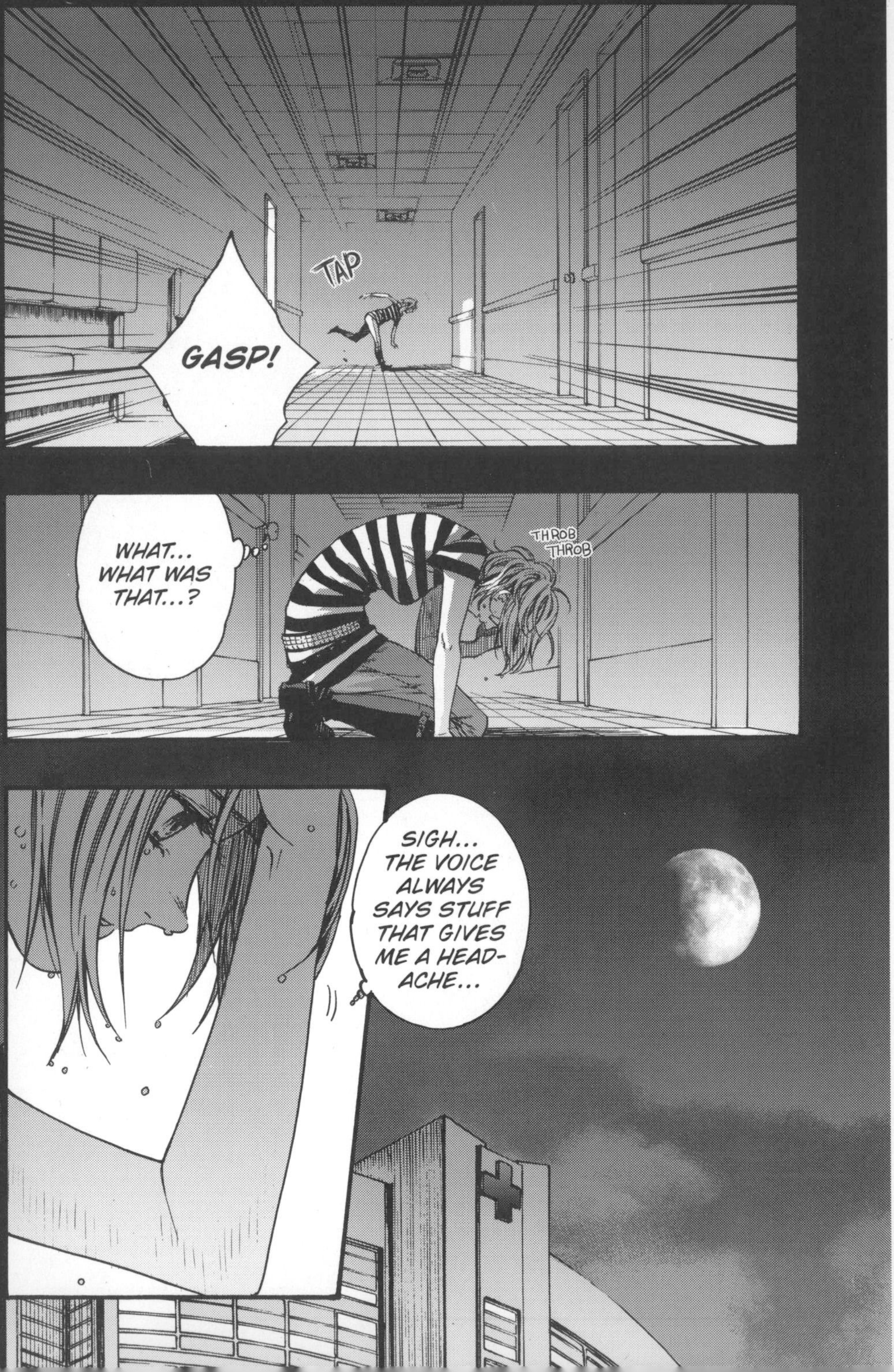

TAP
GASP!
WHAT... WHAT WAS THAT...?
THROB THROB
SIGH... THE VOICE ALWAYS SAYS STUFF THAT GIVES ME A HEAD-ACHE...

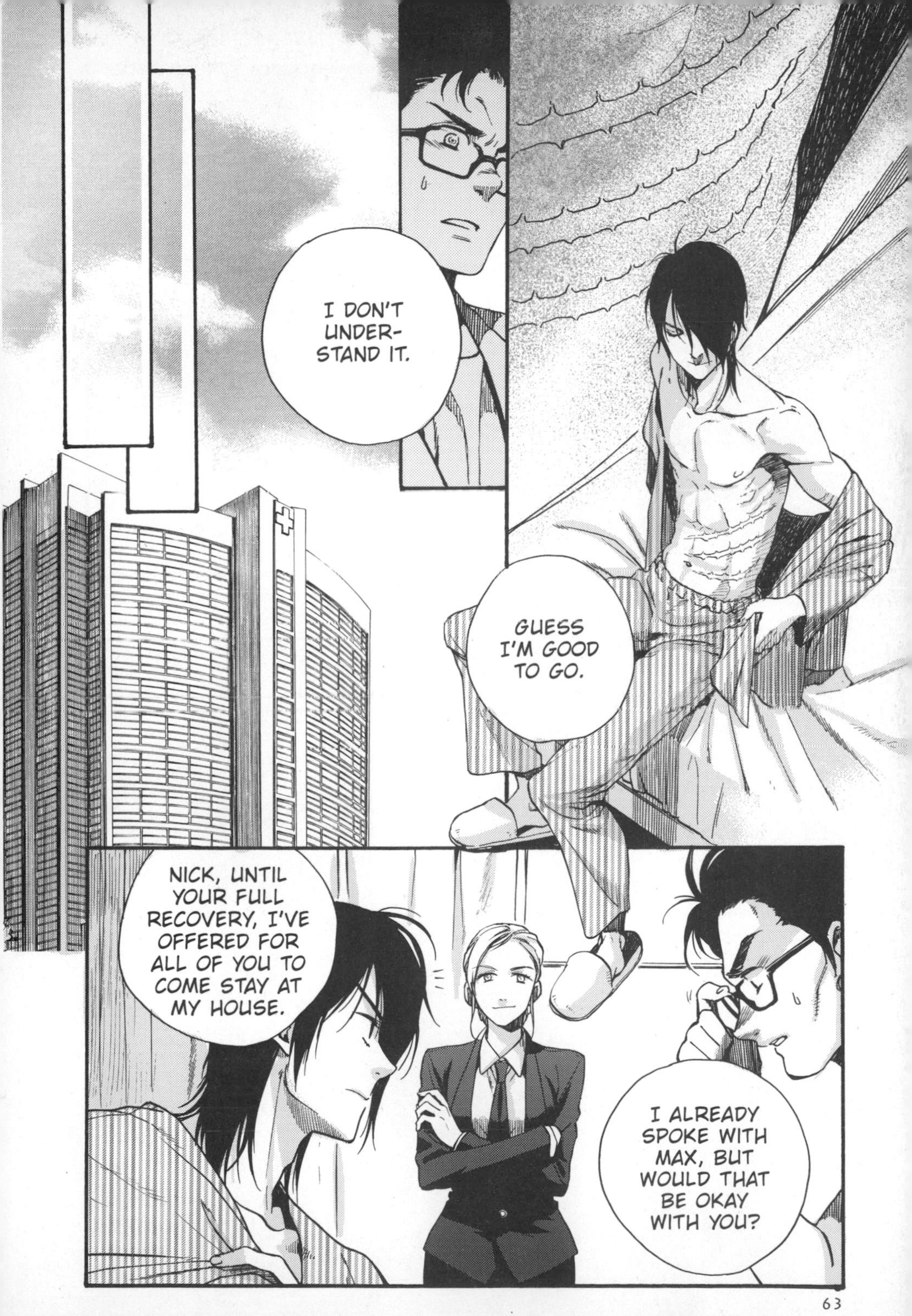
I DON'T UNDER- STAND IT.
GUESS I'M GOOD TO GO.
NICK, UNTIL YOUR FULL RECOVERY, I'VE OFFERED FOR ALL OF YOU TO COME STAY AT MY HOUSE.
I ALREADY SPOKE WITH MAX, BUT WOULD THAT BE OKAY WITH YOU?

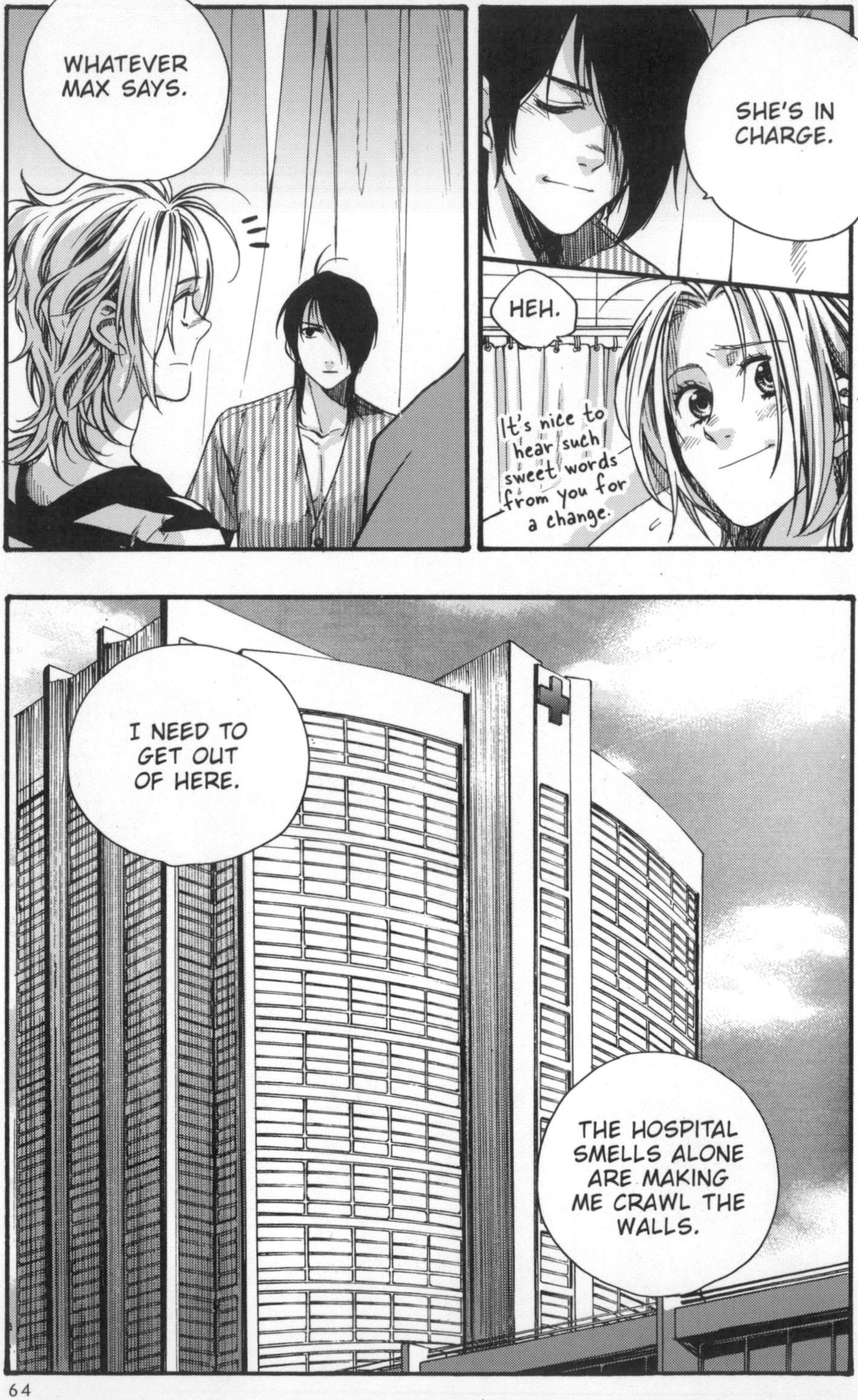
WHATEVER MAX SAYS.
SHE'S IN CHARGE.
HEH.
It's nice to hear such sweet words from you for a change.
I NEED TO GET OUT OF HERE.
THE HOSPITAL SMELLS ALONE ARE MAKING ME CRAWL THE WALLS.

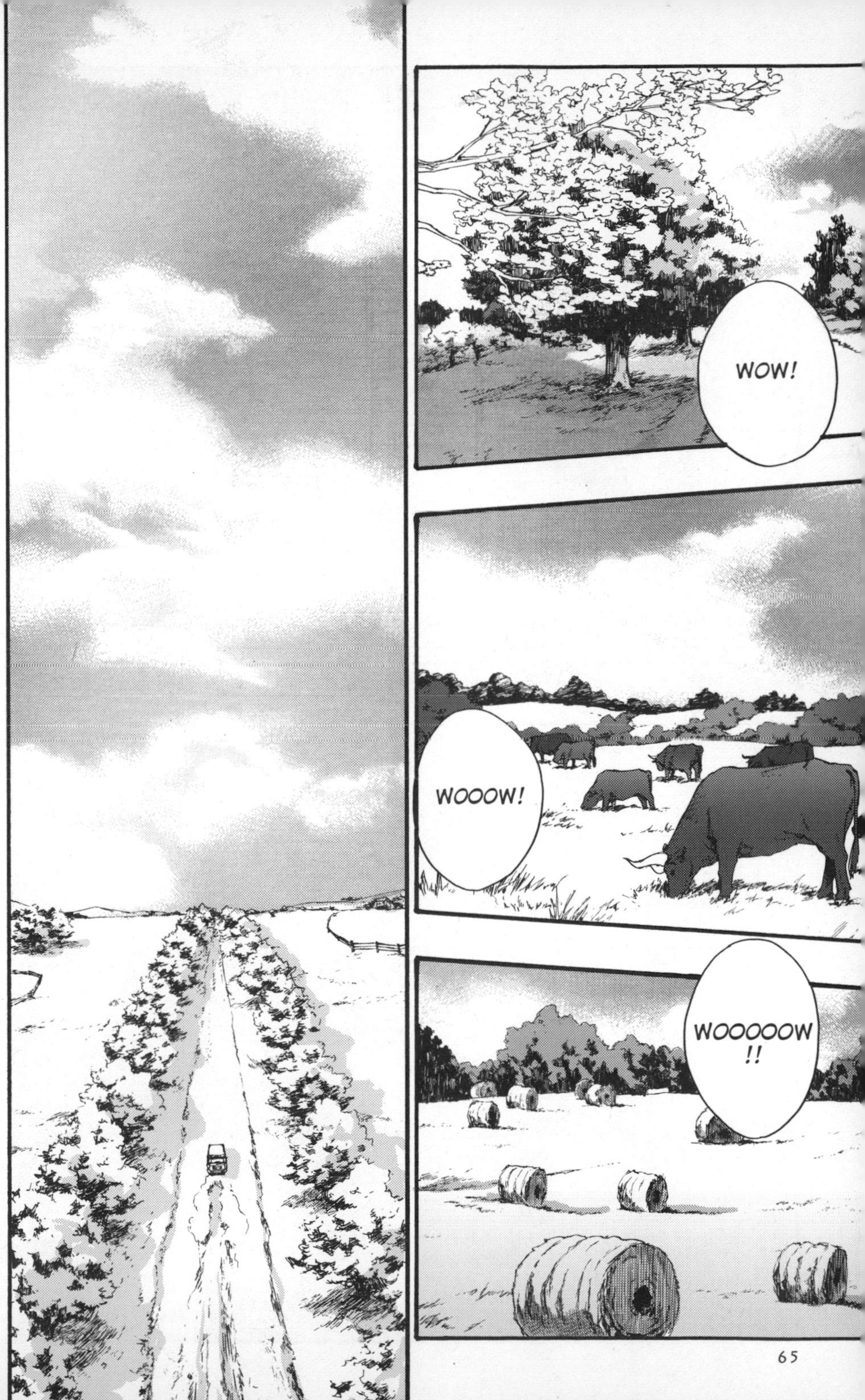
WOW!
WOOOW!
WOOOOOW !!

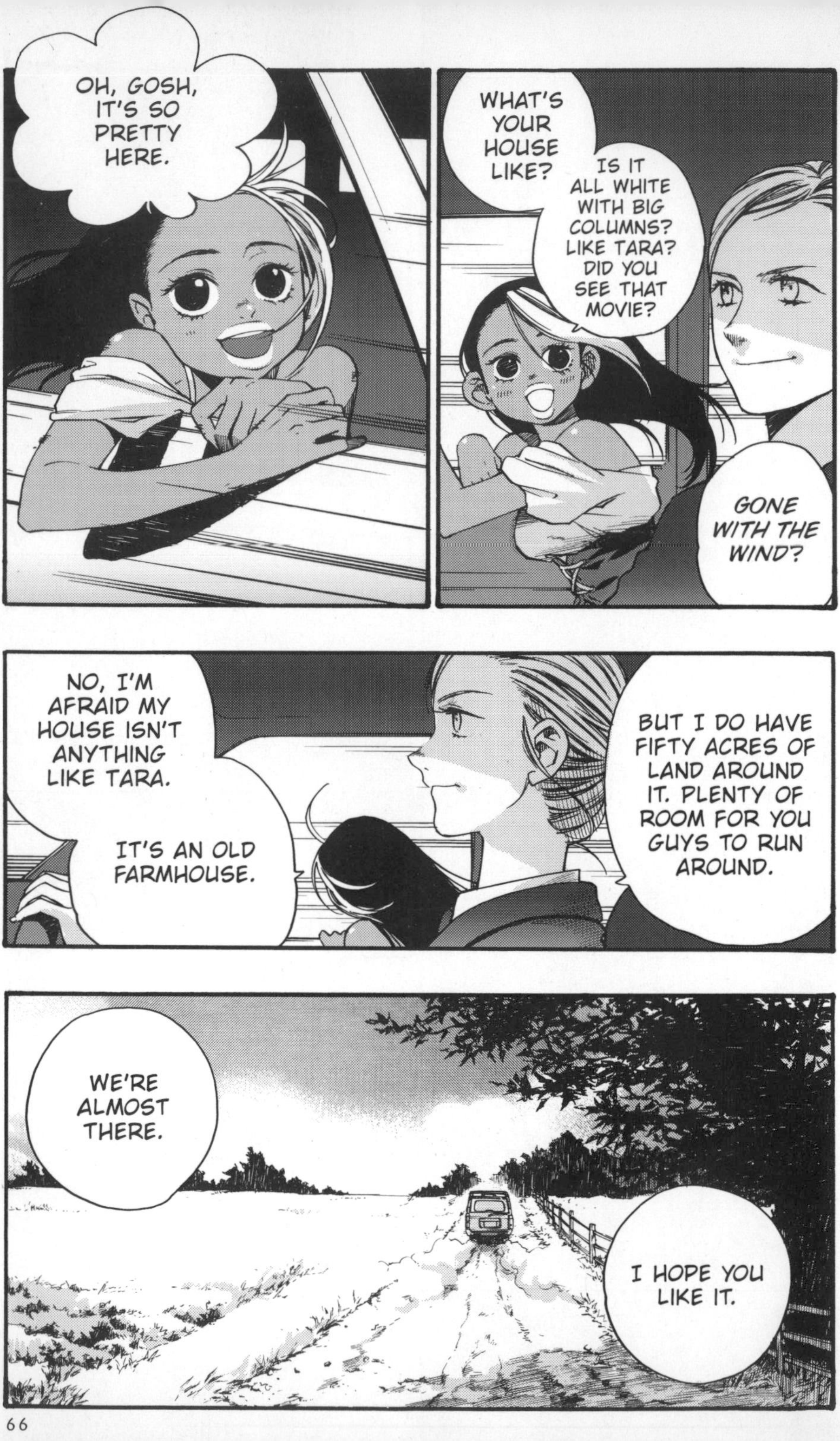
OH, GOSH, IT'S SO PRETTY HERE.
WHAT'S YOUR HOUSE LIKE?
IS IT ALL WHITE WITH BIG COLUMNS? LIKE TARA? DID YOU SEE THAT MOVIE?
GONE WITH THE WIND?
NO, I'M AFRAID MY HOUSE ISN'T ANYTHING LIKE TARA.
IT'S AN OLD FARMHOUSE.
BUT I DO HAVE FIFTY ACRES OF LAND AROUND IT. PLENTY OF ROOM FOR YOU GUYS TO RUN AROUND.
WE'RE ALMOST THERE.
I HOPE YOU LIKE IT.

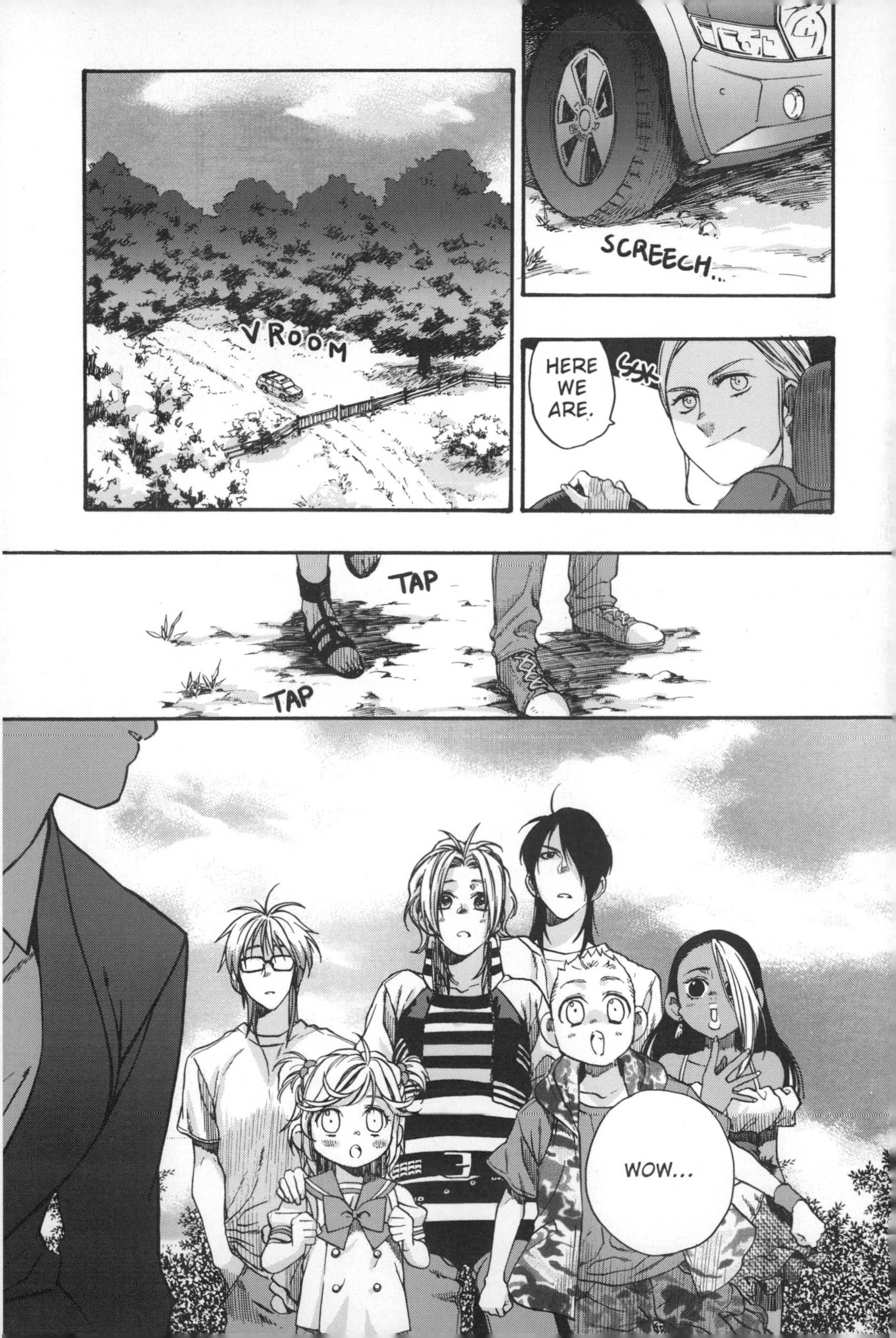
VROOM
SCREECH...
HERE WE ARE.
SSK
TAP
TAP
WOW...

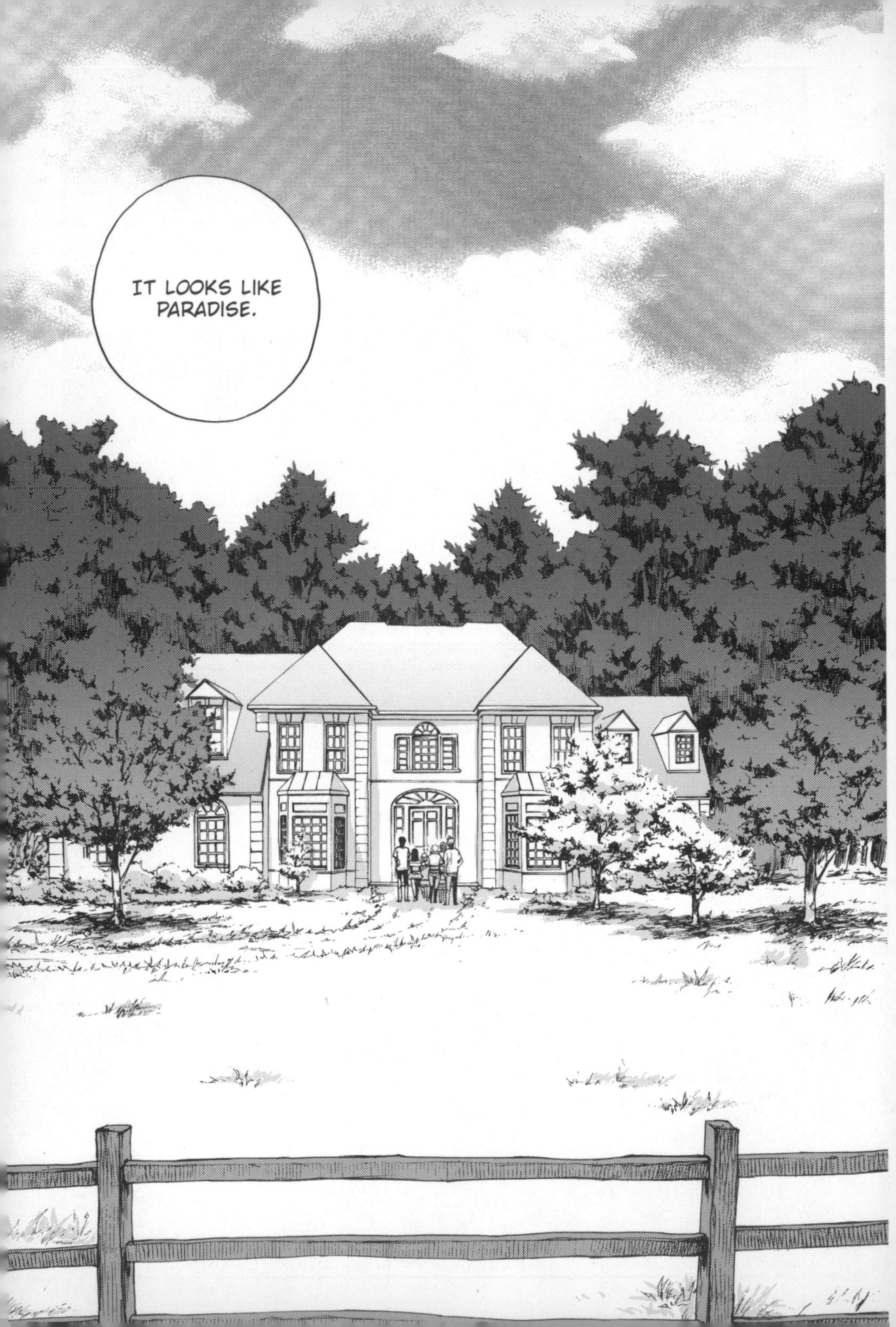
IT LOOKS LIKE PARADISE.

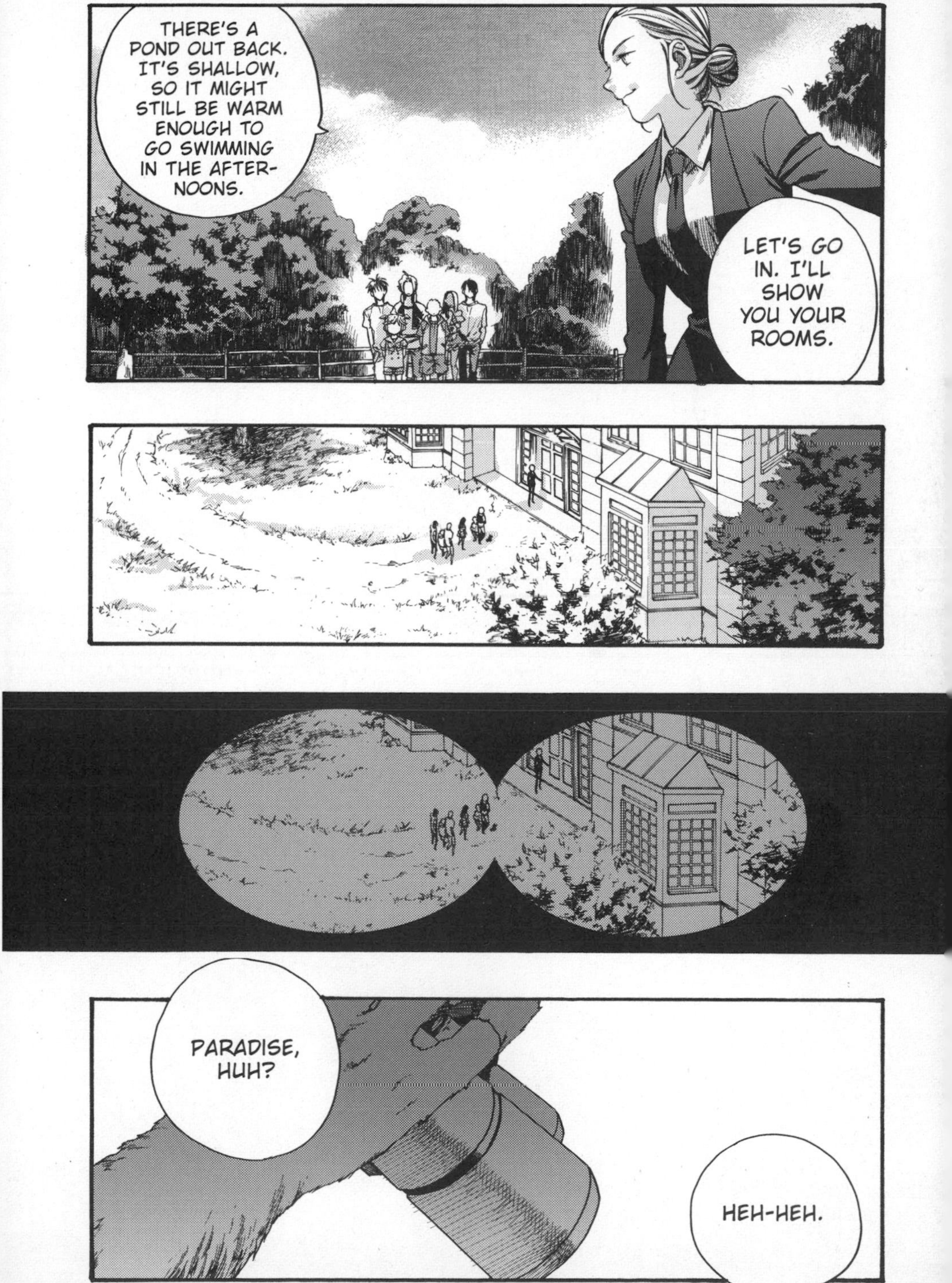
THERE'S A POND OUT BACK. IT'S SHALLOW, SO IT MIGHT STILL BE WARM ENOUGH TO GO SWIMMING IN THE AFTER-NOONS.
LET'S GO IN. I'LL SHOW YOU YOUR ROOMS.
PARADISE, HUH?
HEH-HEH.

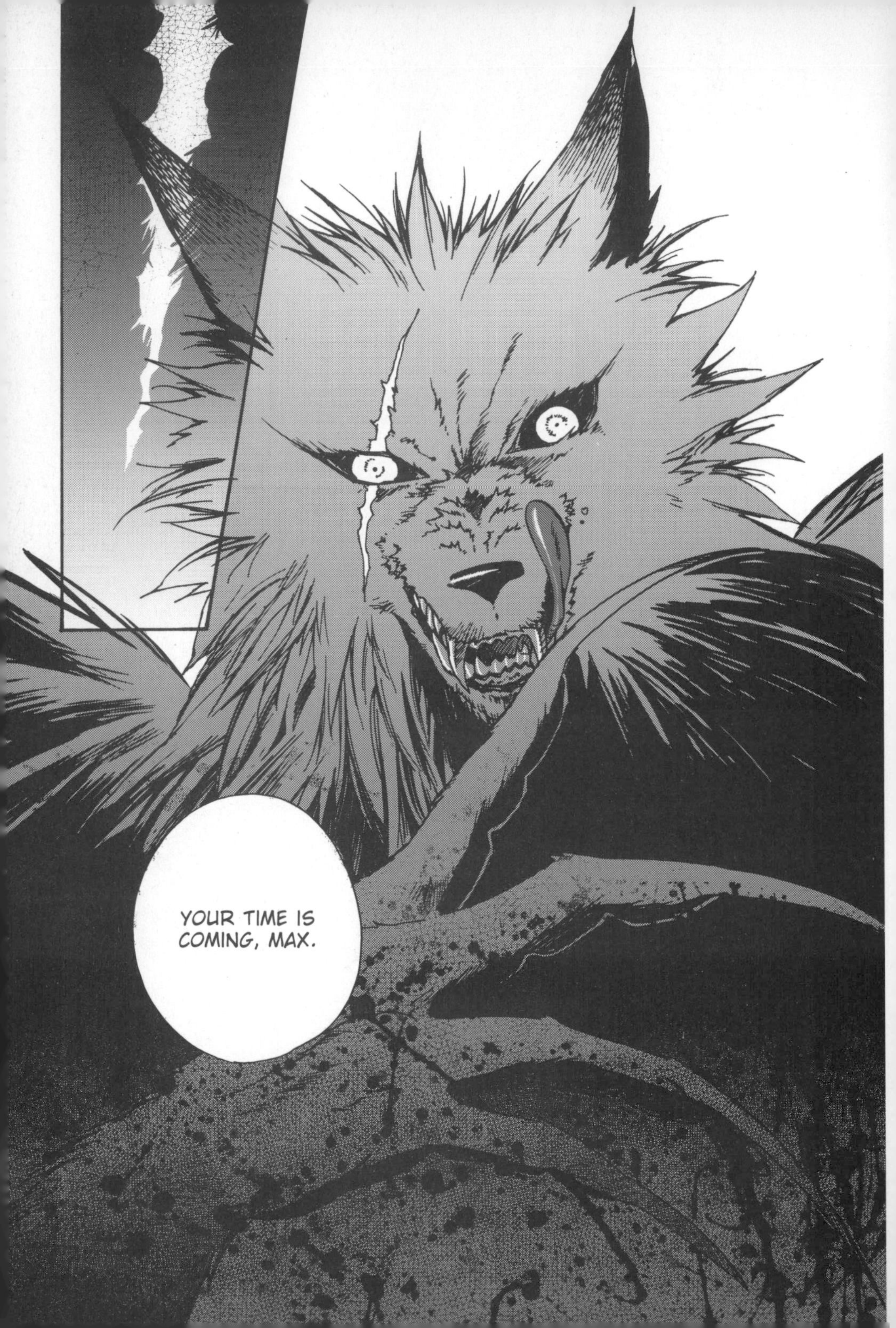
YOUR TIME IS COMING, MAX.

MAXIMUM
RIDE

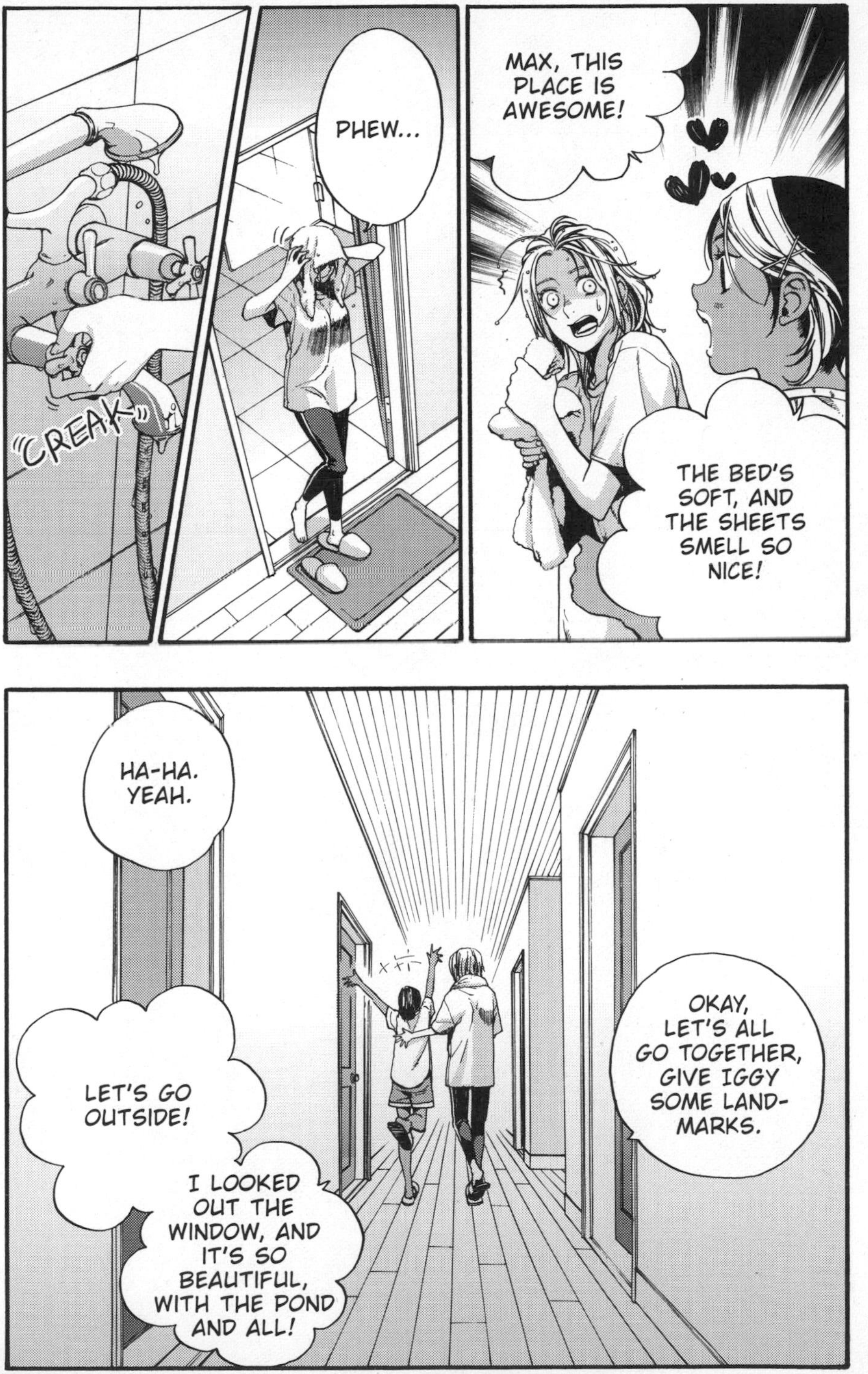
"CREAK"
PHEW...
MAX, THIS PLACE IS AWESOME!
THE BED'S SOFT, AND THE SHEETS SMELL SO NICE!
HA-HA. YEAH.
LET'S GO OUTSIDE!
I LOOKED OUT THE WINDOW, AND IT'S SO BEAUTIFUL, WITH THE POND AND ALL!
OKAY, LET'S ALL GO TOGETHER, GIVE IGGY SOME LAND-MARKS.

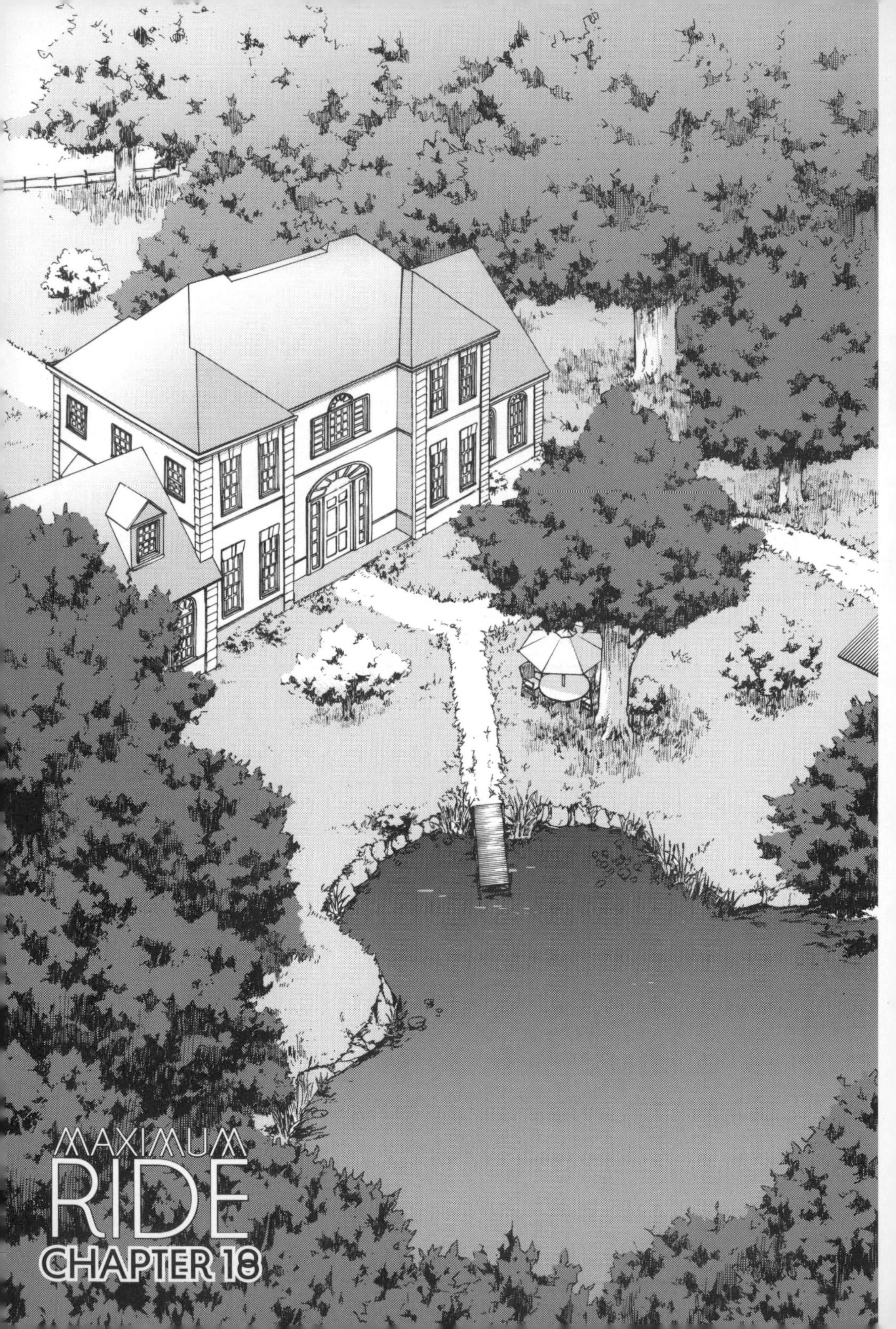

MAXIMUM
RIDE
CHAPTER 18

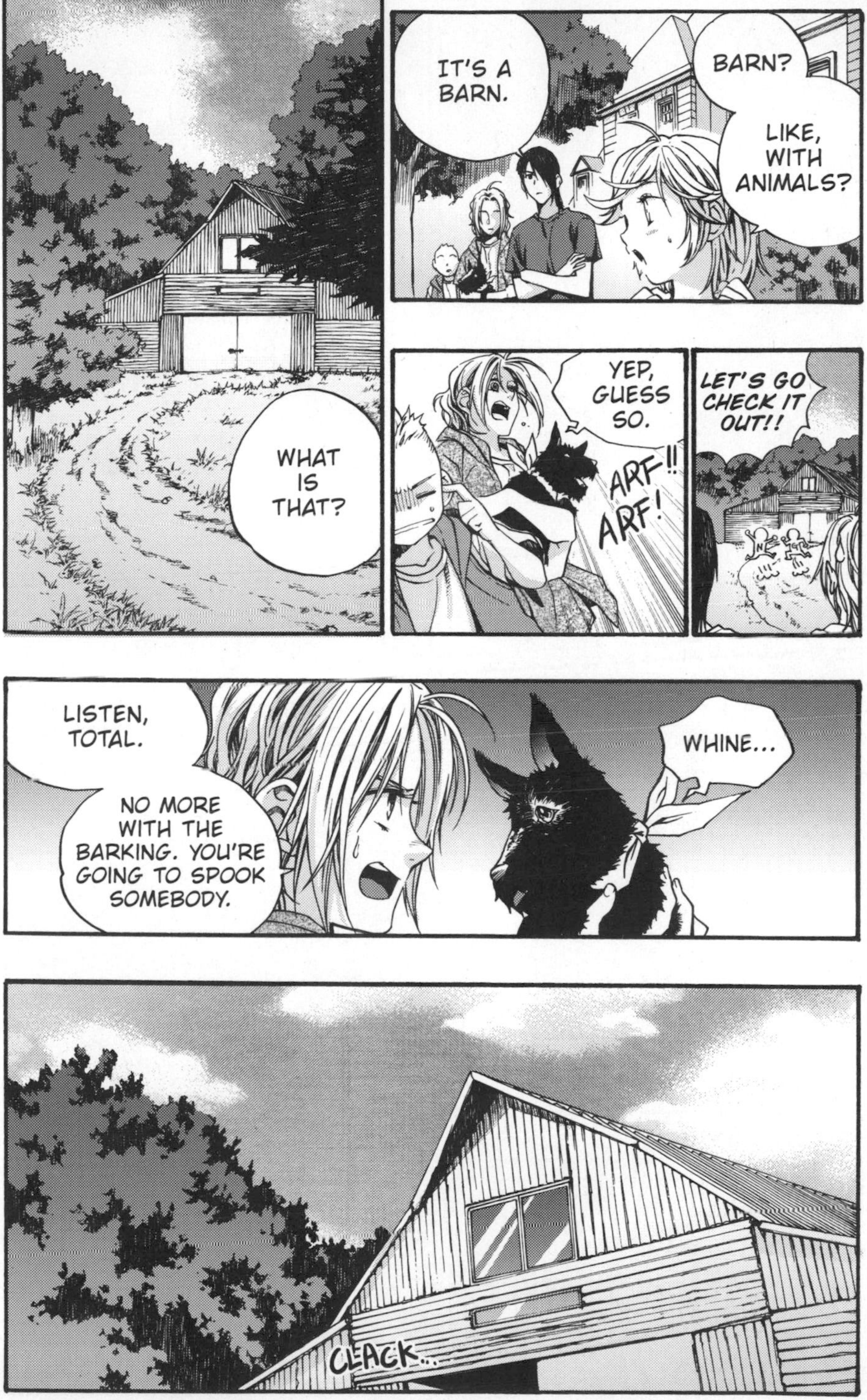
WHAT IS THAT?
IT'S A BARN.
BARN?
LIKE, WITH ANIMALS?
YEP, GUESS SO.
ARF!!
ARF!
LET'S GO CHECK IT OUT!!
LISTEN, TOTAL.
NO MORE WITH THE BARKING. YOU'RE GOING TO SPOOK SOMEBODY.
WHINE...
CLACK...

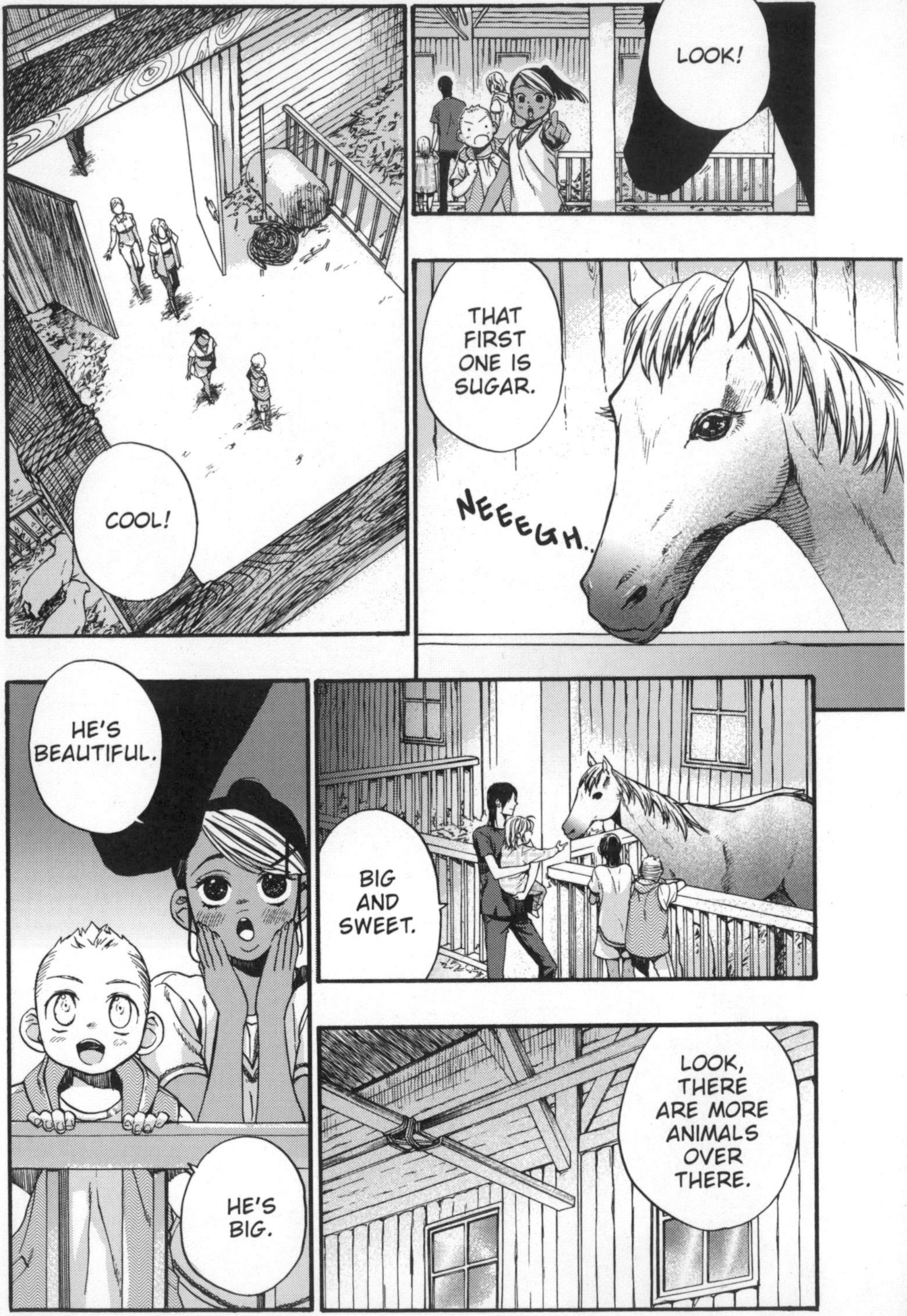
COOL!
LOOK!
THAT FIRST ONE IS SUGAR.
NEEEGH..
HE'S BEAUTIFUL.
HE'S BIG.
BIG AND SWEET.
LOOK, THERE ARE MORE ANIMALS OVER THERE.

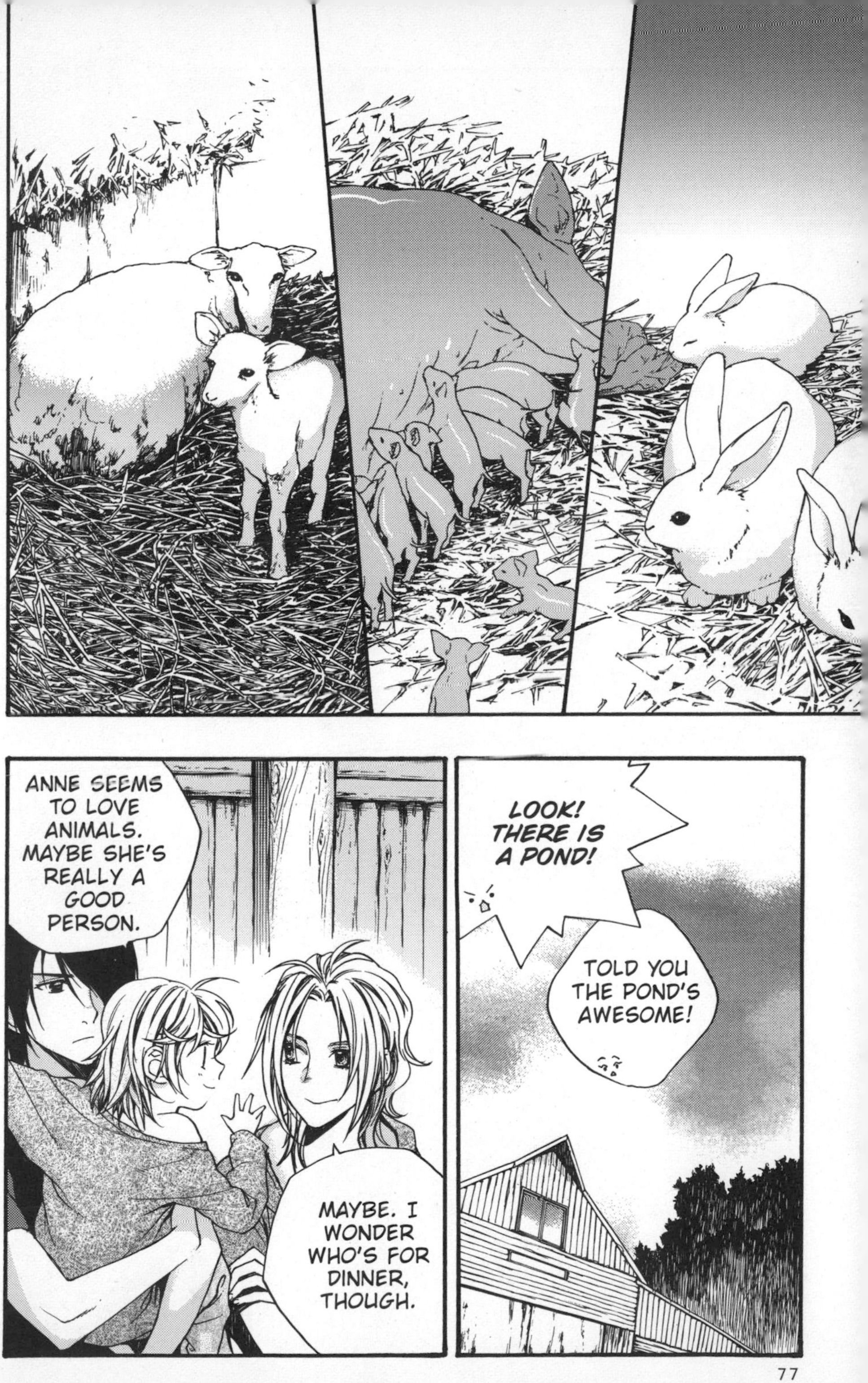
ANNE SEEMS TO LOVE ANIMALS. MAYBE SHE'S REALLY A GOOD PERSON.
MAYBE. I WONDER WHO'S FOR DINNER, THOUGH.
LOOK! THERE IS A POND!
TOLD YOU THE POND'S AWESOME!

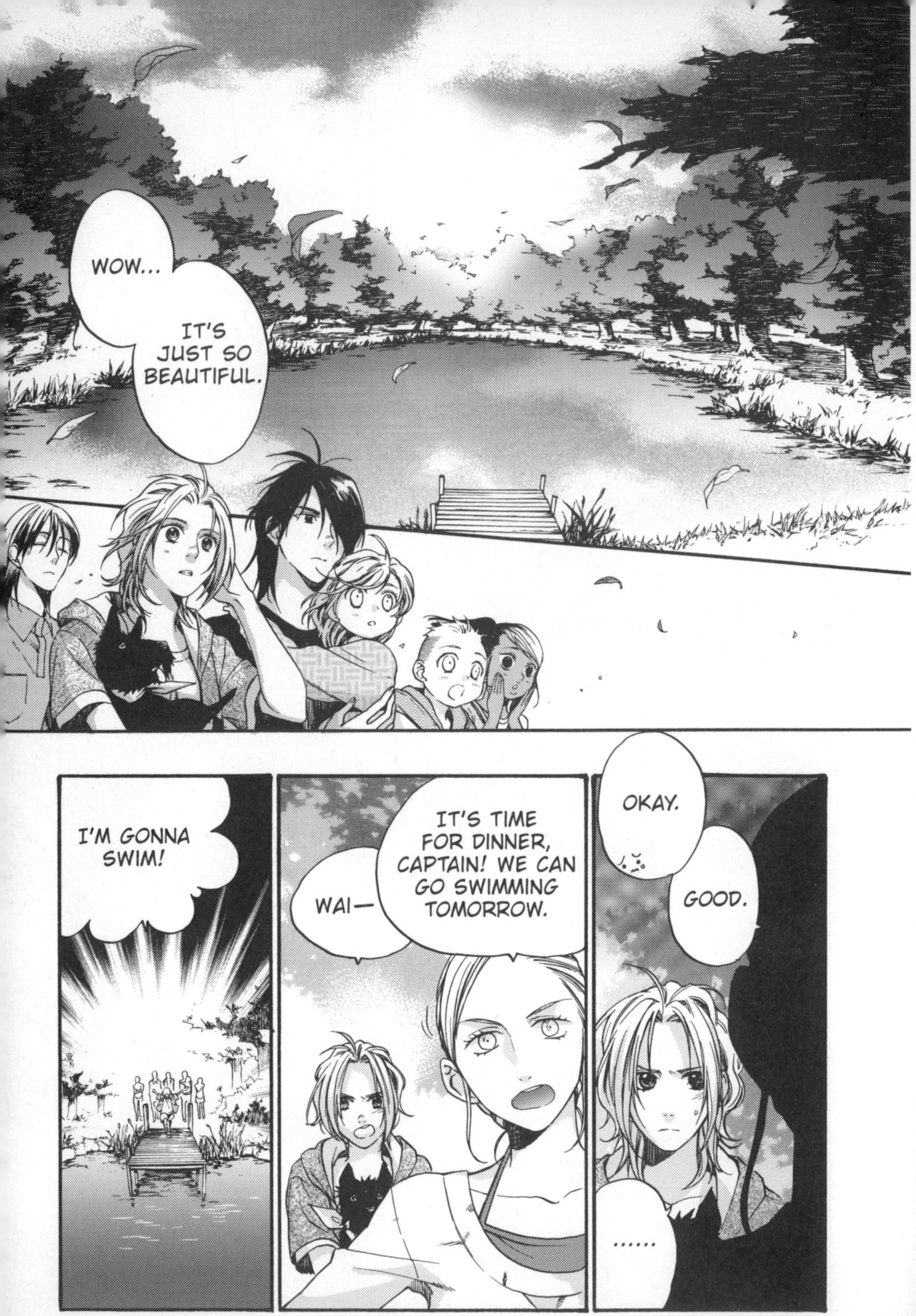
WOW...
IT'S JUST SO BEAUTIFUL.
I'M GONNA SWIM!
WAI—
IT'S TIME FOR DINNER, CAPTAIN! WE CAN GO SWIMMING TOMORROW.
OKAY.
GOOD.
......

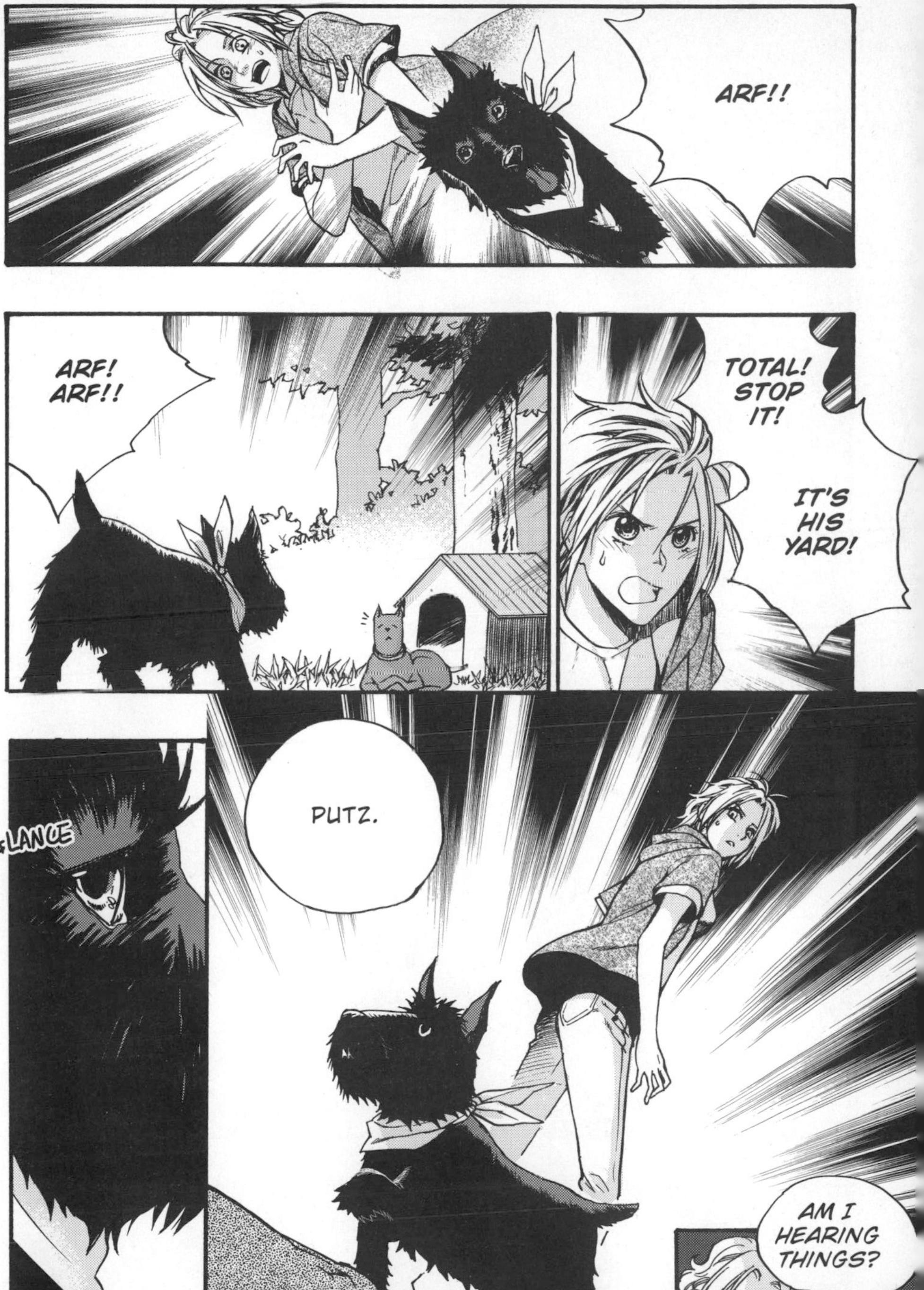
ARF!!
ARF! ARF!!
TOTAL! STOP IT!
IT'S HIS YARD!
GLANCE
PUTZ.
AM I HEARING THINGS?

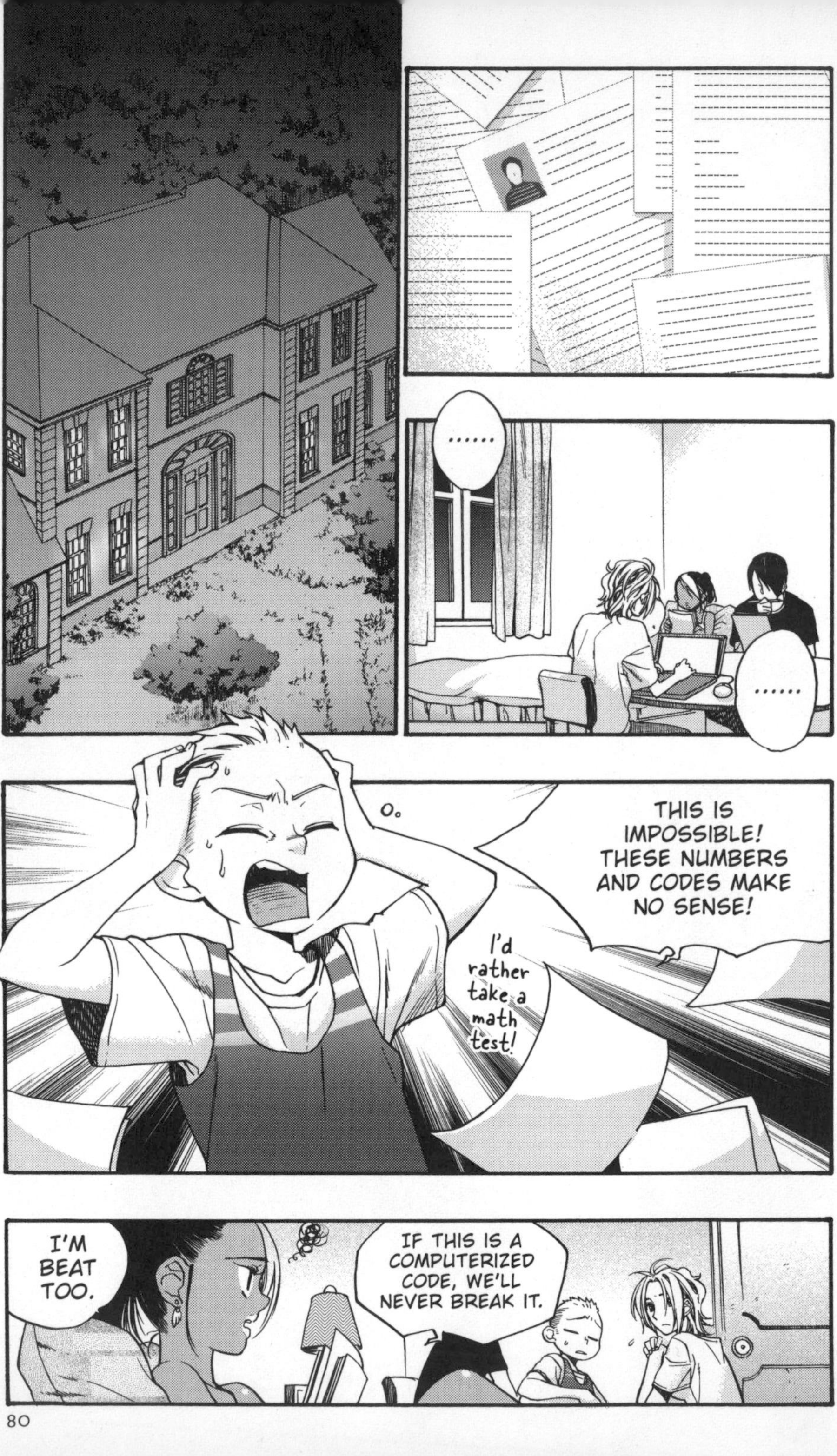
......
......
THIS IS IMPOSSIBLE! THESE NUMBERS AND CODES MAKE NO SENSE!
I'd rather take a math test!
I'M BEAT TOO.
IF THIS IS A COMPUTERIZED CODE, WE'LL NEVER BREAK IT.

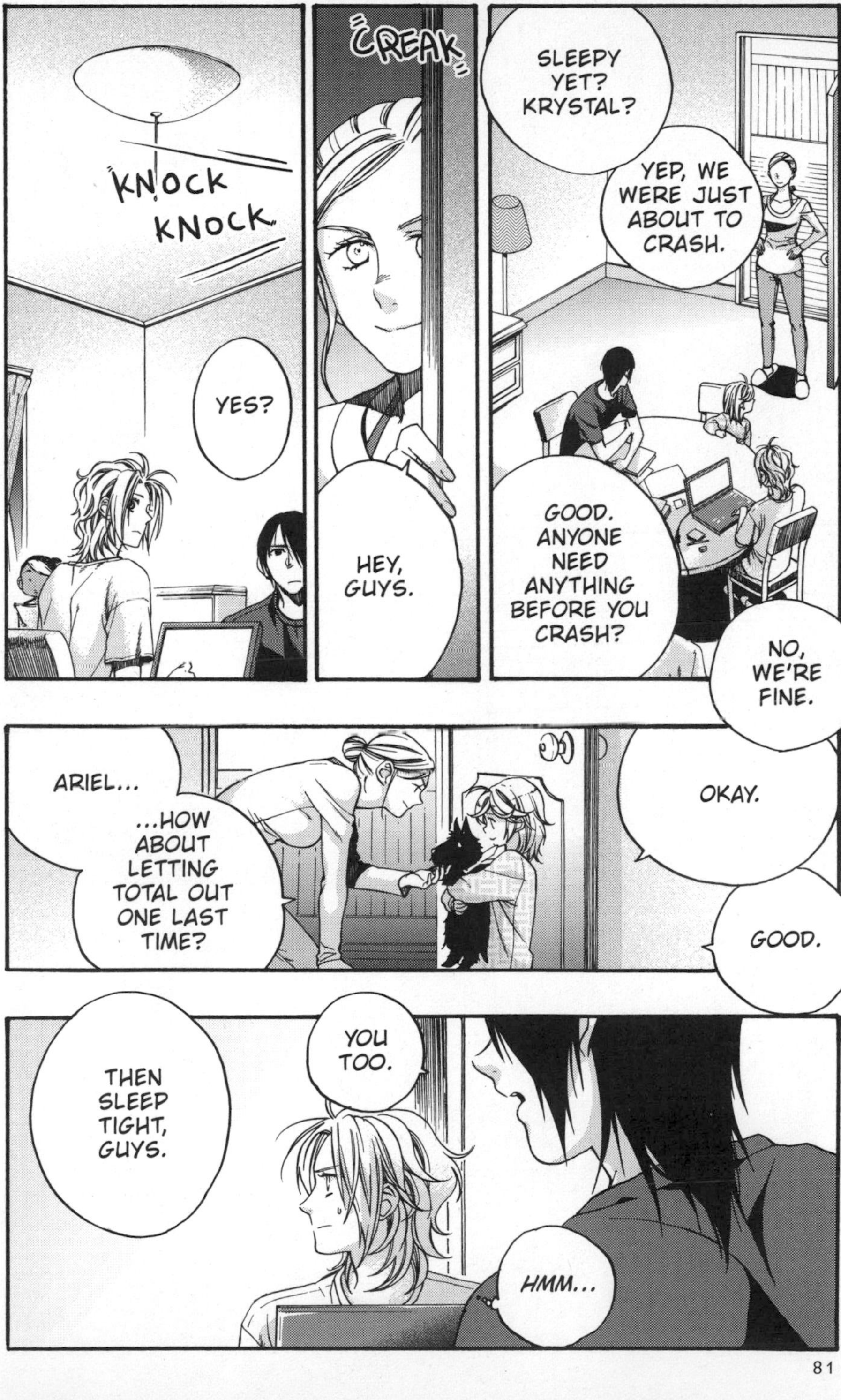
KNOCK KNOCK
YES?
CREAK
HEY, GUYS.
SLEEPY YET? KRYSTAL?
YEP, WE WERE JUST ABOUT TO CRASH.
GOOD. ANYONE NEED ANYTHING BEFORE YOU CRASH?
NO, WE'RE FINE.
ARIEL...
...HOW ABOUT LETTING TOTAL OUT ONE LAST TIME?
OKAY.
GOOD.
THEN SLEEP TIGHT, GUYS.
YOU TOO.
HMM...

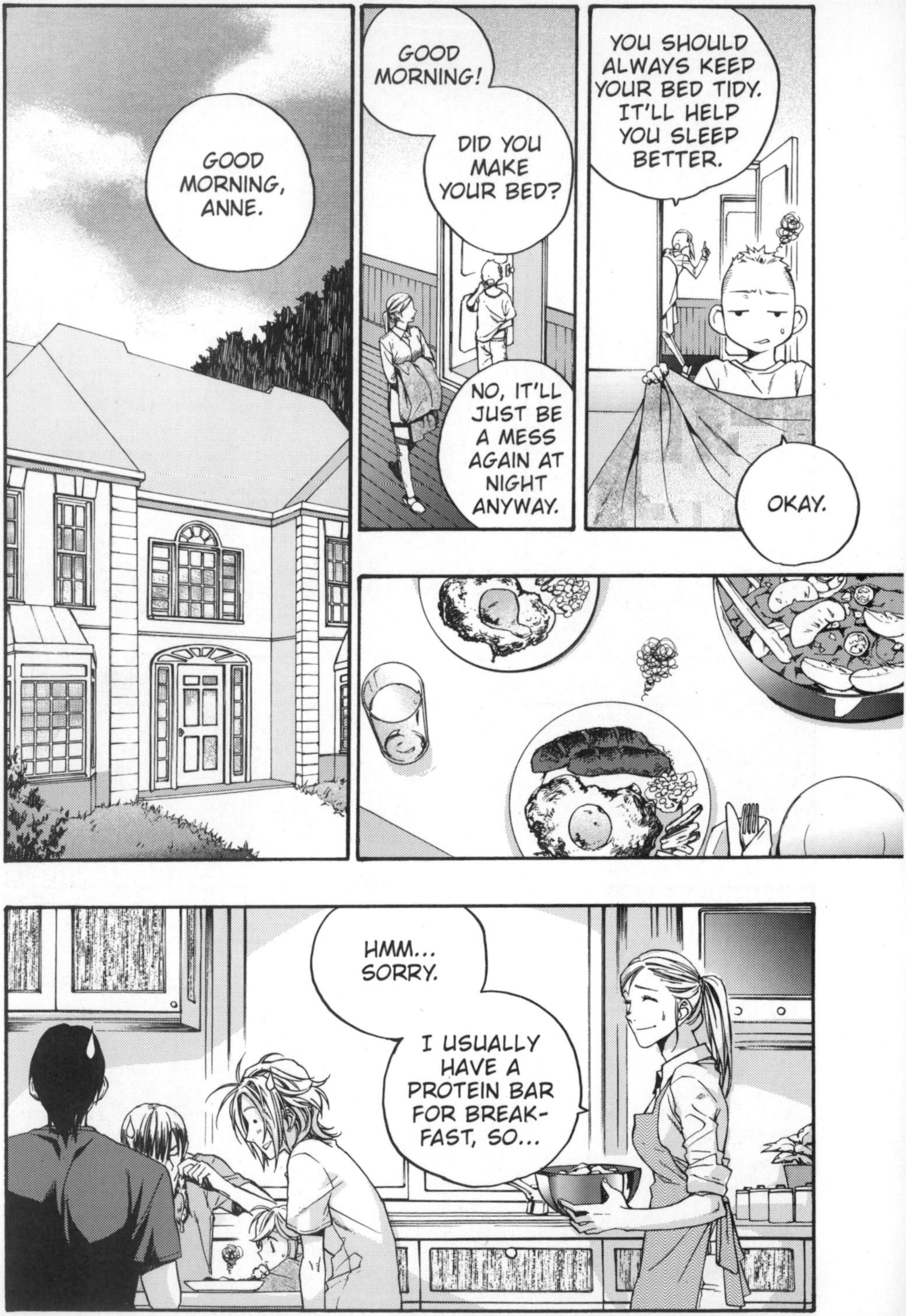
GOOD MORNING, ANNE.
GOOD MORNING!
DID YOU MAKE YOUR BED?
NO, IT'LL JUST BE A MESS AGAIN AT NIGHT ANYWAY.
YOU SHOULD ALWAYS KEEP YOUR BED TIDY. IT'LL HELP YOU SLEEP BETTER.
OKAY.
HMM... SORRY.
I USUALLY HAVE A PROTEIN BAR FOR BREAK-FAST, SO...

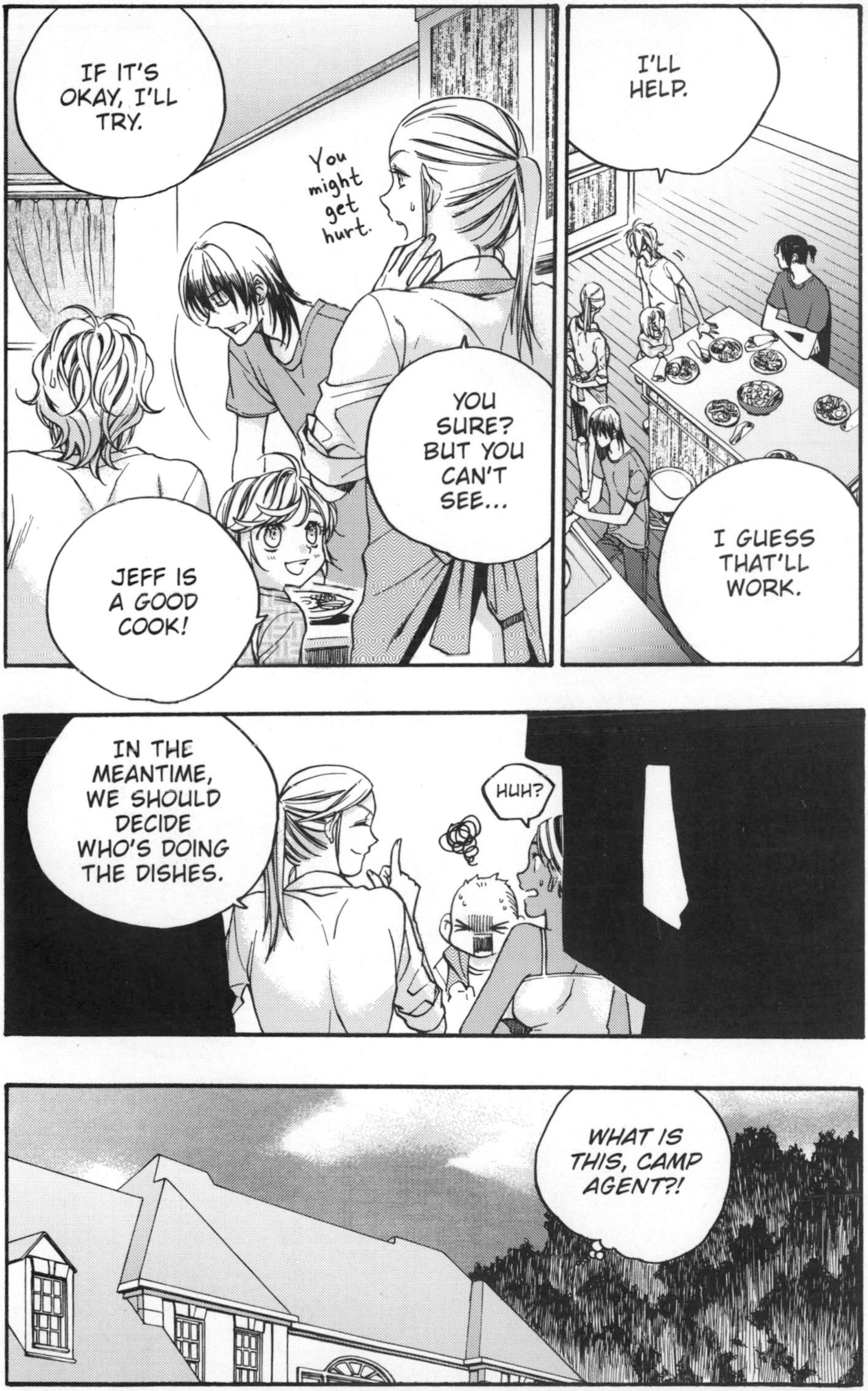
IF IT'S OKAY, I'LL TRY.
You might get hurt.
YOU SURE? BUT YOU CAN'T SEE...
JEFF IS A GOOD COOK!
I'LL HELP.
I GUESS THAT'LL WORK.
IN THE MEANTIME, WE SHOULD DECIDE WHO'S DOING THE DISHES.
HUH?
WHAT IS THIS, CAMP AGENT?!

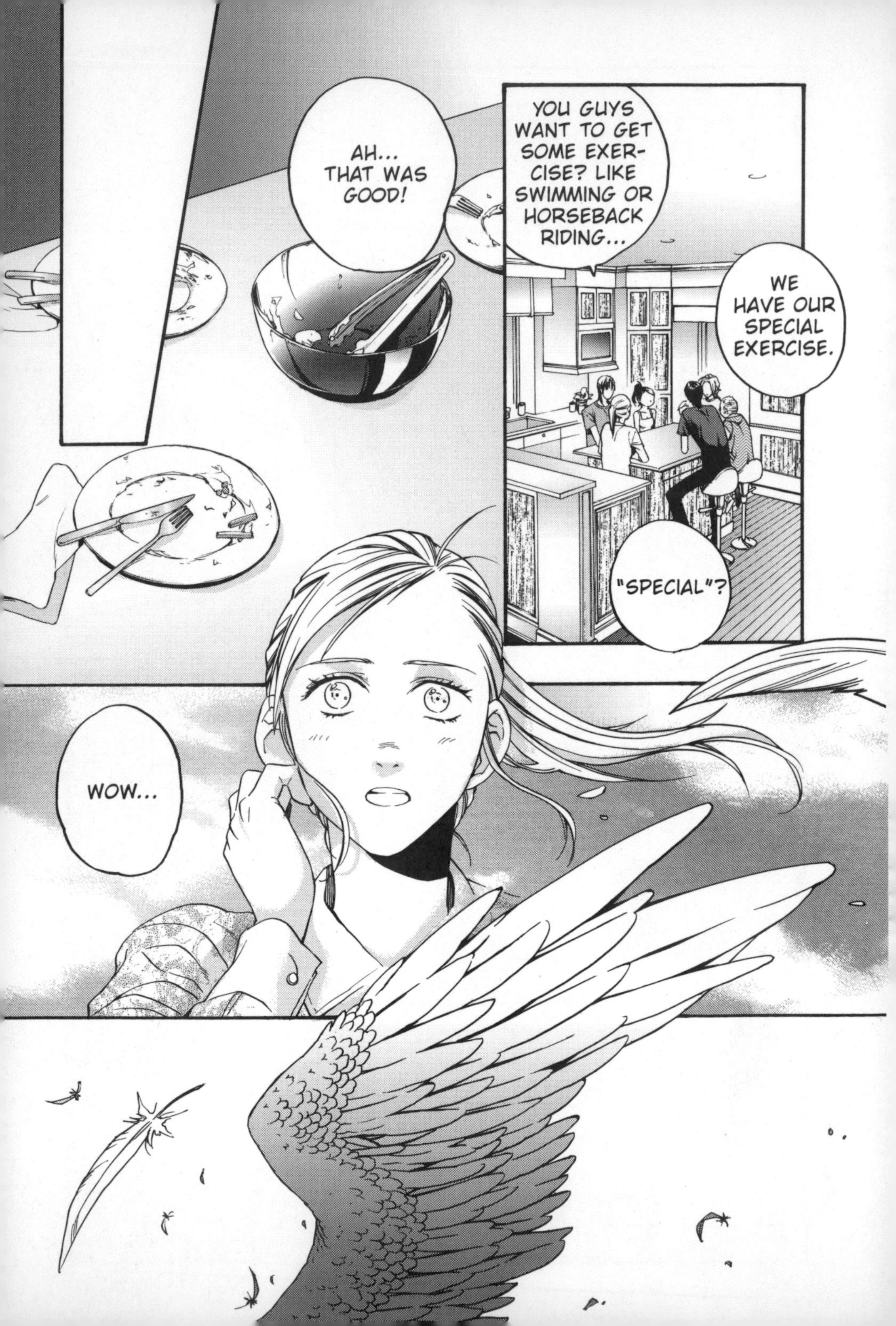
AH... THAT WAS GOOD!
YOU GUYS WANT TO GET SOME EXER-CISE? LIKE SWIMMING OR HORSEBACK RIDING...
WE HAVE OUR SPECIAL EXERCISE.
"SPECIAL"?
WOW...

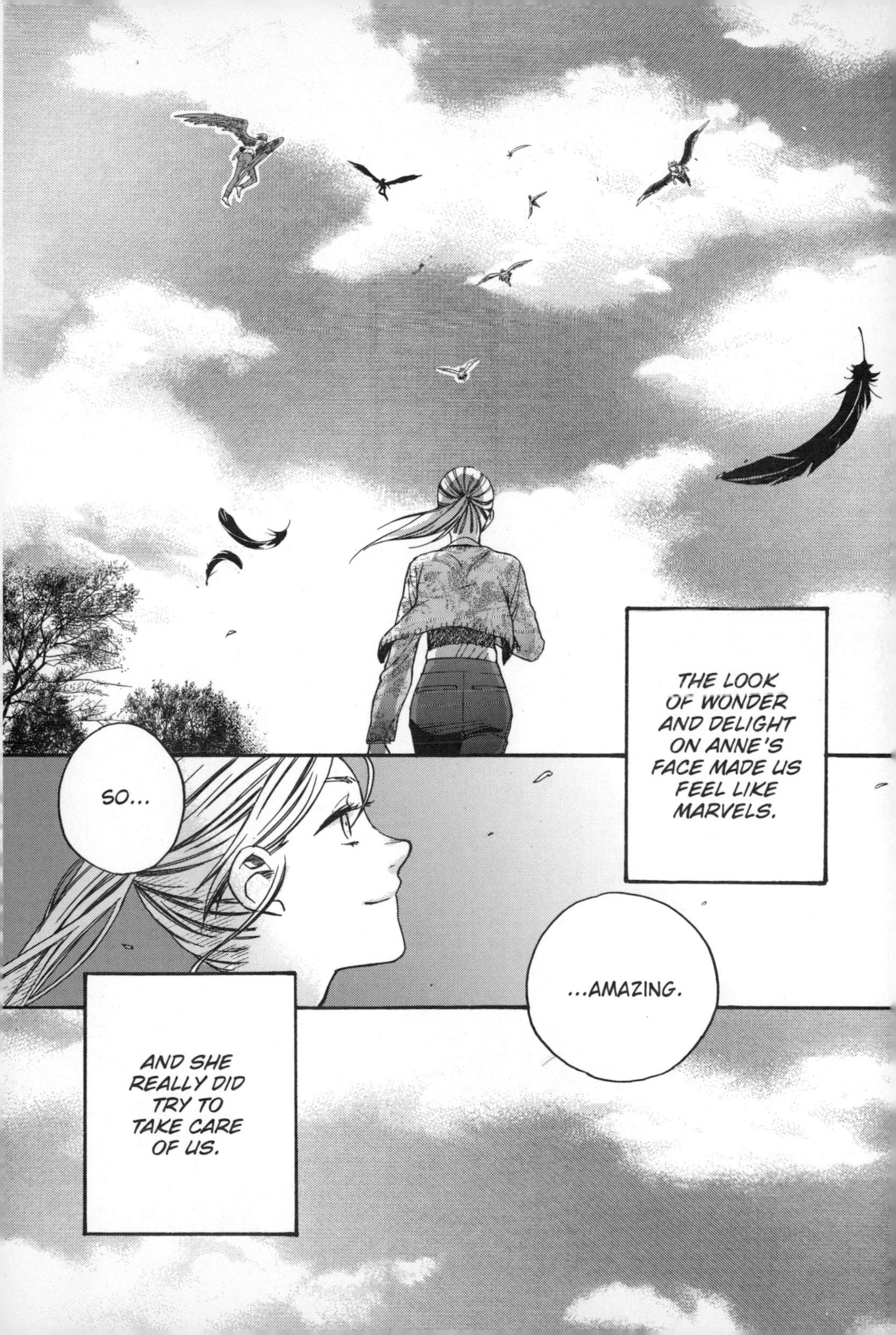
THE LOOK OF WONDER AND DELIGHT ON ANNE'S FACE MADE US FEEL LIKE MARVELS.
SO...
...AMAZING.
AND SHE REALLY DID TRY TO TAKE CARE OF US.

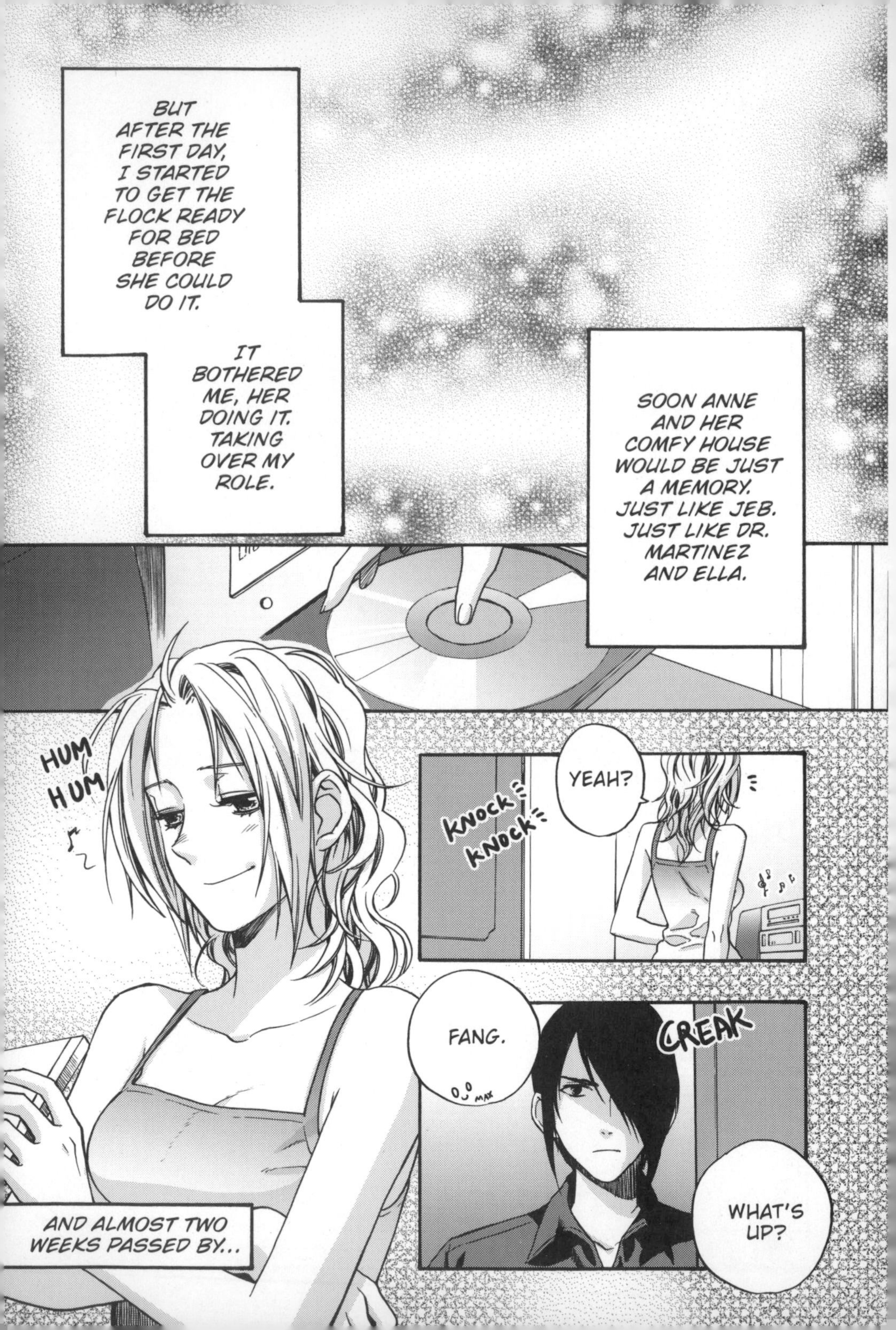
BUT AFTER THE FIRST DAY, I STARTED TO GET THE FLOCK READY FOR BED BEFORE SHE COULD DO IT.
IT BOTHERED ME, HER DOING IT. TAKING OVER MY ROLE.
SOON ANNE AND HER COMFY HOUSE WOULD BE JUST A MEMORY. JUST LIKE JEB. JUST LIKE DR. MARTINEZ AND ELLA.
HUM HUM
AND ALMOST TWO WEEKS PASSED BY...
KNOCK KNOCK
YEAH?
FANG.
CREAK
WHAT'S UP?

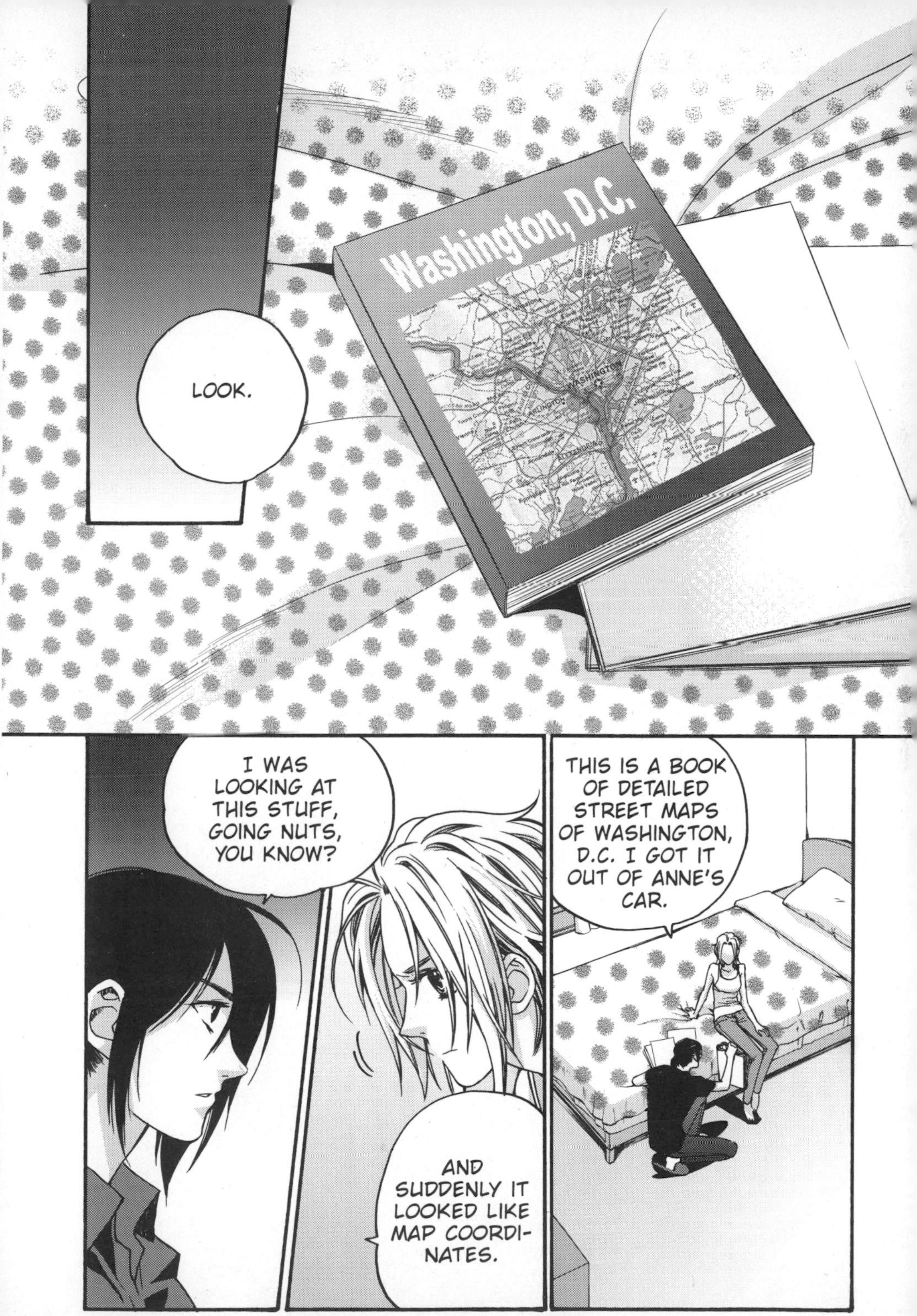
Washington, D.C.
LOOK.
I WAS LOOKING AT THIS STUFF, GOING NUTS, YOU KNOW?
AND SUDDENLY IT LOOKED LIKE MAP COORDI-NATES.
THIS IS A BOOK OF DETAILED STREET MAPS OF WASHINGTON, D.C. I GOT IT OUT OF ANNE'S CAR.

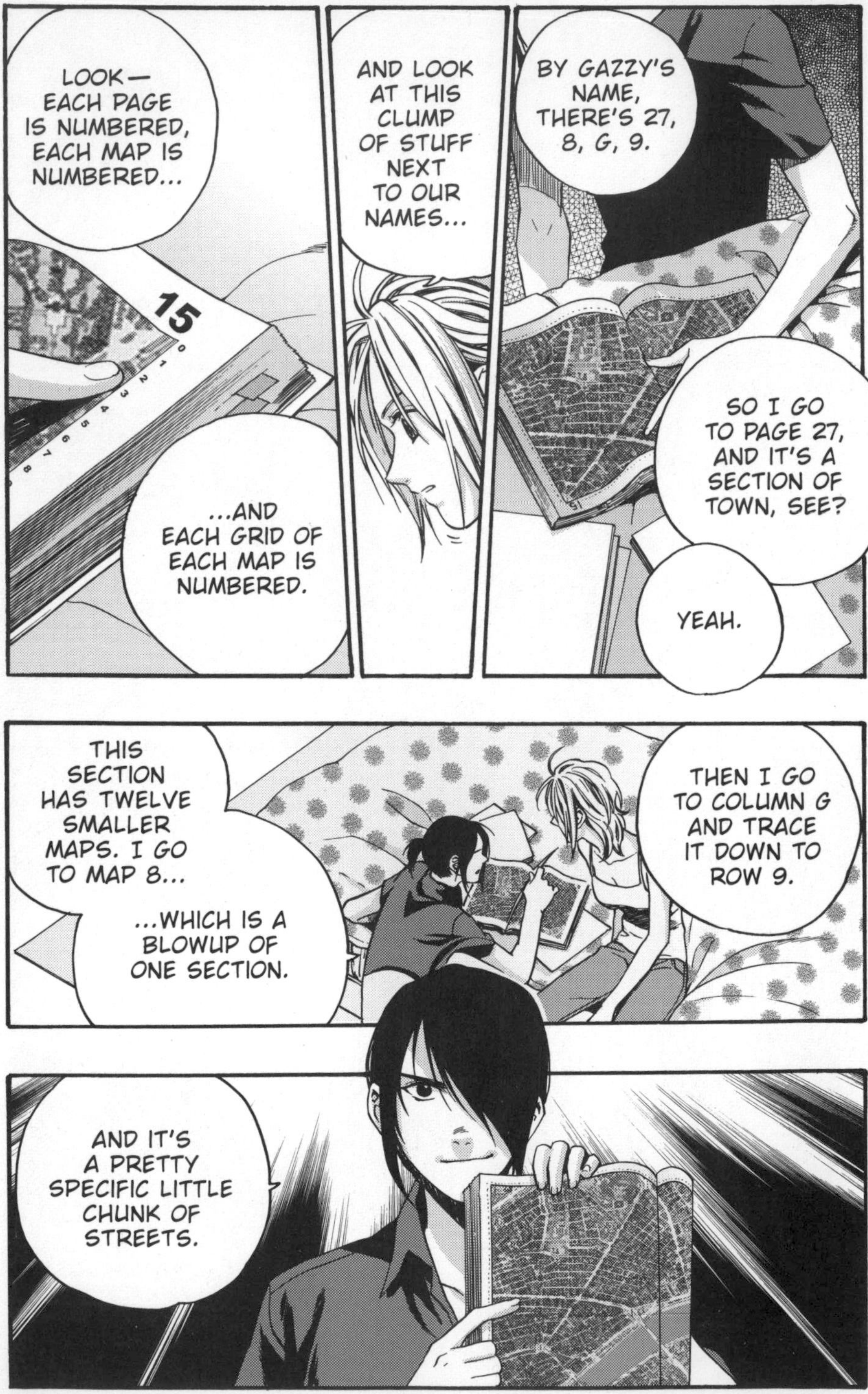
LOOK— EACH PAGE IS NUMBERED, EACH MAP IS NUMBERED...
15
...AND EACH GRID OF EACH MAP IS NUMBERED.
AND LOOK AT THIS CLUMP OF STUFF NEXT TO OUR NAMES...
BY GAZZY'S NAME, THERE'S 27, 8, G, 9.
SO I GO TO PAGE 27, AND IT'S A SECTION OF TOWN, SEE?
YEAH.
THIS SECTION HAS TWELVE SMALLER MAPS. I GO TO MAP 8...
...WHICH IS A BLOWUP OF ONE SECTION.
THEN I GO TO COLUMN G AND TRACE IT DOWN TO ROW 9.
AND IT'S A PRETTY SPECIFIC LITTLE CHUNK OF STREETS.

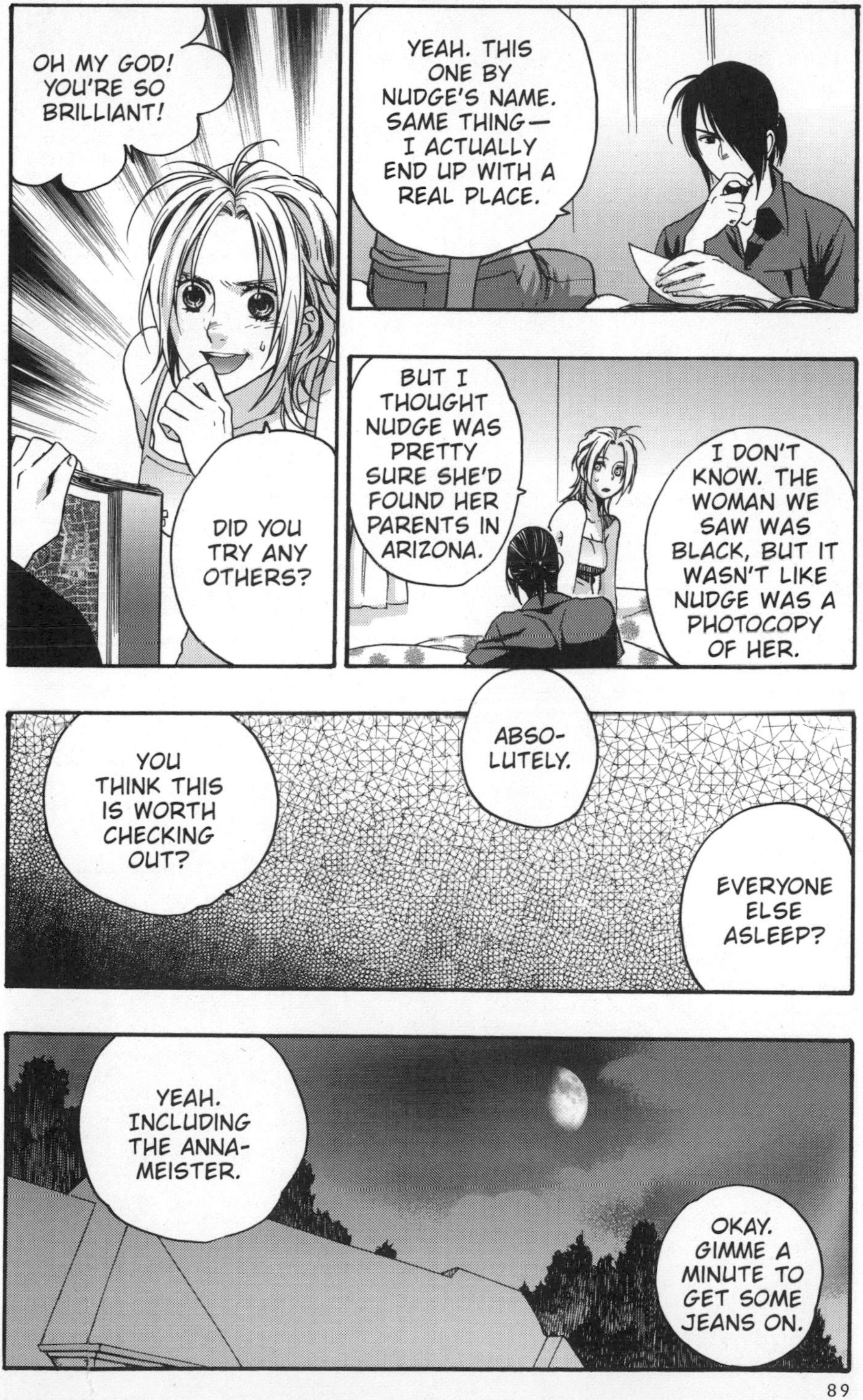
OH MY GOD! YOU'RE SO BRILLIANT!
YEAH. THIS ONE BY NUDGE'S NAME. SAME THING— I ACTUALLY END UP WITH A REAL PLACE.
DID YOU TRY ANY OTHERS?
BUT I THOUGHT NUDGE WAS PRETTY SURE SHE'D FOUND HER PARENTS IN ARIZONA.
I DON'T KNOW. THE WOMAN WE SAW WAS BLACK, BUT IT WASN'T LIKE NUDGE WAS A PHOTOCOPY OF HER.
YOU THINK THIS IS WORTH CHECKING OUT?
ABSO-LUTELY.
EVERYONE ELSE ASLEEP?
YEAH. INCLUDING THE ANNA-MEISTER.
OKAY. GIMME A MINUTE TO GET SOME JEANS ON.

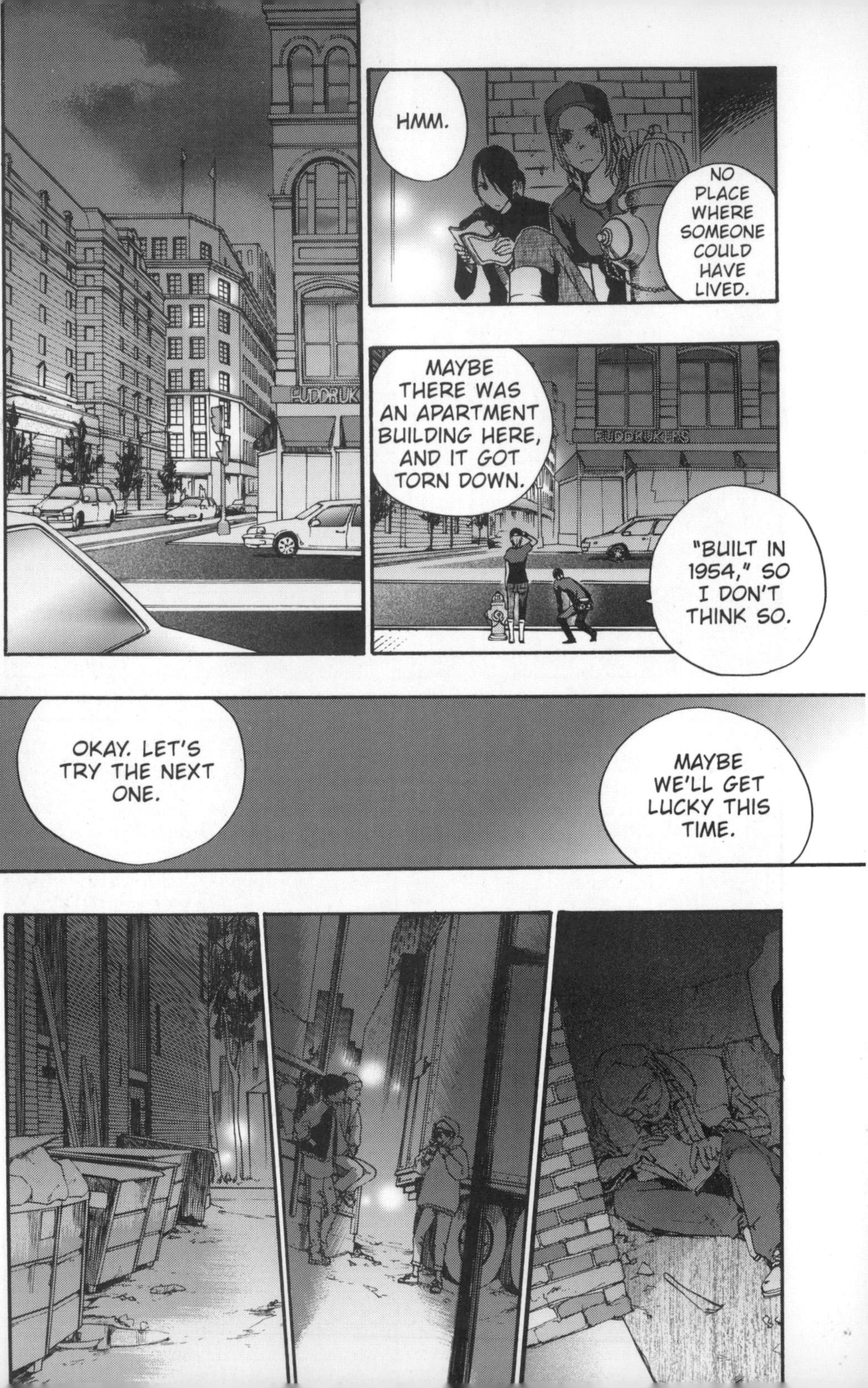
HMM.
NO PLACE WHERE SOMEONE COULD HAVE LIVED.
MAYBE THERE WAS AN APARTMENT BUILDING HERE, AND IT GOT TORN DOWN.
"BUILT IN 1954," SO I DON'T THINK SO.
OKAY. LET'S TRY THE NEXT ONE.
MAYBE WE'LL GET LUCKY THIS TIME.

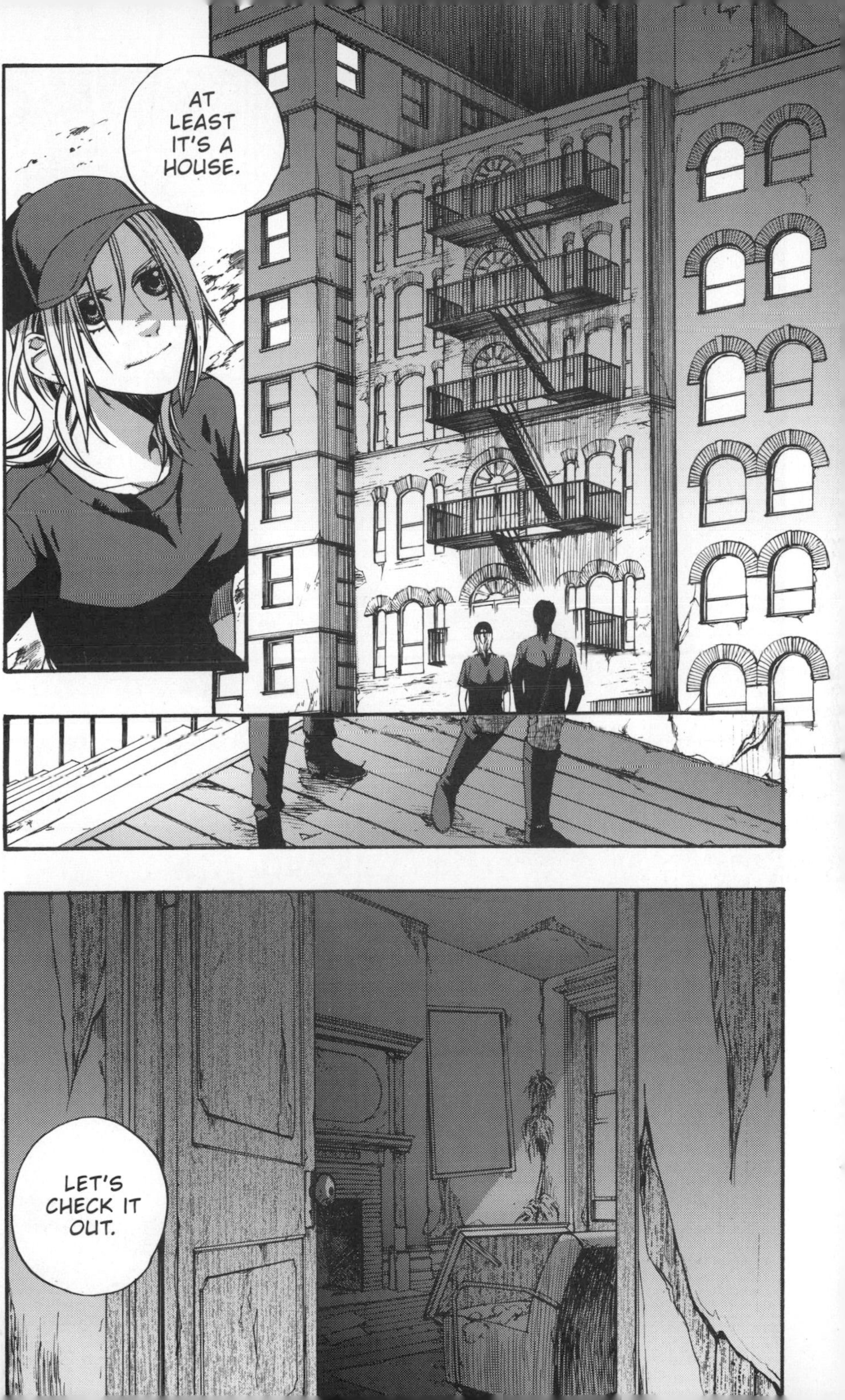
AT LEAST IT'S A HOUSE.
LET'S CHECK IT OUT.

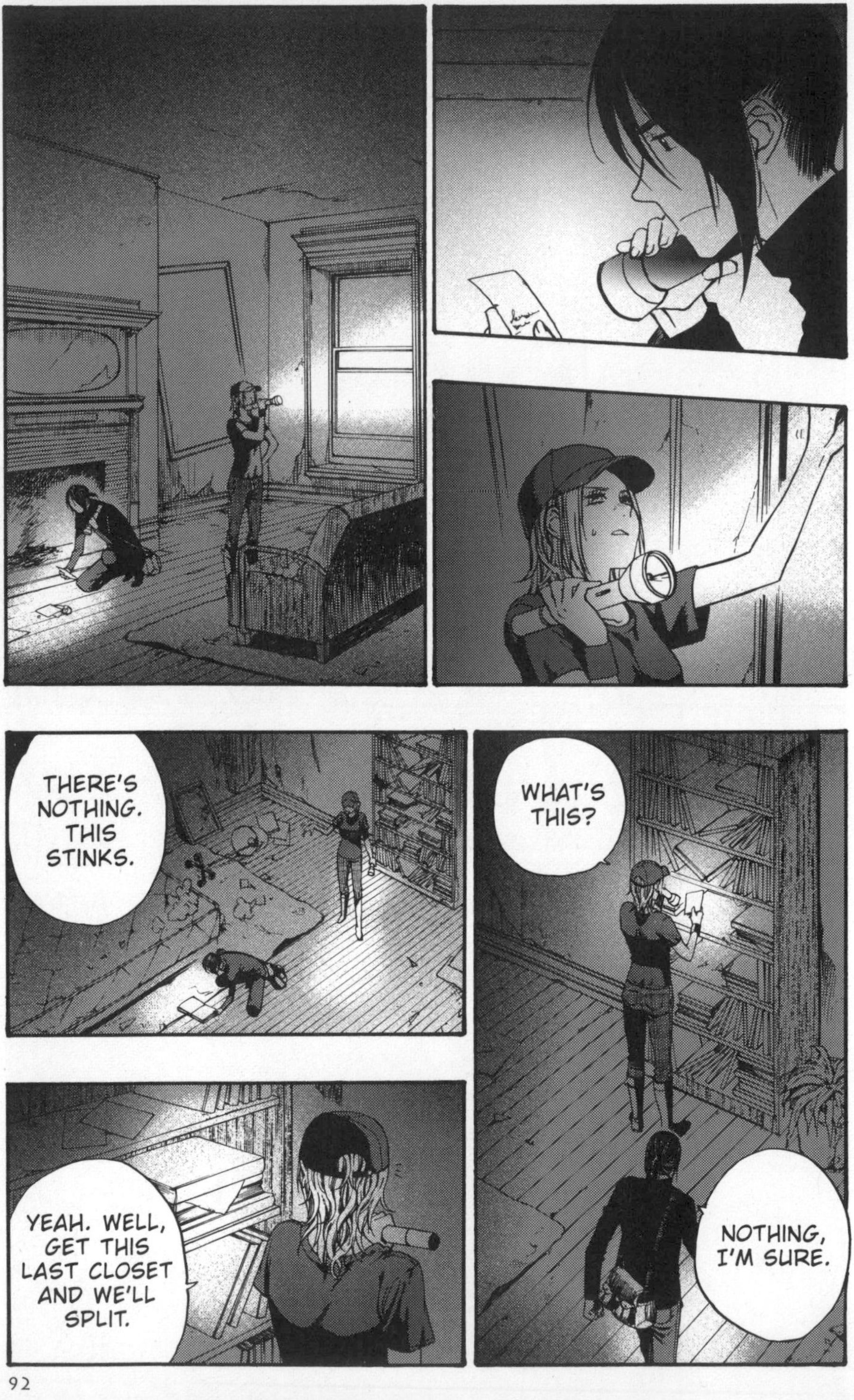
THERE'S NOTHING. THIS STINKS.
WHAT'S THIS?
YEAH. WELL, GET THIS LAST CLOSET AND WE'LL SPLIT.
NOTHING, I'M SURE.

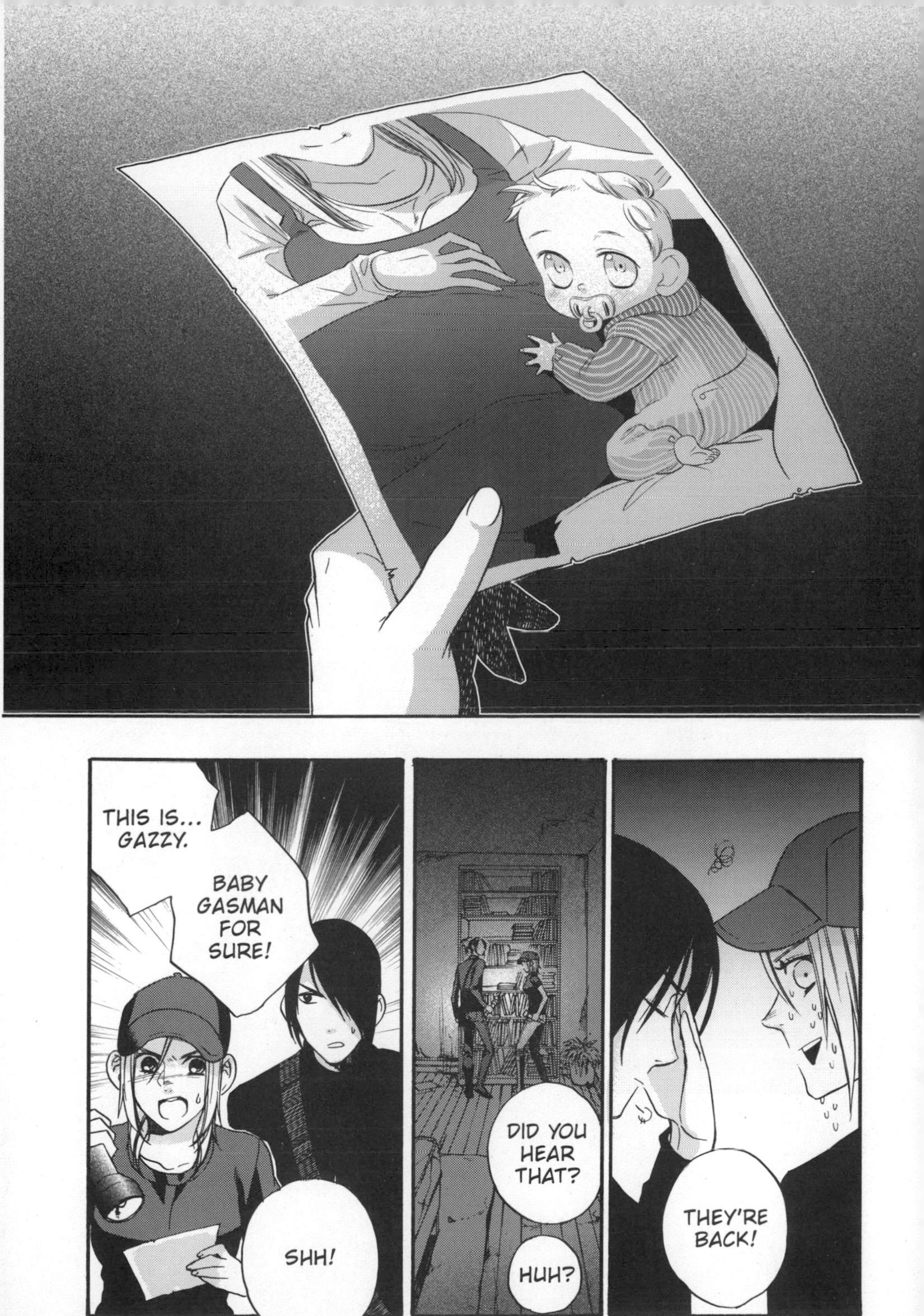
THIS IS... GAZZY.
BABY GASMAN FOR SURE!
SHH!
DID YOU HEAR THAT?
HUH?
THEY'RE BACK!

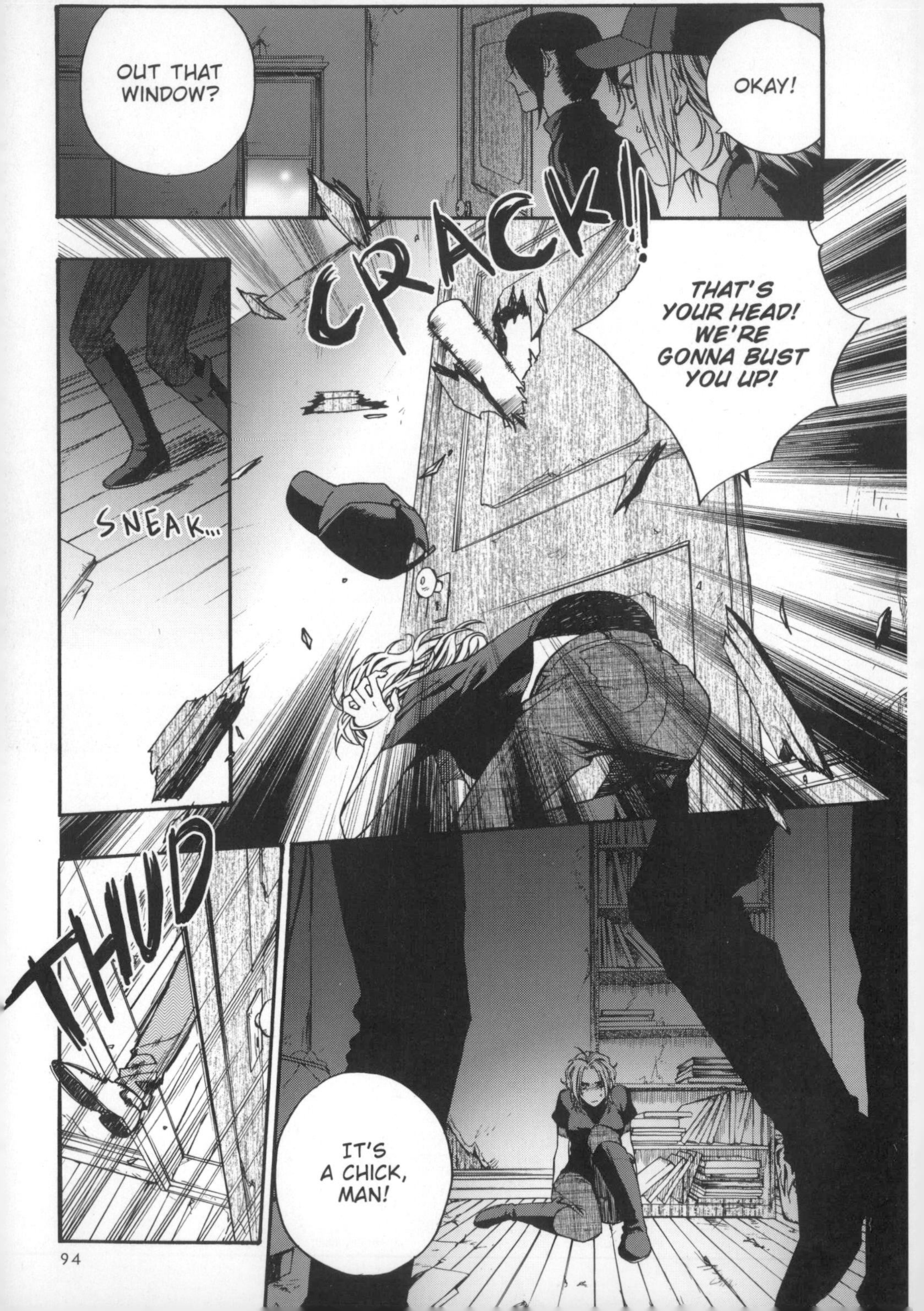
OUT THAT WINDOW?
OKAY!
SNEAK...
CRACK!!
THAT'S YOUR HEAD! WE'RE GONNA BUST YOU UP!
THUD
IT'S A CHICK, MAN!

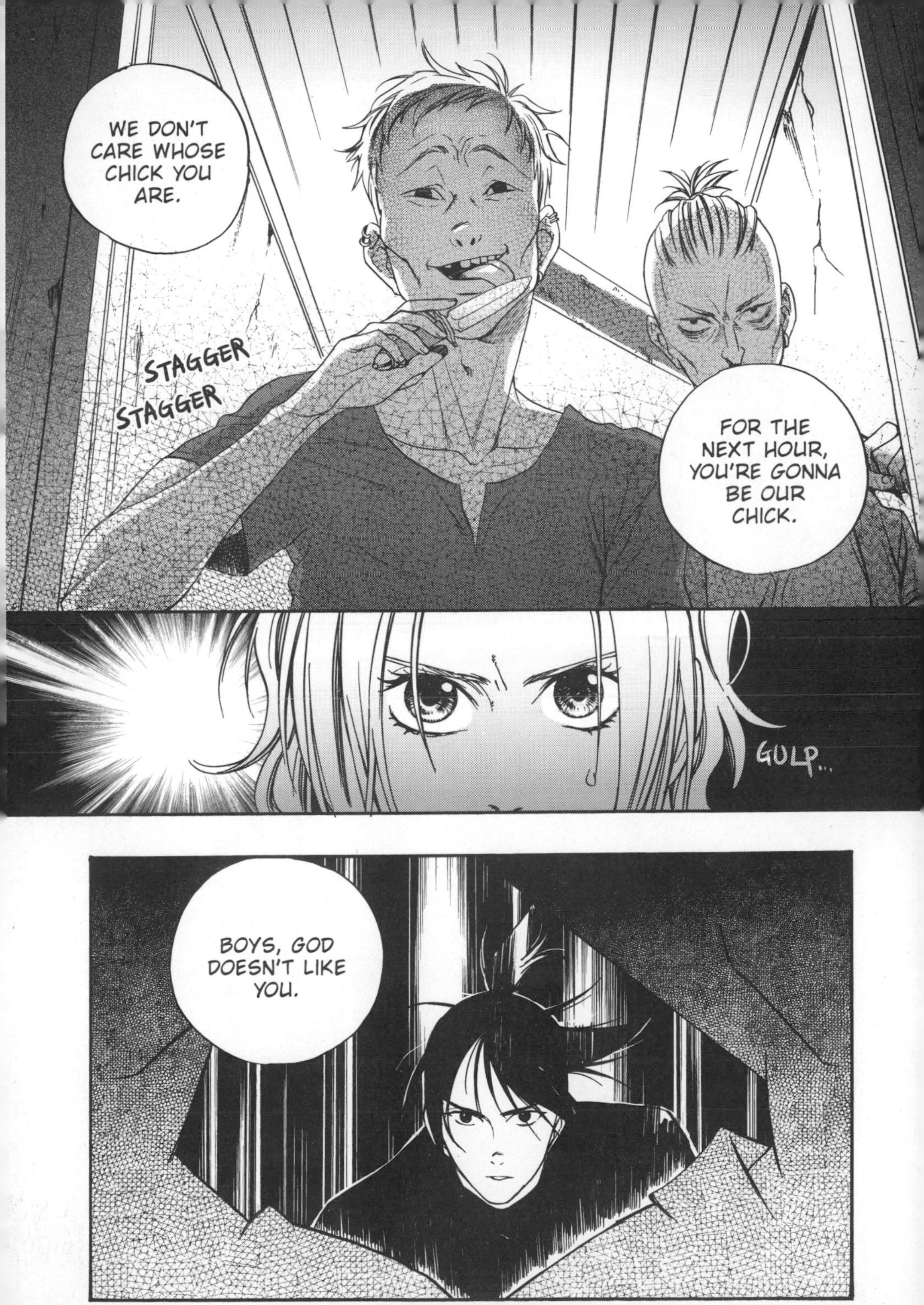
WE DON'T CARE WHOSE CHICK YOU ARE.
STAGGER
STAGGER
FOR THE NEXT HOUR, YOU'RE GONNA BE OUR CHICK.
GULP...
BOYS, GOD DOESN'T LIKE YOU.

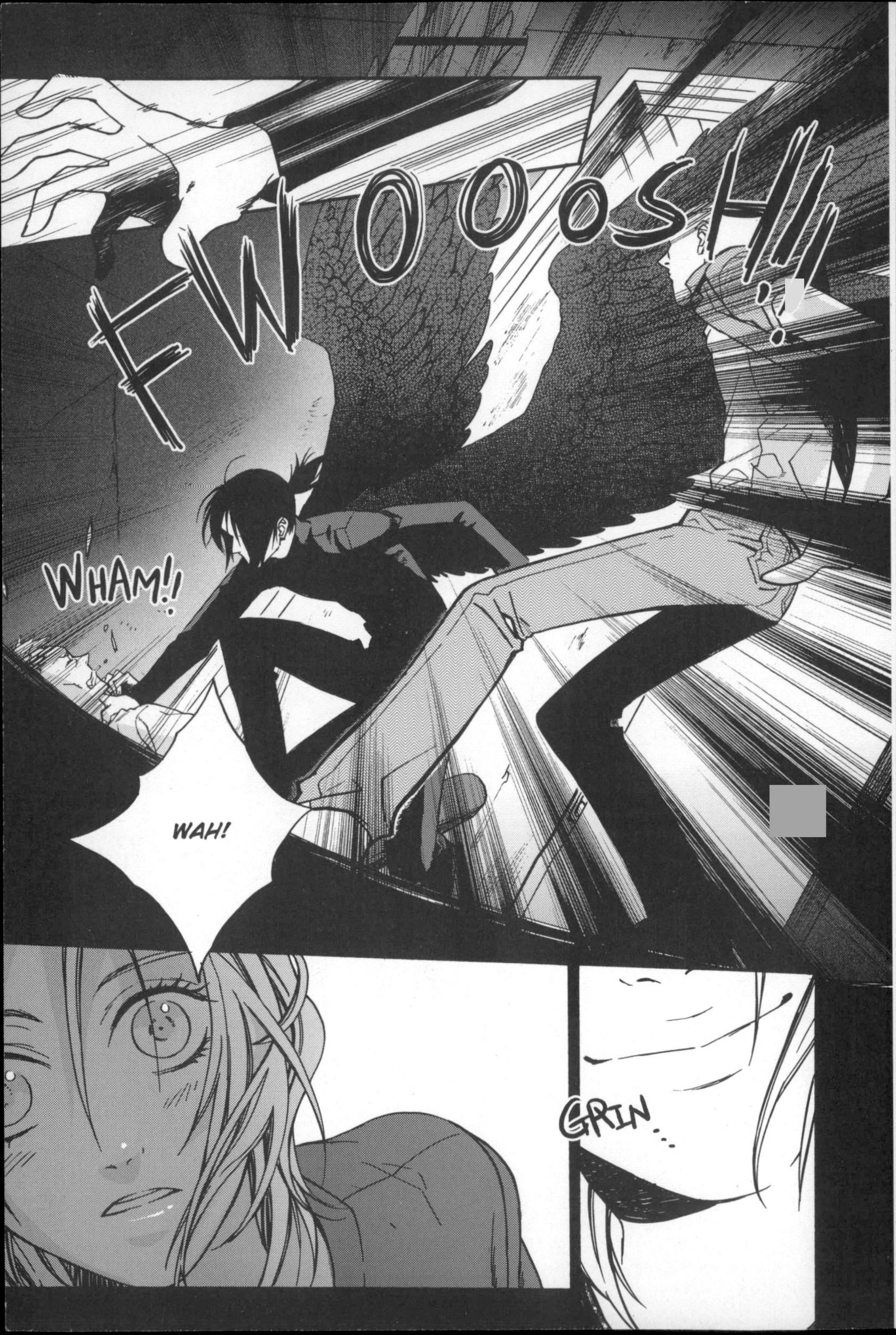
FWOOOSH!!!
WHAM!!
WAH!
GRIN...

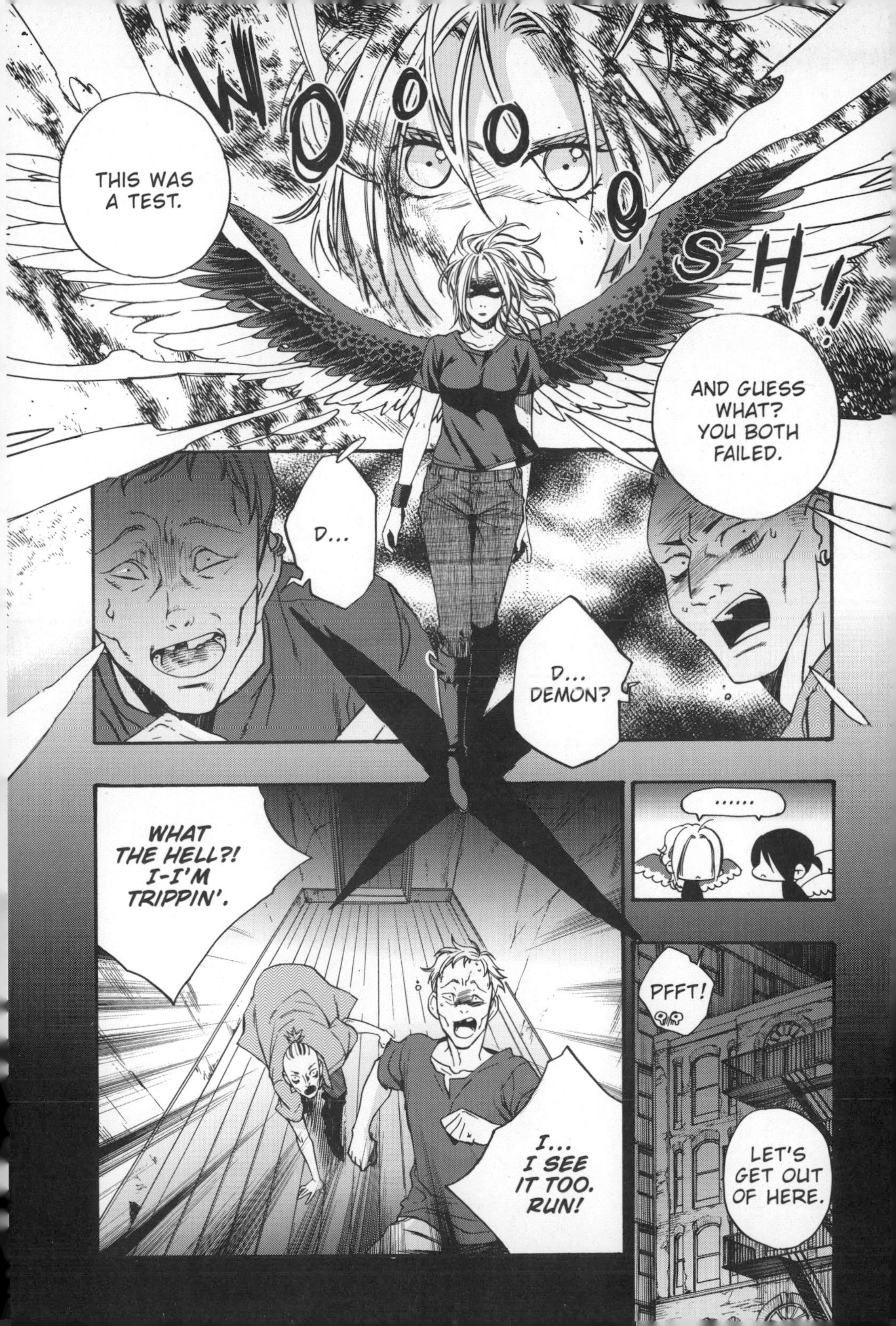
WOOOOOSH!!
THIS WAS A TEST.
AND GUESS WHAT? YOU BOTH FAILED.
D...
D... DEMON?
WHAT THE HELL?! I-I'M TRIPPIN'.
I... I SEE IT TOO. RUN!
......
PFFT!
LET'S GET OUT OF HERE.

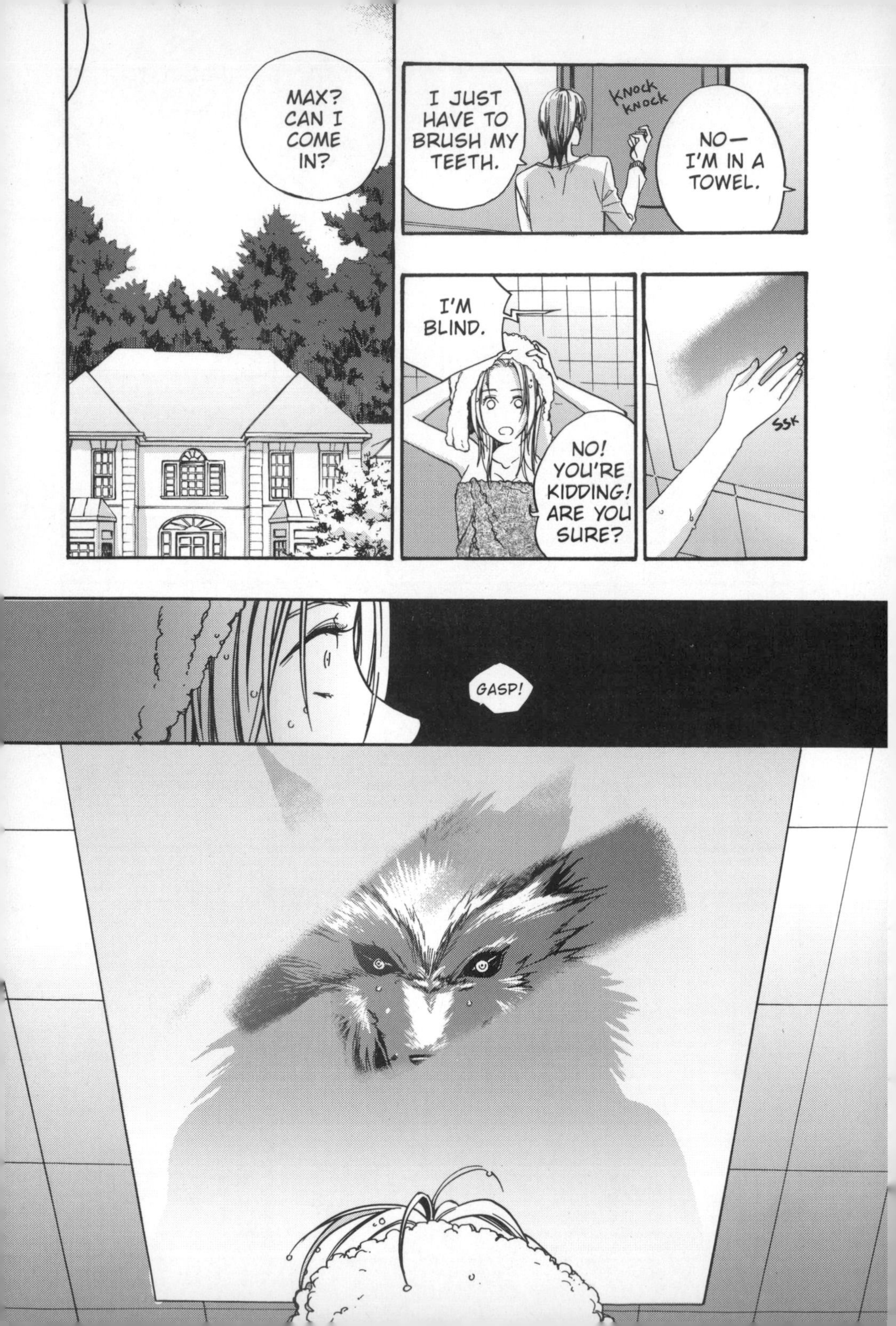
MAX? CAN I COME IN?
I JUST HAVE TO BRUSH MY TEETH.
KNOCK KNOCK
NO— I'M IN A TOWEL.
I'M BLIND.
NO! YOU'RE KIDDING! ARE YOU SURE?
SSK
GASP!

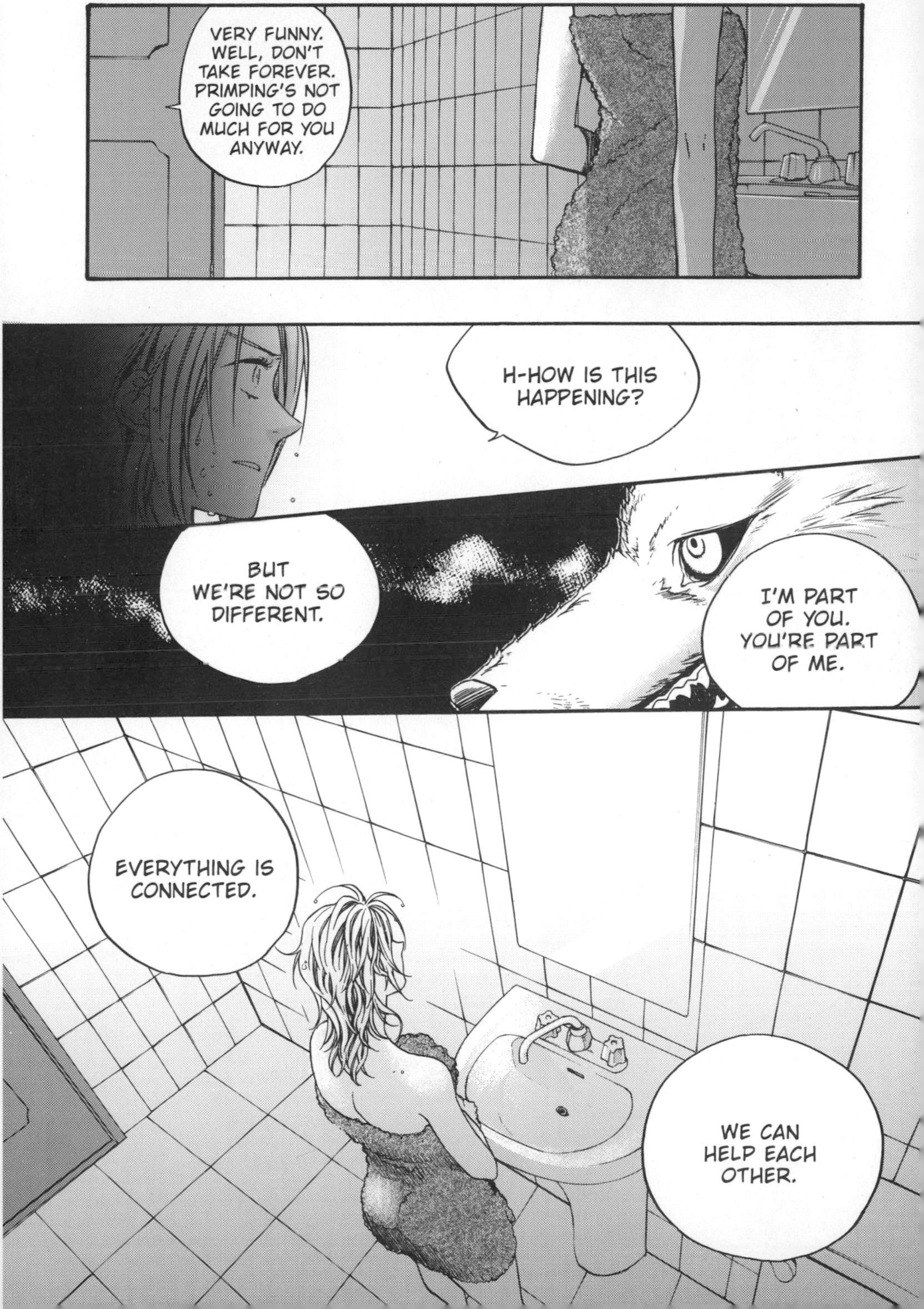
VERY FUNNY. WELL, DON'T TAKE FOREVER. PRIMPING'S NOT GOING TO DO MUCH FOR YOU ANYWAY.
H-HOW IS THIS HAPPENING?
BUT WE'RE NOT SO DIFFERENT.
I'M PART OF YOU. YOU'RE PART OF ME.
EVERYTHING IS CONNECTED.
WE CAN HELP EACH OTHER.

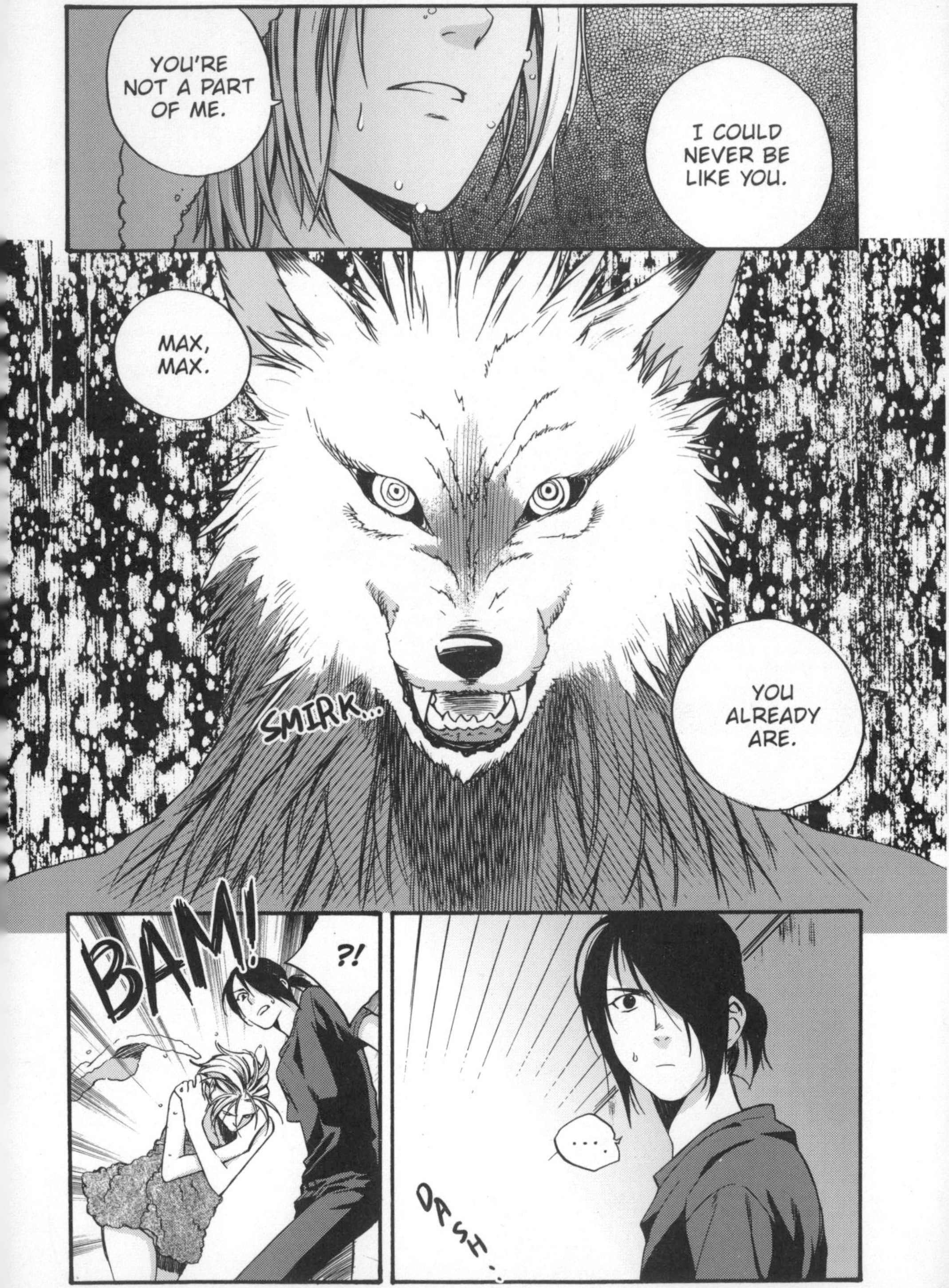
YOU'RE NOT A PART OF ME.
I COULD NEVER BE LIKE YOU.
MAX, MAX.
SMIRK...
YOU ALREADY ARE.
BAM!
?!
...
DASH...

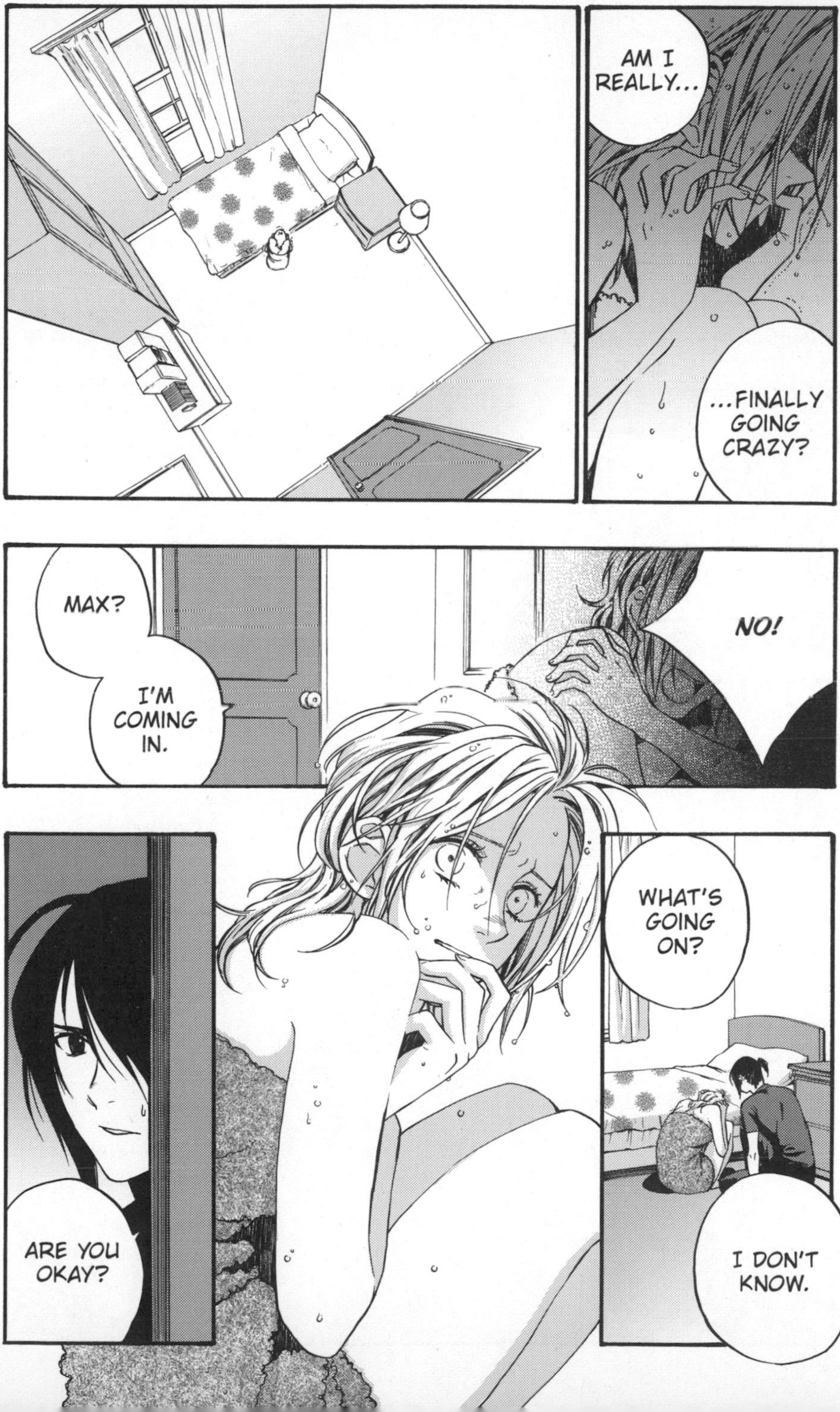
AM I REALLY...
...FINALLY GOING CRAZY?
MAX?
I'M COMING IN.
NO!
ARE YOU OKAY?
WHAT'S GOING ON?
I DON'T KNOW.

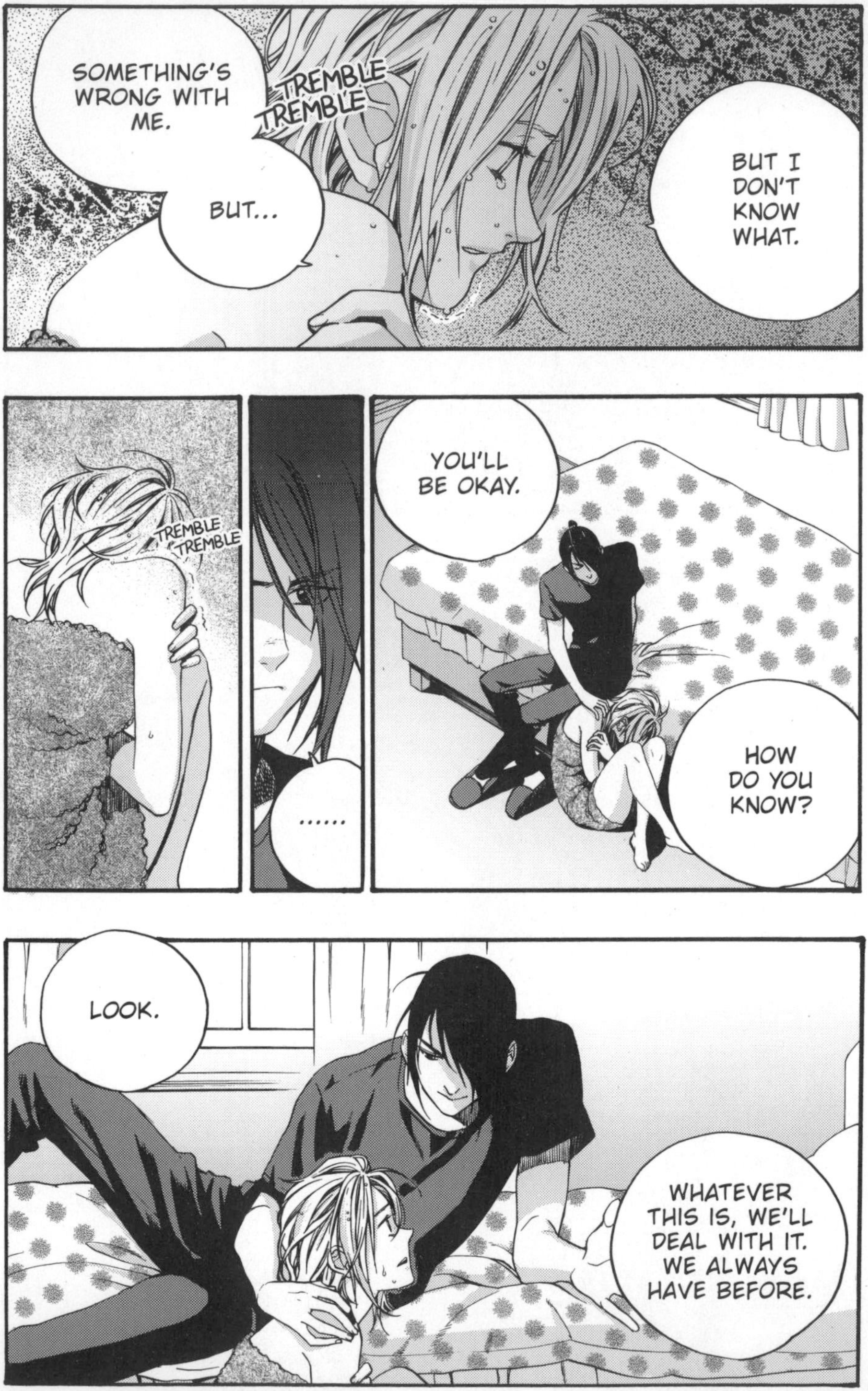
SOMETHING'S WRONG WITH ME.
TREMBLE TREMBLE
BUT...
BUT I DON'T KNOW WHAT.
TREMBLE TREMBLE
......
YOU'LL BE OKAY.
HOW DO YOU KNOW?
LOOK.
WHATEVER THIS IS, WE'LL DEAL WITH IT. WE ALWAYS HAVE BEFORE.

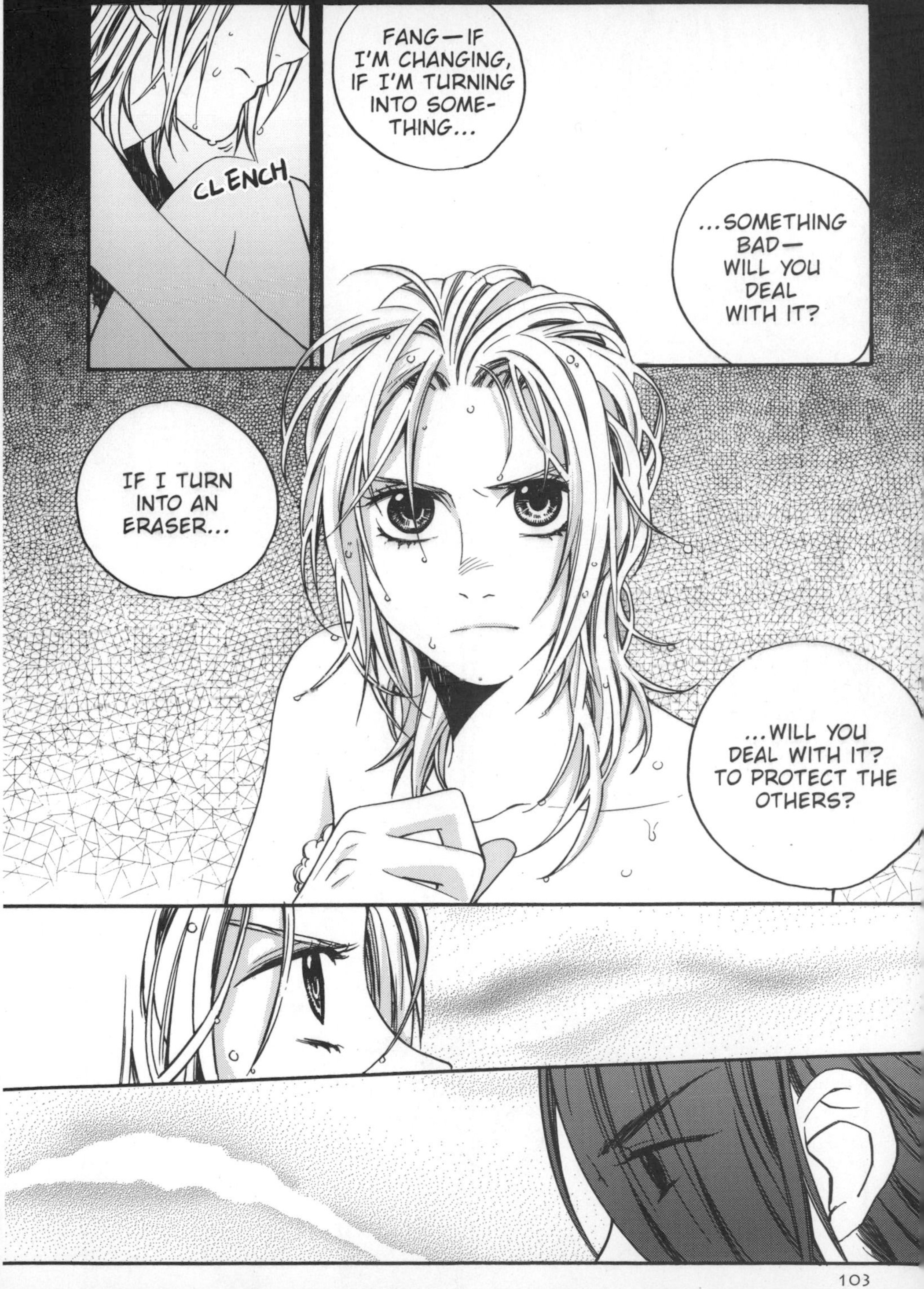
CLENCH
FANG—IF I'M CHANGING, IF I'M TURNING INTO SOME-THING...
...SOMETHING BAD—WILL YOU DEAL WITH IT?
IF I TURN INTO AN ERASER...
...WILL YOU DEAL WITH IT? TO PROTECT THE OTHERS?

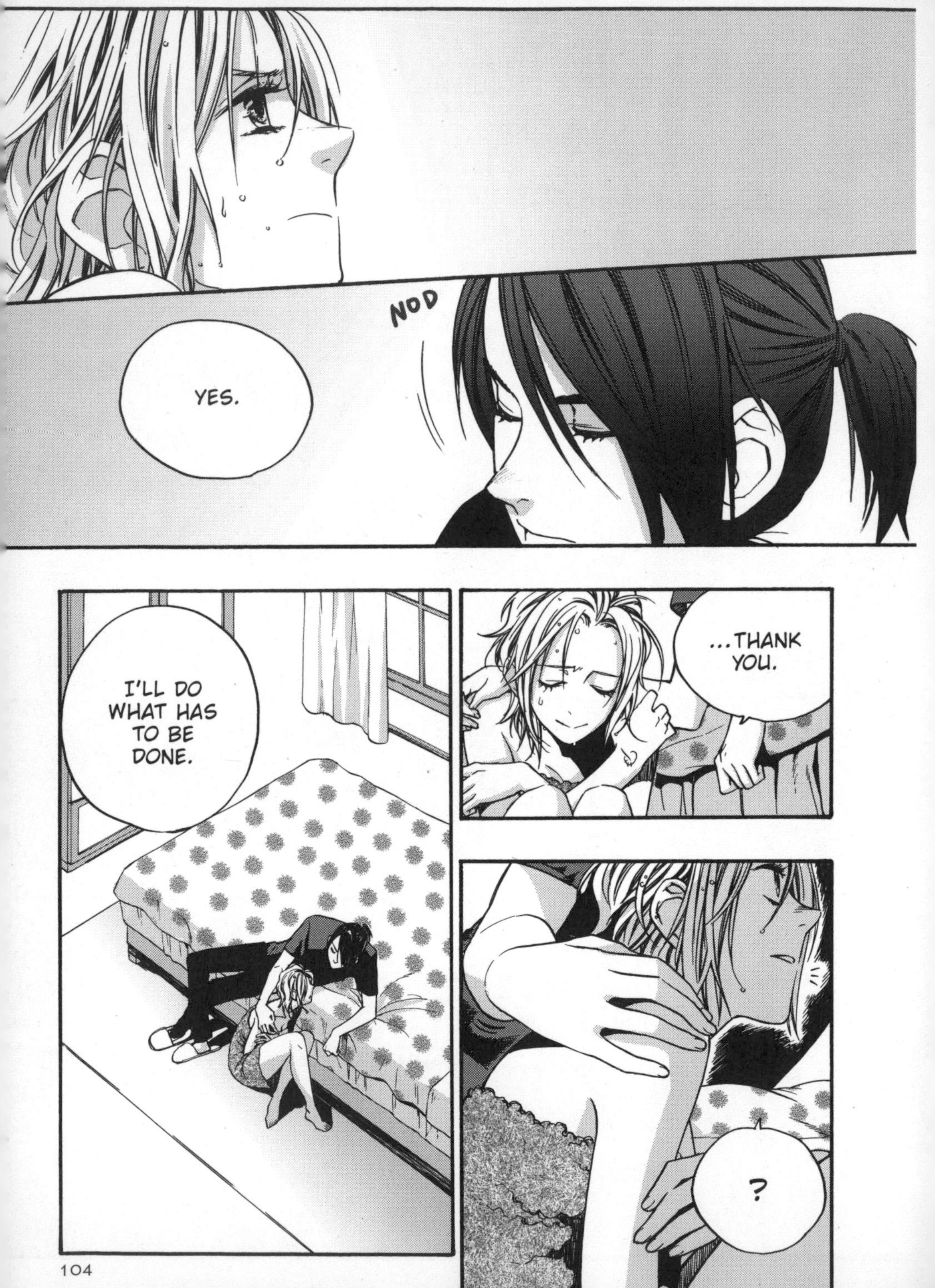
NOD
YES.
I'LL DO WHAT HAS TO BE DONE.
...THANK YOU.
?

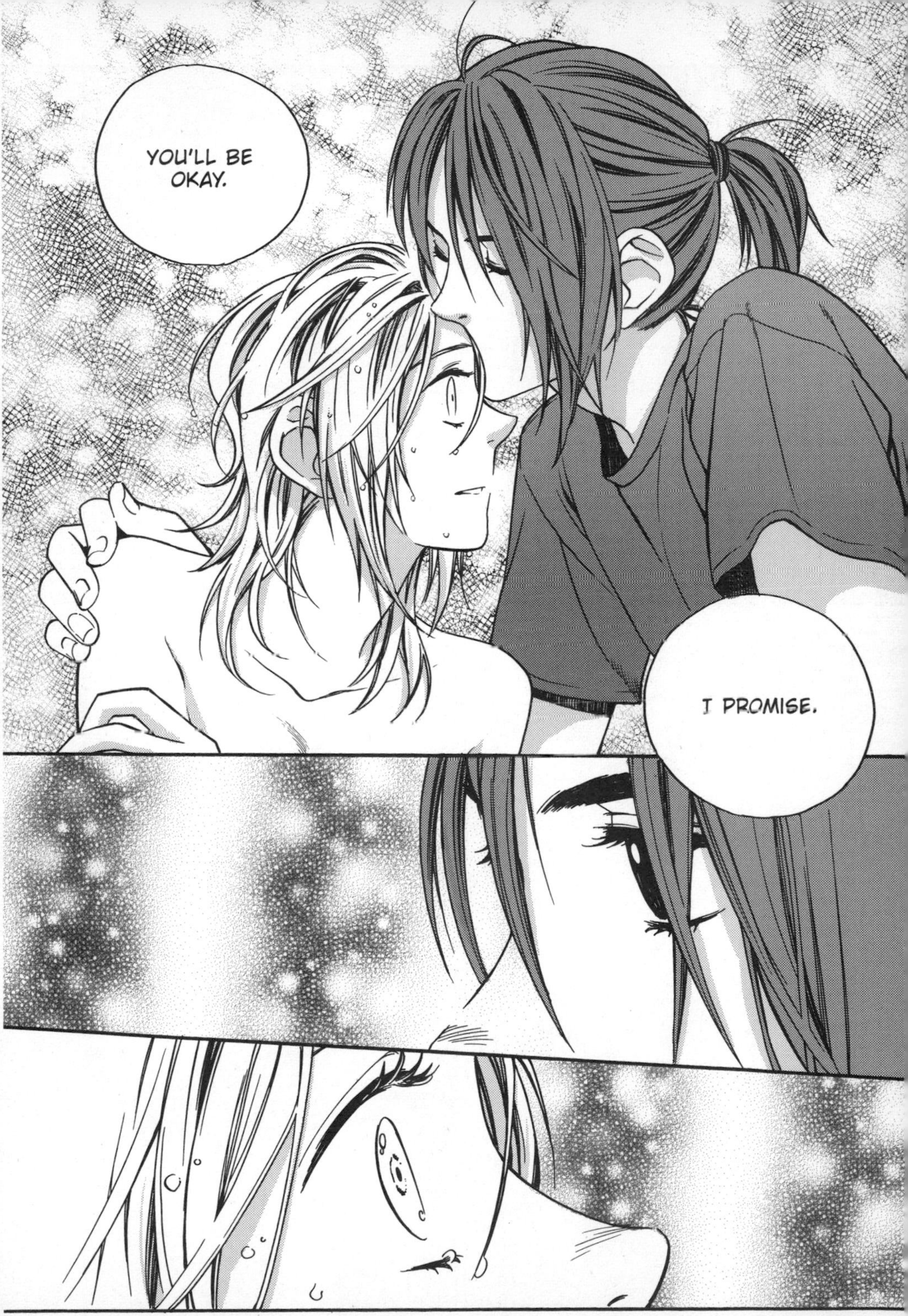
YOU'LL BE OKAY.
I PROMISE.

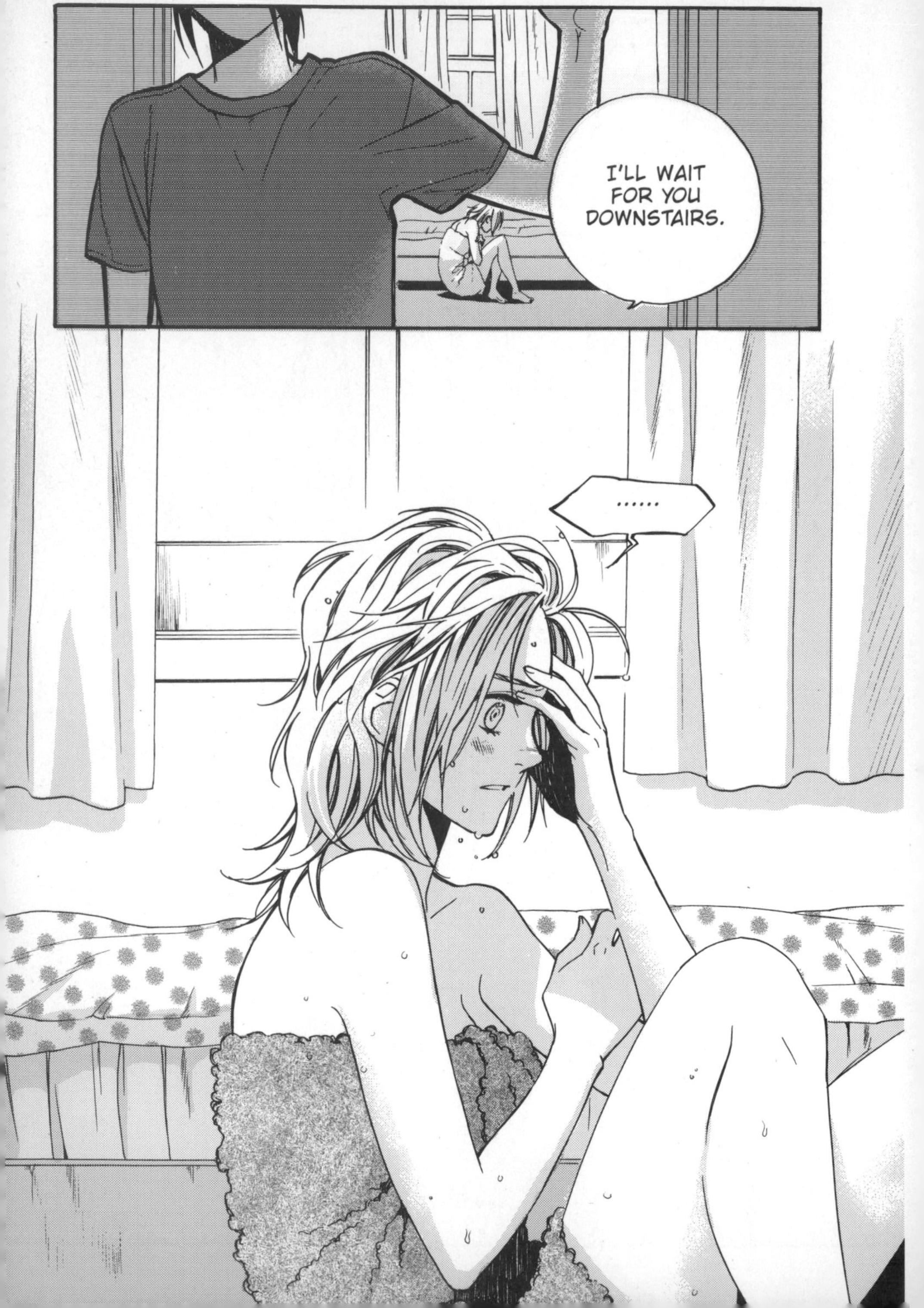
I'LL WAIT FOR YOU DOWNSTAIRS.
......

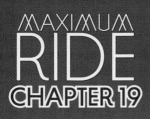
MAXIMUM RIDE
CHAPTER 19

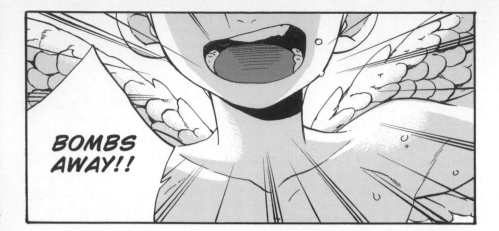

BOMBS
AWAY!!

SPIN.

SHOOOOOO

SPLASH!

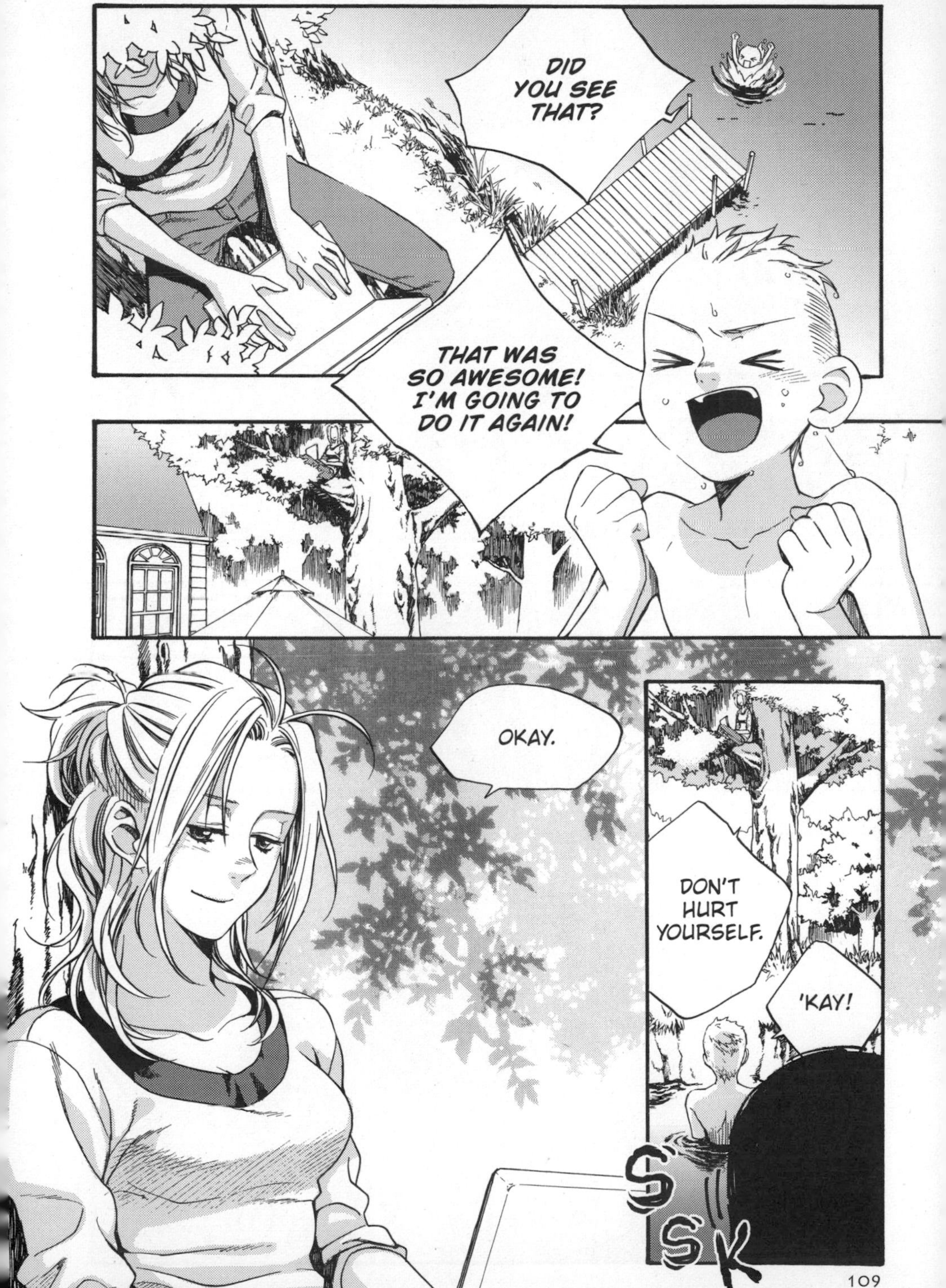
DID YOU SEE THAT?
THAT WAS SO AWESOME! I'M GOING TO DO IT AGAIN!
OKAY.
DON'T HURT YOURSELF.
'KAY!
SSK

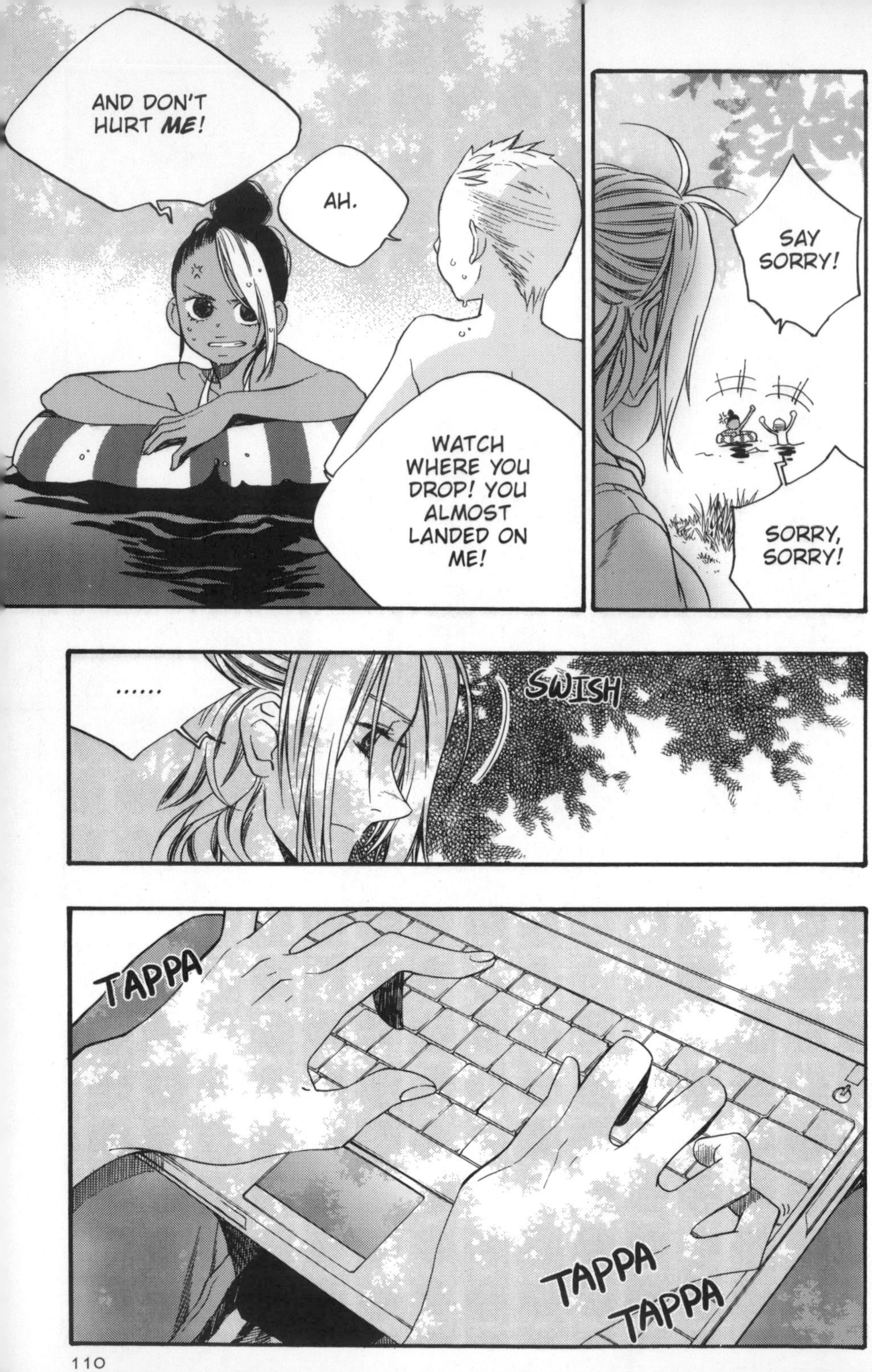

AND DON'T HURT ME!
AH.
WATCH WHERE YOU DROP! YOU ALMOST LANDED ON ME!
SAY SORRY!
SORRY, SORRY!
......
SWISH
TAPPA
TAPPA TAPPA

"FREEZE.,

......

We are searching for a four-year-old girl, who disappeared at the park.

he disappearance of child

TEN KIDS HAVE GONE MISSING IN THE D.C. AREA OVER THE LAST FOUR MONTHS.

DID THE WHITECOATS TAKE THEM AS FODDER FOR THEIR EXPERIMENTS?

I CAN ONLY IMAGINE WHAT THE FAMILIES ARE GOING THROUGH.

WHAT HAPPENED WHEN WE WENT MISSING?

OUR PARENTS CARED, DIDN'T THEY? THEY MISSED US, RIGHT?

MAX!

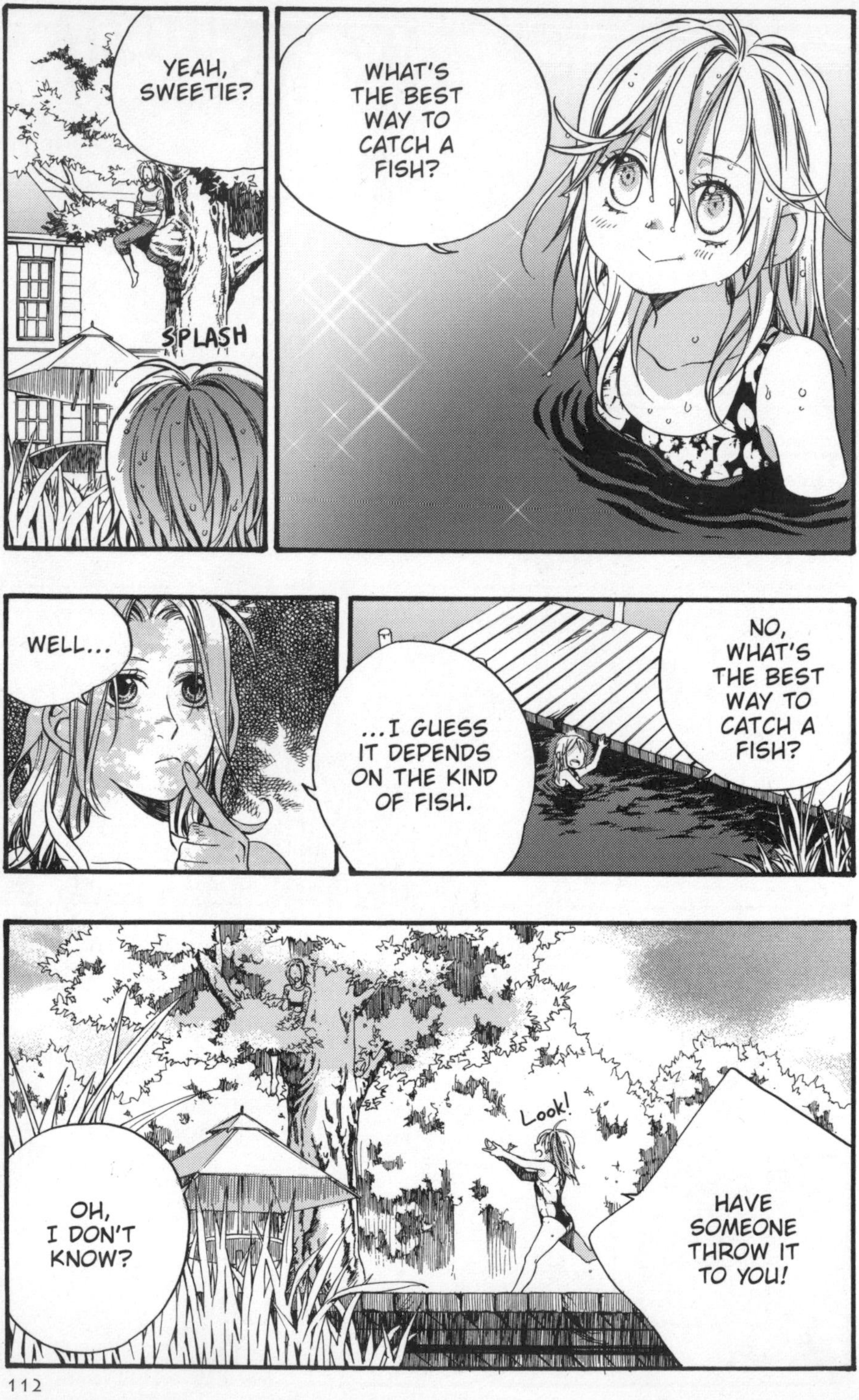
YEAH, SWEETIE?
SPLASH
WHAT'S THE BEST WAY TO CATCH A FISH?
WELL...
...I GUESS IT DEPENDS ON THE KIND OF FISH.
NO, WHAT'S THE BEST WAY TO CATCH A FISH?
OH, I DON'T KNOW?
Look!
HAVE SOMEONE THROW IT TO YOU!

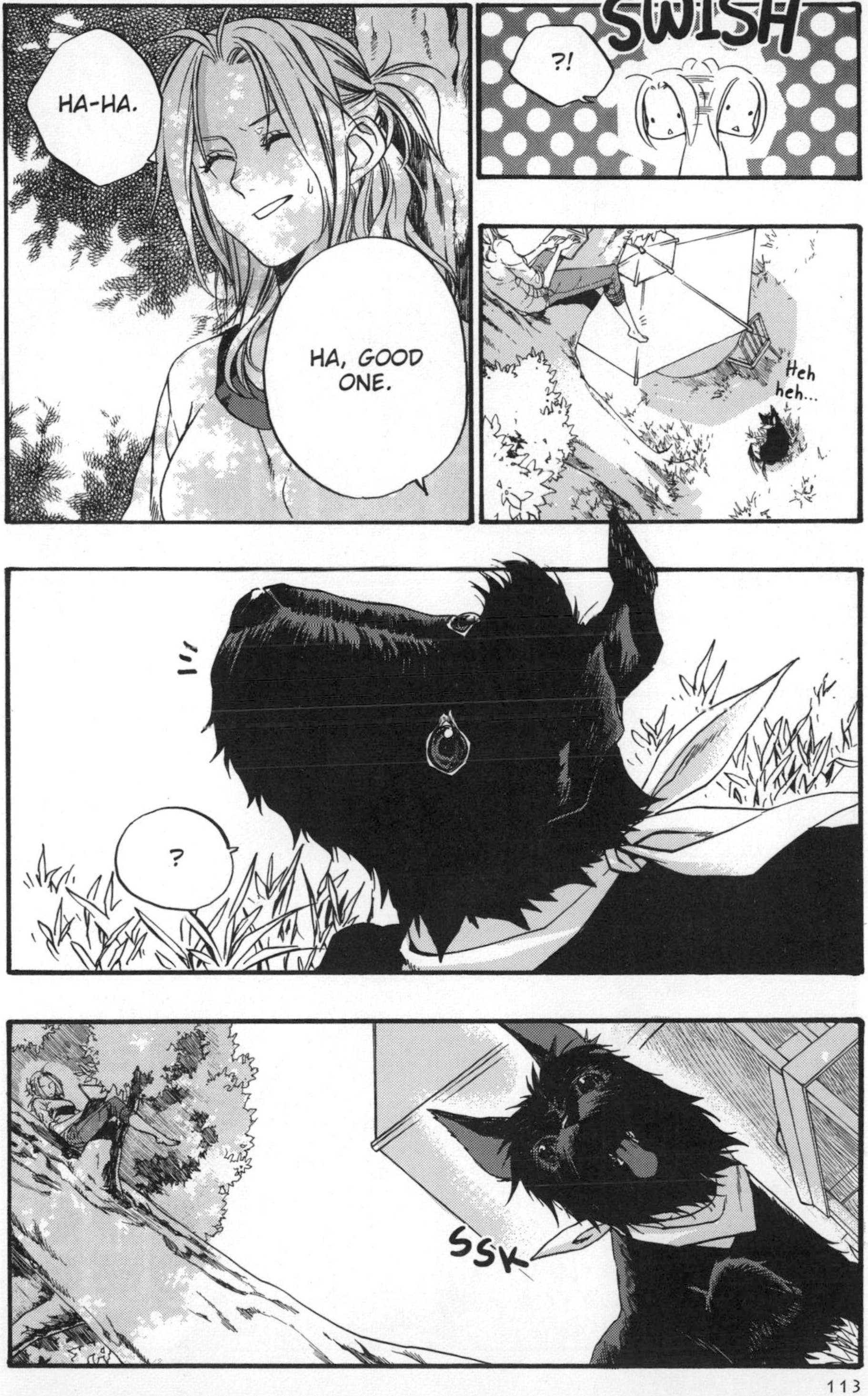
HA-HA.
HA, GOOD ONE.
SWISH
?!
Heh heh...
?
SSK

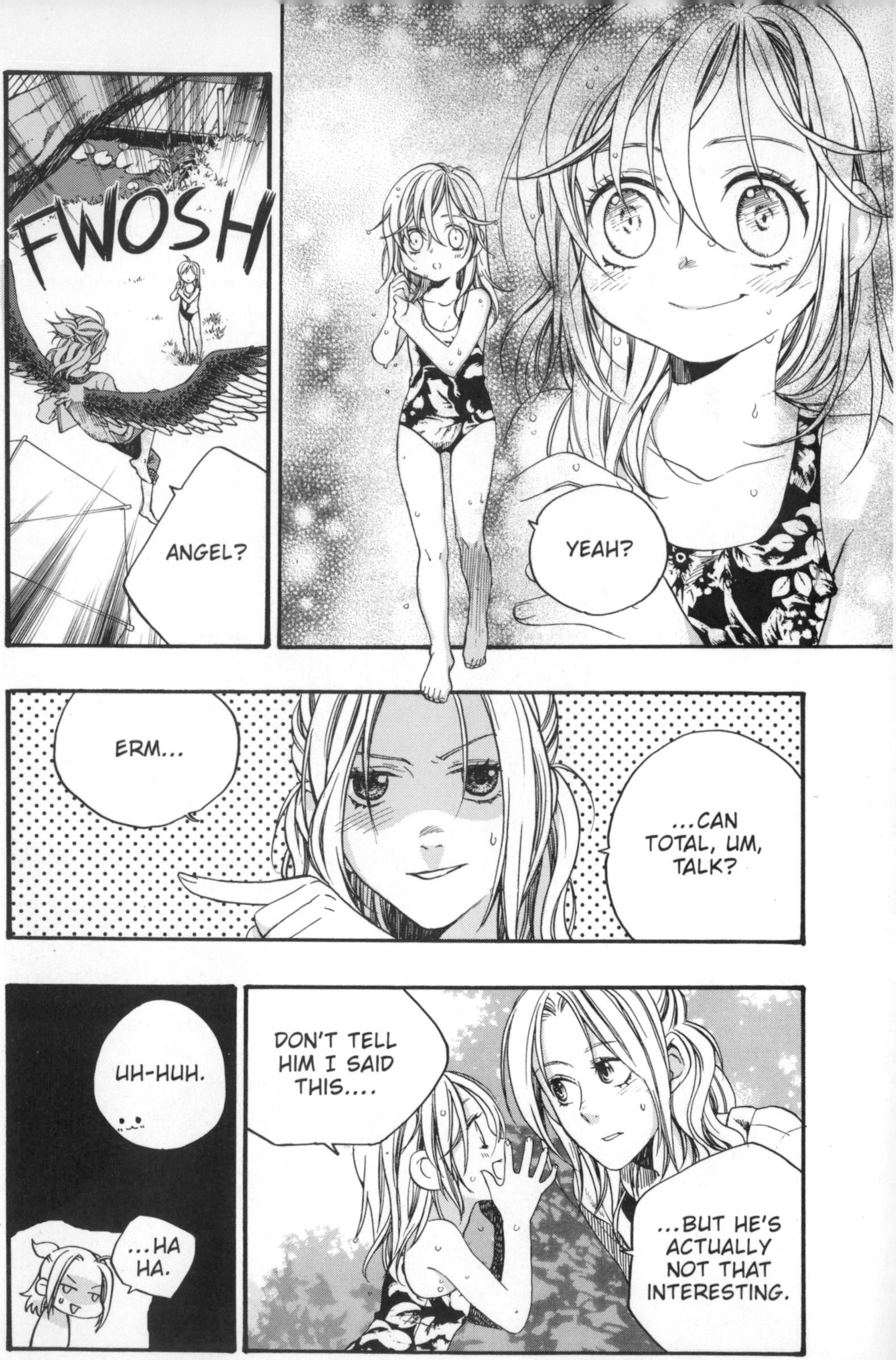
FWOSH
ANGEL?
YEAH?
ERM...
...CAN TOTAL, UM, TALK?
UH-HUH.
...HA HA.
DON'T TELL HIM I SAID THIS....
...BUT HE'S ACTUALLY NOT THAT INTERESTING.

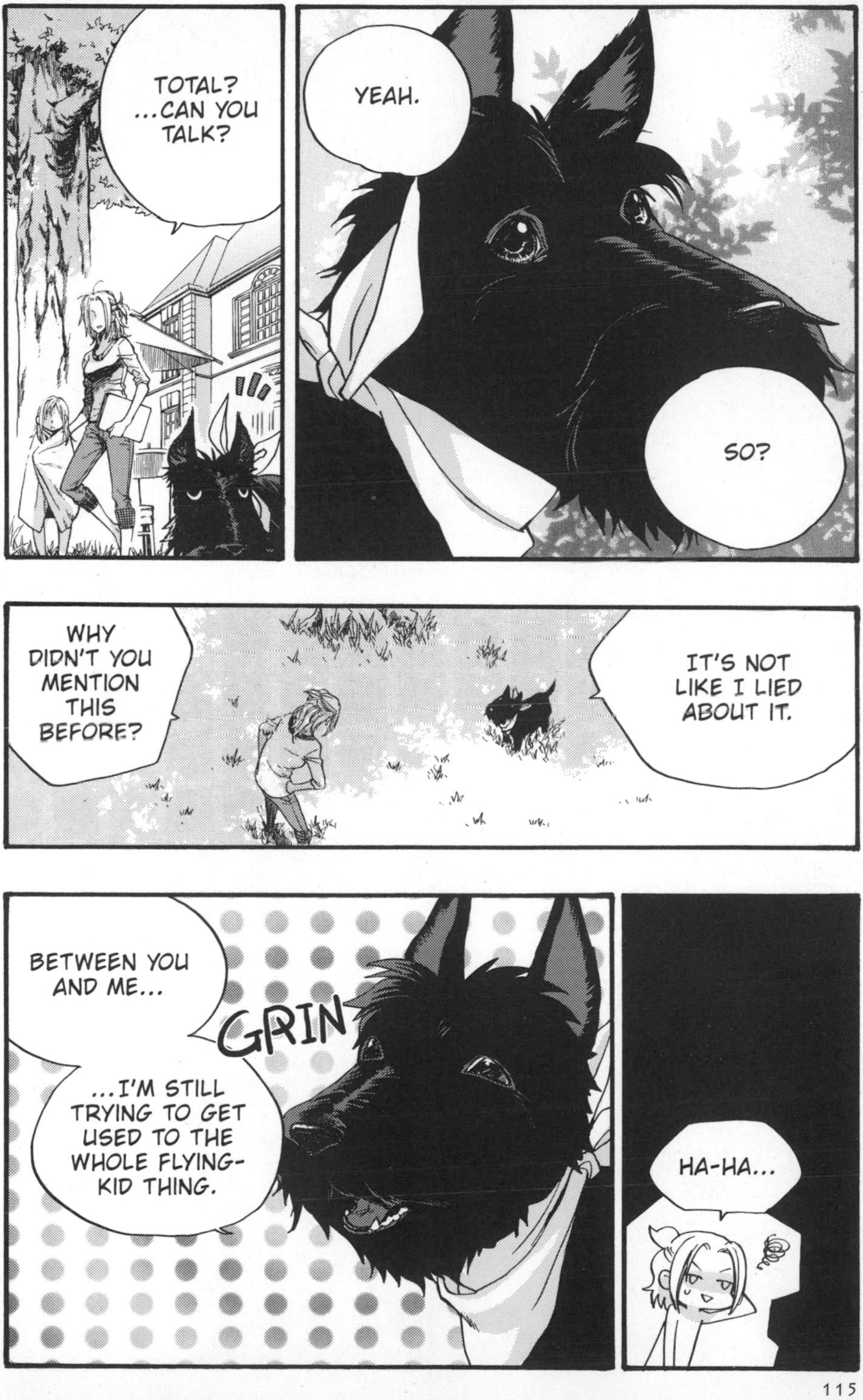
TOTAL? ...CAN YOU TALK?
YEAH.
SO?
WHY DIDN'T YOU MENTION THIS BEFORE?
IT'S NOT LIKE I LIED ABOUT IT.
BETWEEN YOU AND ME...
GRIN
...I'M STILL TRYING TO GET USED TO THE WHOLE FLYING-KID THING.
HA-HA...

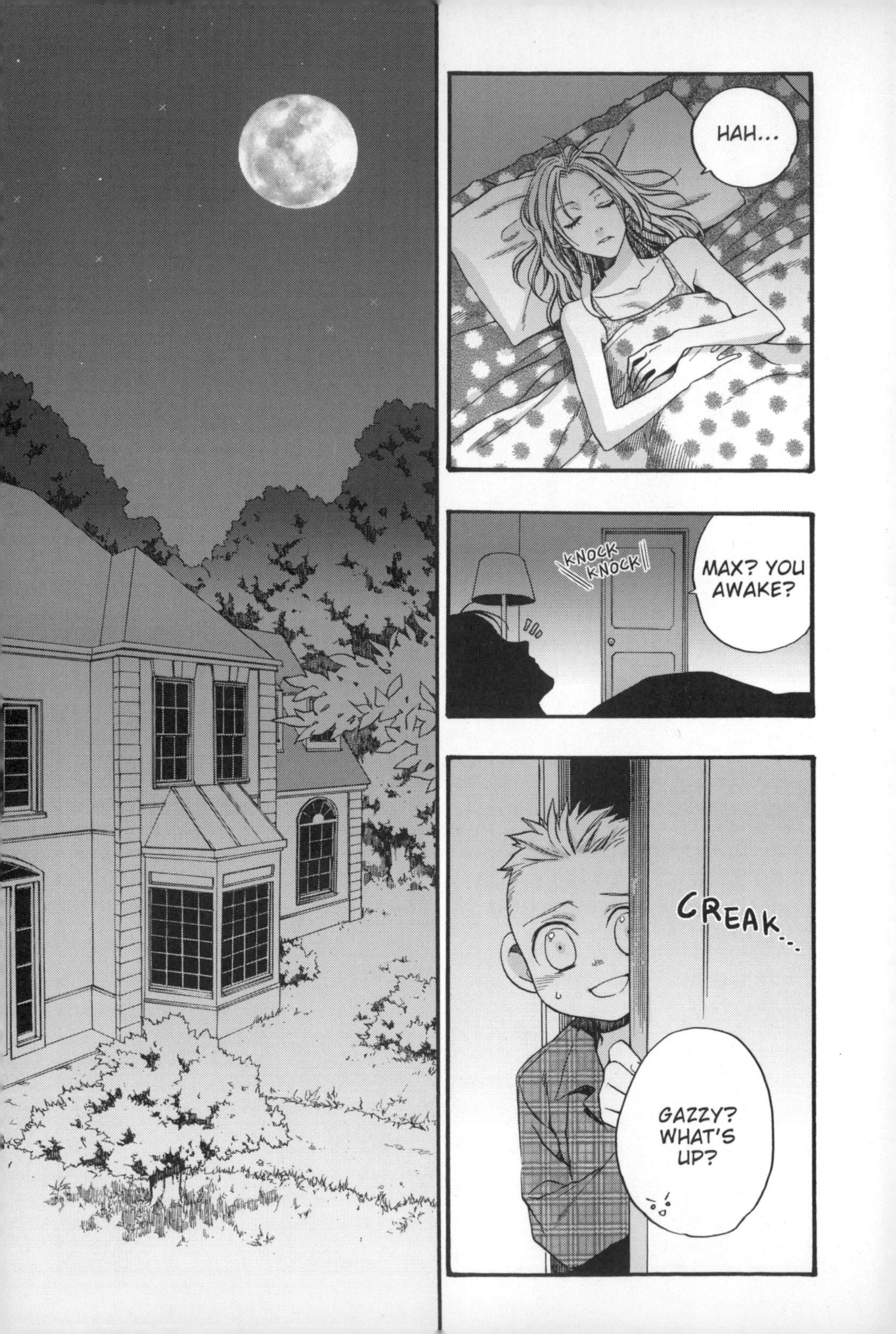
HAH...
KNOCK KNOCK
MAX? YOU AWAKE?
CREAK...
GAZZY? WHAT'S UP?

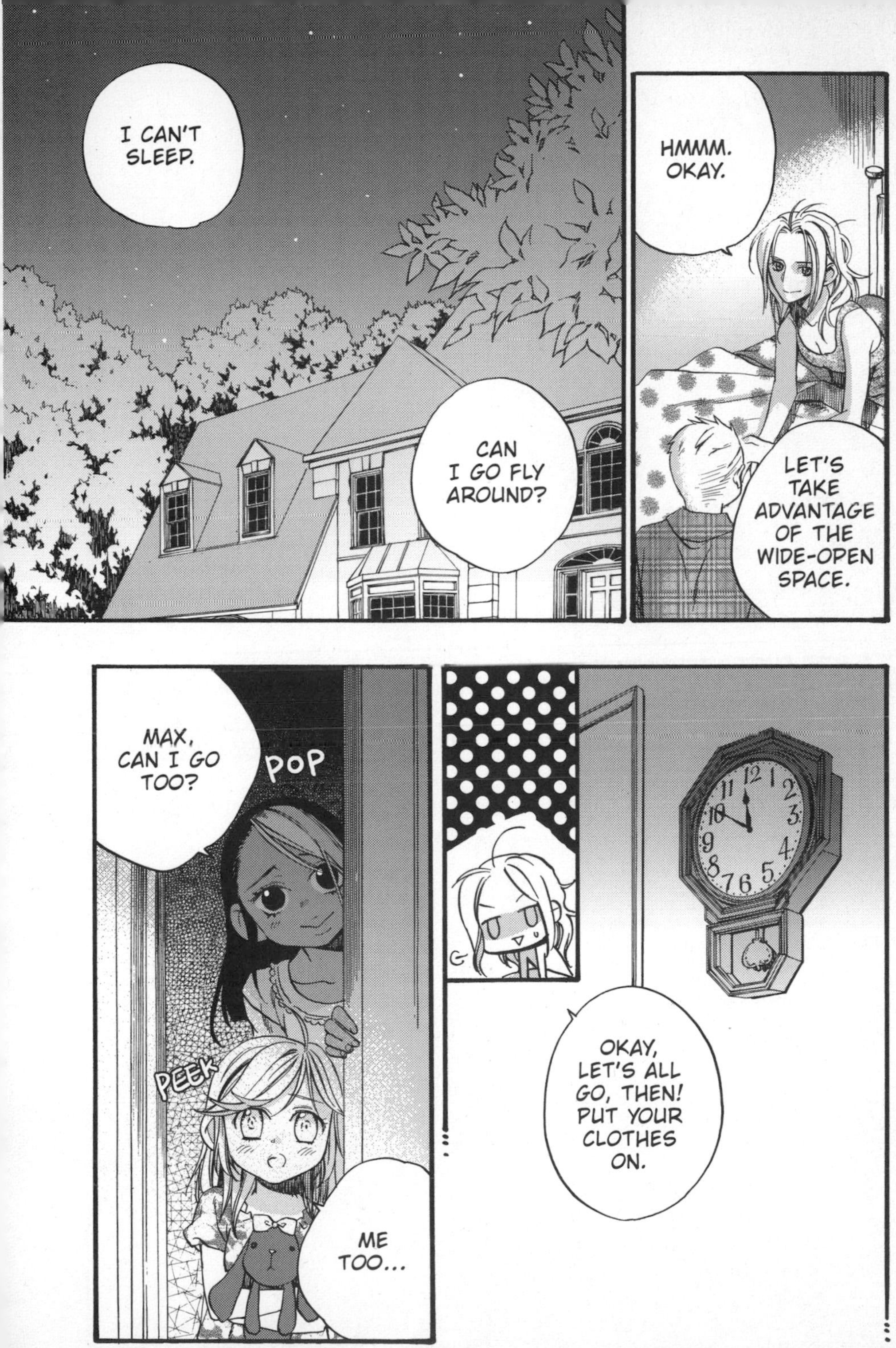
I CAN'T SLEEP.
CAN I GO FLY AROUND?
HMMM. OKAY.
LET'S TAKE ADVANTAGE OF THE WIDE-OPEN SPACE.
MAX, CAN I GO TOO?
POP
PEEK
ME TOO...
OKAY, LET'S ALL GO, THEN! PUT YOUR CLOTHES ON.

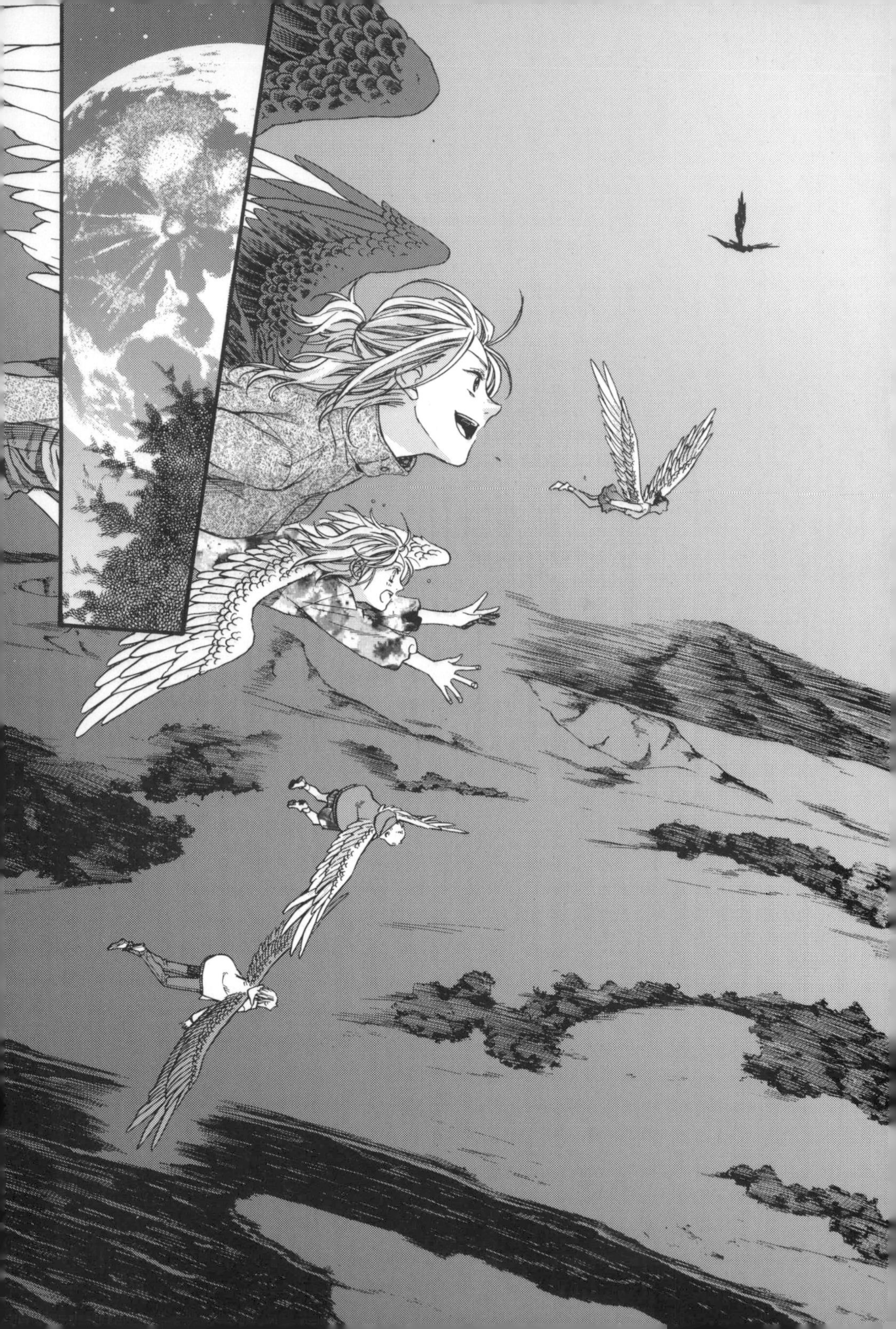

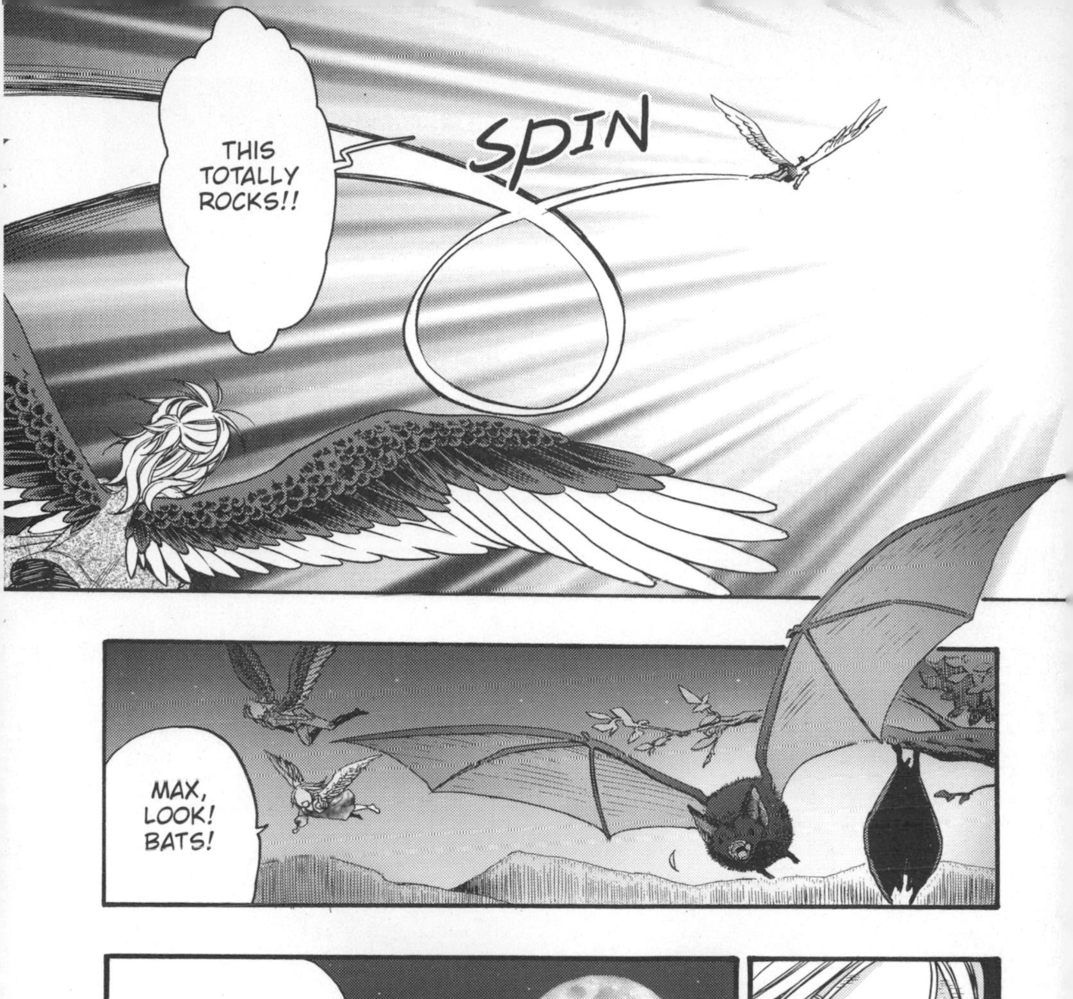
THIS TOTALLY ROCKS!!
SPIN
MAX, LOOK! BATS!
THEY'RE MAMMALS, LIKE WE ARE.
MAMMALS? REALLY?
ARE THEY MORE LIKE US THAN BIRDS? WELL, NOT THE WHOLE EATING-INSECTS THING.

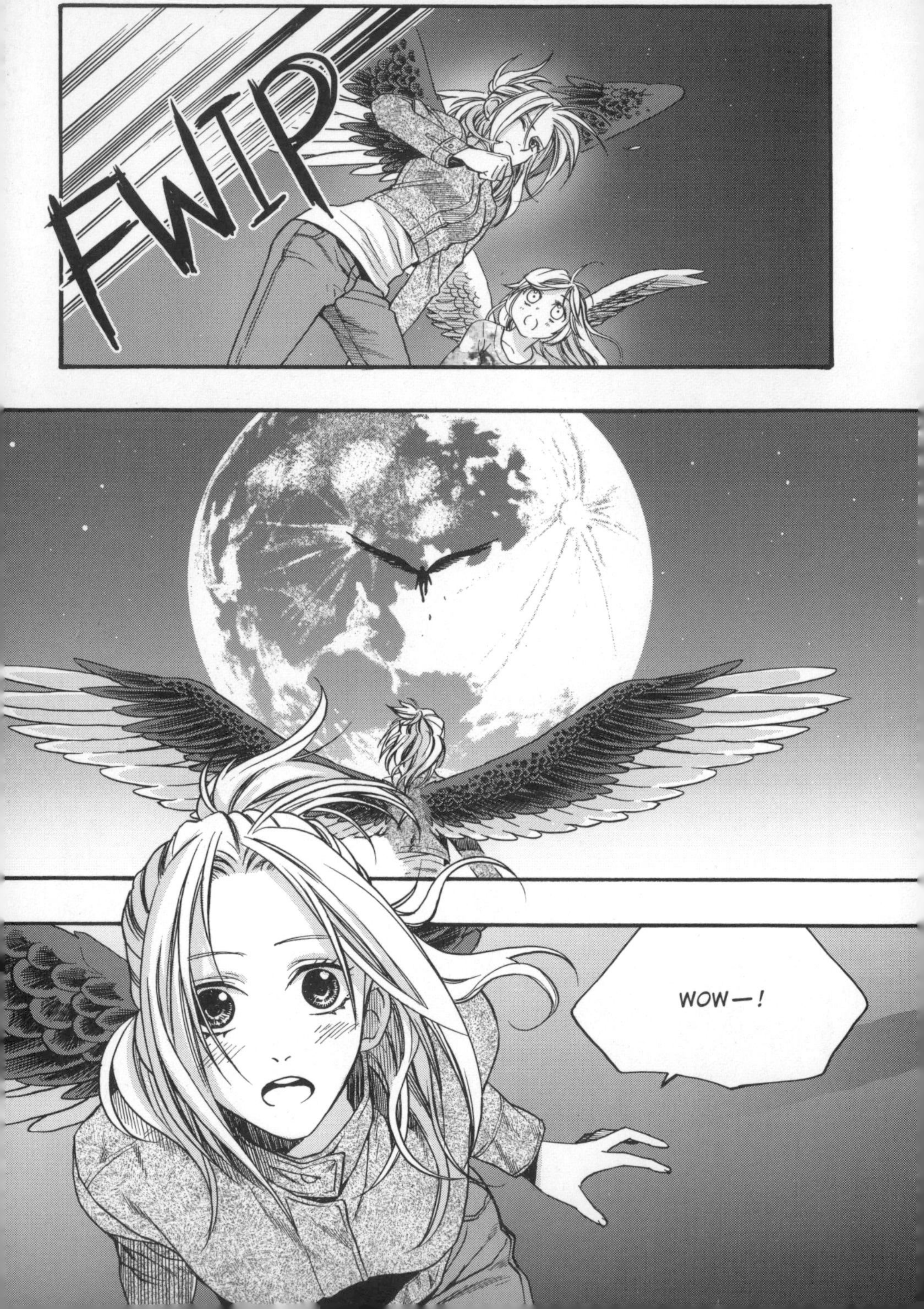
FWIP
WOW—!

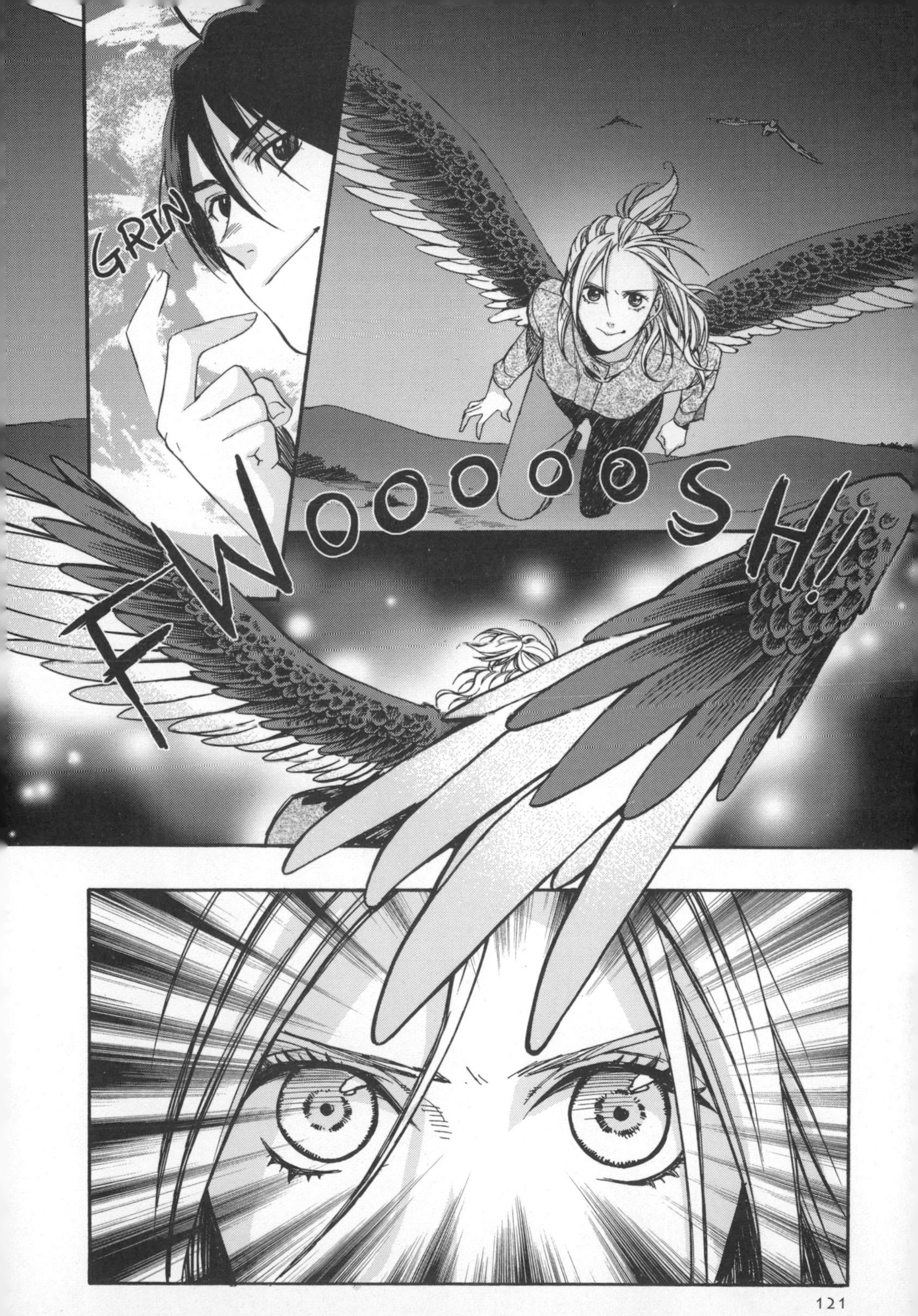
GRIN
FWOOOOOSH!!

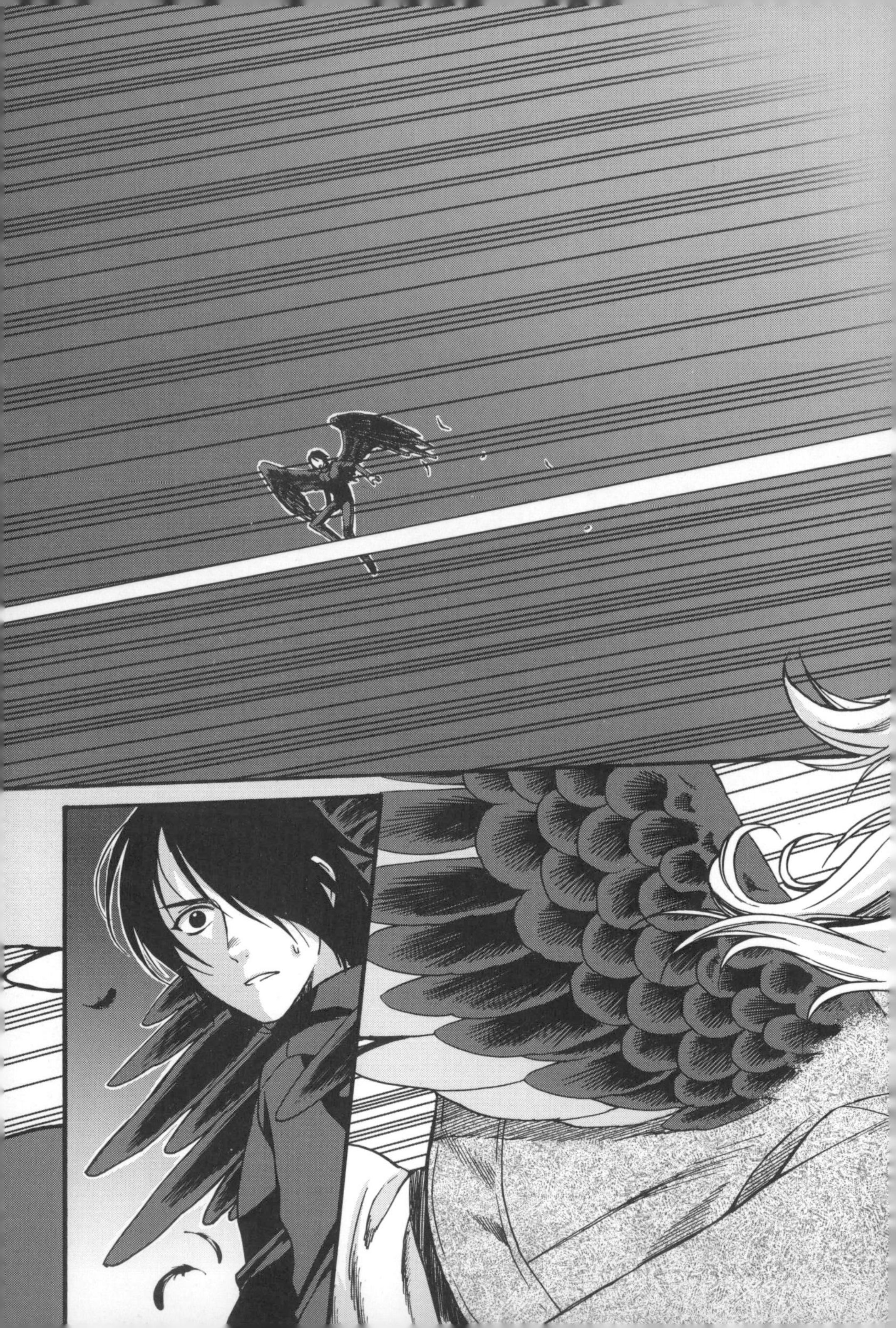

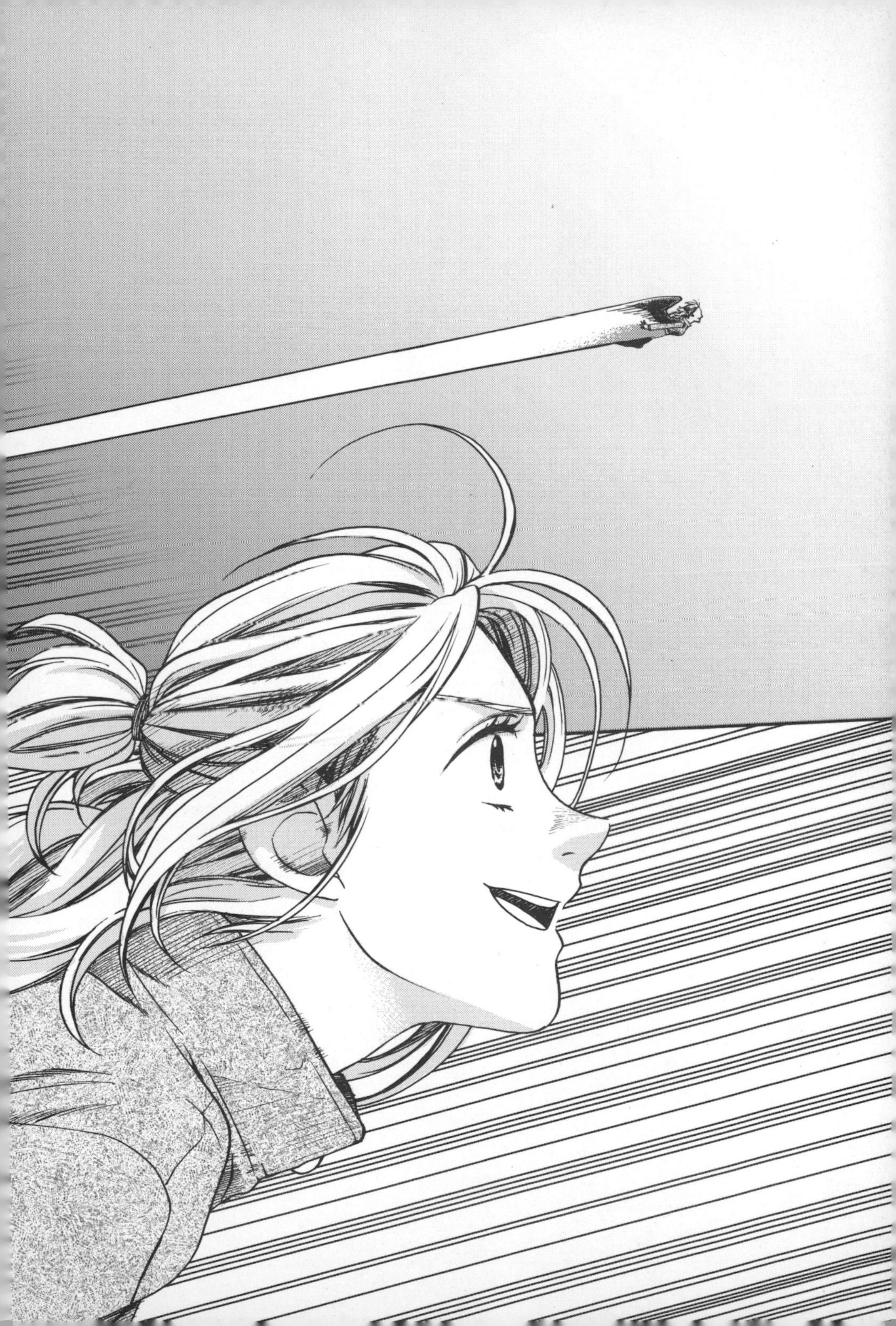

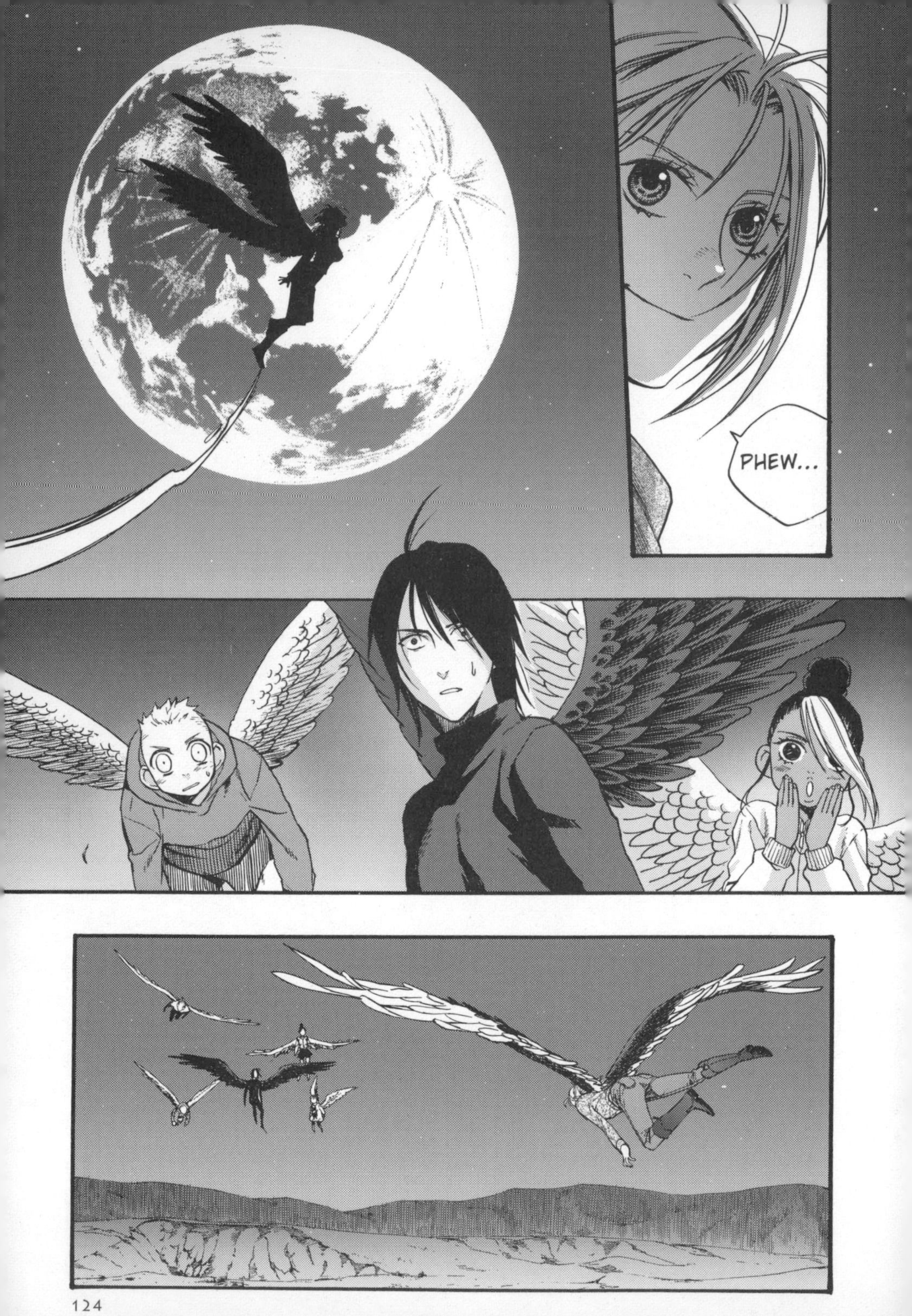
PHEW...

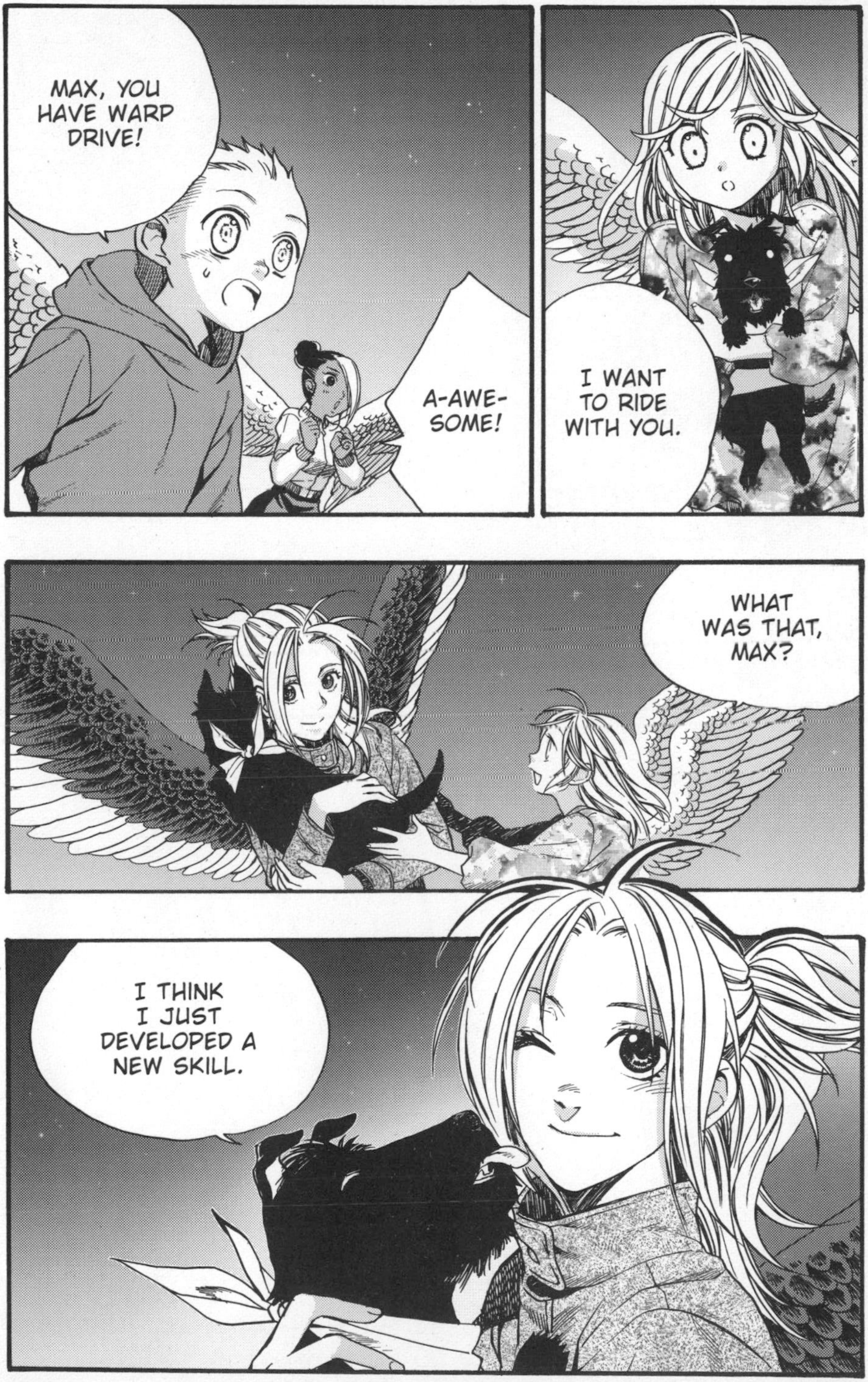
MAX, YOU HAVE WARP DRIVE!
A-AWE-SOME!
I WANT TO RIDE WITH YOU.
WHAT WAS THAT, MAX?
I THINK I JUST DEVELOPED A NEW SKILL.

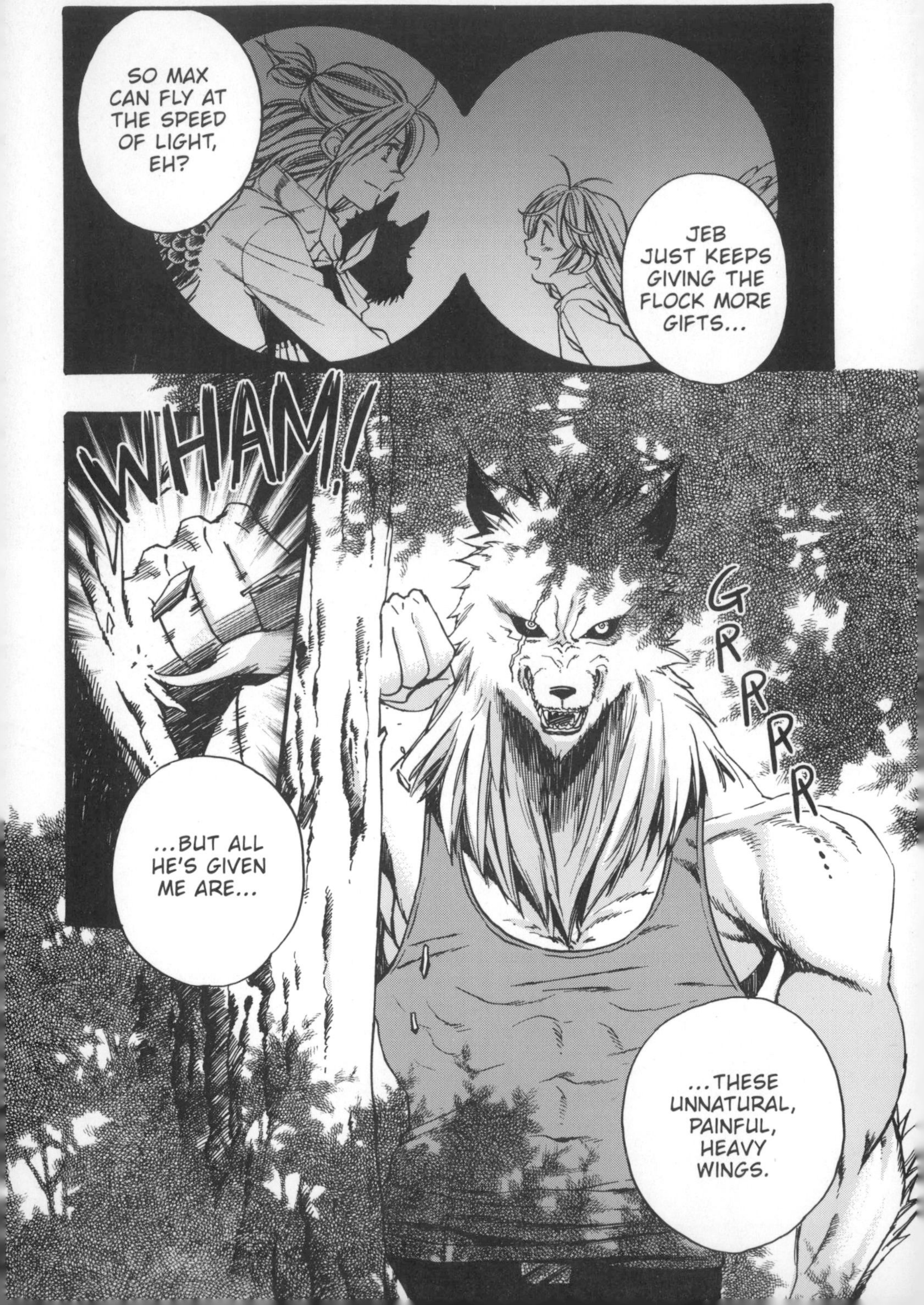
SO MAX CAN FLY AT THE SPEED OF LIGHT, EH?
JEB JUST KEEPS GIVING THE FLOCK MORE GIFTS...
WHAM!
GRRRR...
...BUT ALL HE'S GIVEN ME ARE...
...THESE UNNATURAL, PAINFUL, HEAVY WINGS.

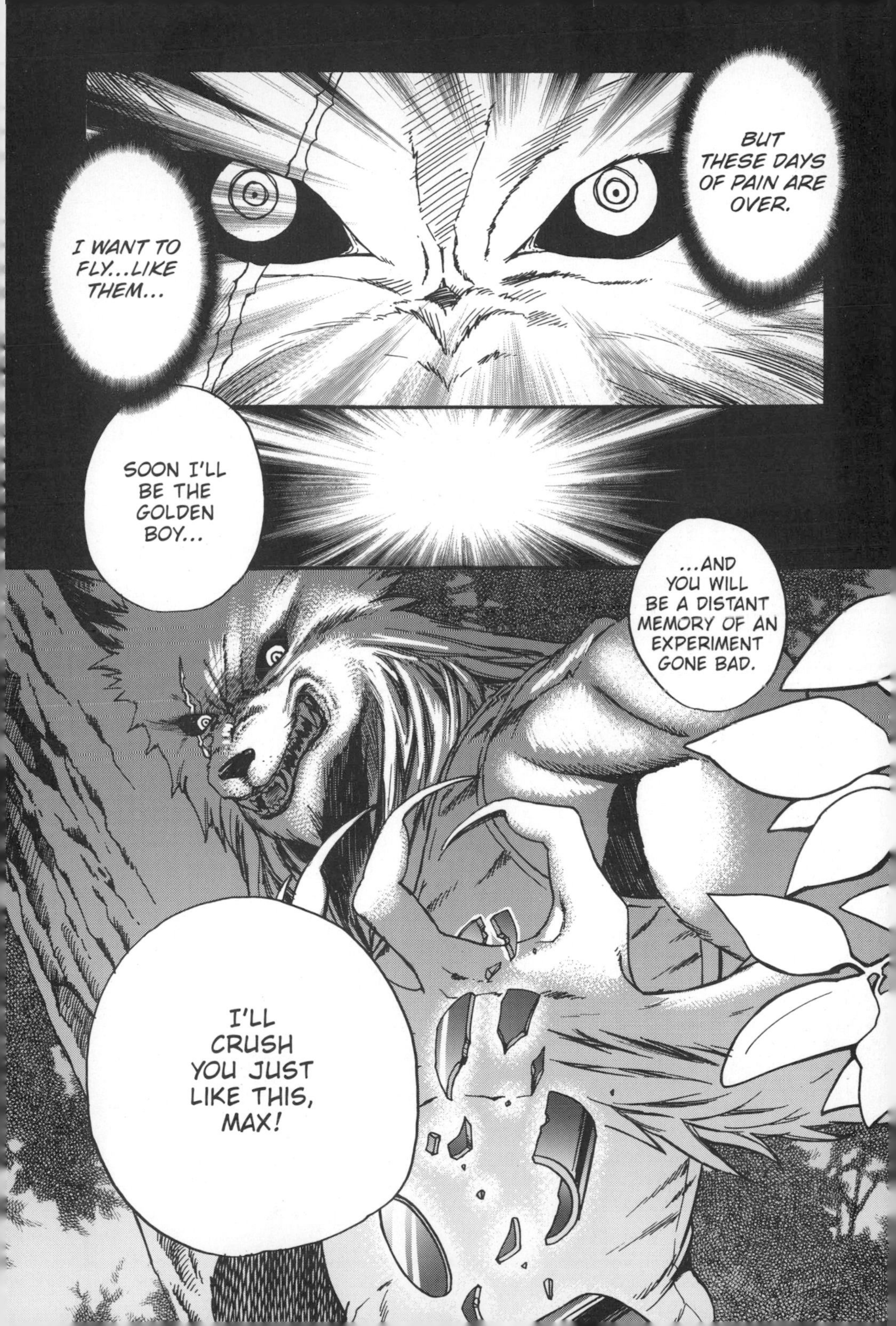
I WANT TO FLY...LIKE THEM...
BUT THESE DAYS OF PAIN ARE OVER.
SOON I'LL BE THE GOLDEN BOY...
...AND YOU WILL BE A DISTANT MEMORY OF AN EXPERIMENT GONE BAD.
I'LL CRUSH YOU JUST LIKE THIS, MAX!

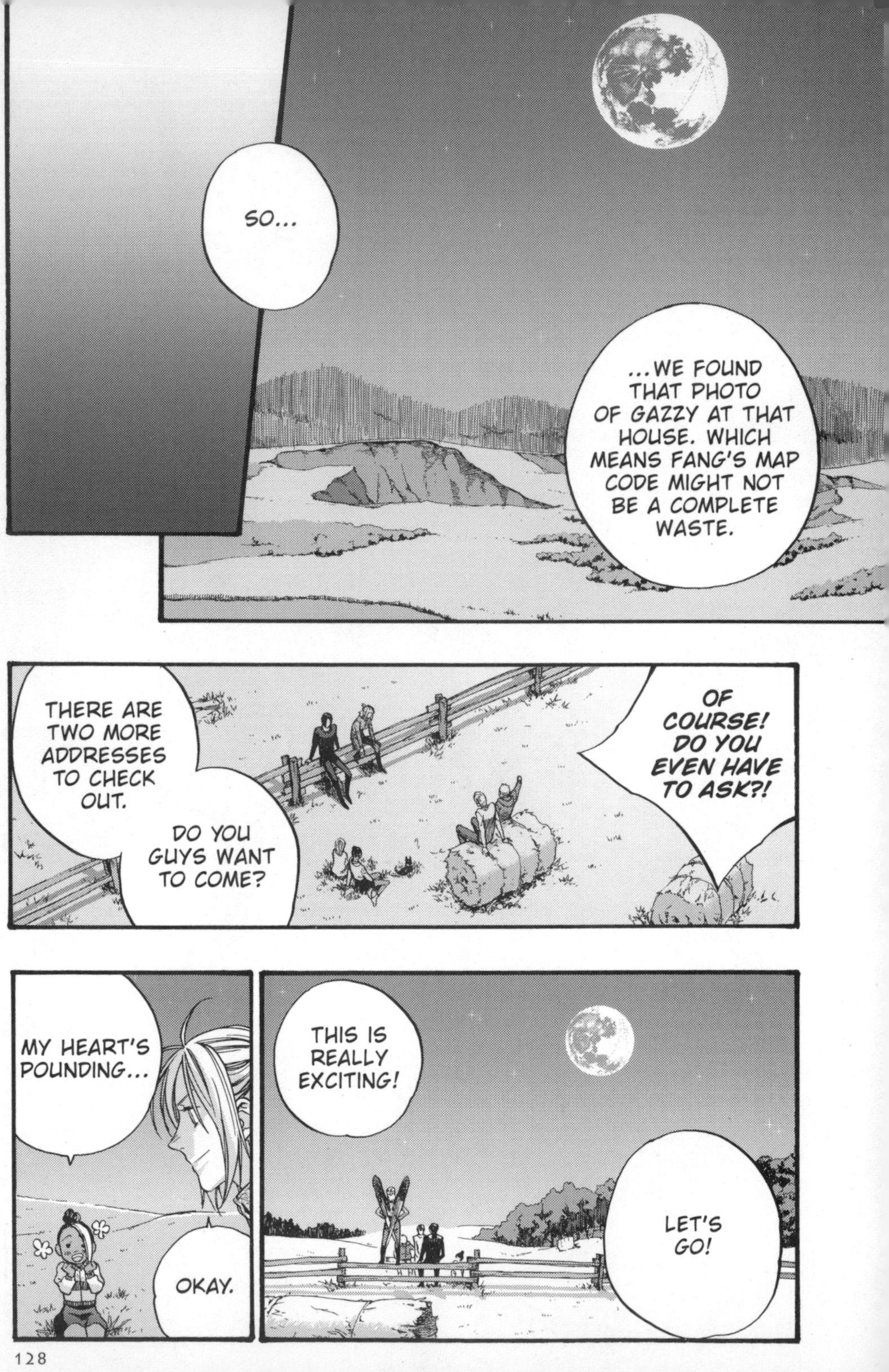
SO...
...WE FOUND THAT PHOTO OF GAZZY AT THAT HOUSE. WHICH MEANS FANG'S MAP CODE MIGHT NOT BE A COMPLETE WASTE.
THERE ARE TWO MORE ADDRESSES TO CHECK OUT.
DO YOU GUYS WANT TO COME?
OF COURSE! DO YOU EVEN HAVE TO ASK?!
MY HEART'S POUNDING...
OKAY.
THIS IS REALLY EXCITING!
LET'S GO!

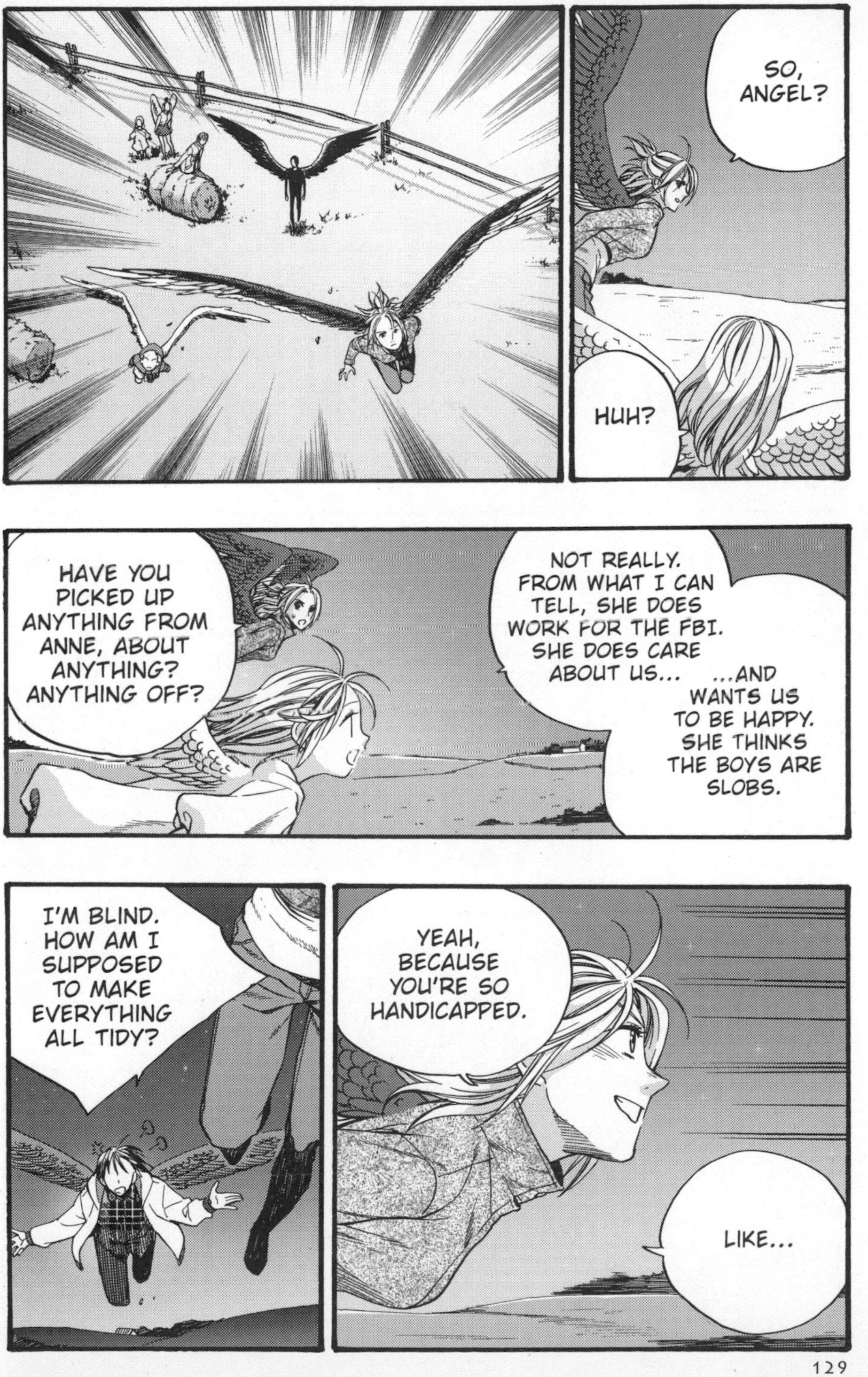
SO, ANGEL?
HUH?
HAVE YOU PICKED UP ANYTHING FROM ANNE, ABOUT ANYTHING? ANYTHING OFF?
NOT REALLY. FROM WHAT I CAN TELL, SHE DOES WORK FOR THE FBI. SHE DOES CARE ABOUT US...
...AND WANTS US TO BE HAPPY. SHE THINKS THE BOYS ARE SLOBS.
I'M BLIND. HOW AM I SUPPOSED TO MAKE EVERYTHING ALL TIDY?
YEAH, BECAUSE YOU'RE SO HANDICAPPED.
LIKE...

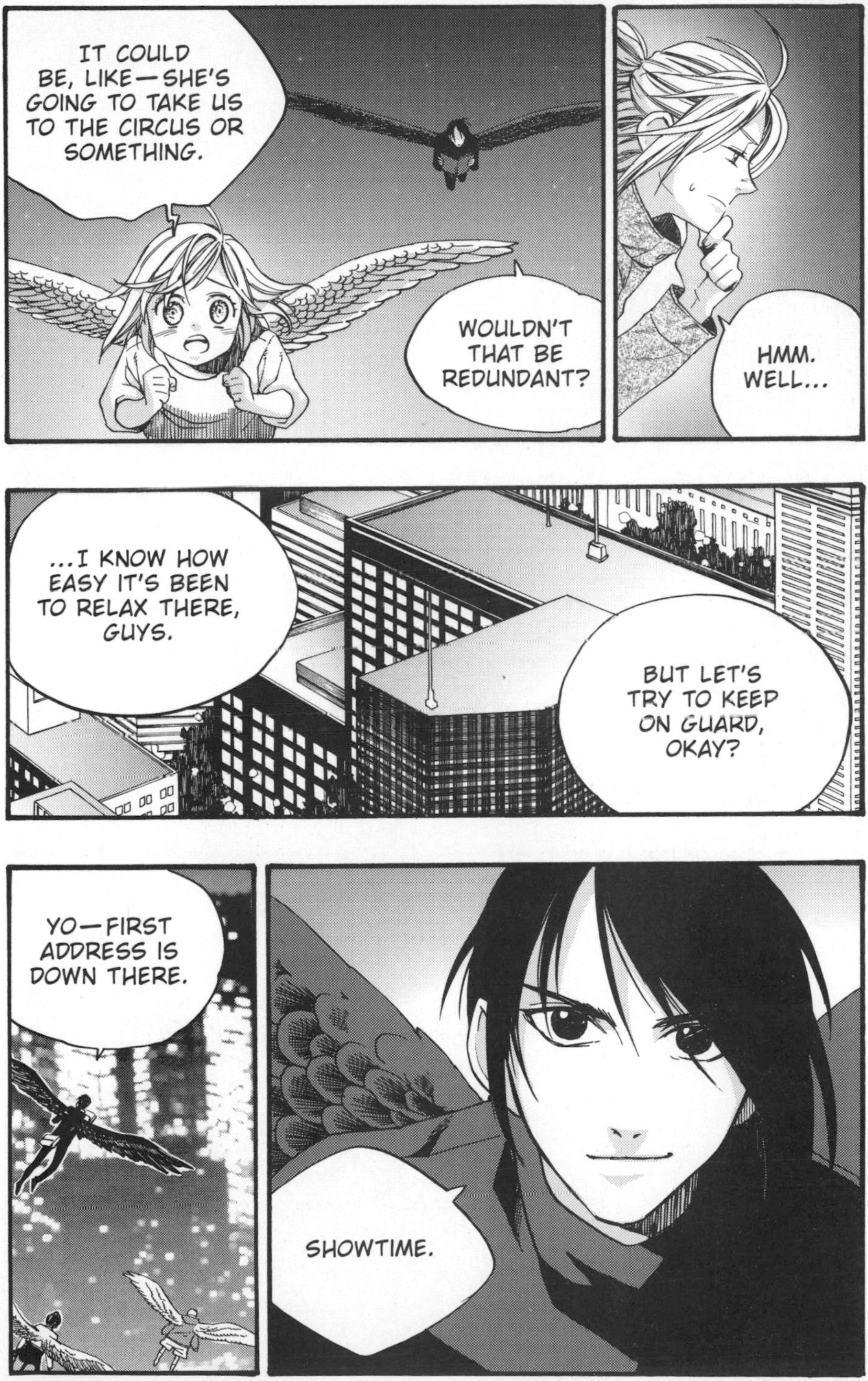
IT COULD BE, LIKE—SHE'S GOING TO TAKE US TO THE CIRCUS OR SOMETHING.
WOULDN'T THAT BE REDUNDANT?
HMM. WELL...
...I KNOW HOW EASY IT'S BEEN TO RELAX THERE, GUYS.
BUT LET'S TRY TO KEEP ON GUARD, OKAY?
YO—FIRST ADDRESS IS DOWN THERE.
SHOWTIME.

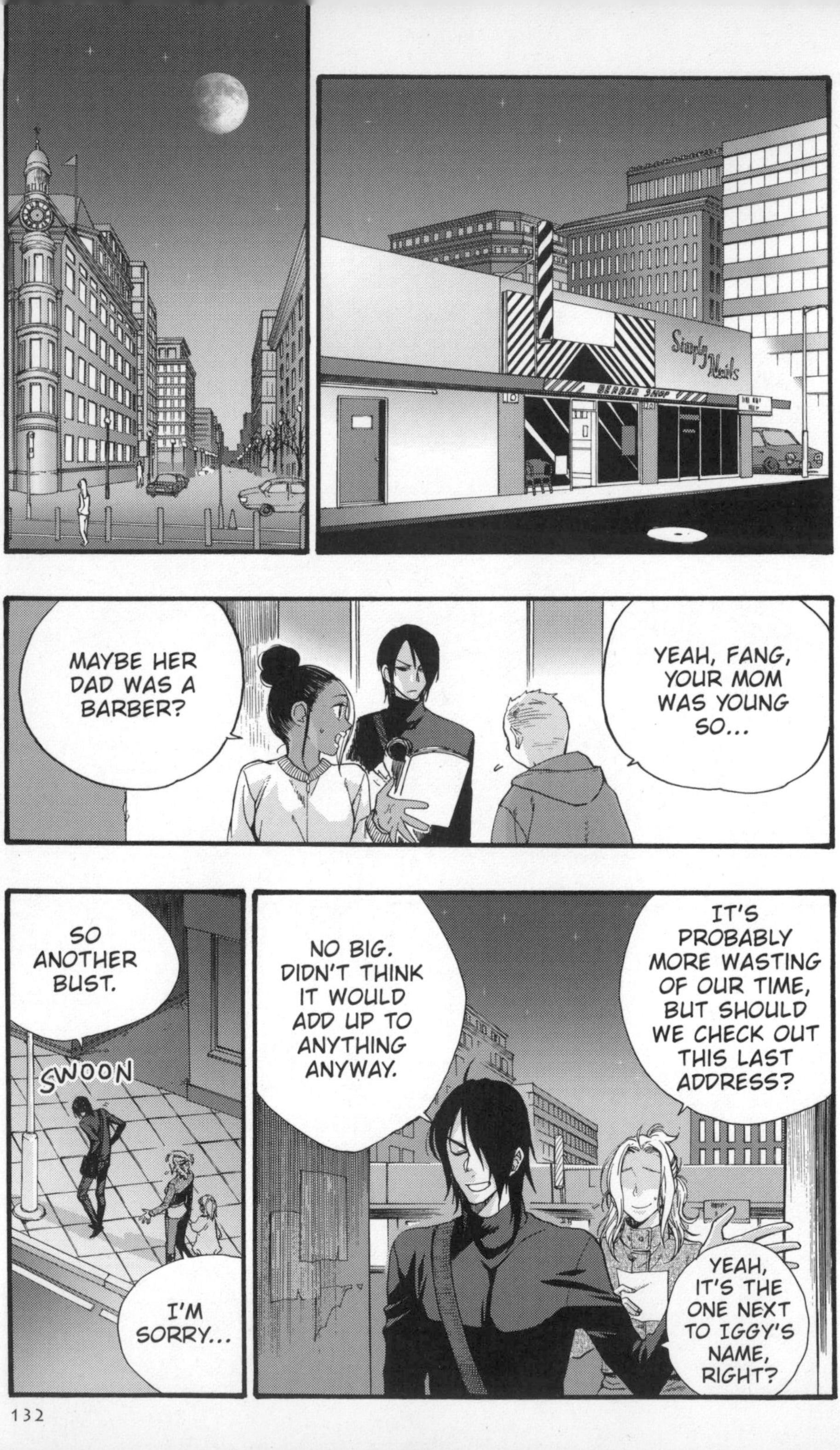
Simply Nails
BARBER SHOP
MAYBE HER DAD WAS A BARBER?
YEAH, FANG, YOUR MOM WAS YOUNG SO...
SO ANOTHER BUST.
SWOON
I'M SORRY...
NO BIG. DIDN'T THINK IT WOULD ADD UP TO ANYTHING ANYWAY.
IT'S PROBABLY MORE WASTING OF OUR TIME, BUT SHOULD WE CHECK OUT THIS LAST ADDRESS?
YEAH, IT'S THE ONE NEXT TO IGGY'S NAME, RIGHT?

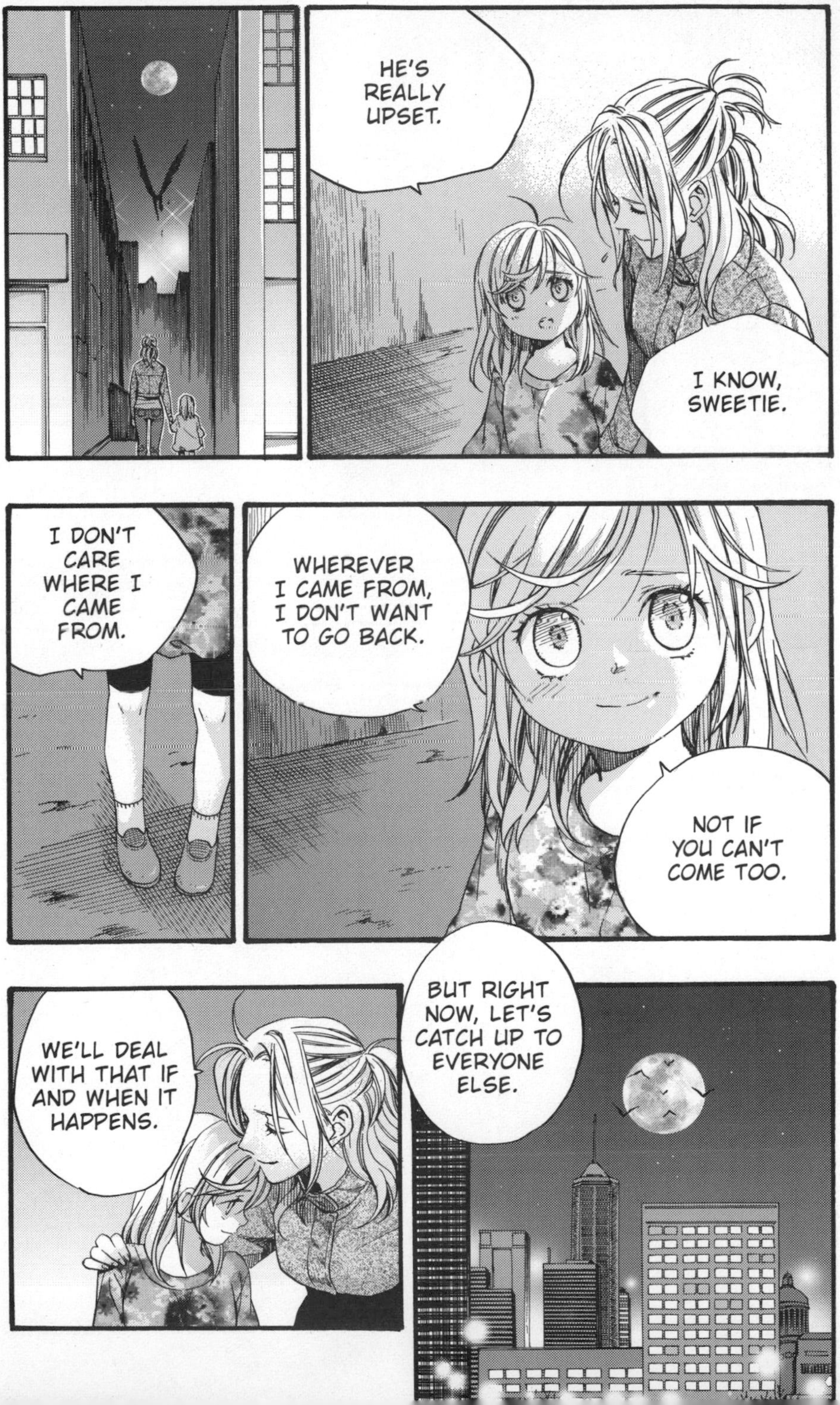
HE'S REALLY UPSET.
I KNOW, SWEETIE.
I DON'T CARE WHERE I CAME FROM.
WHEREVER I CAME FROM, I DON'T WANT TO GO BACK.
NOT IF YOU CAN'T COME TOO.
WE'LL DEAL WITH THAT IF AND WHEN IT HAPPENS.
BUT RIGHT NOW, LET'S CATCH UP TO EVERYONE ELSE.

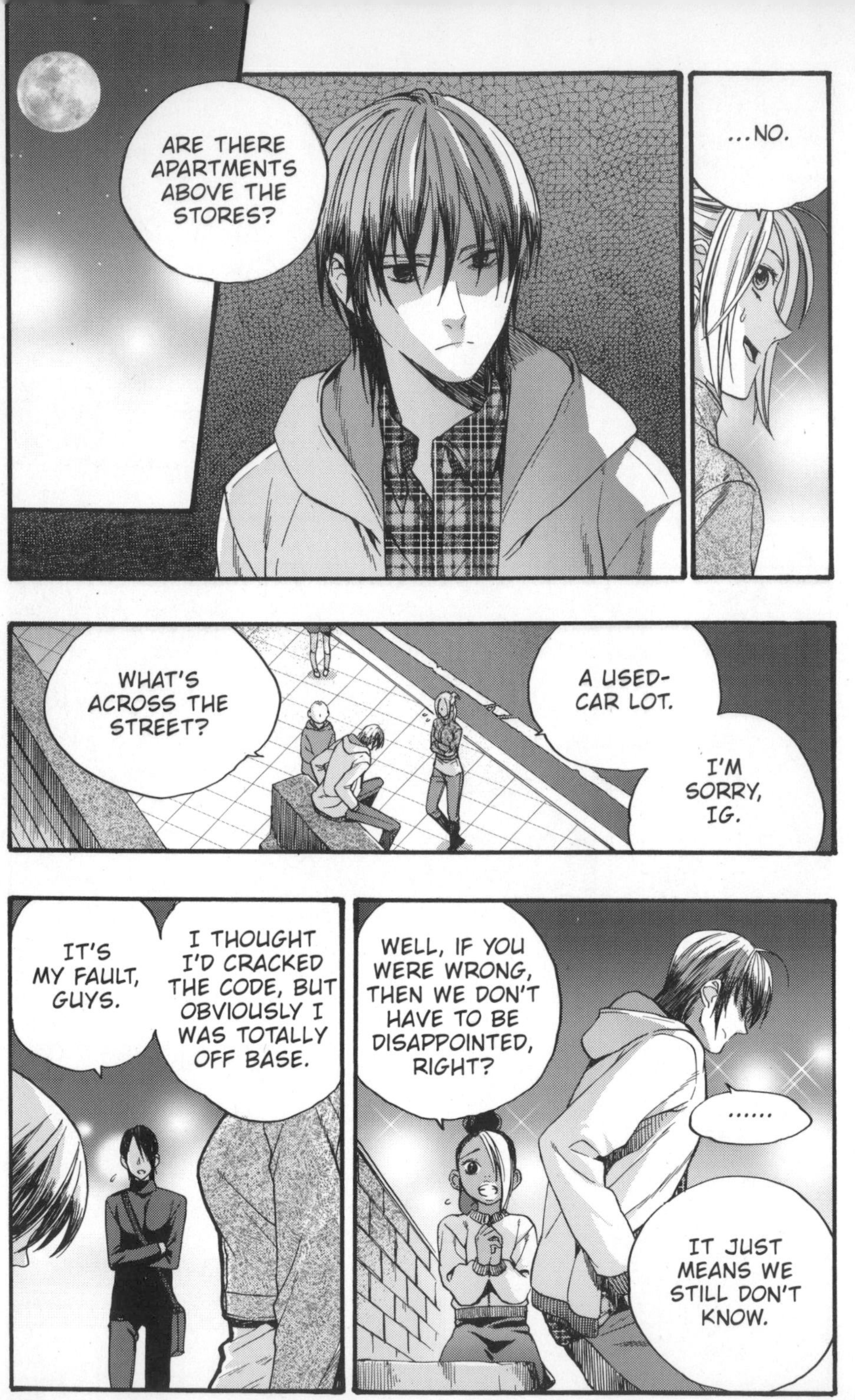
ARE THERE APARTMENTS ABOVE THE STORES?
...NO.
WHAT'S ACROSS THE STREET?
A USED-CAR LOT.
I'M SORRY, IG.
IT'S MY FAULT, GUYS.
I THOUGHT I'D CRACKED THE CODE, BUT OBVIOUSLY I WAS TOTALLY OFF BASE.
WELL, IF YOU WERE WRONG, THEN WE DON'T HAVE TO BE DISAPPOINTED, RIGHT?
......
IT JUST MEANS WE STILL DON'T KNOW.

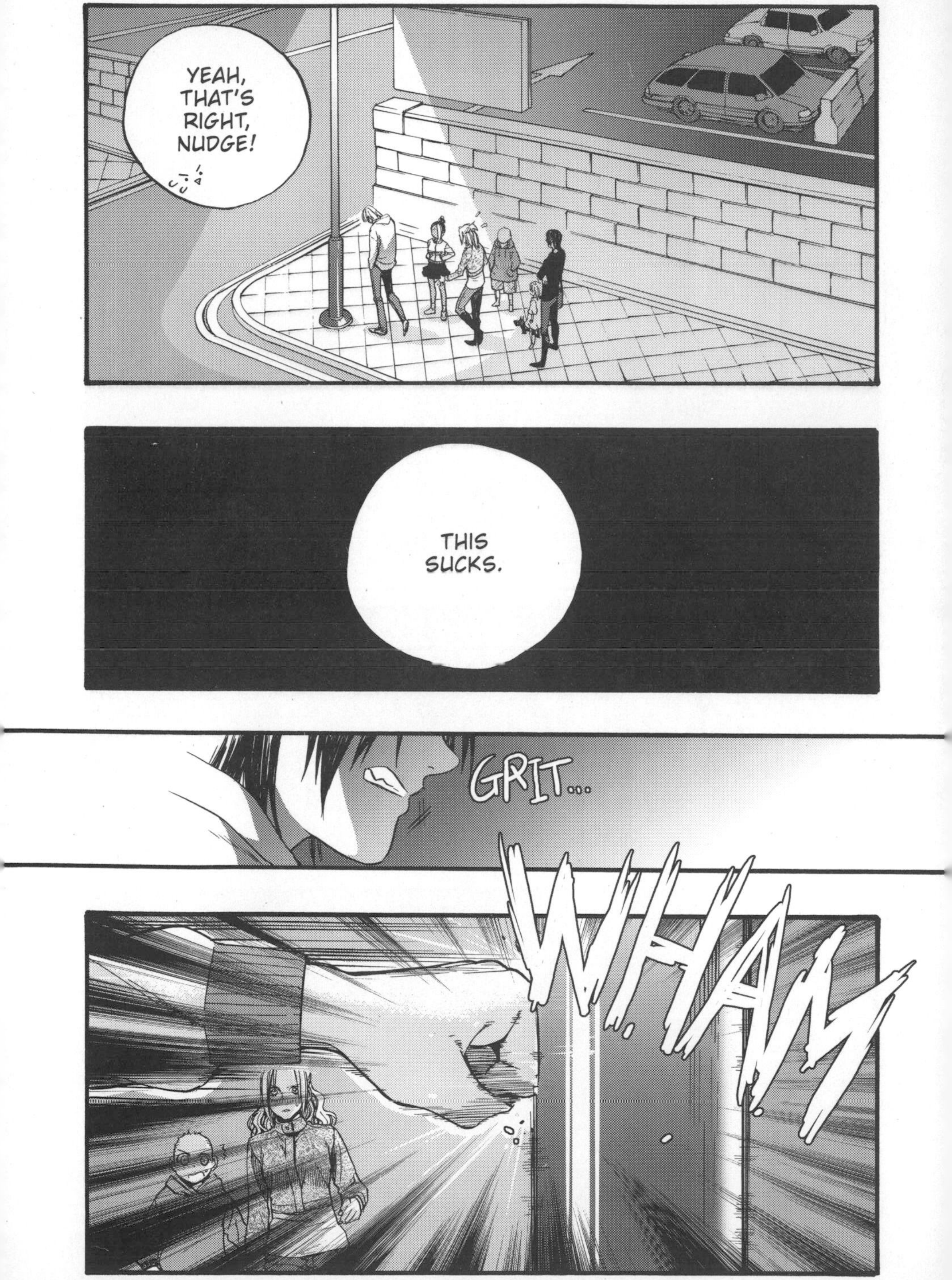
YEAH, THAT'S RIGHT, NUDGE!
THIS SUCKS.
GRIT...
WHAM

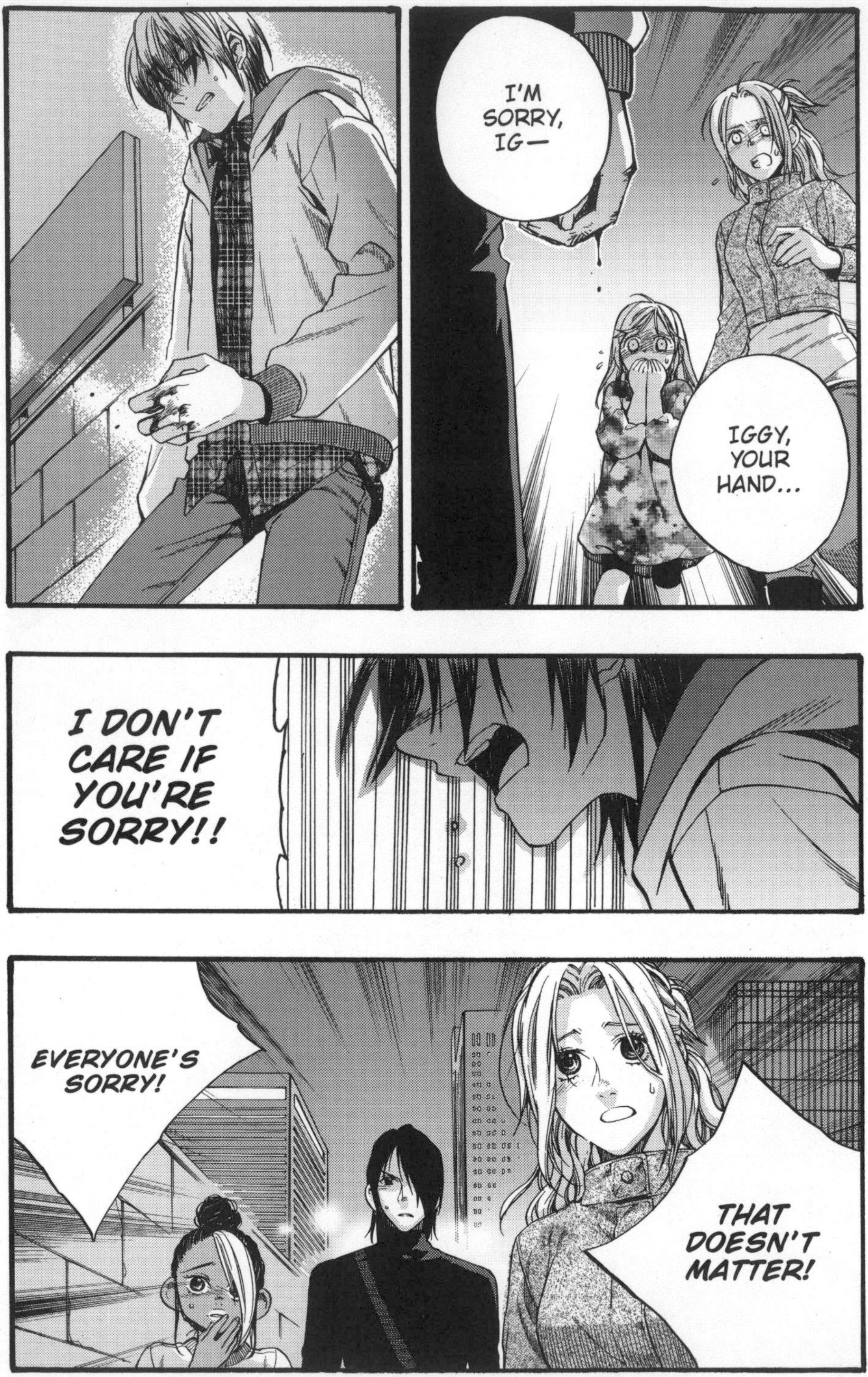
I'M SORRY, IG—
IGGY, YOUR HAND...
I DON'T CARE IF YOU'RE SORRY!!
EVERYONE'S SORRY!
THAT DOESN'T MATTER!

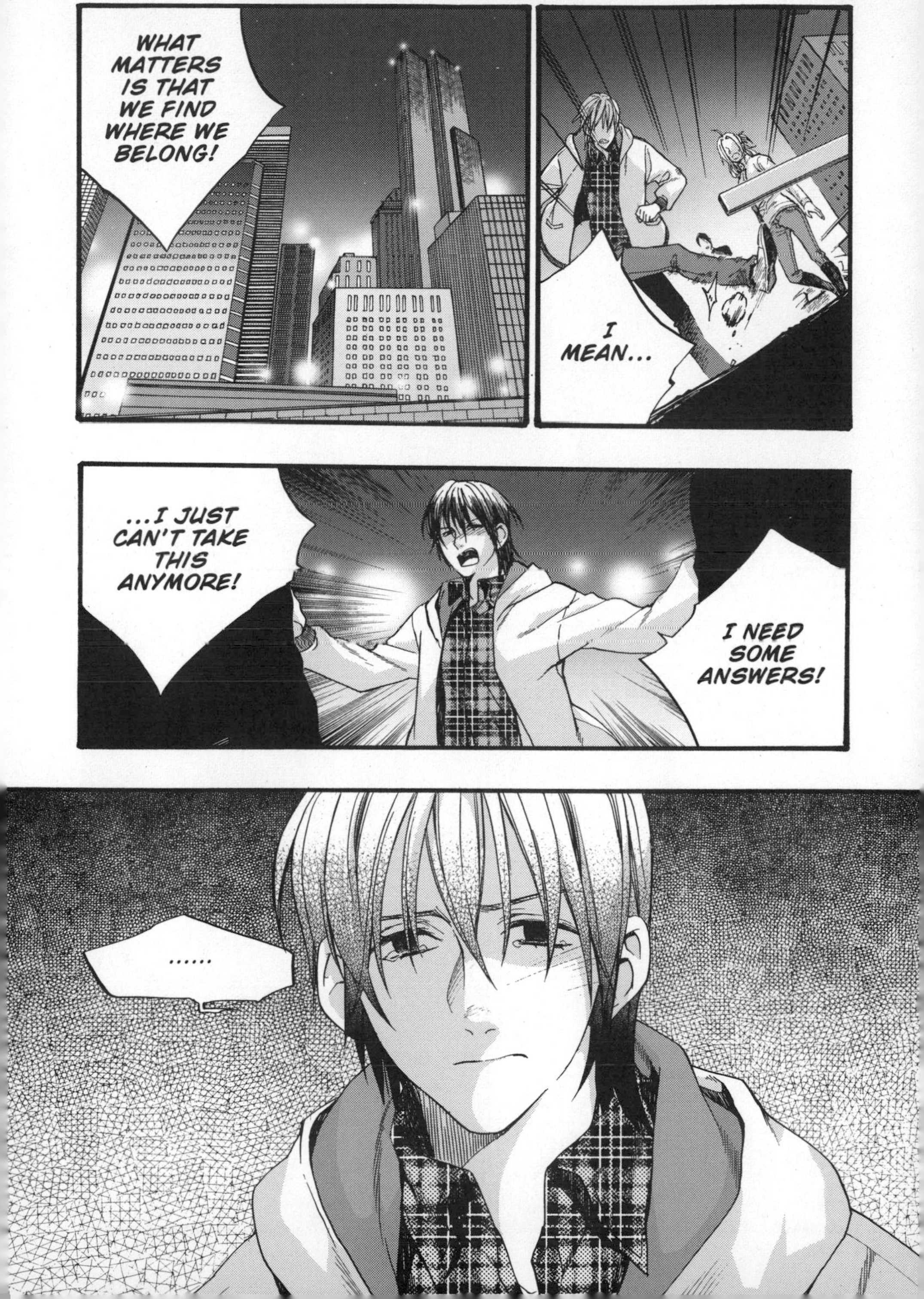
WHAT MATTERS IS THAT WE FIND WHERE WE BELONG!
I MEAN...
...I JUST CAN'T TAKE THIS ANYMORE!
I NEED SOME ANSWERS!
......

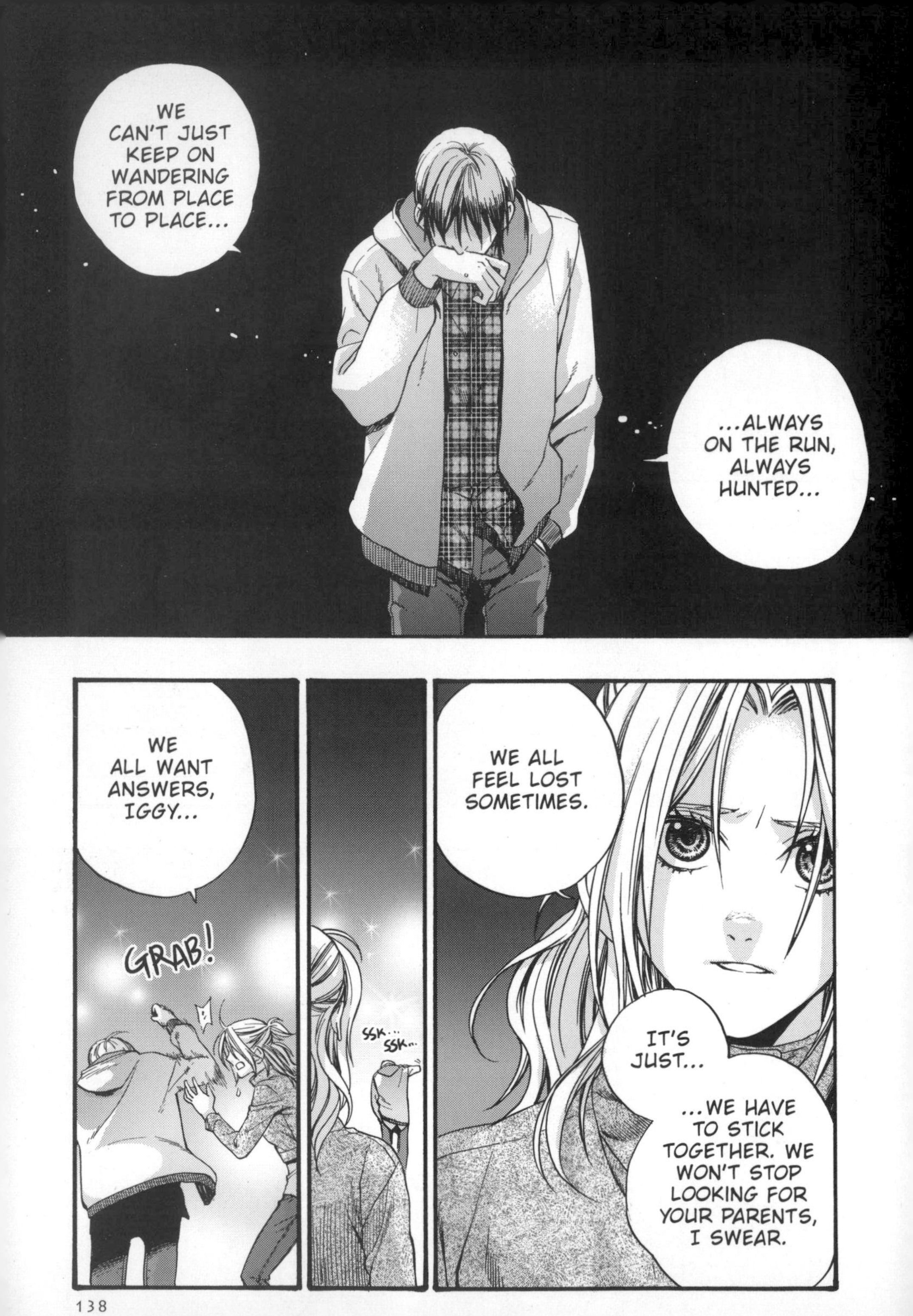
WE CAN'T JUST KEEP ON WANDERING FROM PLACE TO PLACE...
...ALWAYS ON THE RUN, ALWAYS HUNTED...
WE ALL WANT ANSWERS, IGGY...
GRAB!
!
SSK... SSK...
WE ALL FEEL LOST SOMETIMES.
IT'S JUST...
...WE HAVE TO STICK TOGETHER. WE WON'T STOP LOOKING FOR YOUR PARENTS, I SWEAR.

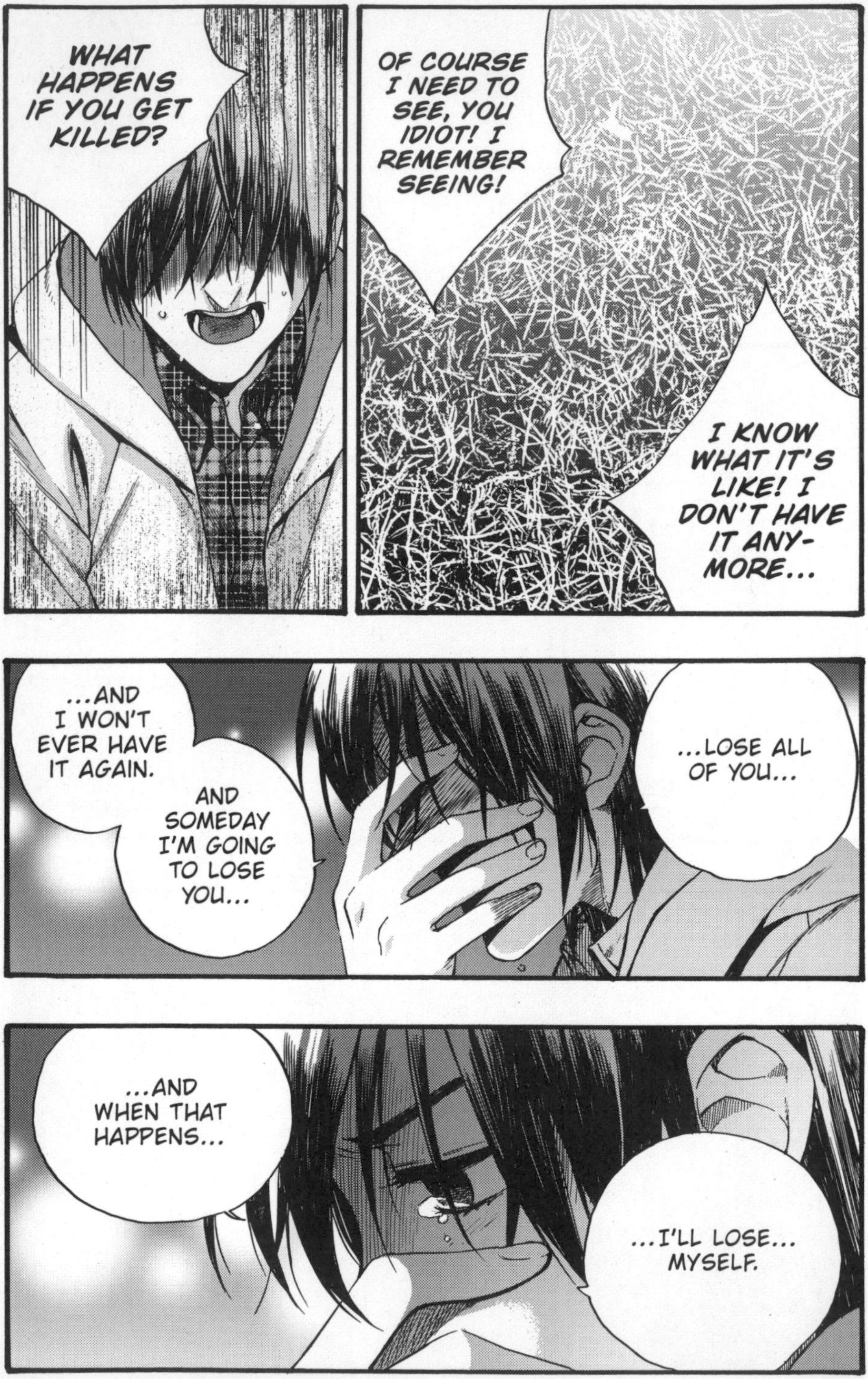
WHAT HAPPENS IF YOU GET KILLED?
OF COURSE I NEED TO SEE, YOU IDIOT! I REMEMBER SEEING!
I KNOW WHAT IT'S LIKE! I DON'T HAVE IT ANY-MORE...
...AND I WON'T EVER HAVE IT AGAIN.
AND SOMEDAY I'M GOING TO LOSE YOU...
...LOSE ALL OF YOU...
...AND WHEN THAT HAPPENS...
...I'LL LOSE... MYSELF.

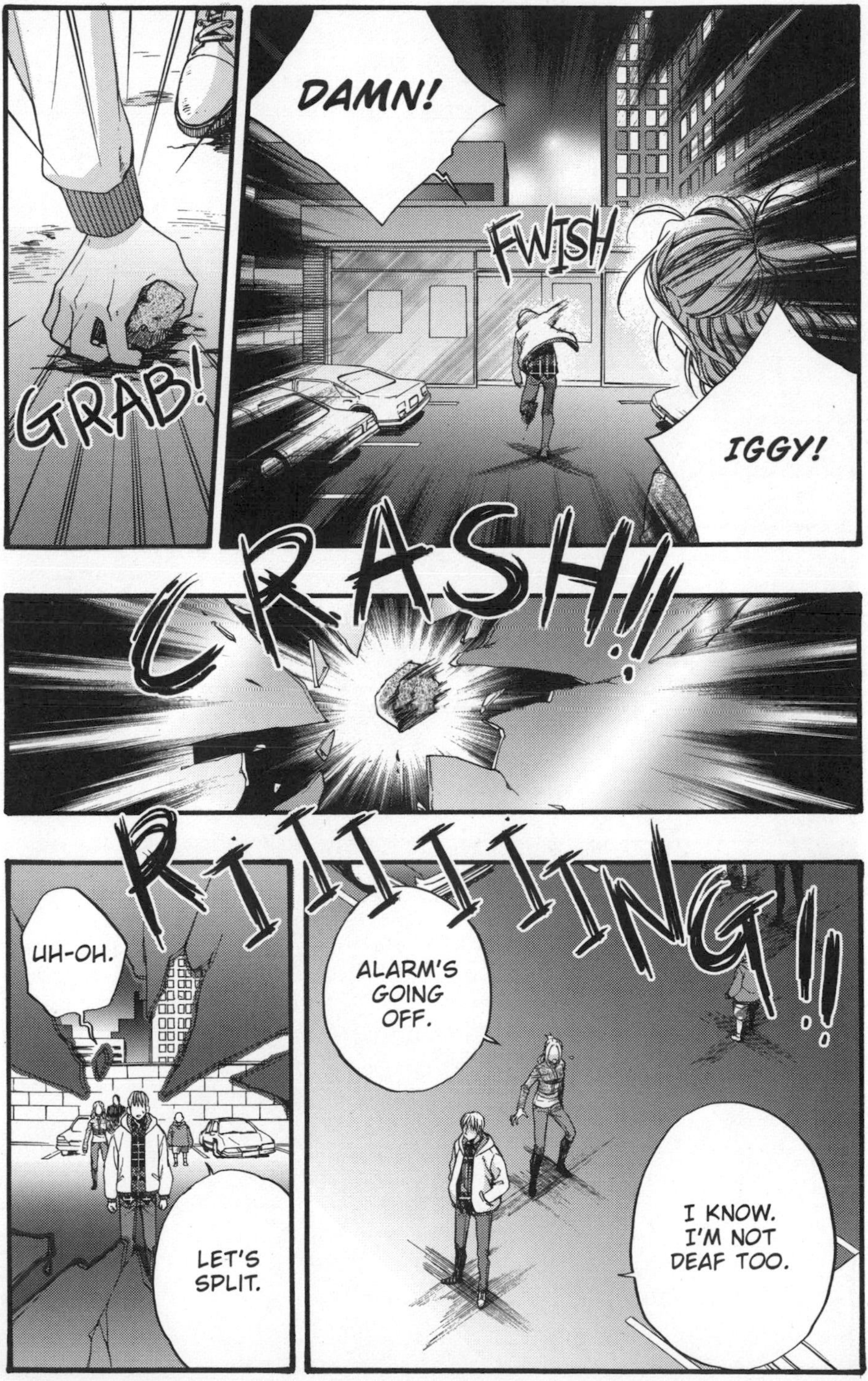
GRAB!
DAMN!
FWISH
IGGY!
CRASH!!
RIIIIING!!
UH-OH.
LET'S SPLIT.
ALARM'S GOING OFF.
I KNOW. I'M NOT DEAF TOO.

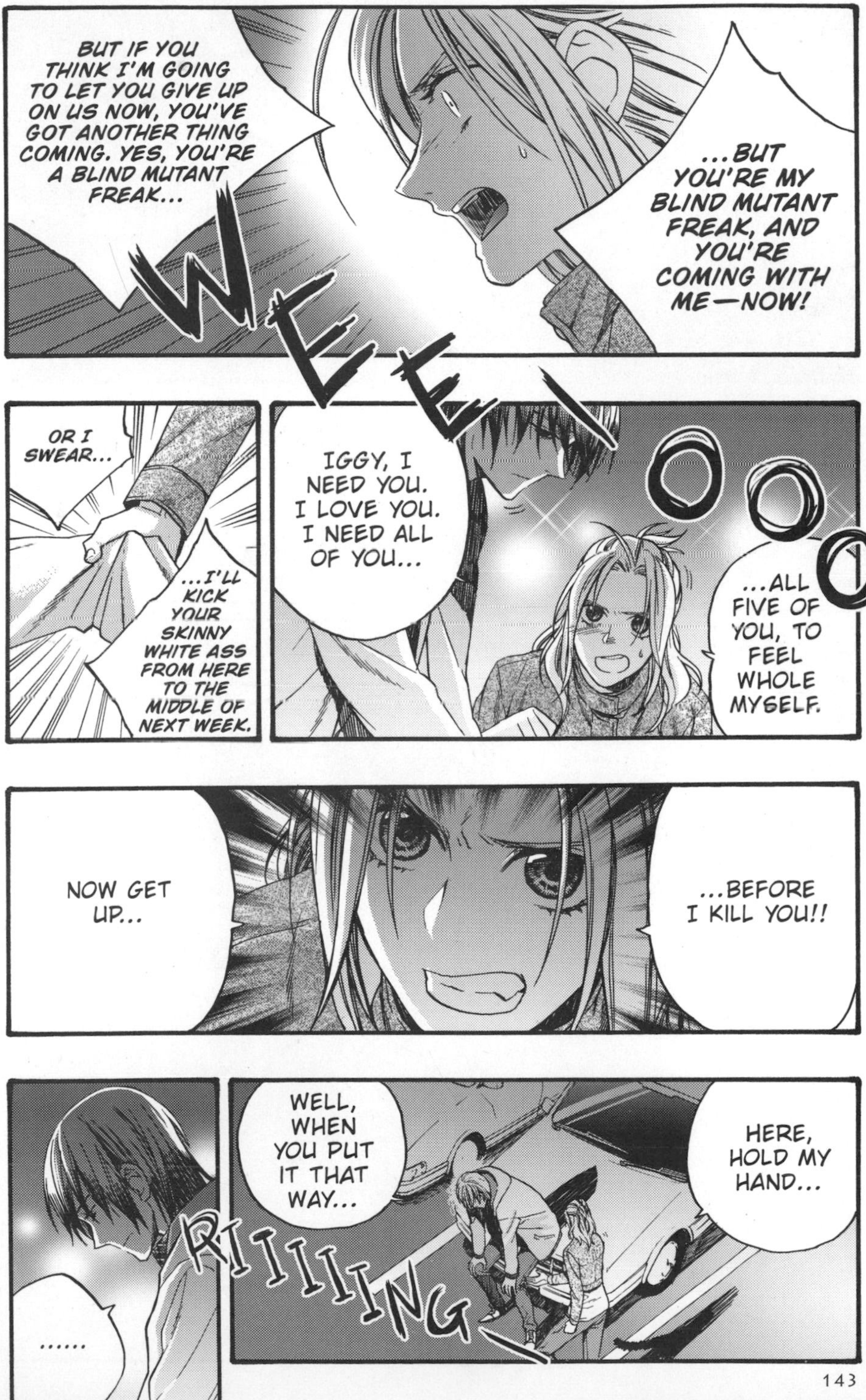
BUT IF YOU THINK I'M GOING TO LET YOU GIVE UP ON US NOW, YOU'VE GOT ANOTHER THING COMING. YES, YOU'RE A BLIND MUTANT FREAK...
...BUT YOU'RE MY BLIND MUTANT FREAK, AND YOU'RE COMING WITH ME—NOW!
WEEEOOOO
OR I SWEAR...
...I'LL KICK YOUR SKINNY WHITE ASS FROM HERE TO THE MIDDLE OF NEXT WEEK.
IGGY, I NEED YOU. I LOVE YOU. I NEED ALL OF YOU...
...ALL FIVE OF YOU, TO FEEL WHOLE MYSELF.
NOW GET UP...
...BEFORE I KILL YOU!!
......
WELL, WHEN YOU PUT IT THAT WAY...
RIIIING
HERE, HOLD MY HAND...

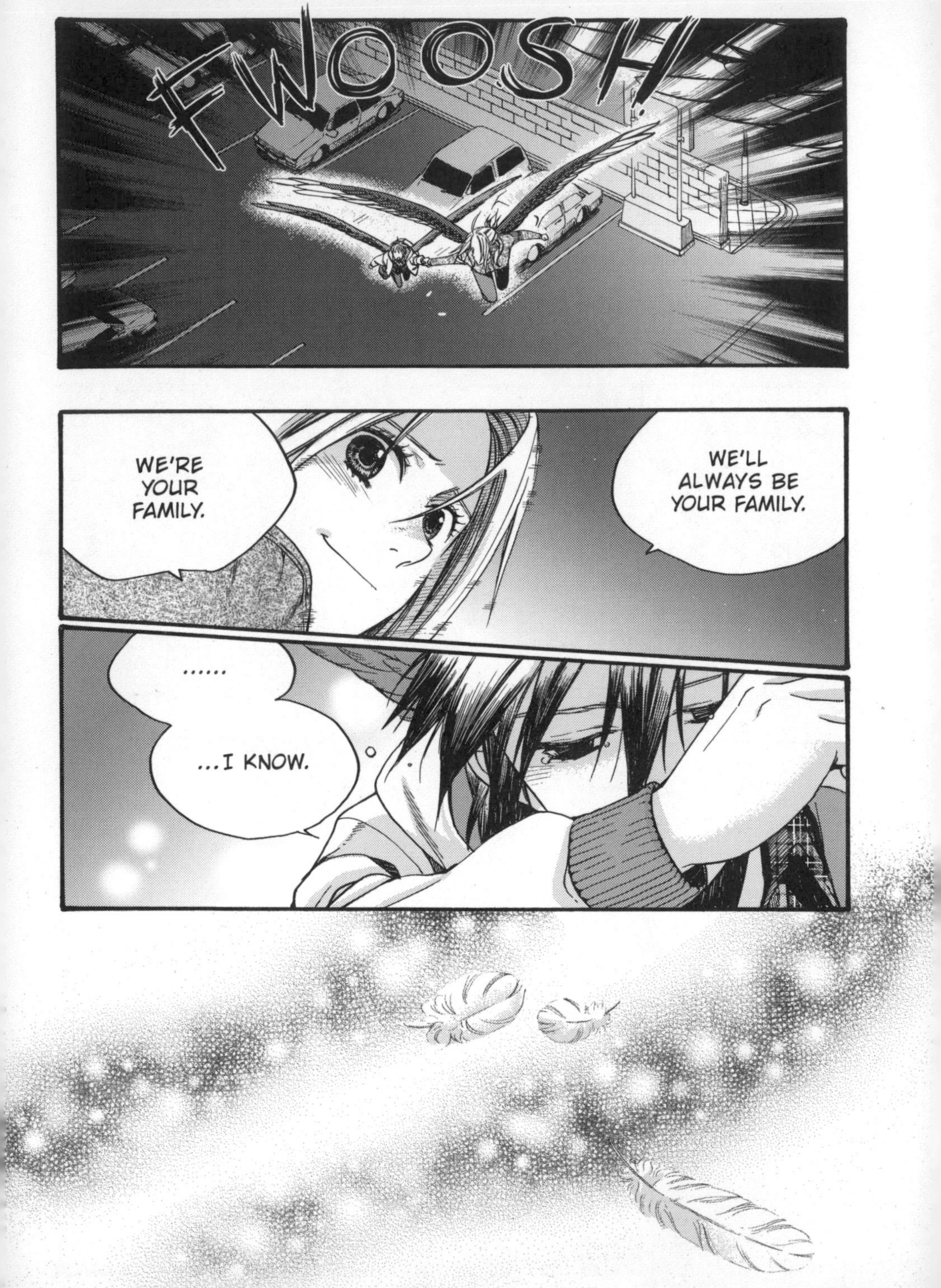
FWOOSH!
WE'RE YOUR FAMILY.
WE'LL ALWAYS BE YOUR FAMILY.
......
...I KNOW.

MAXIMUM
RIDE

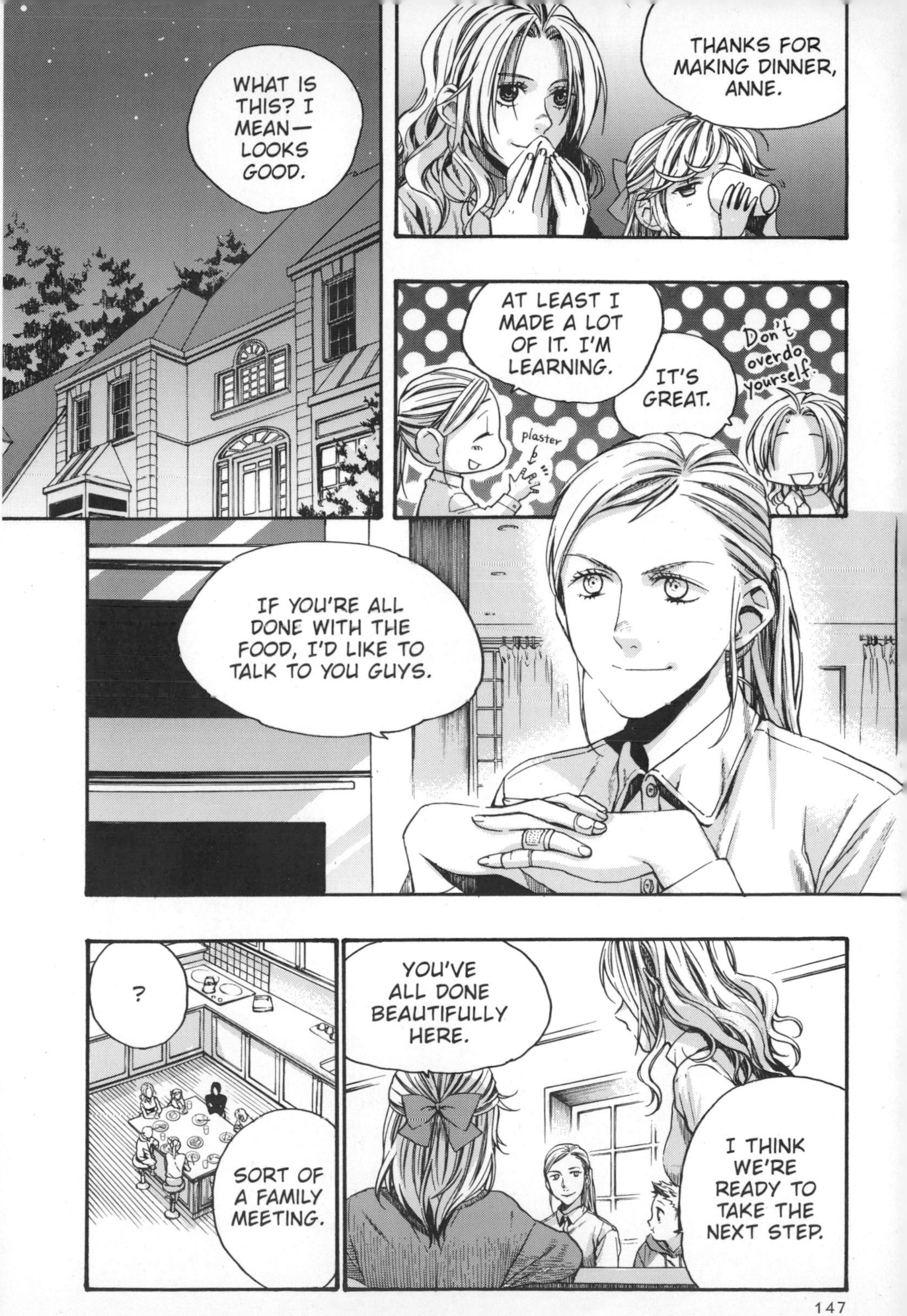
WHAT IS THIS? I MEAN—LOOKS GOOD.
THANKS FOR MAKING DINNER, ANNE.
AT LEAST I MADE A LOT OF IT. I'M LEARNING.
plaster
IT'S GREAT.
Don't overdo yourself.
IF YOU'RE ALL DONE WITH THE FOOD, I'D LIKE TO TALK TO YOU GUYS.
?
SORT OF A FAMILY MEETING.
YOU'VE ALL DONE BEAUTIFULLY HERE.
I THINK WE'RE READY TO TAKE THE NEXT STEP.

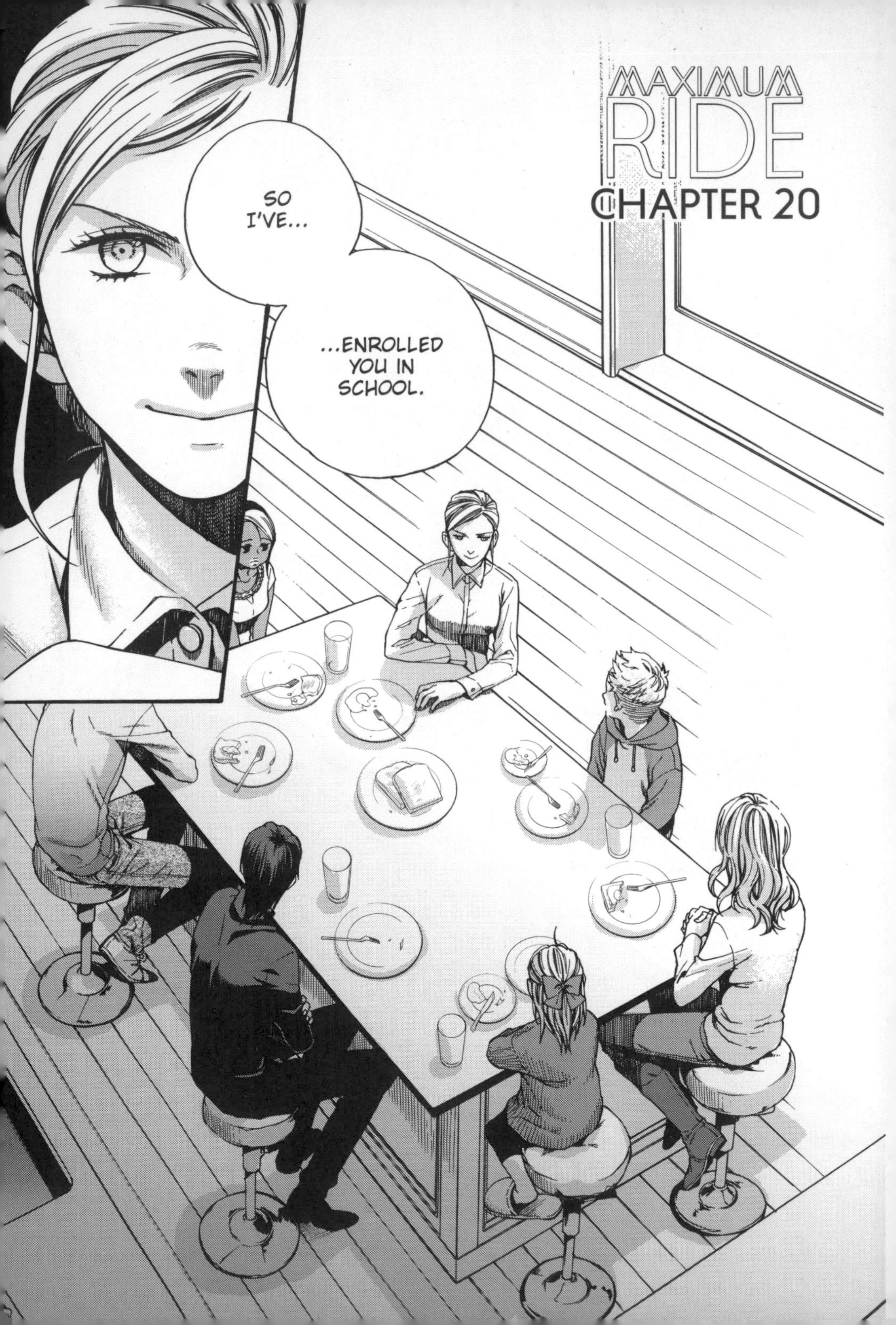
MAXIMUM RIDE
CHAPTER 20
SO I'VE...
...ENROLLED YOU IN SCHOOL.

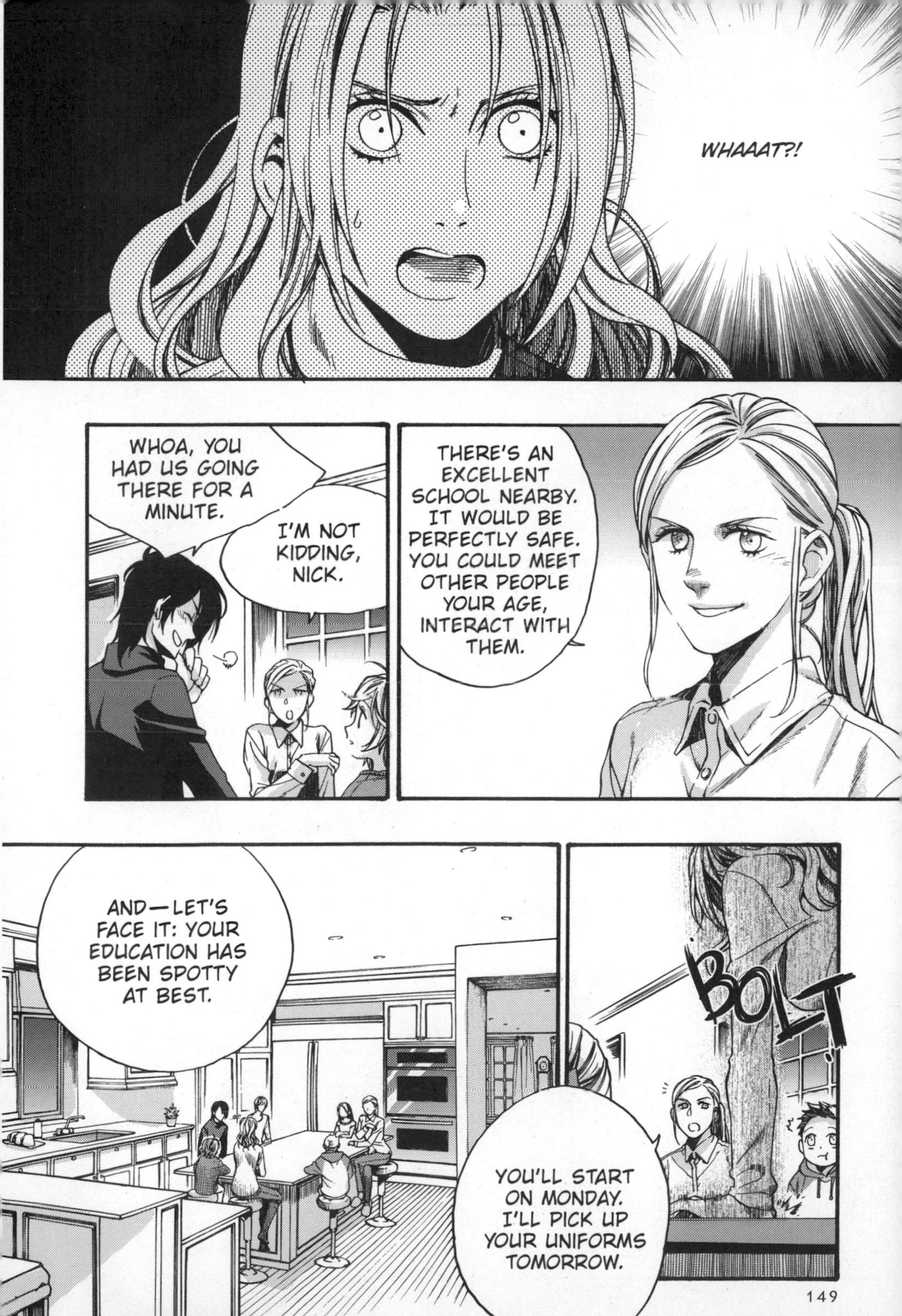
WHAAAT?!
WHOA, YOU HAD US GOING THERE FOR A MINUTE.
I'M NOT KIDDING, NICK.
THERE'S AN EXCELLENT SCHOOL NEARBY. IT WOULD BE PERFECTLY SAFE. YOU COULD MEET OTHER PEOPLE YOUR AGE, INTERACT WITH THEM.
AND—LET'S FACE IT: YOUR EDUCATION HAS BEEN SPOTTY AT BEST.
BOLT
YOU'LL START ON MONDAY. I'LL PICK UP YOUR UNIFORMS TOMORROW.

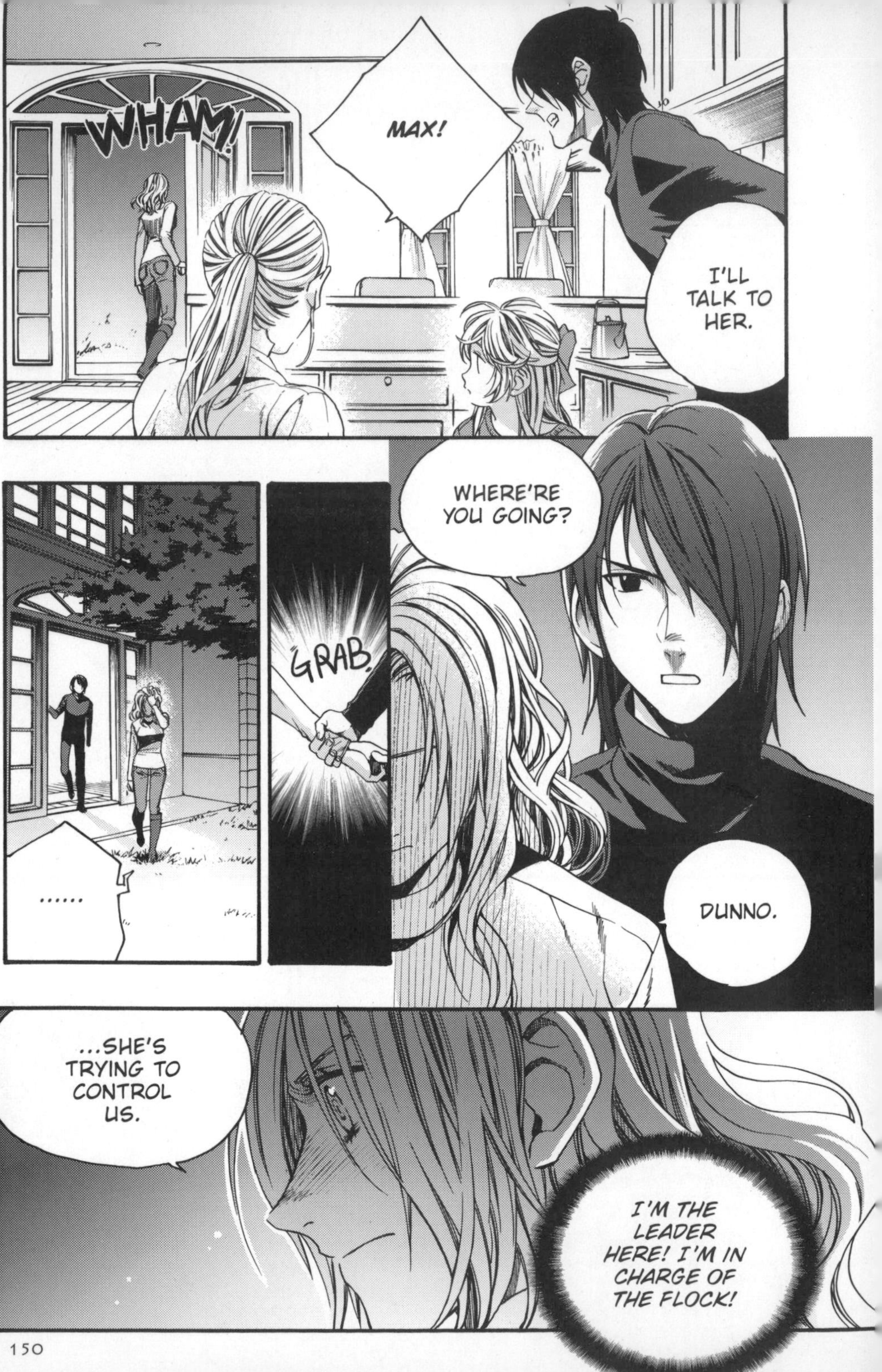
WHAM!
MAX!
I'LL TALK TO HER.
WHERE'RE YOU GOING?
......
GRAB
DUNNO.
...SHE'S TRYING TO CONTROL US.
I'M THE LEADER HERE! I'M IN CHARGE OF THE FLOCK!

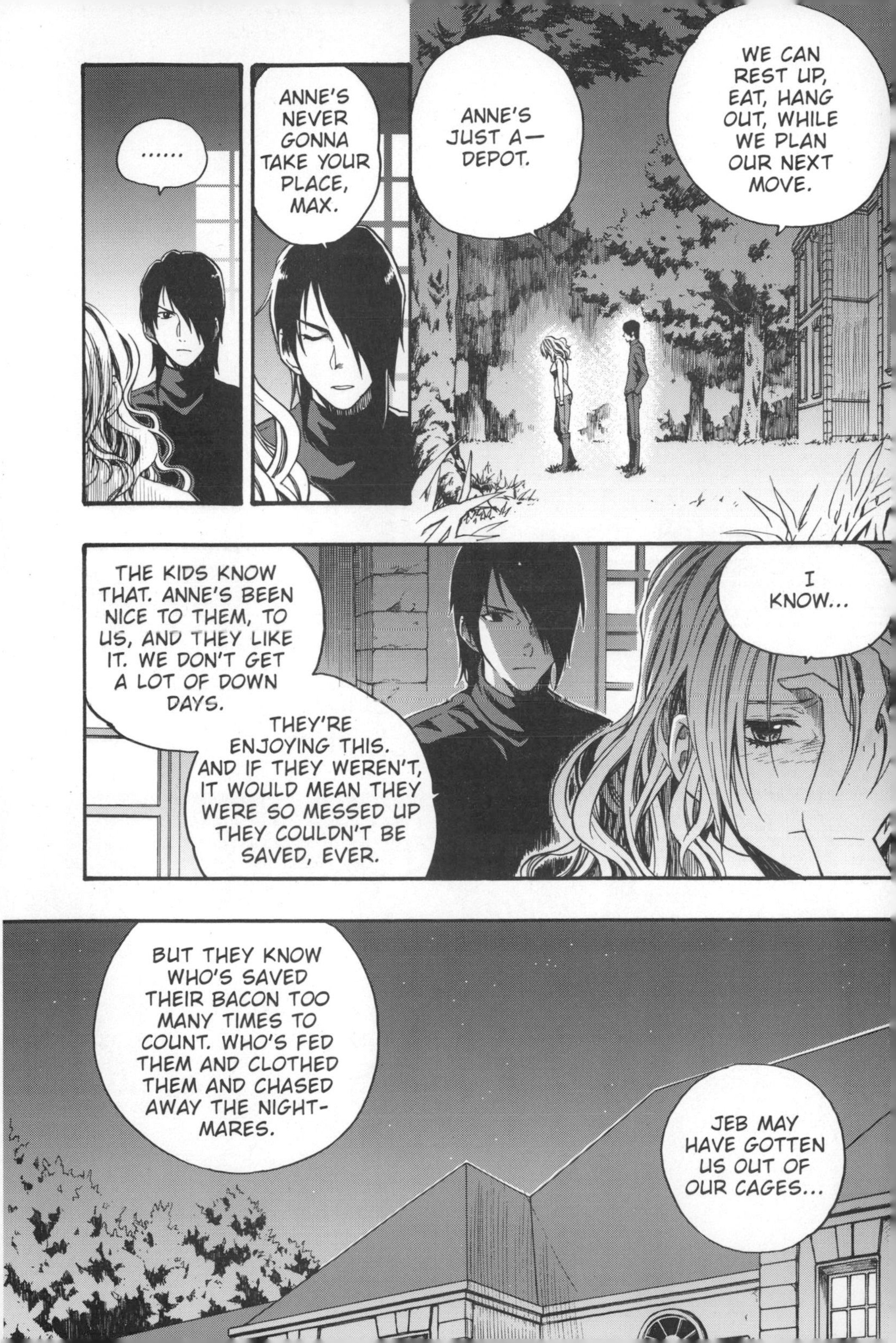
......
ANNE'S NEVER GONNA TAKE YOUR PLACE, MAX.
ANNE'S JUST A— DEPOT.
WE CAN REST UP, EAT, HANG OUT, WHILE WE PLAN OUR NEXT MOVE.
THE KIDS KNOW THAT. ANNE'S BEEN NICE TO THEM, TO US, AND THEY LIKE IT. WE DON'T GET A LOT OF DOWN DAYS.
THEY'RE ENJOYING THIS. AND IF THEY WEREN'T, IT WOULD MEAN THEY WERE SO MESSED UP THEY COULDN'T BE SAVED, EVER.
I KNOW...
BUT THEY KNOW WHO'S SAVED THEIR BACON TOO MANY TIMES TO COUNT. WHO'S FED THEM AND CLOTHED THEM AND CHASED AWAY THE NIGHT-MARES.
JEB MAY HAVE GOTTEN US OUT OF OUR CAGES...

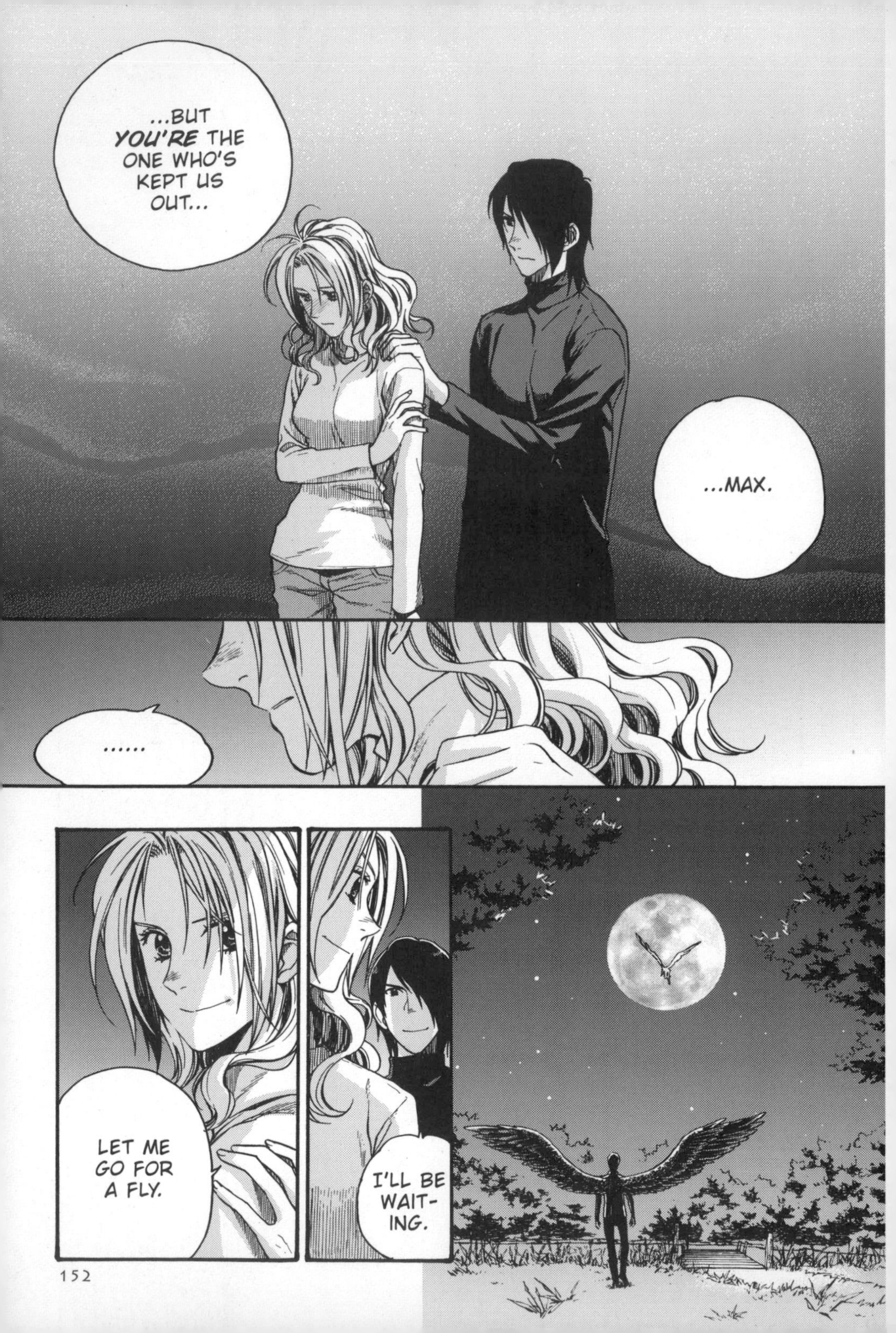
...BUT *YOU'RE* THE ONE WHO'S KEPT US OUT...
...MAX.
......
LET ME GO FOR A FLY.
I'LL BE WAIT-ING.

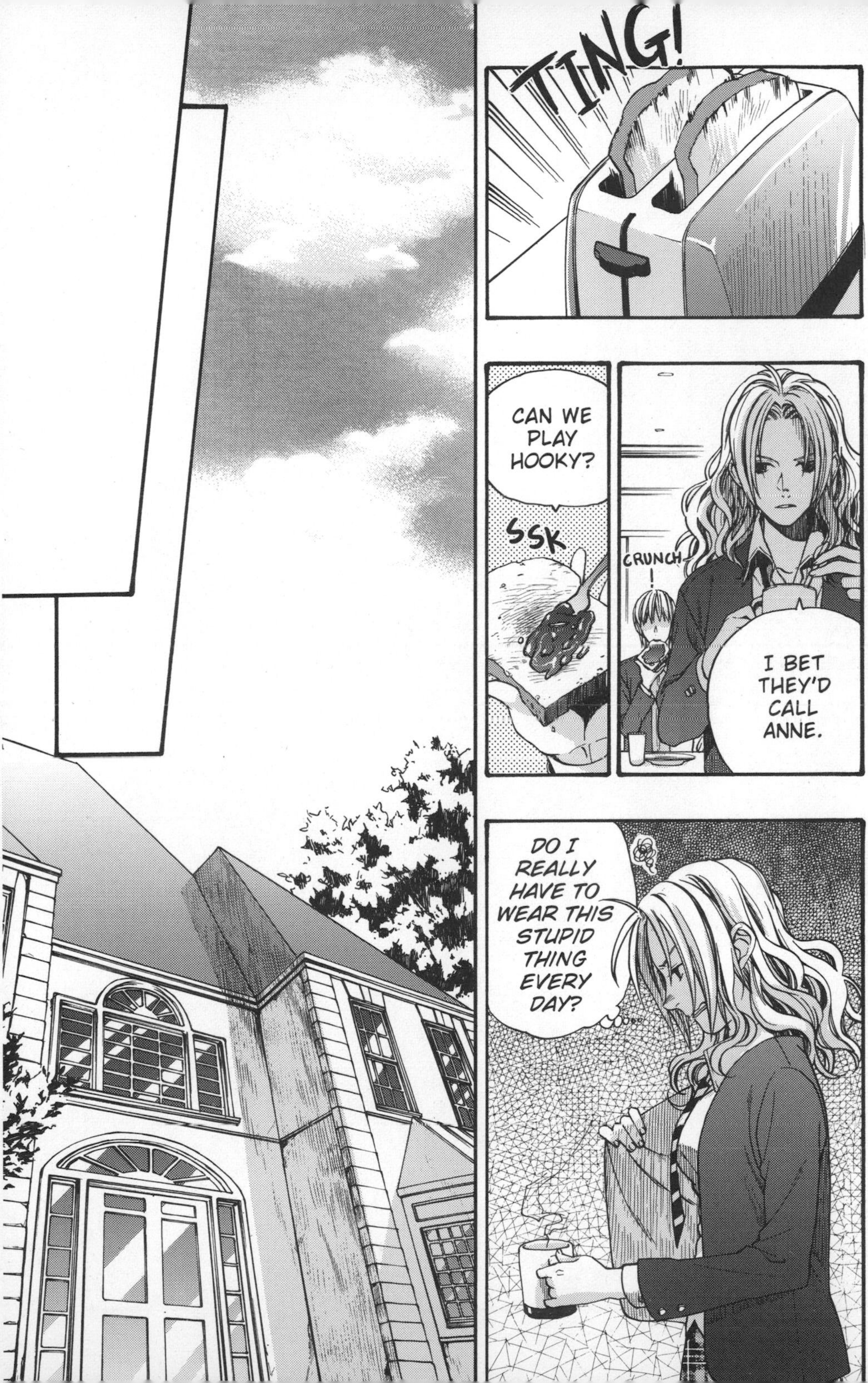
TING!
CAN WE PLAY HOOKY?
SSK
CRUNCH
I BET THEY'D CALL ANNE.
DO I REALLY HAVE TO WEAR THIS STUPID THING EVERY DAY?

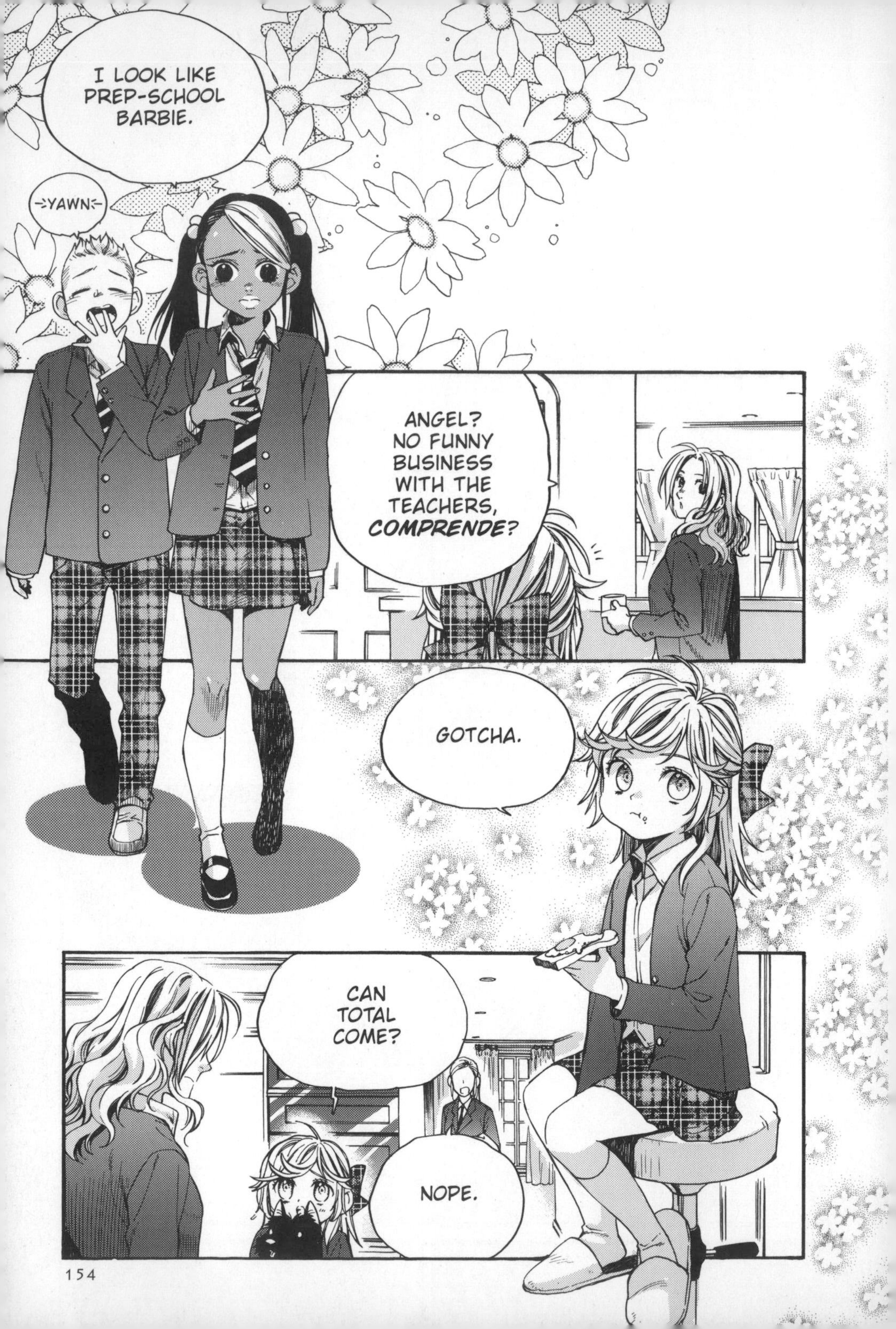
I LOOK LIKE PREP-SCHOOL BARBIE.
YAWN
ANGEL? NO FUNNY BUSINESS WITH THE TEACHERS, *COMPRENDE*?
GOTCHA.
CAN TOTAL COME?
NOPE.

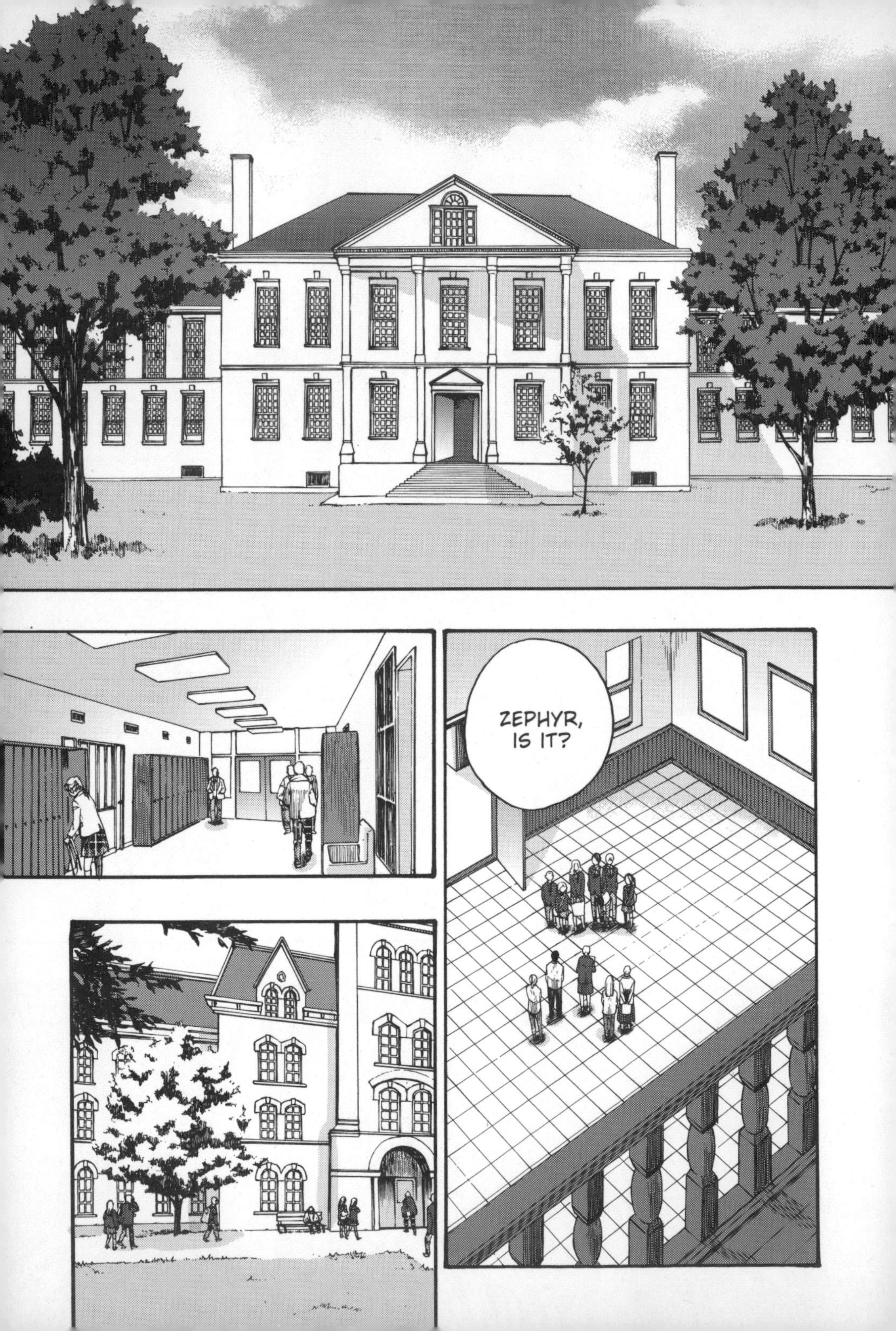
ZEPHYR, IS IT?

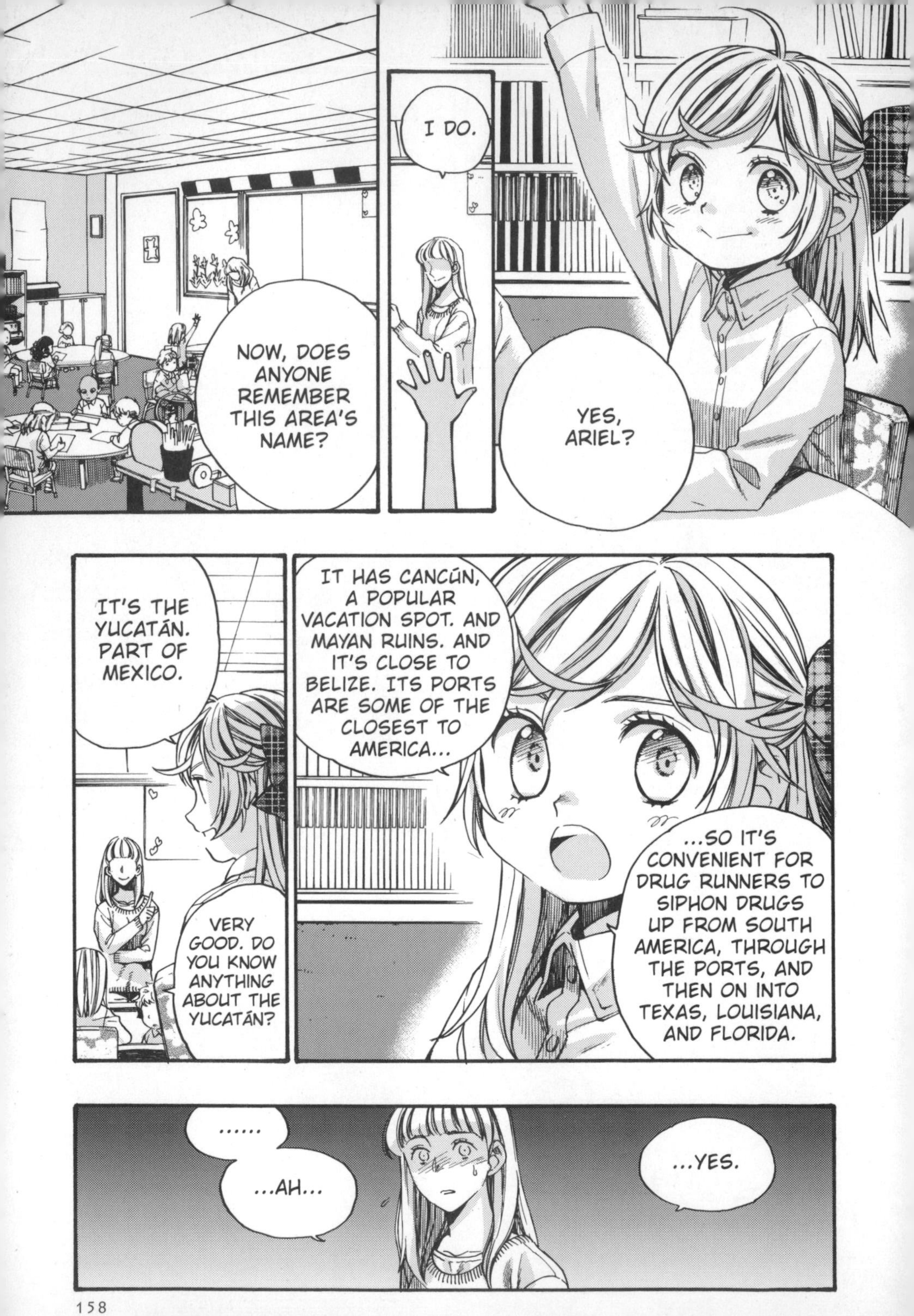

NOW, DOES ANYONE REMEMBER THIS AREA'S NAME?
I DO.
YES, ARIEL?
IT'S THE YUCATÁN. PART OF MEXICO.
VERY GOOD. DO YOU KNOW ANYTHING ABOUT THE YUCATÁN?
IT HAS CANCÚN, A POPULAR VACATION SPOT. AND MAYAN RUINS. AND IT'S CLOSE TO BELIZE. ITS PORTS ARE SOME OF THE CLOSEST TO AMERICA...
...SO IT'S CONVENIENT FOR DRUG RUNNERS TO SIPHON DRUGS UP FROM SOUTH AMERICA, THROUGH THE PORTS, AND THEN ON INTO TEXAS, LOUISIANA, AND FLORIDA.
......
...AH...
...YES.

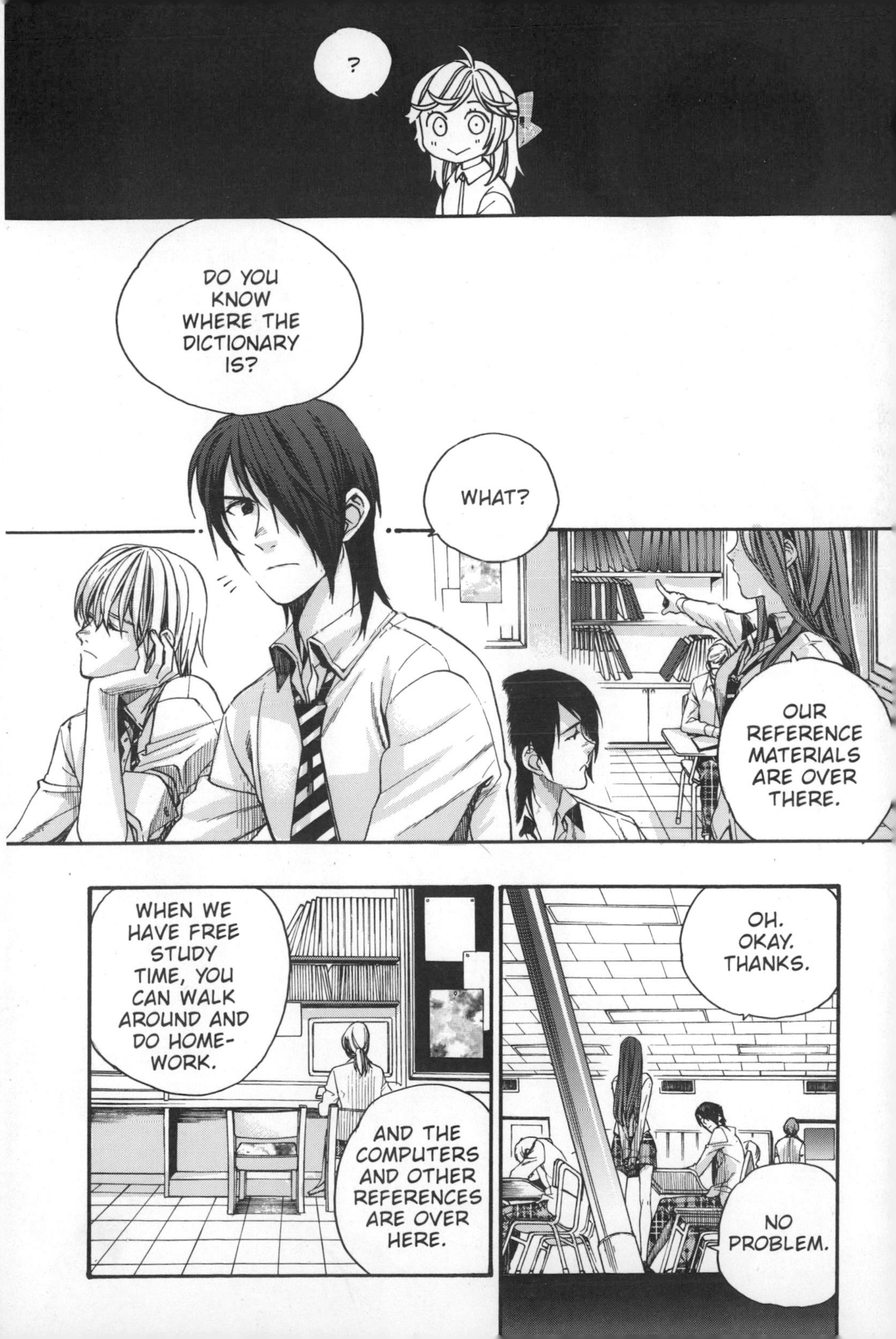
?
DO YOU KNOW WHERE THE DICTIONARY IS?
WHAT?
OUR REFERENCE MATERIALS ARE OVER THERE.
WHEN WE HAVE FREE STUDY TIME, YOU CAN WALK AROUND AND DO HOME-WORK.
AND THE COMPUTERS AND OTHER REFERENCES ARE OVER HERE.
OH. OKAY. THANKS.
NO PROBLEM.

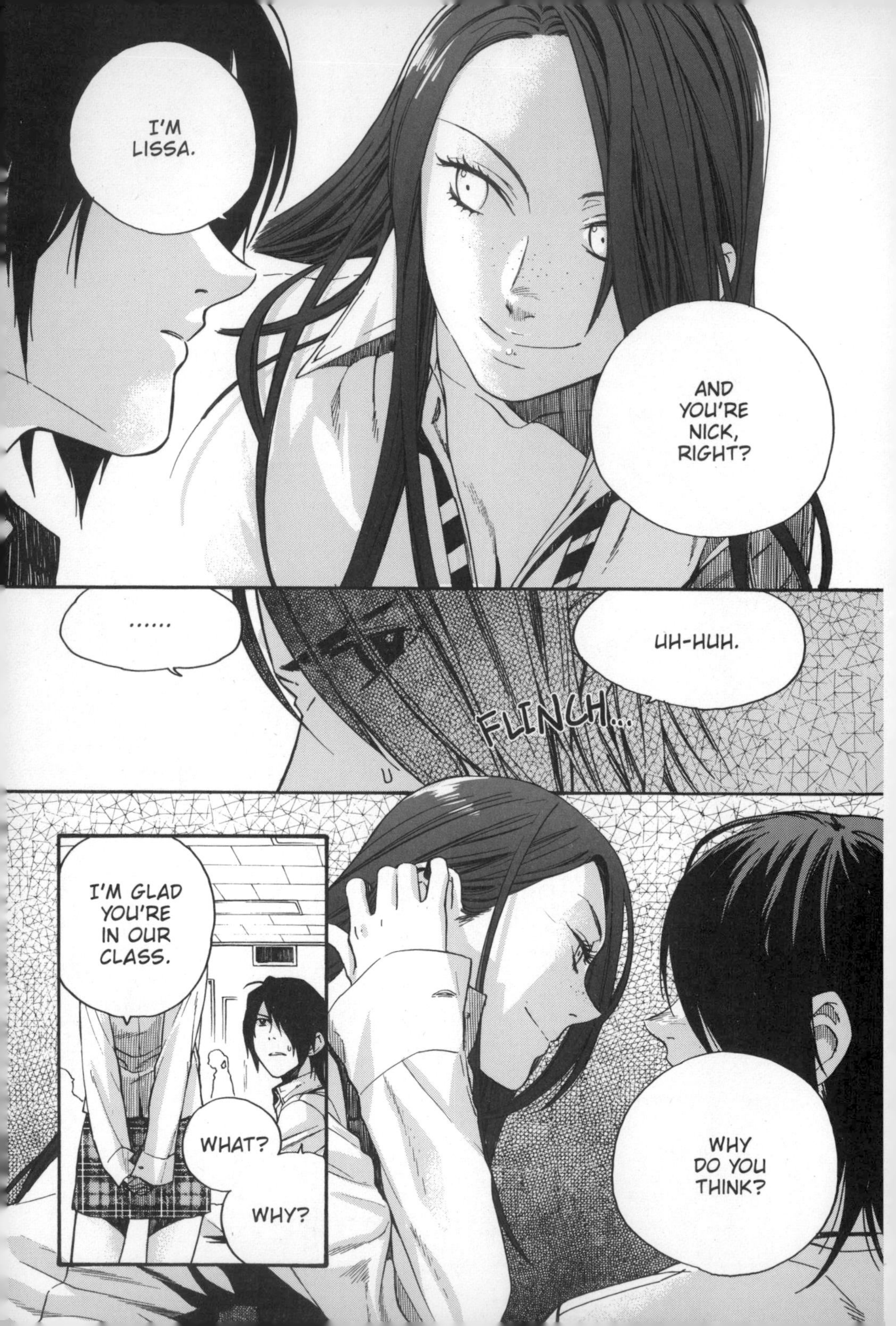
I'M LISSA.
AND YOU'RE NICK, RIGHT?
......
UH-HUH.
FLINCH...
I'M GLAD YOU'RE IN OUR CLASS.
WHAT?
WHY?
WHY DO YOU THINK?

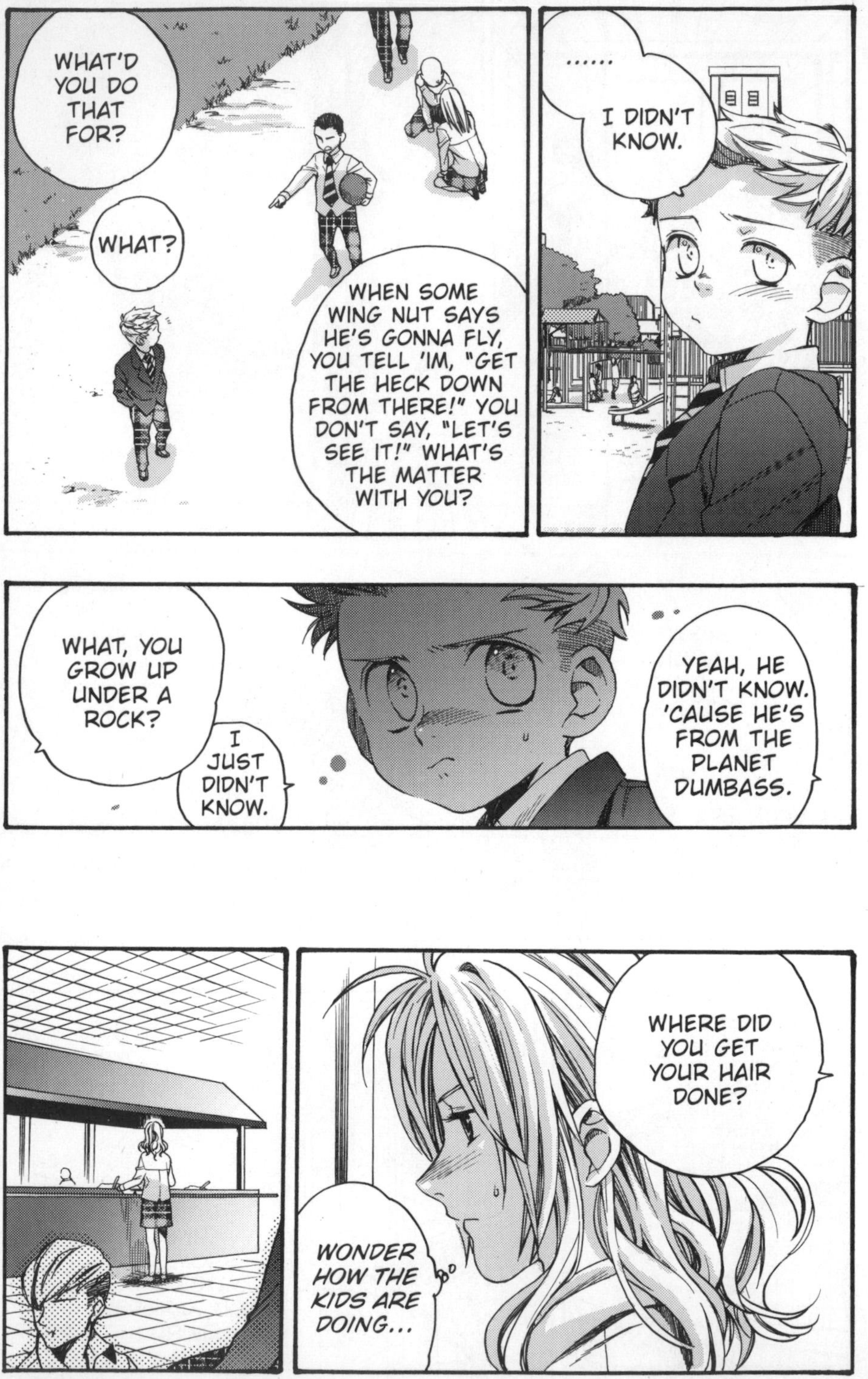
WHAT'D YOU DO THAT FOR?
WHAT?
WHEN SOME WING NUT SAYS HE'S GONNA FLY, YOU TELL 'IM, "GET THE HECK DOWN FROM THERE!" YOU DON'T SAY, "LET'S SEE IT!" WHAT'S THE MATTER WITH YOU?
......
I DIDN'T KNOW.
WHAT, YOU GROW UP UNDER A ROCK?
I JUST DIDN'T KNOW.
YEAH, HE DIDN'T KNOW. 'CAUSE HE'S FROM THE PLANET DUMBASS.
WHERE DID YOU GET YOUR HAIR DONE?
WONDER HOW THE KIDS ARE DOING...

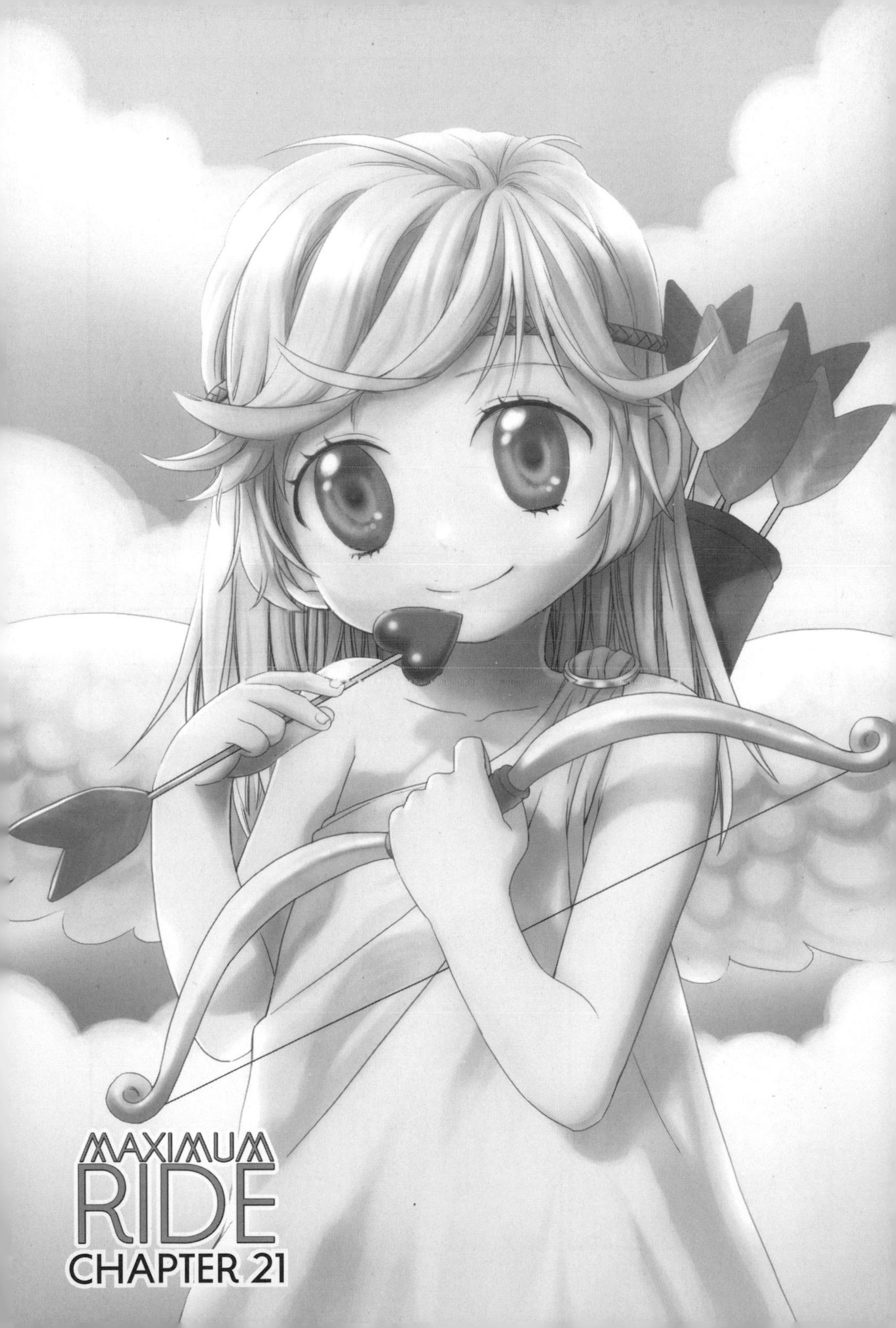
MAXIMUM
RIDE
CHAPTER 21

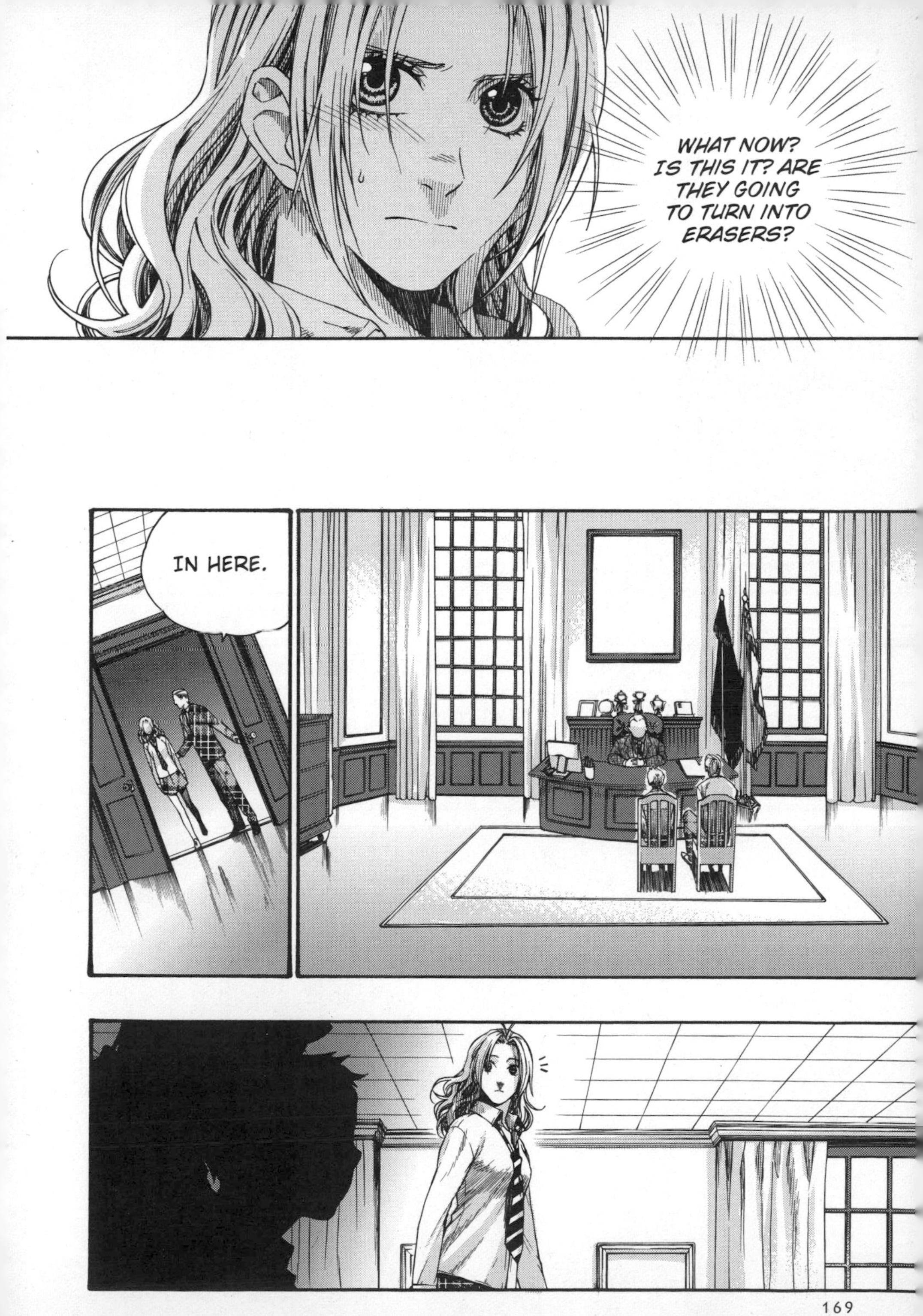
WHAT NOW? IS THIS IT? ARE THEY GOING TO TURN INTO ERASERS?
IN HERE.

173

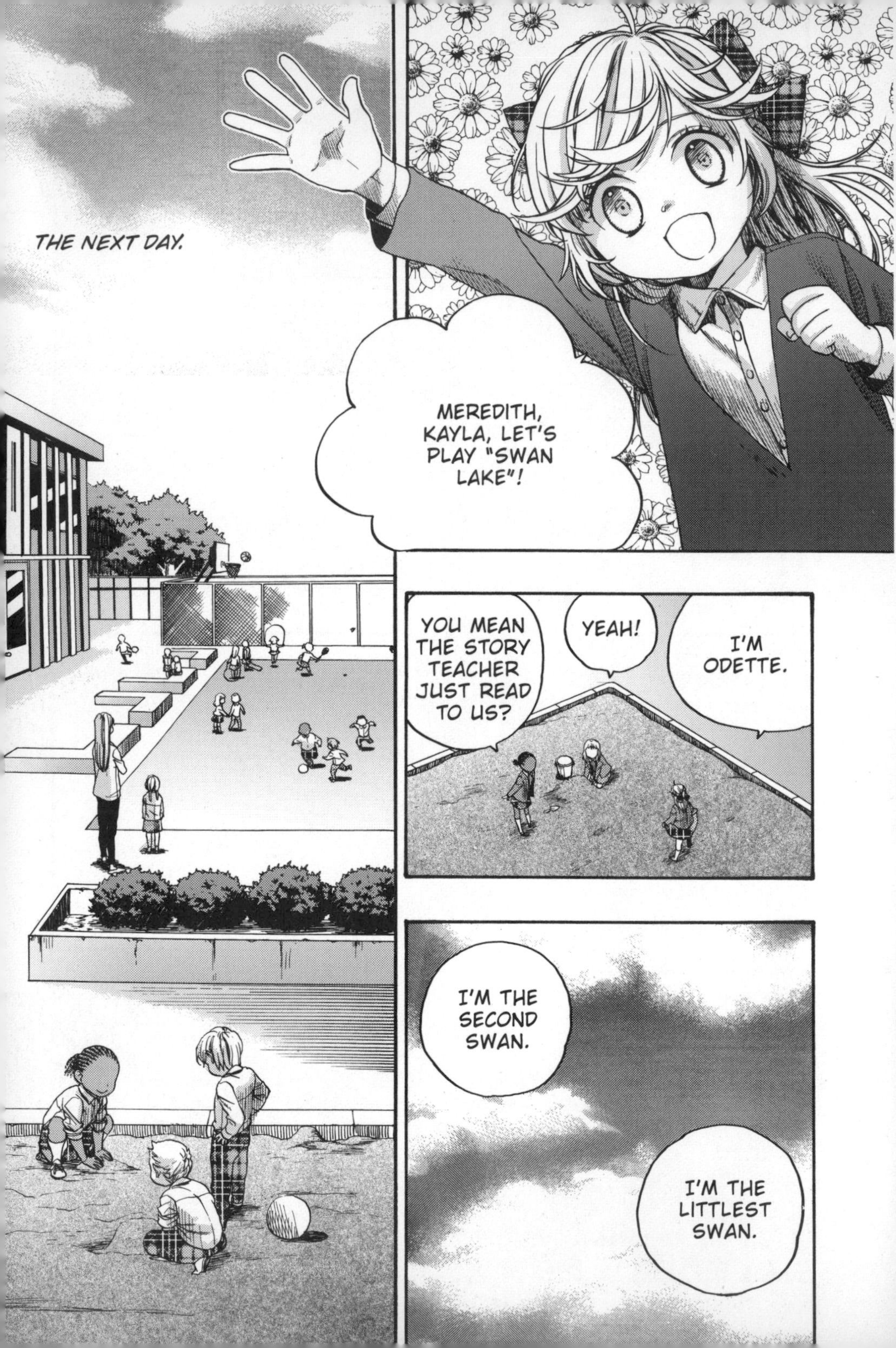
THE NEXT DAY.
MEREDITH, KAYLA, LET'S PLAY "SWAN LAKE"!
YOU MEAN THE STORY TEACHER JUST READ TO US?
YEAH!
I'M ODETTE.
I'M THE SECOND SWAN.
I'M THE LITTLEST SWAN.

YOU CAN HAVE IT.

I'M SAM.

OH, OKAY. THANKS.

YOU'RE IN MY LANGUAGE ARTS CLASS.

AH...

UM...

HE'S CUTE.

WHERE DID YOU MOVE FROM?

UH...

MISSOURI.

WOW. MIDWEST. THIS MUST BE PRETTY DIFFERENT FOR YOU.

YEP.

SO, ARE YOU DOING SCHOOL-WORK OR MORE OF A PERSONAL PROJECT?

UM...

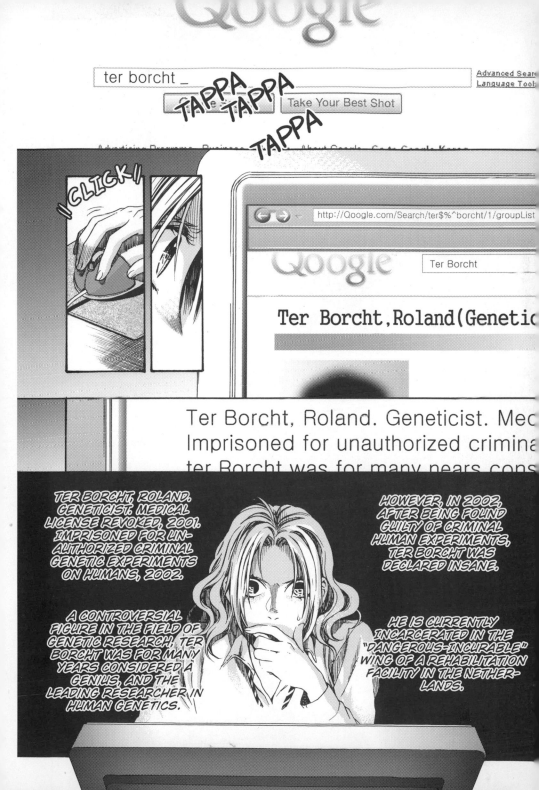

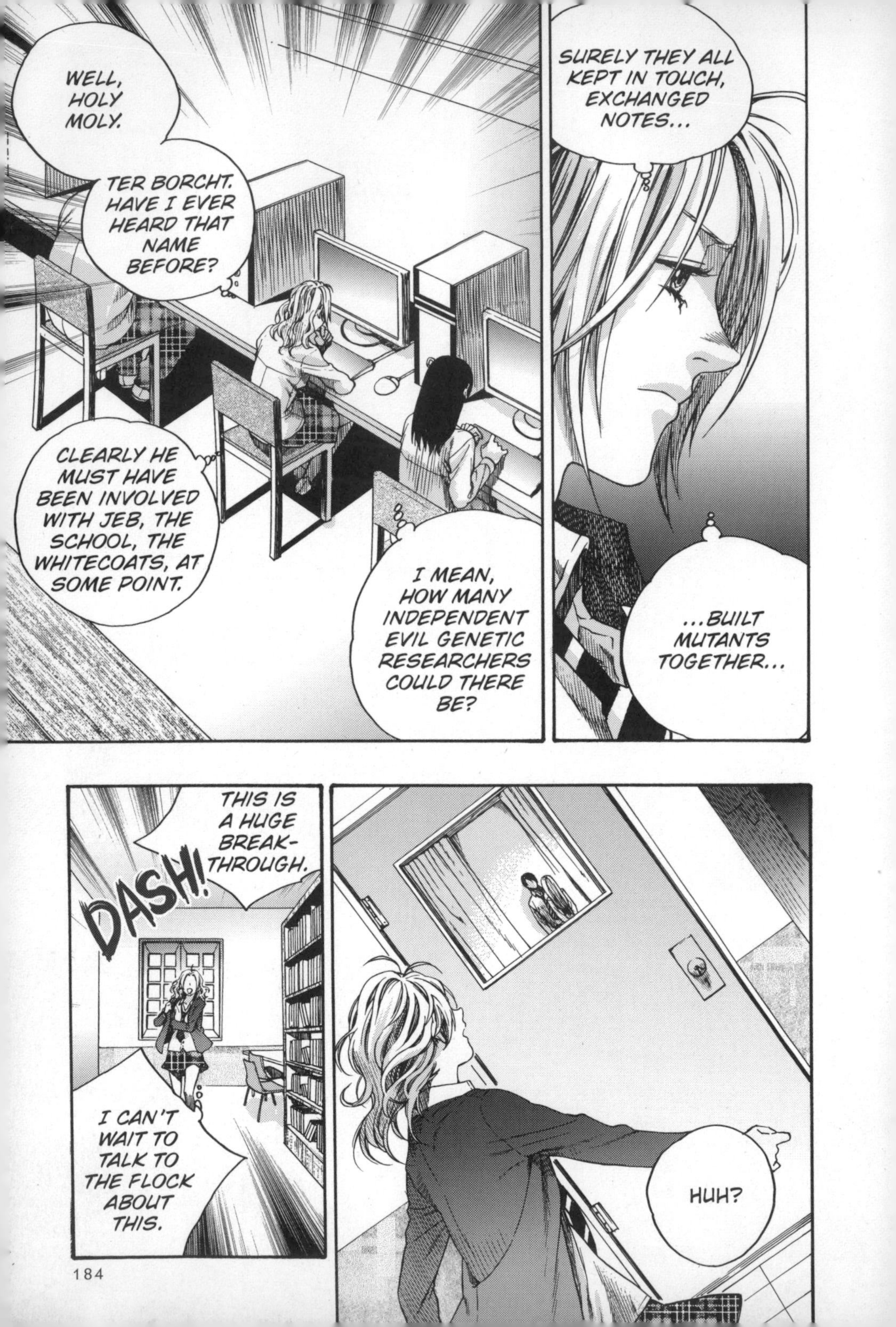
WELL, HOLY MOLY.
TER BORCHT. HAVE I EVER HEARD THAT NAME BEFORE?
CLEARLY HE MUST HAVE BEEN INVOLVED WITH JEB, THE SCHOOL, THE WHITECOATS, AT SOME POINT.
I MEAN, HOW MANY INDEPENDENT EVIL GENETIC RESEARCHERS COULD THERE BE?
SURELY THEY ALL KEPT IN TOUCH, EXCHANGED NOTES...
...BUILT MUTANTS TOGETHER...
THIS IS A HUGE BREAK-THROUGH.
DASH!
I CAN'T WAIT TO TALK TO THE FLOCK ABOUT THIS.
HUH?

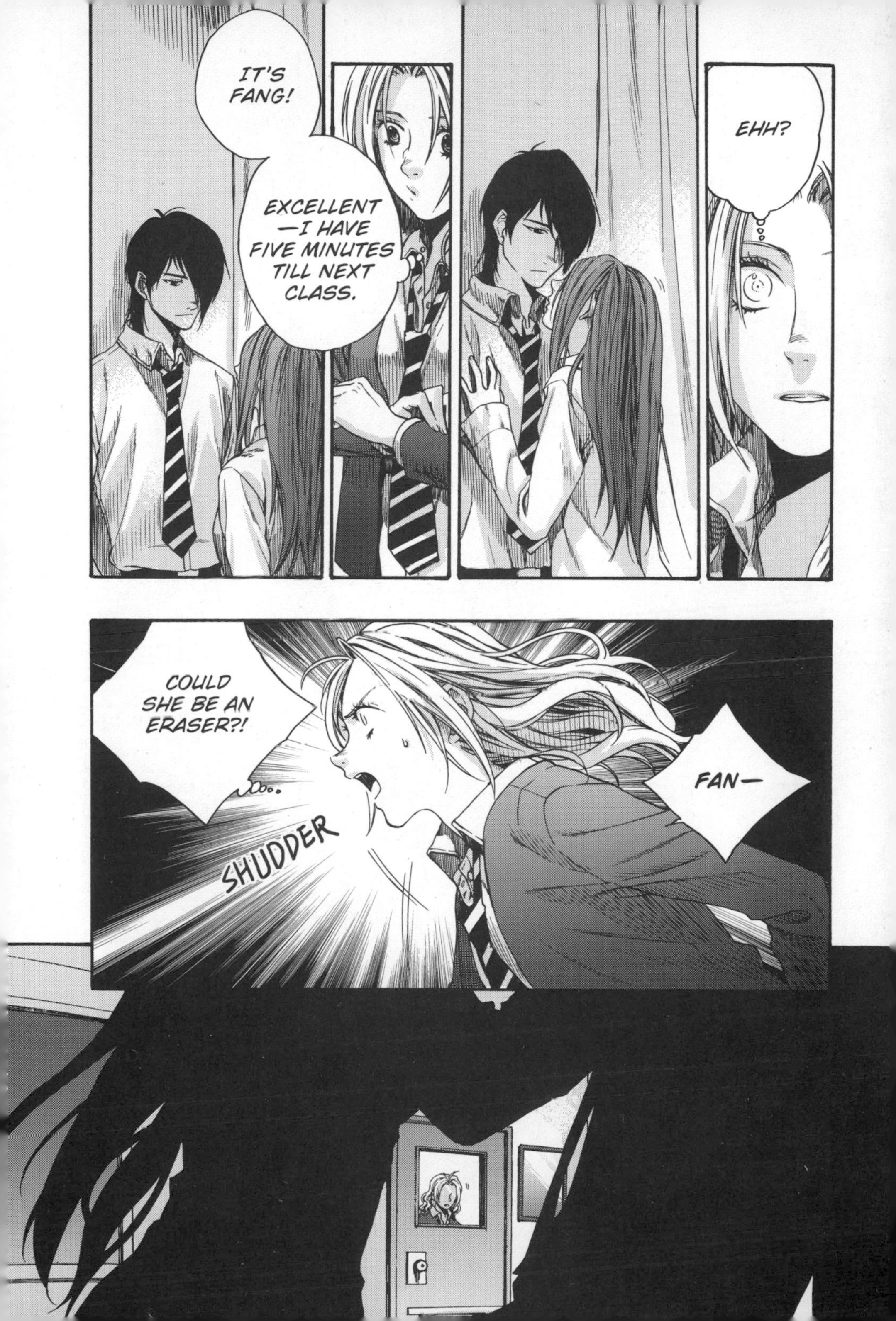
IT'S FANG!
EXCELLENT—I HAVE FIVE MINUTES TILL NEXT CLASS.
EHH?
COULD SHE BE AN ERASER?!
SHUDDER
FAN—

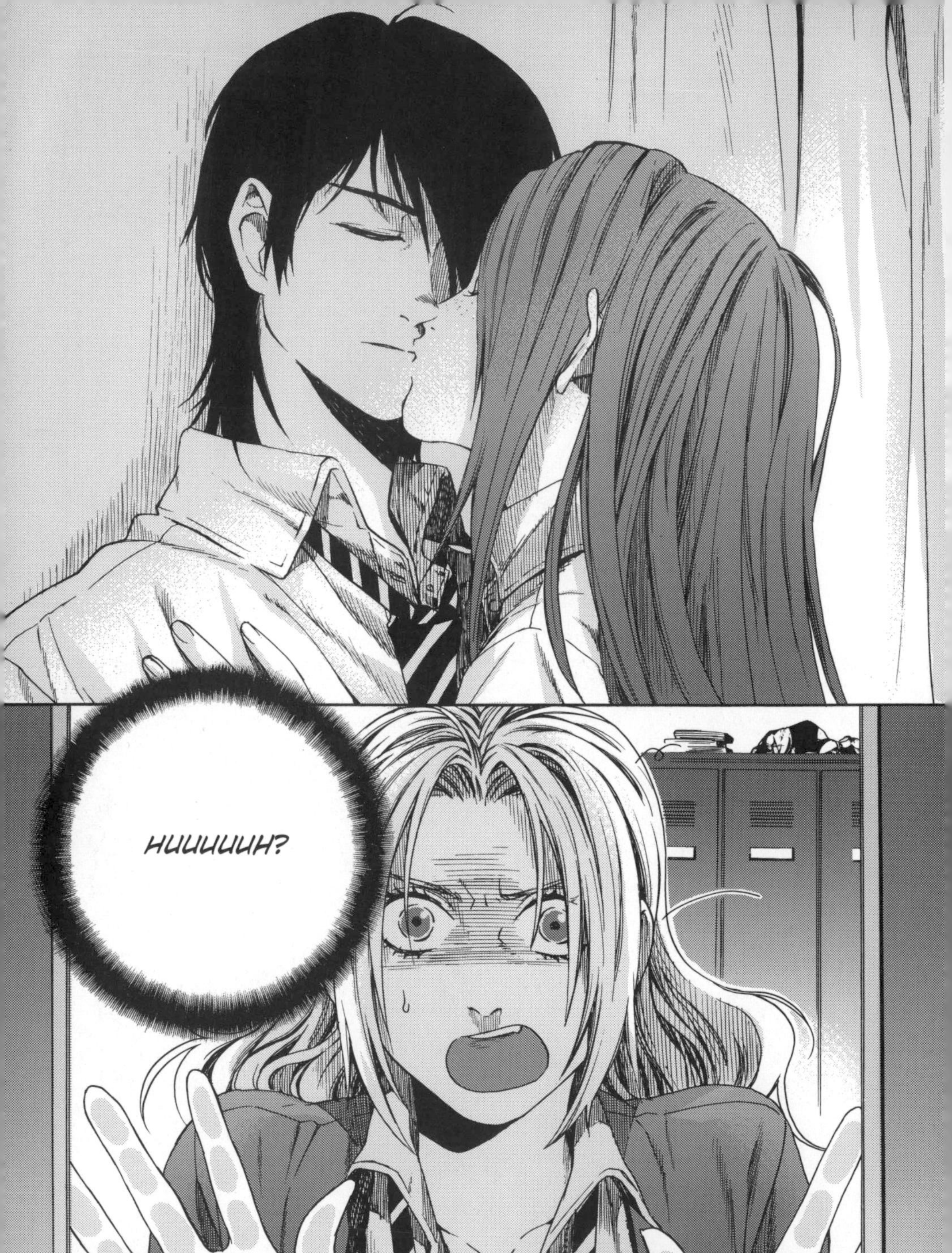
HUUUUUUH?

MAXIMUM RIDE
CHAPTER 22

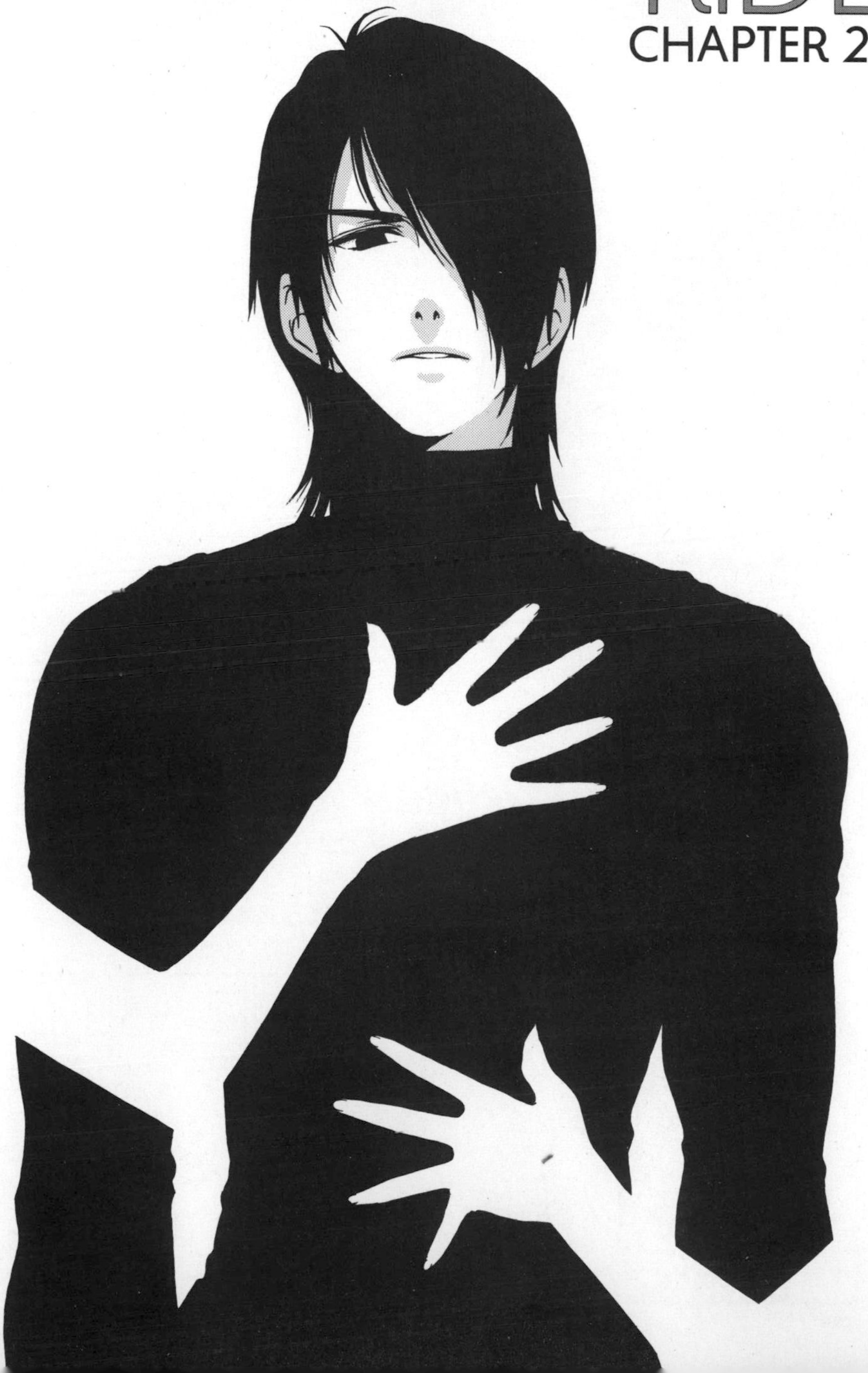

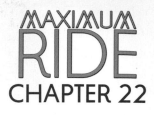

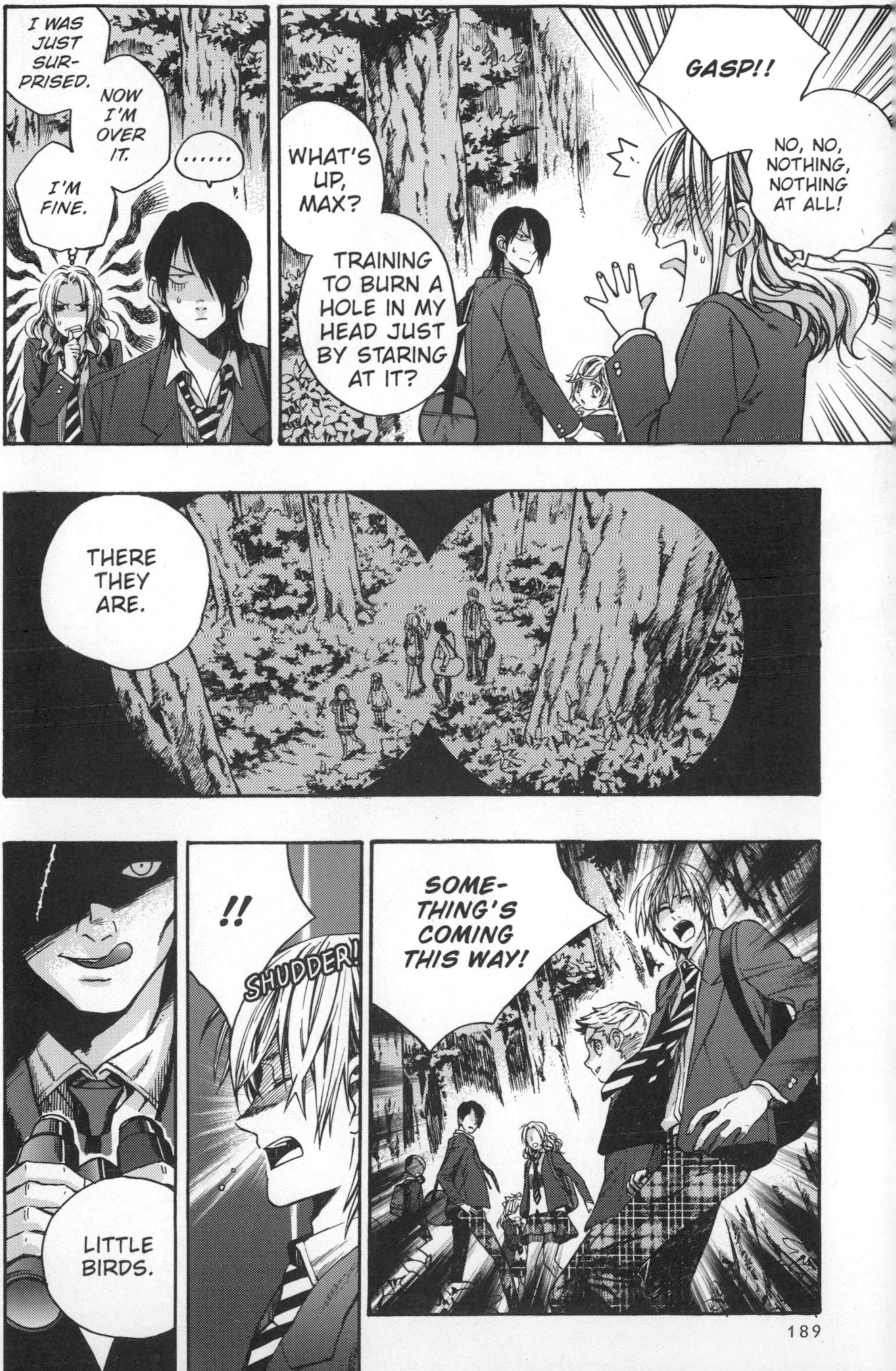
I WAS JUST SURPRISED.
NOW I'M OVER IT.
I'M FINE.
....
WHAT'S UP, MAX?
TRAINING TO BURN A HOLE IN MY HEAD JUST BY STARING AT IT?
GASP!!
NO, NO, NOTHING, NOTHING AT ALL!
THERE THEY ARE.
LITTLE BIRDS.
!!
SHUDDER!
SOMETHING'S COMING THIS WAY!

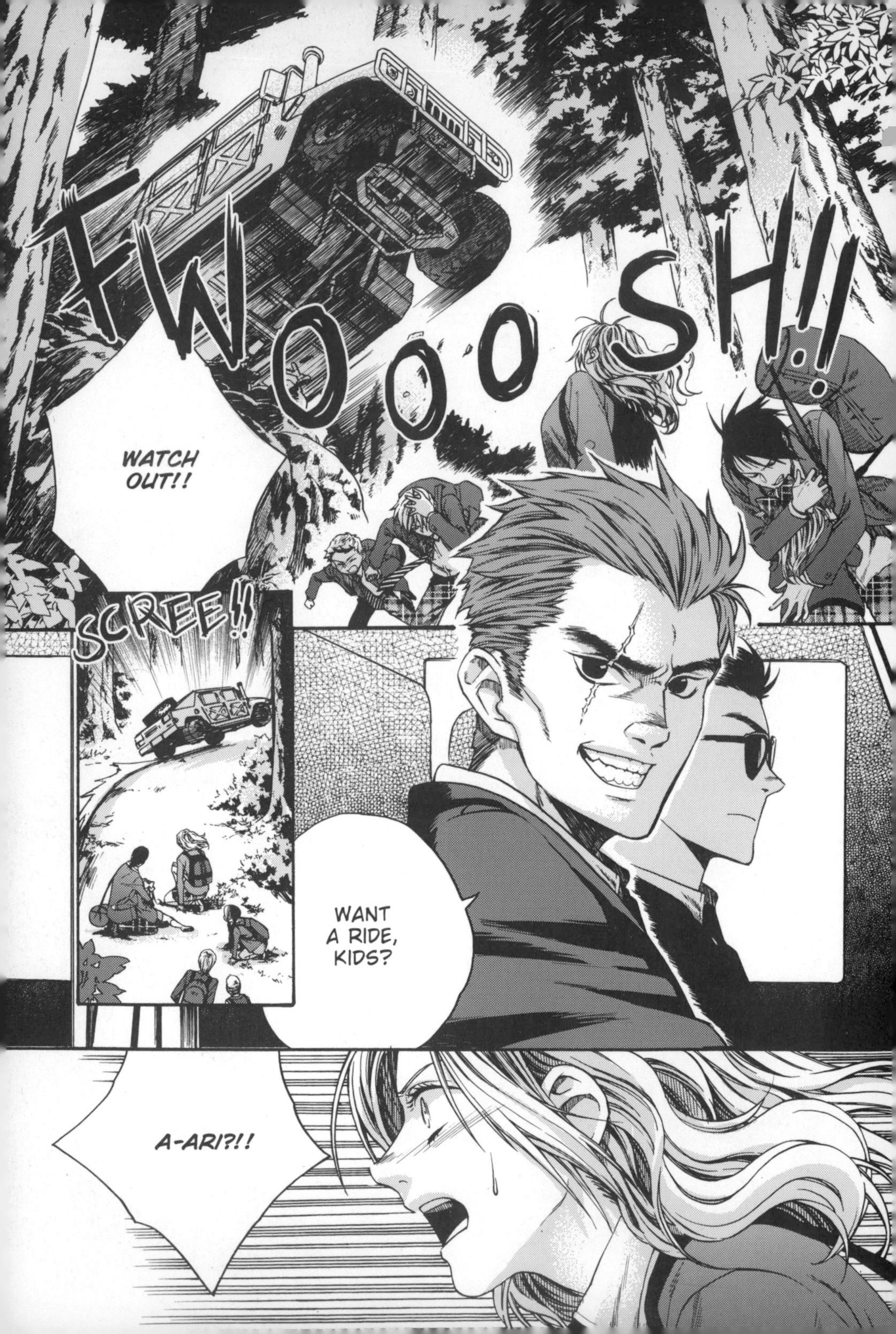
TWOOOSH!!
WATCH OUT!!
SCREE!!
WANT A RIDE, KIDS?
A-ARI?!!

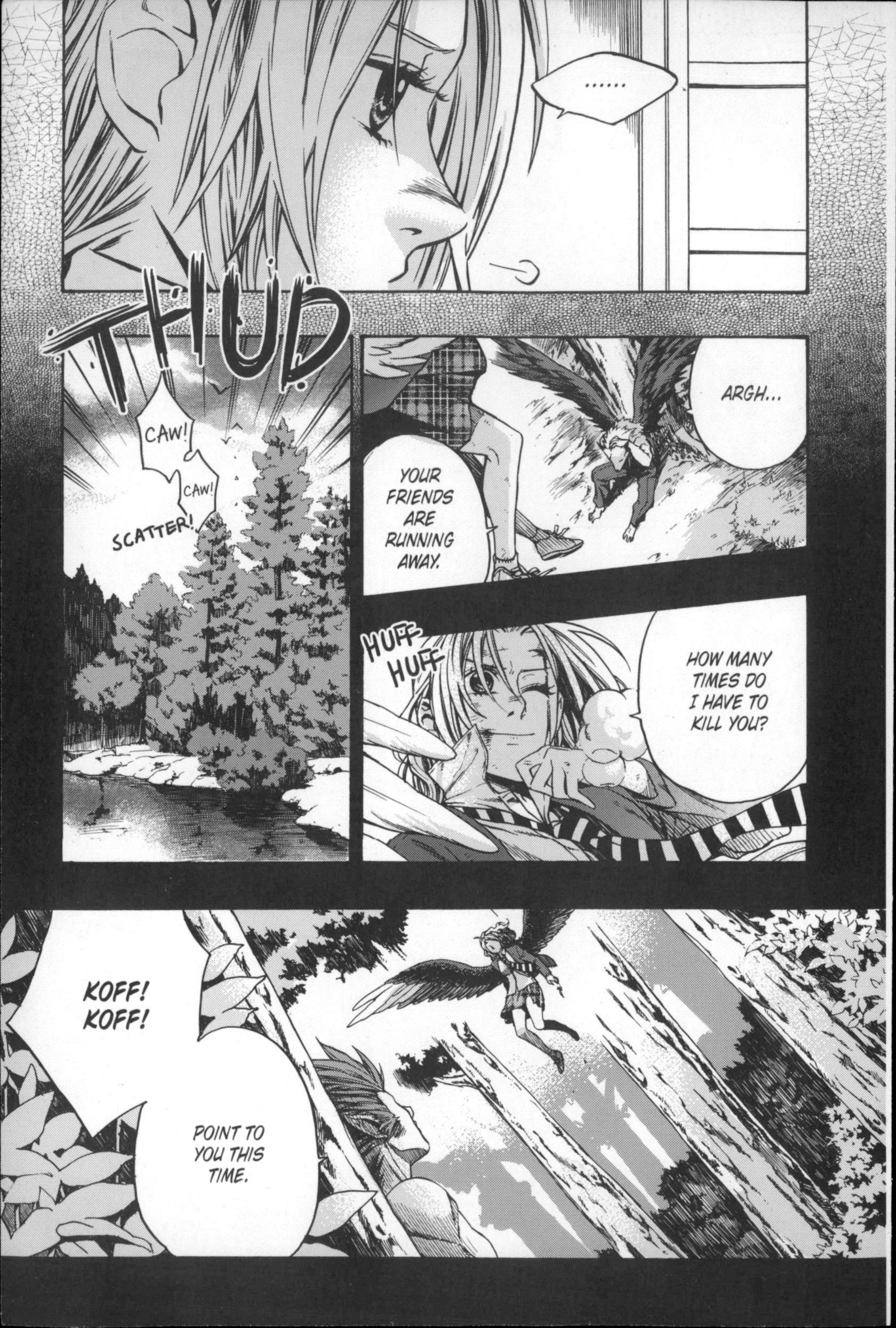
......
THUD
CAW!
CAW!
SCATTER!
YOUR FRIENDS ARE RUNNING AWAY.
ARGH...
HUFF HUFF
HOW MANY TIMES DO I HAVE TO KILL YOU?
KOFF! KOFF!
POINT TO YOU THIS TIME.

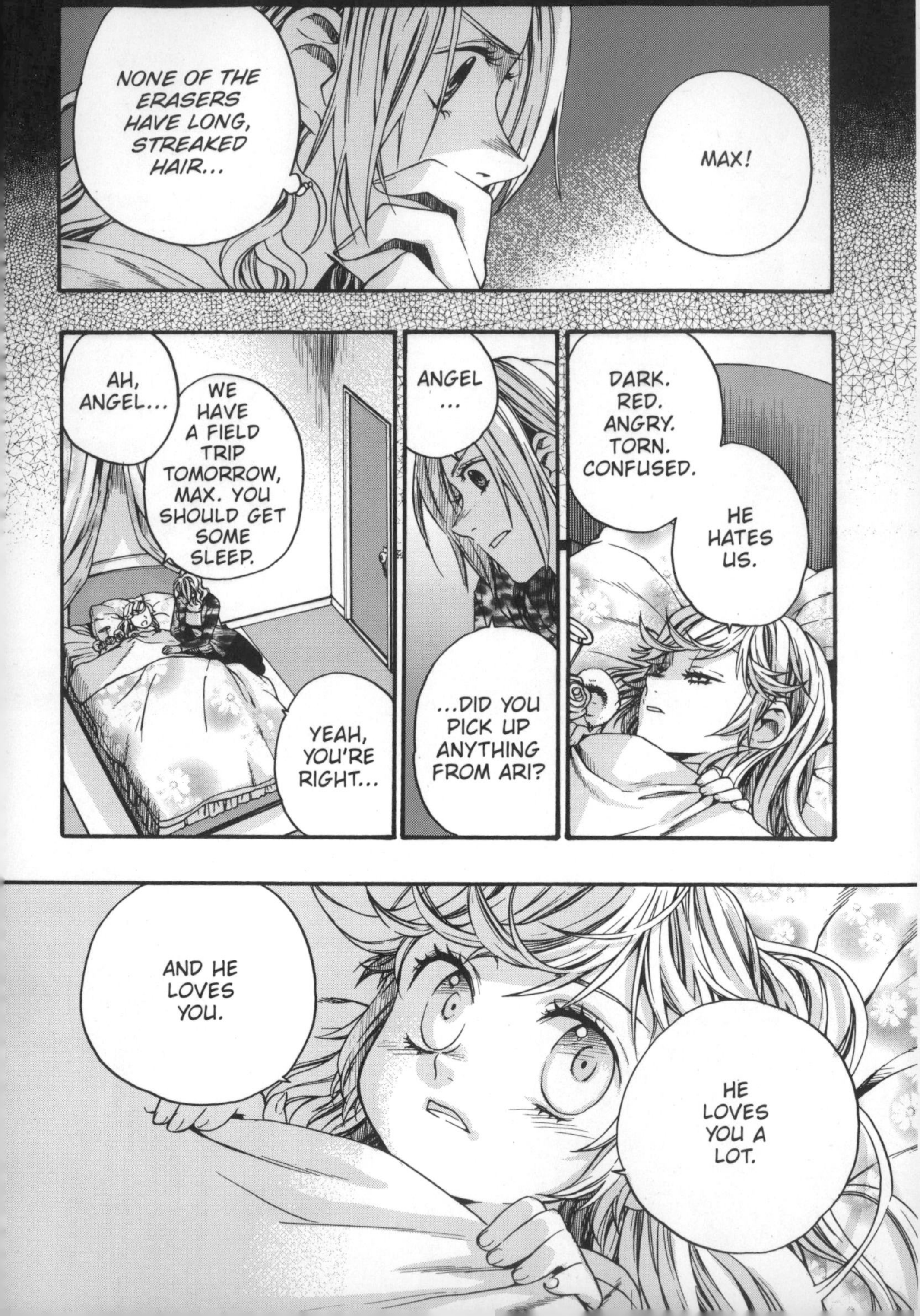
NONE OF THE ERASERS HAVE LONG, STREAKED HAIR...
MAX!
AH, ANGEL...
WE HAVE A FIELD TRIP TOMORROW, MAX. YOU SHOULD GET SOME SLEEP.
YEAH, YOU'RE RIGHT...
ANGEL ...
...DID YOU PICK UP ANYTHING FROM ARI?
DARK. RED. ANGRY. TORN. CONFUSED.
HE HATES US.
AND HE LOVES YOU.
HE LOVES YOU A LOT.

SO A FIELD TRIP IS BASICALLY JUST A TOUR?

IT'S A SPECIAL TREAT!

NO CLASSES, NO HOME-WORK TODAY!

AH, THAT'S ANGEL'S CLASS.

HELLO. YOU'RE ARIEL'S FRIENDS, RIGHT?

IT'S ARIEL'S BIG SISTER!

ARIEL WENT TO THE BATH-ROOM!

ANGEL!

WHERE IS SHE?!

MAX!

HI.

HI, UH, ARIEL.

I GOT LOST. MR. DANNING BROUGHT ME BACK.

IT'S THE REAL PRESI-DENT!

I'VE ONLY SEEN HIM ON TV!

MURMUR

......

MURMUR MURMUR

MURMUR

HE'S SO MUCH COOLER!

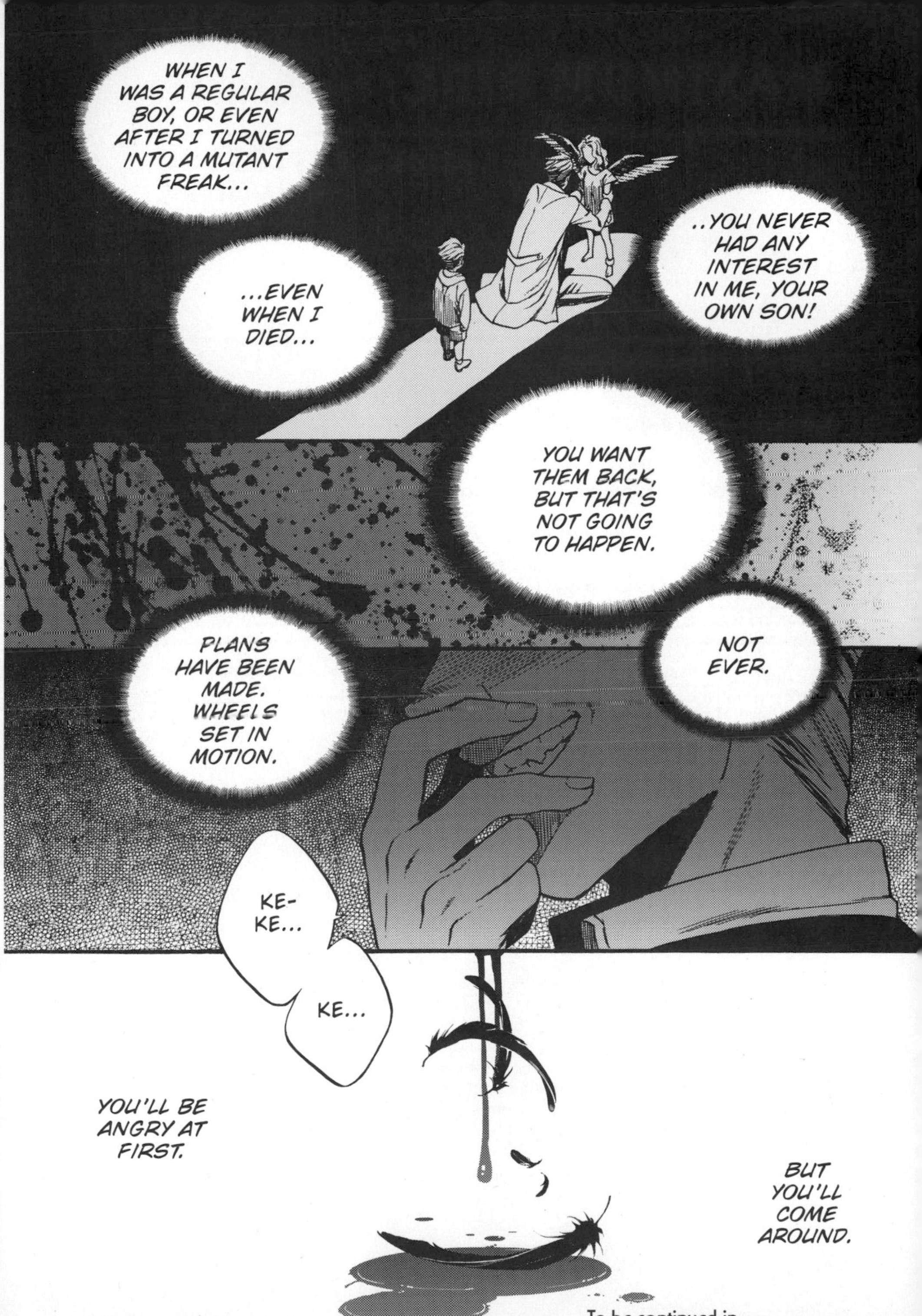
WHEN I WAS A REGULAR BOY, OR EVEN AFTER I TURNED INTO A MUTANT FREAK...
...EVEN WHEN I DIED...
..YOU NEVER HAD ANY INTEREST IN ME, YOUR OWN SON!
YOU WANT THEM BACK, BUT THAT'S NOT GOING TO HAPPEN.
PLANS HAVE BEEN MADE. WHEELS SET IN MOTION.
NOT EVER.
KE-KE...
KE...
YOU'LL BE ANGRY AT FIRST.
BUT YOU'LL COME AROUND.

To be continued in
MAXIMUM RIDE, Vol. 4!

MAXIMUM RIDE: THE MANGA ③

JAMES PATTERSON
& NaRae Lee

Adaptation and Illustration: NaRae Lee

Lettering: Abigail Blackman

Published by Arrow Books in 2010

5 7 9 10 8 6 4

MAXIMUM RIDE, THE MANGA, Vol. 3 © SueJack, Inc. 2010

Illustrations © Hachette Book Group, Inc., 2010

James Patterson has asserted his right under the Copyright, Designs and Patents Act, 1988 to be identified as the author of this work

First published in Great Britain in 2010 by
Arrow Books
Random House, 20 Vauxhall Bridge Road,
London SW1V 2SA

www.randomhouse.co.uk

Addresses for companies within The Random House Group Limited can be found at:
www.randomhouse.co.uk/offices.htm

The Random House Group Limited Reg. No. 954009

A CIP catalogue record for this book is available from the British Library

ISBN 9780099538424

The Random House Group Limited supports the Forest Stewardship Council® (FSC®), the leading international forest-certification organisation. Our books carrying the FSC label are printed on FSC®-certified paper. FSC is the only forest-certification scheme supported by the leading environmental organisations, including Greenpeace. Our paper procurement policy can be found at: www.randomhouse.co.uk/environment

Printed and bound in Germany by GGP Media GMBH, Pößneck

Also by James Patterson

Maximum Ride series
The Angel Experiment • School's Out Forever •
Saving the World and Other Extreme Sports •
The Final Warning • Max • Fang • Angel • Nevermore

Witch & Wizard series
Witch & Wizard (*with Gabrielle Charbonnet*) •
The Gift (*with Ned Rust*) • The Fire (*with Jill Dembowski*) •
The Kiss (*with Jill Dembowski*)

Daniel X series
The Dangerous Days of Daniel X (*with Michael Ledwidge*) •
Watch the Skies (*with Ned Rust*) • Demons and Druids (*with Adam Sadler*) • Game Over (*with Ned Rust*) •
Armageddon (*with Chris Grabenstein*)

Middle School novels
Middle School: The Worst Years of My Life (*with Chris Tebbetts*) •
Middle School: Get Me Out of Here! (*with Chris Tebbetts*) •
Middle School: My Brother Is a Big, Fat Liar (*with Lisa Papademetriou*) • Middle School: How I Survived Bullies, Broccoli, and Snake Hill (*with Chris Tebbetts*)

I Funny
I Funny (*with Chris Grabenstein*) • I Even Funnier (*with Chris Grabenstein, to be published December 2013*)

Treasure Hunters
Treasure Hunters (*with Chris Grabenstein, to be published September 2013*)

Confessions series
Confessions of a Murder Suspect (*with Maxine Paetro*) •
Confessions: The Private School Murders (*with Maxine Paetro, to be published October 2013*)

Graphic novels
Daniel X: Alien Hunter (*with Leopoldo Gout*) • Maximum Ride: Manga Vol. 1–6 (*with NaRae Lee*)

For more information about James Patterson's novels, visit
www.jamespatterson.co.uk

Or become a fan on Facebook

MAX
A MAXIMUM RIDE NOVEL

James Patterson

NOBODY SAID SAVING THE WORLD WOULD BE EASY.

Until now, Max and the flock have lived a lonely existence: hunted down, tortured, and pushed to the fringe of society. Always on the run, they have never been able to live a normal life. But things are changing.

The flock have finally found acceptance for their extraordinary skills. They don't have to hide away and longer – far from it: now everyone wants to see just what they can do. But fame and fortune always come at a price, and Max isn't ready for all the glitz and glamour just yet. Meanwhile, sinister forces are plotting their attack, putting more than just the flock in danger.

Something deadly is lurking in the depths of the ocean. As the flock uncover a terrible secret set to threaten the world, can they save the day or is this a disaster too tough to tackle, even for them?

FANG
A MAXIMUM RIDE NOVEL

James Patterson

**A TERRIFYING PROPHECY. AN UNDYING LOVE.
THE ULTIMATE SACRIFICE.**

Maximum Ride is used to surviving – living constantly under threat from evil forces sabotaging her quest to save the world – but nothing has ever come as close to destroying her as the horrifying prophecy that Fang will be the first to die. Fang is Max's best friend, her soulmate, her partner in leadership of her flock of bird kids. A life without him is a life unimaginable.

Max's desperate desire to protect Fang brings the two closer together than ever. But when a newly created winged boy, the magnificent Dylan, is introduced into the flock, their world is upended yet again. Raised in a lab like the others, Dylan exists for only one reason: he was designed to be Max's perfect other half.

Thus unfolds a battle of science against soul, perfection versus passion, that terrifies, twists, and turns . . . and meanwhile, the apocalypse is coming.

ANGEL
A MAXIMUM RIDE NOVEL

James Patterson

HOW DO YOU SAVE EVERYTHING AND EVERYONE YOU LOVE . . .

Max Ride and her best friends have always had one another's backs. No matter what. Living on the edge as fugitives, they never had a choice. But now they're up against a mysterious and deadly force that's racing across the globe – and just when they need one another the most, Fang is gone. He's creating his own gang that will replace everyone – including Max.

WHEN YOU CAN'T BE TOGETHER . . .

Max is heartbroken over losing Fang, her soulmate, her closest friend. But with Dylan ready and willing to fight by her side, she can no longer deny that his incredible intensity draws her in.

BUT YOU CAN'T STAY APART?

Max, Dylan, and the rest of their friends must soon join with Fang and his new gang for an explosive showdown in Paris. It's unlike anything you've ever imagined . . . or read.

For everything you need to know about the
bestselling Maximum Ride series, as well as
games, videos, competitions and much, much
more, go to the Maximum Ride website:

www.maximumride.co.uk